S
Zahn

Zahn, Timothy.

Star wars.
Allegiance.

DATE			

BY TIMOTHY ZAHN

The Blackcollar
A Coming of Age
Cobra
Spinneret
Cobra Strike
Cascade Point and Other Stories
The Backlash Mission
Triplet
Cobra Bargain
Time Bomb and Zahndry Others
Deadman Switch
Warhorse
Cobras Two
Distant Friends
Conquerors' Pride
Conquerors' Heritage
Conquerors' Legacy
The Icarus Hunt
Angelmass
Manta's Gift
Starsong and Other Stories
DRAGONBACK BOOK 1: Dragon and Thief
DRAGONBACK BOOK 2: Dragon and Soldier
DRAGONBACK BOOK 3: Dragon and Slave
DRAGONBACK BOOK 4: Dragon and Herdsman
The Green and the Gray
Night Train to Rigel
Blackcollar: The Judas Solution

STAR WARS: Heir to the Empire
STAR WARS: Dark Force Rising
STAR WARS: The Last Command
STAR WARS: The Hand of Thrawn, Book 1: Specter of the Past
STAR WARS: The Hand of Thrawn, Book 2: Vision of the Future
STAR WARS: Survivor's Quest
STAR WARS: Outbound Flight
STAR WARS: Allegiance

ALLEGIANCE

STAR WARS

ALLEGIANCE

Timothy Zahn

DEL REY BALLANTINE BOOKS
NEW YORK

Published in the United States by Del Rey Books, an imprint of The Random House Publishing Group, a division of Random House, Inc., New York.

DEL REY is a registered trademark and the Del Rey colophon is a trademark of Random House, Inc.

ISBN 978-0-345-47738-5

Printed in the United States of America on acid-free paper

www.starwars.com
www.delreybooks.com

2 4 6 8 9 7 5 3 1

First Edition

Book design by Katie Shaw

In memory of Katie,
and for her sisters Allie and Emily,
for their love and courage and strength.

ACKNOWLEDGMENTS

The idea for the Hand of Judgment came out of a casual conversation with 501st Legion founder Albin Johnson at StellarCon in March, 2004. Though his original idea was different from that which I eventually used, it was a conversation that got the creative spark going.

Often a writer's mind functions like a giant food processor, taking in thoughts and ideas from everywhere and then mixing and matching the pieces until something new (or at least unrecognizable) emerges. On the rare occasions when we're actually able to trace something directly to its source, it's only right we acknowledge it.

Thanks, Albin.

Dramatis Personae

Barshnis Choard; governor, Shelsha sector (human male)

Caaldra; mercenary (human male)

Carlist Rieekan; general, Rebel Alliance (human male)

Cav'Saran; patroller chief of Janusar on Ranklinge (human male)

Chewbacca; copilot, *Millennium Falcon* (Wookiee male)

Daric LaRone; stormtrooper

Darth Vader; Dark Lord of the Sith

Han Solo; captain, *Millennium Falcon* (human male)

Joak Quiller; stormtrooper pilot

Kendal Ozzel; captain, Imperial Star Destroyer *Reprisal* (human male)

Korlo Brightwater; scout stormtrooper

Leia Organa; Princess and Rebel (human female)

Luke Skywalker; Jedi and Rebel (human male)

Mara Jade; Emperor's Hand (human female)

Mon Mothma; Supreme Commander, Rebel Alliance (human female)

Palpatine; Emperor, Galactic Empire (human male)

Saberan Marcross; stormtrooper

Shakko; captain, pirate ship *Cavalcade* (human male)

Tannis; pilot, pirate ship *Cavalcade* (human male)

Taxtro Grave; stormtrooper sharpshooter

Thillis Slanni; director of planning for Shining Hope (Ishi Tib male)

Vak Somoril; senior officer, Imperial Security Bureau (human male)

Vilim Disra; chief administrator, Shelsha sector (human male)

Ydor Vokkoli; head of Freedonna Kaisu (Mungra male)

Yeeru Chivkyrie; head of Republic Redux (Adarian male)

ALLEGIANCE

Chapter One

THE IMPERIAL STAR DESTROYER *REPRISAL* SLIPPED SILENTLY THROUGH the blackness of space, preparing itself for action against the Rebel forces threatening to tear the galaxy apart.

Standing on the command walkway, his hands clasped behind him, Captain Kendal Ozzel gazed out at the planet Teardrop directly ahead, a mixture of anticipation and dark brooding swirling through him. As far as he was concerned the entire planet was a snake pit, crawling with smugglers, third-rate pirate gangs, and other dregs of society. If *he'd* been in command of the Death Star instead of that idiot Tarkin, he mused, *he* would have picked someplace like Teardrop instead of Alderaan for the weapon's first serious field test.

But he hadn't been in charge; and now both Tarkin and the Death Star were gone, blown to shrapnel off Yavin 4. In a single, awful moment the Rebel Alliance had morphed from a minor nuisance to a bitter enemy.

And Imperial Center had responded. Less than three days ago the word had come down to show no mercy to either the Rebels or their sympathizers.

Not that Ozzel would have shown any mercy at any rate. Eliminating Rebels, and Rebel sympathizers, had become the best and fastest way to success in the Imperial fleet. Perhaps all the way to an admiral's rank bars. "Status?" he called behind him.

"Forty-seven standard minutes to orbit, sir," the navigation officer called from the crew pits.

Ozzel nodded. "Keep a sharp watch," he ordered. "No one gets off that planet."

He glowered at the faintly lit disk ahead of them. "No one," he added softly.

"Luke?" Han Solo called from the *Millennium Falcon*'s cockpit. "Come on, kid—move it. We're on a tight schedule here."

"They're in!" Luke Skywalker's voice came back. "Ramp's sealed."

Han already knew that from his control board readouts, of course. If the kid stuck around, he'd have to learn not to clutter the ship's atmosphere with unnecessary chatter. "Okay, Chewie, hit it," he said.

Beside him Chewbacca gave a rolling trill of acknowledgment, and the *Falcon* lifted smoothly off the hard-packed Teardrop ground.

Apparently not smoothly enough. From behind, Han heard a couple of muffled and rather indignant exclamations. "Hey!" someone shouted.

Han rolled his eyes as he fed power to the sublight engines. "This is *absolutely* the last time we take on passengers," he told his partner firmly.

Chewbacca's reply was squarely to the point and a shade on the disrespectful side.

"No, I mean it," Han insisted. "From now on, if they don't pay, they don't fly."

From behind him came footsteps, and he glanced back as Luke dropped into the seat behind Chewbacca. "They're all settled," he announced.

"Great," Han said sarcastically. "Once we make hyperspace, I'll take their drink orders."

"Oh, come on," Luke chided him. "Anyway, you think *this* bunch is stiff, you should have seen the ones who got out on the earlier transports. These are just the techs who were in charge of packing up the last few crates of equipment."

Han grimaced. Crates which were currently filling the *Falcon*'s holds, leaving no room for paying cargo even if he managed to find some on the way to the rendezvous. This was going to be a complete, 100 percent charity run, like everything else he and Chewbacca had done for Luke and his new friends in the Rebel Alliance. "Yeah, well, I've seen plenty of useless techs before," he muttered.

He was waiting for Luke to come to the techs' defense when a splatter of laserfire ricocheted off the rear deflector. "What the—" he snarled, throwing the *Falcon* into a tight drop loop.

The instinctive maneuver probably saved their skins. Another burst shot through the space they'd just left, this one coming from a different direction. Han twisted the ship back around, hoping fleetingly that their passengers were still strapped in, then took a second to check the aft display.

One glance at the half dozen mismatched ships rising behind them was all he needed. "Pirates," he snapped to the others, throwing power to the engines and angling the ship upward. Facing pirates deep inside a planet's gravity well, with no cover and no chance of quick escape to hyperspace, was about the worst situation a pilot could encounter.

And even the *Falcon* couldn't outmaneuver this many ships forever. "Chewie, get us up and out," he said, throwing off his straps. "Come on, Luke."

The kid was already on it, heading down the cockpit tunnel at a dead run. Han followed, rounding the corner in time to see Luke duck past the passengers crammed into the wraparound seat and head up the ladder to the upper quad laser station. "Captain?" one of the passengers called.

"Save it," Han shot back, grabbing the ladder and sliding down toward the lower quads. He caught himself as the gravity around him did its ninety-degree shift, then dropped into the seat.

It looked even worse from down here than it had from the cockpit. A second wave of pirate ships had joined the first, this group pumping laserfire all around the edges of the first group, forming a deadly cylinder of death around the *Falcon*'s flight vector. They were trying to force their prey to stay on that line so that the first group could chase them down.

Well, they were in for a surprise. Keying the quads with one hand, he snagged his headset with the other and jammed it on. "Luke?"

"I'm here. Any particular strategy, or do we just start with the biggest and see how fast we can blow them apart?"

Han frowned as he got a grip on the control yoke, an odd idea whispering at him. The way that second wave was positioned . . . "You go for that big lead ship," he said. "I'm going to try something cute."

Luke's reply was a blast of laserfire squarely into the lead pirate's bow.

The other ship swerved violently in reaction—clearly, they hadn't expected this kind of firepower from a simple light freighter. The pilot recovered quickly, though, settling the ship back into its position in the battle array. The entire lead wave moved closer together, closing ranks to get maximum protection from their overlapping shields. Han watched closely, waiting for the obvious next move, and heard the twitter from his display board as the lead ships all shifted shield power to double-front.

Which meant they'd just unavoidably lowered the strength of their aft shields. Perfect. "Chewie—dip and waffle," he ordered into his comm. The *Falcon* dropped suddenly in response, and for a second the rear wave of ships was visible past the edges of the first wave's shields. Han was ready, firing a double burst past the lead wave into the flank of the biggest second-wave ship, sending it into a violent swerve as its primary maneuvering system was blown to bits.

And as it did, the laserfire that had been forming that part of the *Falcon*'s entrapment ring sprayed with shattering force across the sterns of the lead-wave ships.

It was everything Han could have hoped for. Two of the smaller ships veered instantly and violently out of formation as their engine sections blew up. The first ricocheted a glancing blow off one of the other pirates on its way to oblivion, while the second slammed full-tilt into another. They fell away together, with Luke taking advantage of the distraction to blow one of the other lead ships into fiery dust.

Then, to Han's shock and disbelief, the *Falcon* dropped and turned into a curving arc back toward the planet's surface. "Chewie?" he snarled. "What in—"

The Wookiee growled a warning. Frowning, Han craned his neck to look in that direction as the familiar shape of an Imperial Star Destroyer swung into view around the dark edge of the planetary disk.

"Han!" Luke gasped.

"I see it, I see it," Han said, his mind racing. Clearly, the Rebel cell on Teardrop had gotten out just in time.

Except that the last half a dozen members of that cell were currently sitting a couple of meters directly above him in the *Falcon*'s lounge. If the Imperials caught them here . . .

Then his brain caught up to him, and he understood what Chewbacca had been doing with that last maneuver. "Luke, shut down," he ordered, slapping the switches on his own quads. The last thing he wanted was for the Imperials to do a power scan and see that the *Falcon* had this kind of weaponry. "Chewie, give me comm."

There was a click— "Emergency!" he called, putting desperation into his voice. "Incoming freighter *Argos* requesting assistance from Teardrop planetary defenses."

There was no answer from the ground, of course. Given the shady character of most of the planet's residents and visitors, Han wasn't even sure they *had* a real defense force down there. But then, he didn't especially care if anyone on Teardrop heard him or not. All he cared about was—

"Freighter *Argos*, state your intention and emergency," a clipped military voice responded.

"Medical mercy team from Briston, responding to the recent groundquake on Por'ste Island," Han called back. Behind the *Falcon*, he saw, the remaining pirate ships were re-forming to continue the attack. Apparently they hadn't noticed Teardrop's newest visitor. "We're under attack—I think they're pirates."

"*Argos*, acknowledged," the voice said. "Hold your present course."

"But if I do—"

He never got to finish his token protest. Behind him a two-by-two group of brilliant green turbolaser bolts sliced across the pirates' formation, blasting four of the ships into rubble.

This time they got the message. The survivors broke formation and headed off in all directions, some back toward the ground, others trying to escape into hyperspace.

Neither option worked. Calmly, systematically, precisely, the Star Destroyer continued to fire, blasting the pirates one by one until the *Falcon* was flying alone.

"Now what?" Luke murmured in Han's earphone.

Han ignored him. "Many thanks, Captain," he called. "Glad to see the Empire is taking this pirate problem seriously."

"You're welcome, *Argos*," a new voice said. "Now turn around and go home."

"What?" Han demanded, trying to sound both outraged and stunned. "But, Captain—"

"That's an order, *Argos*," the other cut him off tartly. "As of right now Teardrop is under Imperial interdiction. Go back to Briston and wait until the block has been lifted."

Han allowed himself a sigh. "Understood," he murmured, careful to maintain a straight face. Sometimes a particularly clever and perceptive man could sense a satisfied grin even over an audio comm channel. Not that this particular Imperial appeared to be either clever *or* perceptive. "You heard him, pilot," he continued. "Turn us around. Again, Captain, thanks for the rescue."

He climbed out of the quad seat and headed back up the ladder. "Captain Solo, I demand to know what's happening," one of the passengers said stiffly as Han crossed the lounge on his way back to the cockpit.

"We're taking you to the rendezvous," Han told him, putting on his best puzzled-and-innocent look. "Why?"

Before the other could recover enough to try the question again, Han had made his escape.

Chewbacca had them well on their way out of Teardrop's gravity well by the time Han dropped into his seat. "Nice move, Chewie," he said as he keyed for a status report. The attack had added a few new dents to the aft armor plating, but considering how many there were already it wasn't likely anyone would notice. "It's always nice when we can obey an Imperial order. For a change."

Behind them, Luke came into the cockpit. "He actually bought it?" he asked, leaning over Han's shoulder to gaze out at the Star Destroyer in the distance.

"Why not?" Han countered. "He saw us heading in, and we *told* him we were heading in. Sometimes you just have to help people think what you want them to."

"I suppose," Luke said, still sounding doubtful. "They still might have decided to board and search us."

"Not a chance," Han said. "Just because they ride around in big fancy ships doesn't make them smart. They're here to hunt Rebels, not inspect cargo. Once Chewie had us turned back inward, the only real question was whether the captain would feel like giving his gunners some target practice."

"Too bad they'll never know what they missed," Luke murmured, taking a last look and then sitting back down. "Sure glad you two are on *our* side."

Han frowned over his shoulder. But Luke was peering at the nav computer display, apparently completely oblivious to what he'd just said. Han shifted his gaze to Chewbacca, to find the Wookiee looking sideways at *him*. "What?" he demanded.

The other shrugged his massive shoulders and turned back to his board. Han glanced at Luke again, but the kid had apparently missed the byplay completely.

He turned back to his board, a sour taste in his mouth. *Our side.* Luke's side, in other words. *And* Princess Leia Organa's side, *and* General Rieekan's, and probably the whole blasted Rebellion's.

Trouble was, Han couldn't for the life of him remember when the Rebellion had become *his* side.

So he'd dusted those TIE fighters off Luke during that lunatic Yavin battle. Big deal. That had been strictly a favor to the kid, and maybe a little payback for the way the Imperials had dragged him aboard the Death Star and then walked all over the *Falcon* with their grubby feet. He didn't mind the Rebels being grateful for that.

But it didn't mean he'd enlisted in the Big Cause.

Chewbacca was all set to do so, of course. His personal history with the Empire, plus the way they had treated his people in general, had left him with a deep hatred for them. He would enlist in the Rebellion in a heartbeat if Han gave the okay.

But Han wasn't going to let anyone's passion drive him on this one. Not Chewie's, and certainly not Luke's. He had his own life to lead.

The Star Destroyer was settling into orbit as the *Falcon* made the jump to lightspeed.

With a final burst, more felt than really heard, the *Reprisal*'s turbolasers fell silent.

Seated on the portside bench in the number three stormtrooper drop ship, Daric LaRone notched up his helmet's audio enhancers, wondering if the battle might be continuing with a more distant set of the Star Destroyer's weapons banks. But he could hear nothing, and after a moment he eased the enhancement back down again. "Wonder what that was all about," he murmured.

Beside him, Saberan Marcross shrugged slightly, the movement eliciting a slight crackle from his armor. "Maybe the Rebels tried to make a run for it," he murmured back.

"If they did, they didn't get very far," Taxtro Grave commented from his seat on the starboard bench, shifting his grip on his long BlasTech T-28 repeating sniper rifle.

"Look at the bright side," Joak Quiller suggested from beside him. "If they're all dead, we can cancel this op and go someplace more promising."

"Whoever's talking back there, stow it," an authoritative voice called from the front of the drop ship.

"Yes, sir," Marcross answered for all of them.

LaRone leaned out slightly to look at the scowling officer seated by Lieutenant Colf. Emblazoned across his chest were the rank bars of a major; above the insignia was a face LaRone couldn't remember ever seeing before. "Who *is* that?" he asked, keeping his voice low.

"Major Drelfin," Marcross whispered back. "ISB."

LaRone leaned back again, a chill running through him. The Imperial Security Bureau was the darkest and most brutal of Emperor Palpatine's tools. "What's he doing on the *Reprisal*?"

"Someone up the chain must have decided we needed extra help," Marcross said. His tone was carefully neutral, but LaRone knew him well enough to recognize the contempt beneath the words. "They brought in a few ISB men to direct the assault."

LaRone grimaced. "I see," he said, matching the other's tone.

From the drop ship's cockpit came a warning buzz. "Stand by for drop," the pilot called. "Drop in five."

LaRone looked across the aisle at Quiller, noting the other's subtle squirming. Quiller was himself an excellent pilot, and consequently a rotten passenger. "Easy," he murmured.

Quiller cocked his head slightly, and LaRone smiled at the strained-patient expression he knew the other was giving him from behind the anonymous white helmet faceplate.

Abruptly the bench lurched beneath him, and the drop ship was away.

Behind his own faceplate LaRone's smile faded, his thoughts drifting back to that fateful day ten standard years ago when the Imperial recruiters had come to Copperline and set up shop. In his mind's eye he saw himself joining with the other teens as they flocked around the booth, dazzled by the presentation, the crisp uniforms, and the unspoken but obvious implication that this was the best and quickest way off their dead-end little world.

Only this time, in his daydream, LaRone said no.

He'd believed in the Empire at first. He really had. He'd been ten when the Fleet and infantry had come in force and spent five months clearing out the pirate nests that had plagued Copperline for decades. Eight years later, when the recruiters had come, he'd jumped at the chance to join such a noble group of people. Three years after that, when he'd been offered a spot in the elite Imperial stormtrooper corps, he'd jumped even harder, working and sweating and praying for the chance to be worthy of this ultimate challenge.

For six years everything had gone well. He'd served with all his heart and strength, fighting against the forces of evil and chaos that threatened to destroy Emperor Palpatine's New Order. And he'd served with distinction, or so at least his commanders had thought.

For LaRone himself, awards and citations meant nothing. He was wearing the white armor, and he was making a difference. That was what mattered.

But then had come Elriss, where an entire town had had to stand out in the pouring rain for six hours while their identities were double- and triple-checked. After that had come Bompreil, and all those terrible civilian casualties as they'd fought to root out a Rebel cell.

And then had come Alderaan.

LaRone shifted uncomfortably on the bench. The details still weren't entirely clear, but the official reports all agreed that the planet had been a center of Rebel strength, and that it had been destroyed only when it defied an order to surrender the traitors.

LaRone certainly couldn't fault the motivation. The Rebels were growing ever stronger, ever bolder, ever more dangerous. They had to be stopped before they destroyed everything the Emperor had created, and dragged the galaxy back into more of the chaos of the Clone Wars era.

But surely the entire *planet* couldn't have been on the Rebels' side. Could it?

And then the quiet rumors had started. Some said that Alderaan hadn't been a Rebel base at all, that its destruction had been nothing more than a field test of the Empire's new Death Star. Others whispered that Grand Moff Tarkin, the Death Star's borderline-psychotic commander, had destroyed all those billions of people over a personal grudge between him and Bail Organa.

But it almost didn't matter what the reason was. The bottom line was that the response had been light-years beyond any provocation the Rebels could possibly have put together.

Something was happening to the Empire that LaRone had served so long and so well. Something terrible.

And LaRone himself was stuck right in the middle of it.

"Ground in three minutes," Major Drelfin called from the front of the drop ship. "Stormtroopers, prepare to deploy."

LaRone took a deep breath, forcing the doubts away. He was an Imperial stormtrooper, and he would do his duty. Because that was all that mattered.

The first of the speeder bike drop ships came to a cautious hover a couple of meters off the ground. As the ramps came down Korlo Brightwater gunned his Aratech 74-Z Speeder Bike and roared out into the afternoon sunlight.

"TBR Four-seven-nine, pull it back," the tart voice of his commander, Lieutenant Natrom, growled in his ear. "Re-form to Search Pattern Jenth."

"Four-seven-nine: acknowledged," Brightwater said, taking a quick look around as he turned into a wide circle that would bring him back to the rest of the scout troopers still maneuvering their way out of the transport. They'd come in on a ground-skimming course just to the north of a set of low, tree-sprinkled hills, with the edge of their target town a couple of hundred meters away on the far side. Activating his helmet's sensors, he gave the hills a quick but careful scan as he circled back toward the transport. There didn't seem to be activity anywhere, of any sort, which struck him as highly suspicious. The hills included a picnic area, several walking paths, and half a dozen trees that had been patiently nurtured and manipulated over the decades into an elaborate children's climbing structure. *Someone* from town ought to be taking his or her leisure out here on such a fine, quiet afternoon.

But there was no one. Something, apparently, was keeping the townspeople indoors today.

Such as the news of an imminent Imperial raid?

Brightwater shook his head in irritation. So the whole thing was a bust. The word had leaked, and any Rebels who might have been hiding here were halfway to the Outer Rim by now. "Command; TBR Four-seven-nine," he called into his comm. "No activity in staging area. The operation may be blown. Repeat, the operation—"

"Scout troopers, you are cleared to secure the perimeter," an unfamiliar voice cut in.

Brightwater frowned. "Command, did you copy?" he asked. "I said the lack of activity—"

"TBR Four-seven-nine, you will restrict your comments to tactical reports," the new voice again interrupted. "All transports: move in."

Brightwater craned his neck. The stormtrooper drop ships were visible now high above him, dropping toward the ground like hunting avians moving for the kill.

Only there wasn't anything down here worth killing anymore.

A movement to his right caught his eye, and he looked back as his partner, Tibren, came alongside. Brightwater lifted his hand in mute question; the other scout shook his head in equally silent warning.

Brightwater scowled. But Tibren was right. Whoever this idiot was running things, he was either too single-minded or too stupid to see reason. Nothing now for the stormtroopers to do but go along for the ride and treat the whole thing as just another training exercise. He nodded Tibren an acknowledgment and gunned his speeder toward his designated containment sector.

By the time they'd finished their encirclement the drop ships were down, their heavy guns sweeping over the rows of mostly single-story buildings, their hatches disgorging their complements of stormtroopers and uniformed command officers. Brightwater kept his speeder moving, watching with professional interest as the troops formed themselves into a double ring and converged on the town. For a change, everything seemed to be going perfectly, without even the small glitches that normally accompanied an operation this size. It really was a pity there weren't any Rebels left in town to appreciate it.

The stormtroopers and officers disappeared from view, heading between and into the buildings, and Brightwater shifted his attention to the area outside the scout troopers' perimeter. The Rebels had almost certainly fled the planet, but there were occasional cells with more audacity than brains who elected to stay behind and try to put together an ambush.

Brightwater rather hoped this bunch had gone that route. It would keep the afternoon from being a complete waste, and it would give the stormtroopers the chance to blast them out here in the open instead of having to sort them out from the civilians.

He had curved to the crest of the nearest hill, his helmet sensors on full power, when he heard the sound of blasterfire from behind him. He swung his speeder sharply around, searching the perimeter on the far side of town. But all the scout troopers over there were still on their speeders, with no indication that anyone was shooting at them. There was another volley of blasterfire, and this time he realized that it was coming from inside the town itself.

He brought his speeder to a halt, frowning. The volleys had been replaced by a less organized stutter, but the shots all carried the distinctive pitch of the stormtroopers' own BlasTech E-11 rifles. Where was the cacophonous mix of military, sporting, and self-defense weaponry that was practically the trademark of the Rebel Alliance?

And then, with a sudden chill, he understood.

He revved his speeder back to full speed, twisting its nose down the hills and toward town. What in the name of the Emperor did they think they were *doing*?

"TBR Four-seven-nine, return to your post," Lieutenant Natrom's voice said in his earphone.

Brightwater flicked out his tongue to the comm's selector control, switching to the squad's private frequency. "Sir, something's happening in town," he said urgently. "Request permission to investigate."

"Permission denied," Natrom said. His voice was under rigid control, but Brightwater could hear the anger beneath it. "Return to your post."

"Sir—"

"That's an order, TBR Four-seven-nine," Natrom said. "It won't be repeated."

Brightwater took a deep breath. But he knew Natrom, and he knew that tone. Whatever was happening, there was nothing either of them could do about it. "Yes, sir," he said. Taking another deep breath, trying to calm himself, he turned his speeder back around.

The sun had set over the western horizon before the blasterfire finally came to an end.

Chapter Two

THE FIRING RANGE WAS DESERTED WHEN LaRONE ARRIVED. DESERTED, that was, except for Grave, standing in the booth at the far end with his T-28 propped against his armored shoulder. "Grave," LaRone greeted the other solemnly. "How are you doing?"

For a minute Grave didn't answer. He kept firing, coolly and methodically, completing the pattern the range had set up for him. LaRone watched the monitor as Grave hit crossmark after crossmark with the kind of accuracy expected of stormtrooper snipers.

He wondered whether Grave had been called on to use that skill earlier that day.

Finally, the blaster fell silent. Grave held his sharpshooter's pose another couple of seconds as the echoes faded away, then laid the weapon down on the shelf in front of him and pulled off his helmet. "It was like something out of the Clone Wars," he said, not turning around to face his friend. "The whole town—everyone. Slaughtered where they stood."

"I know," LaRone said soberly. "I was just talking to Korlo Brightwater—you know, the speeder scout? He told me he'd heard the official report's going to say the Rebels launched an ambush during the search."

"Not a chance," Grave said firmly. "I was on rooftop sniper-suppression duty, and I didn't see a single person so much as poke his nose up there. Even Rebels are smart enough to go for the high ground in a fight."

"Maybe," LaRone agreed, feeling a twinge of doubt. "Still, I suppose there *could* have been Rebel activity in one of the sections of town I didn't see."

"Of course there *could* have been," Grave retorted. "And since none of us could see everything, everyone can persuade himself that's what happened. Typical ISB foggery." He snapped his T-28 back up to his shoulder and fired off another half a dozen rounds. "Only they couldn't stuff up our ears, could they?" he growled as he lowered the weapon again. "And every shot *I* heard came from an E-11."

"I know," LaRone conceded. "So were there *ever* any Rebels in that town? Or was this nothing but some bizarre object lesson?"

Grave shook his head. "You tell me, LaRone," he said. "All I know—" He broke off. "Well, from what I could see, it looked like the first ones to be targeted were the aliens."

"That was how it went down with my squad, too," LaRone said heavily. "Not that anyone ever gave an order nearly that specific. The ISB men just pointed and ordered us to shoot."

"And then watched to see if any of you shot to miss?"

LaRone felt his stomach tighten. That thought had never even occurred to him. "Are you suggesting this might have been a test of *us*?"

Grave shrugged. "From what I've heard, ISB never liked the idea of opening up the ranks to volunteers like us. They wanted to keep the stormtroopers strictly clones."

LaRone snorted. "That was nine years ago. They really should have gotten over it by now."

"Normal people would have," Grave said sourly. "But this is ISB we're talking about." He eyed LaRone. "I hope you shot especially straight today."

"I did my duty," LaRone said stiffly. "Grave, you don't suppose ISB knows something we don't, do you? Like maybe they *were* all Rebel sympathizers in there?"

"You mean like everyone on Alderaan?"

LaRone's throat tightened. Alderaan. "Grave, what's happening to us?" he asked quietly. "What's happening to the Empire?"

"I don't know," Grave said. "Maybe it's the Rebels. Maybe they're pushing so hard, all the loose seams are starting to break." His lips compressed tightly. "Or maybe the Empire's always been like this. Maybe we just didn't notice until Alderaan."

"So what do we do about it?"

"We don't *do* anything, LaRone," Grave said, a warning tone in his voice. "What *can* we do?"

Join the Rebellion? The thought flashed through LaRone's mind. But it was a preposterous idea, and he knew it. He and the others had sworn an oath to defend the Empire and its citizens, and there was no way any of them were going to collaborate with people trying to collapse the whole thing back to chaos. "I don't know," he said. "But this isn't what I signed up for."

"What you signed up for was to obey orders," Grave said, turning back to the firing line. Popping out his blaster's power pack, he pulled a fresh one from his belt and slid it into place. "You *certainly* didn't sign up to let ISB haul you off for seditious thinking."

"That's for sure," LaRone agreed, a shiver running through him. Translation: don't ever talk this way again.

"Because we're supposed to be getting a complete ISB tactical unit in a day or two," Grave went on. "Their own transports, their own chain of command, probably their own stormtroopers, too."

"Where'd you hear that?"

"Marcross, of course," Grave said, a wry smile peeking almost reluctantly from behind all his seriousness. "Where *he* gets all this stuff, I haven't a clue."

"You think he could be ISB himself?"

"Not a chance," Grave said firmly. "He's way too nice a guy for that. No, he just likes to keep his ear to the sky."

"I suppose," LaRone said. "Regardless, it sounds like someone's getting serious about this Rebel hunt."

"That's fine with me," Grave said. "And I intend to be ready next time we run into some *real* Rebels." Turning, he put his helmet back on and keyed for a fresh target.

He was halfway through the new pattern when LaRone slipped quietly out of the booth.

*   *   *

The reception was in full swing, the grand ballroom of Moff Glovstoak's palace glittering with elaborate lighting and flowing banners and soft music played by a balcony ring of live musicians. Only slightly less glittering were the rich and powerful filling the room, their collective conversation adding a muted counterpoint to the music. There were at least five hundred men and women present, Mara Jade estimated as she drifted serenely past and through the little knots of conversation, the elite of the elite of the entire sector. Glovstoak was definitely pulling out all the limiters tonight.

It made one wonder where he was getting the credits to pay for it.

"Ah—Countess Claria."

Mara turned. An older man in a general's uniform was coming through the crowd toward her, a younger man in simple formalwear in tow. "Hello again, General Deerian," Mara greeted him with a smile, her eyes flicking over his companion. Mink Bollis, she identified him, one of Glovstoak's aides. Good—if the inner circle was starting to arrive, the moff himself should be close behind. "I thought you were on your way to inspect the buffet."

"I was, but then I ran into Master Bollis," General Deerian said, indicating the younger man. "Remembering our earlier conversation about your world's pirate problems, I thought he might be able to offer some help."

"Countess," Bollis greeted her, scooping up her right hand and kissing it in Old Core fashion. His predator's gaze took in her green eyes and red-gold hair, shifted to her shoulder sculpt with its interwoven mound of cascading flowers, then dropped still farther to her slender figure encased in its low-cut gown. Pirates and pirate problems, clearly, were the last thing on his mind. "I assure you that Moff Glovstoak and the entire sector government stand ready to assist you in your need. Why don't we find a quiet corner where you can give me some details of your situation?"

"That would be—" Mara broke off, letting an uncertain frown pass briefly across her face before smoothing it out. "That would be wonderful."

"Are you all right?" Deerian asked.

"I just felt a little strange there for a moment," Mara said. She let the odd look flicker across her face again, this time adding a slight unsteadiness to her poise.

"Perhaps you should sit down for a while," Deerian said, eyeing her closely. "Ambrostine can sneak up on you if you're not used to it."

"I thought I was," Mara said, adding a little throatiness to her voice. In actual fact, she was quite familiar with both ambrostine and the symptoms that came from drinking too much of it.

And Bollis, at least, apparently also knew about the loss of inhibitions that was the next stage. "Let me take you someplace where you can lie down," he offered, his eyes glittering a little brighter. He moved to her side, reaching for her arm to assist her.

To Mara's mild surprise, Deerian got there first. "Moff Glovstoak will be expecting you to assist with his guests," the general reminded Bollis as he deftly moved Mara away from the younger man. "I know the palace— I'll find her a place where she'll be safe."

Before Bollis could find the right words for a polite protest, Deerian had eased Mara around a couple dressed completely in shimmersilk and headed for one of the side doors.

Outside the ballroom, the hallways were deserted except for the pairs of liveried guards standing watch at each intersection. None of them stopped or challenged Deerian as he led her into a darkened office two corridors away. "My field offices get their furniture from the same supplier Moff Glovstoak uses for his underlings," he told Mara as he turned the light on low and led her to the room's conversation circle. "I can assure you from personal experience that these couches are just the thing for a quick nap."

"Right now, I think I could sleep in a gravel pit," Mara murmured, slurring the words slightly as she let her eyelids droop. "Thank you."

"No problem, Countess," Deerian said as he helped her stretch out on one of the couches. "As I said, ambrostine is a subtle enemy."

"I meant—you know."

He smiled down at her. "No problem there, either," he assured her. "You're, what? Eighteen? Nineteen?"

"Eighteen."

Deerian's smile turned a bit brittle. "I have a granddaughter that age," he said. "I wouldn't want her alone with Bollis, either. Sleep as long as you want, Countess. I'll make sure you're not disturbed."

He left, closing the door behind him. Rolling off the couch, Mara crossed the room and pressed her ear to the door, running through the audio enhancement techniques the Emperor had taught her.

Even with that assistance she could hear only about every other word Deerian was saying to the nearest guard pair. But she could tell he was instructing them in no uncertain terms to make sure no one bothered the young lady. The conversation ended, and Deerian's footsteps faded away in the direction of the ballroom. Readjusting her hearing to normal, Mara turned off the light and glided back across the room.

Time to go to work.

In her admittedly short career so far as the Emperor's Hand, Mara had noted the odd mixture of caution and sloppiness displayed by many of the Empire's top politicians. Glovstoak was no exception. Even here on the palace's tenth floor, the windows were protected by an intruder warning grid; at the same time, there was a local release for that grid tucked away beneath the sill so that the office's occupant could get fresh air without having to call to the main security office for clearance. A moment's study gained her the key, and with the grid disabled she slid the window carefully open and leaned out.

Aside from the guards walking their rounds far below and the distant aircars patrolling the outer perimeter of the palace grounds, no one was visible. Stretching out to the Force, she got a grip on the package she'd hidden earlier beneath one of the decorative bushes lining the outer wall and pulled.

For a moment nothing happened. She focused harder, and this time the handle came free and floated swiftly upward, its connecting cord trailing behind it. A moment later it was in her hands, and at a touch of a button the motors inside began reeling in the cord and the much heavier black-wrapped package at the far end.

A minute later the package was inside, its contents spread on the office floor. Two minutes after that, she had exchanged her flowing gown for a gray combat suit, her delicate flowery shoulder sculpt for a shoulder-slung

Stokhli spray stick, and her embroidered waist sash for a belt and a lightsaber.

The packet also included a tube of compressed air and an inflatable-mannequin duplicate of her, dressed in formalwear identical to that she had been wearing moments before. She set it up and arranged it on the couch as a decoy for any prying eyes; with her real gown out of sight beneath the desk, she headed back to the window and slipped outside.

Mara had been introduced to the spray stick only a few months earlier, and in that time had worked hard to master it and add it to her already extensive repertoire of tools and weapons. This entire gambit, in fact, was one she'd practiced over and over again at her training center in the Imperial Palace. Straddling the windowsill, she pointed the device at an upward angle along the outer wall and squeezed the thumb trigger.

There was a sharp hiss, and the spray stick snapped back against its shoulder sling as a jet of fine mist shot out the far end. As it hit the air, the mist turned into a roiling flow of liquid that quickly solidified against the stonework, forming a twist-surfaced bridge that could be climbed. Shutting off the spray, Mara rotated the stick out of her way on its strap and started up.

She had to pause twice to spray additional length to her private pathway before she reached the twentieth floor and Glovstoak's private quarters. His windows were protected by the same intruder grid she'd found in the office, with the same built-in weakness. Stretching with the Force through the transparisteel, she first shut off the grid and then tripped the catch. A minute later she was inside.

The quarters were deserted, Glovstoak and all his people downstairs at the grand party. Still, Mara stayed alert as she moved silently between the rooms. The moff could easily have left a droid or two to watch over his private possessions.

But droids could be scanned or reprogrammed, and Glovstoak apparently wasn't willing to take that kind of chance. Instead he had chosen to rely on two highly sophisticated alarms on his concealed walk-in safe.

Sophisticated from his point of view, anyway. The professional thieves the Emperor had brought in to instruct Mara in their craft would have laughed at both systems. Mara herself, not nearly so experienced, merely smiled, and had both neutralized within ten minutes.

After all the preliminaries, getting the safe itself open was almost an anticlimax. Two minutes later she pulled open the heavy door and stepped inside.

One wall of the safe had been taken over entirely by data card file cabinets, containing the sector's duplicate administration records. Interesting enough, certainly, but even if Glovstoak had been careless enough to leave a data trail that would show his alleged financial irregularities, it would take a small army of accountants to sniff it out. Instead Mara headed toward the back of the safe, looking for more personal items.

And there she found the evidence she needed.

For a long moment she gazed at the half dozen artworks sitting in the beam of her glow rod. At first glance the private collection seemed rather puny, especially considering the number of flats, sculptures, tressles, and volmans decorating the public areas of the palace.

Mara wasn't fooled. The pieces downstairs were grandiose but relatively cheap. More importantly, they were comfortably within the budget of an honest administrator of Glovstoak's position.

The six pieces in the safe were something else entirely. Any one of them would fetch upward of a hundred million credits from the galaxy's wealthiest private collectors, no questions asked. Taken together, they were probably worth three times the value of Glovstoak's palace and everything in it.

Which meant that the Emperor's suspicions were correct. Glovstoak was skimming the top off the tax revenues he was sending to Imperial Center.

Picking up one of the flats, Mara turned it around. In the light from her glow rod the back surface appeared to be plain and unmarked. But there was a little thing art dealers did that Glovstoak might not be aware of. Tuning her glow rod to a specific frequency of ultraviolet light, she tried again.

There it was: a complete listing of all the dealers and auction houses and brokers through whose hands the flat had traveled throughout its long history.

Mara smiled. The dealers made these lists invisible to avoid introducing such crass commercialism into the carefully nurtured elegance of their world. Professional art thieves routinely obliterated the markings in order to make their new acquisitions harder to trace. Glovstoak hadn't done that, which immediately told her he hadn't obtained the art through a professional. Interesting.

She made a note of the last listing—Peven Auction House, Crovna—and set the flat back where she'd found it. She made a similar check of two more of the artworks, then left the safe, closing the door and reactivating the alarms behind her.

The trip down the wall was much easier and faster than the trip up had been. The solidified Stokhli spray would evaporate in another couple of hours, leaving no trace even if Glovstoak's men thought to look.

She was back in her gown, the rest of her gear hidden again behind its ground-level bush, when the office door eased open a cautious crack. "Countess?" Deerian's voice called quietly.

"Yes, General," she called back, sitting up on the couch and stretching. "Please, come in."

"I trust you're feeling better?" the other said, stepping into the doorway.

"Much better," she assured him, smiling as she crossed to him. "Thank you for your thoughtfulness."

"My pleasure," he said, smiling back as he offered her his arm. "Shall we return to the reception?"

"Yes, indeed," she said, taking his arm.

And let's hope everyone enjoys it, she thought as they headed past the watchful sentries. *It's the last party Glovstoak will ever throw.*

Chapter Three

MARCROSS'S INFORMATION, AS USUAL, TURNED OUT TO BE CORRECT. Six days after the Teardrop massacre an ISB tactical unit arrived aboard the *Reprisal*.

They arrived in force, too: ten full squads, including officers, troopers, droids, even their own intel analysis group. More disturbing to LaRone were the two squads of stormtroopers who came with them.

"Which means that whatever *they* do—shoot up another town, or worse—they'll be wearing *our* armor, which means the whole storm-trooper corps will get the blame for it," he warned Quiller and Grave as the three of them gazed down from the observation walkway into Hangar Bay 5. The ISB people had brought a strange assortment of vehicles with them, from light freighters to old and outmoded military transports and even a dilapidated pleasure yacht.

"Not that we're not blamed for everything anyway," Quiller added with an edge of bitterness. "Comes of our always catching the tough ones."

"Which comes of our being the Empire's finest," Grave countered with a touch of pride. "We *certainly* have better transports than these clowns."

"What, you mean *those*?" Quiller asked, pointing at the cluster of ships below them. "Don't you believe it, buddy, not for a minute. That Suwantek TL-1800, for instance—see those crimp marks on the engine nozzles?"

"Which one are we talking about?" LaRone asked, frowning at the unfamiliar designs.

"That flat, angular job with the oversized sublight engines," Quiller said, pointing. "Usually the 1800's a piece of junk—holds together okay, but it's slow, badly armed, and poorly shielded. The nav computer glitches a lot, too."

"Sounds perfect for the ISB," Grave murmured. "Let's turn 'em loose and let 'em get lost."

"Like I said, don't believe it," Quiller said. "Those engines have been upgraded probably six ways from Imperial Center, and odds are everything else beneath the plating has, too. Ditto for the rest of the ships."

"You suppose they run under false IDs?" LaRone asked.

Quiller snorted. "They probably have whole racks full of them," he said. "We may be the Empire's finest, but you'd never know it when ISB gets up from the budget table."

"You have a problem with the ISB, soldier?" a dark voice demanded from behind them.

LaRone felt his stomach knot up. It was Major Drelfin, the ISB man who'd ordered the massacre on Teardrop.

"No, sir, not at all," Quiller assured him quickly.

"Glad to hear it," Drelfin said as he stalked toward them, his hand resting on the grip of his holstered blaster. "Now, you have exactly five seconds to tell me what you're doing in a restricted area."

"We're Imperial stormtroopers, sir," LaRone told him, fighting to keep the proper level of military respect in his voice. "We're allowed access everywhere aboard ship."

"Really," Drelfin said, his gaze flicking over LaRone's fatigues. "Why aren't you in armor?"

"We've been permitted a bit of latitude in that area, sir," LaRone said, choosing his words carefully. Regulations unequivocally stated that stormtroopers were always to be in armor whenever outside their barracks section. But Captain Ozzel resented their presence aboard his ship, and didn't like seeing armored men wandering around during their off hours. Since the stormtrooper commanders had, in turn, refused to confine their men to barracks when they were off duty, they'd come to a more unofficial arrangement.

"Permitted by whom?" Drelfin demanded. "Your lieutenant? Your major?"

"Is there a problem here, Major?" a new voice said from the far end of the observation gallery.

LaRone turned to find Marcross and Brightwater walking toward them, the latter with a rag tucked into the pocket of his fatigues and grease stains on his hands.

"What *is* this, the Kiddie Klub meeting room?" Drelfin growled. "Identify yourselves."

"Stormtrooper TKR 175," Marcross said, an edge of both pride and challenge in his voice. "This is TBR 479."

"Also not in armor, I see," Drelfin growled. "Also apparently ignorant of the regulations regarding off-limit areas."

He shifted his glare back to LaRone. "Or is it that you border-world recruits don't know how to read the regulations in the first place?"

"As I said, sir—" LaRone began.

"—you didn't think regulations applied to you," Drelfin finished sarcastically. "I trust you know better now?"

"Yes, sir," Brightwater said. He touched LaRone's arm. "Come on, LaRone. You were going to help me change the steering vanes on my speeder."

"LaRone?" Drelfin echoed, his voice suddenly strange. "*Daric* LaRone? TKR 330?"

LaRone glanced at Marcross, noting the sudden crease in the other's forehead. "Yes, sir," he said.

"Well, well," Drelfin said softly. Without warning, he drew his blaster. "I've been going over the records of the Teardrop operation," he continued, an unpleasant tightness at the corners of his eyes as the weapon came to a halt pointed at LaRone's stomach. "Your squad was ordered to execute some Rebel sympathizers. You deliberately missed your shots. That's dereliction of duty."

LaRone felt his throat tighten. So someone had noticed his lack of precision shooting that day. This was not good. "My duty is to protect and preserve the Empire and the New Order," he said, forcing his voice to stay calm.

"Your *duty* is to obey orders," Drelfin countered.

"They were unarmed and nonthreatening civilians," LaRone said. "If there were charges or suspicions concerning them, they should have been arrested and brought to trial."

"They were Rebel sympathizers!"

Quiller took a step forward. "Sir, if you have a complaint against this man—"

"Stay out of this, stormtrooper," Drelfin warned. "You're in enough trouble as it is."

"What sort of trouble?" Marcross asked.

"You're out of uniform, you're in a restricted area without authorization—" Drelfin nodded at LaRone. "—and you're obviously friendly with a traitor to the Empire."

"*What?*" Grave demanded. "That's insa—"

"With all due respect, Major, TKR 2014 is correct," Marcross cut him off. "Regulations require that a charge of this magnitude be brought immediately to the attention of the senior stormtrooper officer."

"Let me explain something, TKR 175," Drelfin growled. "We're the Imperial Security Bureau. What we say is principle; what we decide is regulation; what we do is law."

"And whoever you order shot is dead?" LaRone retorted.

"So you *do* understand," Drelfin said, the corners of his mouth quirking upward in a death's-head smile. "*I* was in command of that operation, which means *I* will decide what to do with you. Not your lieutenant; not your major; certainly not your stupid Captain Ozzel."

He stepped up and pressed the muzzle of his blaster into LaRone's forehead. It was an unfamiliar design, LaRone noted distantly: large and nasty, with an odd-looking attachment at the end of the barrel. "And if I choose to summarily execute you for treason—" His finger tightened visibly on the trigger.

He was bluffing, a small part of LaRone's mind knew. He was toying with his victim in one of the macabre games that these small-minded, sadistic little men enjoyed so much.

But LaRone was an Imperial stormtrooper, ruthlessly trained in the arts of combat and survival, and those deeply embedded reflexes knew nothing about ISB mind games. His left hand snapped up of its own accord, slapping Drelfin's wrist and knocking the blaster away from his forehead.

It was probably the last thing Drelfin expected. He stumbled with the impact, snarling a curse as he tried to swing the weapon back on target. But even as he did so LaRone's right hand came up, catching the other's wrist and giving it an extra push. For a single, nerve-racking fraction of a second the blaster was again pointing at LaRone's face; then it was past, overcorrecting and swinging wide to LaRone's left. He swiveled on his right foot, spinning himself halfway around as he held on to the major's wrist, and a second later he had Drelfin hunched over, his arm twisted around, the blaster pointed harmlessly at the ceiling. "What was that about ISB whims being law?" he ground out.

"LaRone, are you *insane*?" Brightwater demanded, his eyes bulging.

"Maybe," LaRone said. His anger was draining away, and to his dismay he realized that Brightwater was right. If he hadn't been in trouble before, he was certainly there now. "But that'll be for the *proper* procedure to determine," he added. Reaching up, he twisted the blaster out of Drelfin's grip, then let go of his arm.

Drelfin straightened up, his eyes staring vibroblades at LaRone, his face contorted with rage, his mouth working with soundless curses.

His left hand gripping a small hold-out blaster.

And this time, LaRone knew, it was no game. There was a soft flash, a muted blast—

Without a sound, Drelfin collapsed silently to the deck.

For a long, frozen moment, no one moved or spoke. LaRone stared at the crumpled body, then at the major's blaster still in his hand, his mind struggling to believe the evidence of his eyes. No—something else had surely happened. The major must have had a stroke or heart attack, or perhaps been shot from concealment by some unknown party. That hadn't even sounded like a real blaster shot, for pity's sake—

"Oh, no," Brightwater murmured, sounding stunned.

LaRone swallowed hard; and with that, the bubble of wild speculation burst, and the cold reality flooded in on him. Daric LaRone, with all his high-minded prattlings about duty and honor, had just gunned down a man in cold blood.

Not just a man. An officer. An ISB officer.

And in that second frozen moment, he knew he was dead.

The others knew it, too. "It was self-defense," Quiller said, his voice shaking in a way LaRone had never heard from him in even the most desperate combat situations. "You all saw it. Drelfin drew first."

"You think ISB will care?" Grave bit out.

"I just meant—"

"They won't care," Marcross said, his voice tight as he looked quickly around the observation deck. "The question is, how serious are they going to be about tracking us down?"

"Wait a second," Brightwater said. "What do you mean, *us?*"

"He's right, Marcross," LaRone agreed, his heart starting to pound in reaction. "There's no *us* here—there's just *me*. None of you did anything."

"I doubt ISB will care about *that*, either," Quiller muttered.

"Of course they'll care," Marcross said heavily. "They'll care that none of us did anything to stop you."

"There wasn't any *time*—"

"Quiet, LaRone," Grave cut in. "He's right. We're all for the jump on this one."

"Not if they can't identify us," Brightwater suggested, looking furtively around. "There's no one else here, and he was shot with his own gun. Maybe they'll even think it was suicide."

Grave snorted. "Oh, come *on*. An ISB major, at the height of his twisted little career? They kill other people, not themselves."

"There's only one thing to do," LaRone said. Taking a long step to the side, he brought up his blaster to cover them. "On the floor, all of you."

None of them moved. "Nice gesture," Grave said. "But it won't work."

"I've got the blaster," LaRone said, lifting the weapon for emphasis. "There's no way you can stop me, and regulations don't require you to throw away your lives for nothing."

"No, LaRone, Grave's right," Marcross said, shaking his head. "They'll torture us, and as soon as they find out we knew you wouldn't shoot we'll be right back in the grinder."

"Besides, you can't fly one of those ISB ships by yourself," Quiller said quietly. "At the very least *I* have to come with you."

"At the very least we *all* have to," Grave said, his voice heavy. "And we're wasting time."

"I can't let you do this," LaRone protested. "I can't ask you to give up everything this way. You'll have to leave the Empire, become fugitives—"

"We haven't got a choice," Grave said. "Besides, after what happened on Teardrop, I'm not sure I'll ever be comfortable wearing my armor again."

"And as for leaving the Empire," Quiller added soberly, "it seems to me the Empire left us first. At least the Empire we thought we were signing up to serve." He looked at Brightwater. "So: Brightwater. Raise and call to you."

Brightwater grimaced. "I'm not ready to give up on the Empire quite yet," he said. "But I also don't want to sit around waiting for ISB to put me under their hot lights. What's the plan?"

LaRone looked down at Drelfin's crumpled form, trying to kick his brain back up to speed. "First thing is to hide the body," he said. "One of those storage lockers over there ought to do it. Quiller, which ship are we taking?"

"The Suwantek," Quiller said, pointing to the ship they'd been discussing earlier. "Considering our combined mechanical skills, we're going to want the most reliable ship we can get. If they were thoughtful enough to leave the systems on standby, I can have it prepped in ten minutes."

"We can't leave while the *Reprisal*'s in hyperspace," Brightwater said.

"Maybe there's another way," LaRone said, an audacious idea tickling the back of his mind. "Go get it prepped—Grave, Brightwater, you go with him. Marcross and I will deal with the body."

The storage lockers were well packed, but with a little tweaking they were able to make enough room for Drelfin's body. By the time they finished and descended to the hangar deck level Quiller and the others were already inside the Suwantek. Trying to look casual, LaRone touched Marcross's arm and headed toward the boarding ramp.

No one challenged them as they strode along, a circumstance that struck LaRone as both suspicious and ominous. They were halfway across before it occurred to him that with the ISB's restrictions in place there probably wasn't anyone in the hangar bay monitor room to watch the parade. They reached the ship without incident and climbed up into a small but nicely furnished crew lounge. Raising and sealing the ramp, they headed for the bridge.

Quiller was in the pilot's seat, his fingers tapping here and there as he brought the ship to full life. "Where are Grave and Brightwater?" Marcross asked as he sat down beside Quiller in the copilot's seat.

"Checking to make sure no one's sleeping aboard," Quiller said. "Okay, we're ready." He peered over his shoulder at LaRone. "You said you had an idea?"

LaRone nodded, sat down behind Marcross at the astrogation/comm station, and gave the controls a quick scan. In-hangar comm . . . there. Squaring his shoulders, trying to put himself in the mind-set of an ISB thug, he keyed it on. "This is Major Drelfin," he said in his best impression of Drelfin's voice. "We're ready."

"Sir?" a slightly puzzled voice came back.

"I said we're ready to go," LaRone said, putting some bite into his voice. "Bring the *Reprisal* out of hyperspace so we can launch."

"Ah . . . one moment, sir."

The comm went silent. "*That* was your big trick?" Quiller muttered.

"Give him a minute," LaRone said, trying to sound more confident than he felt. If they had to blast their way out of here—

"Major, this is Commander Brillstow," a new voice put in. "I see no ship departures on my schedule."

"Of course you don't," LaRone growled. "And you won't put anything in your log report, either. Now kindly drop out of hyperspace so we can get on with this."

He held his breath. Quiller was right, of course; standing orders would certainly require that the deck officer clear any such unscheduled request with the captain, or at least check with someone in Drelfin's own contingent.

But the Imperial Security Bureau ran under its own rules, and everyone in the Fleet knew it. If Commander Brillstow had heard enough stories of ISB displeasure . . .

And to his relief and surprise, the mottled hyperspace sky outside the hangar bay faded into the star-flecked blackness of realspace. "Acknowledged, Major," Brillstow said, his voice stiff and formal. "You're cleared to launch."

LaRone switched off the comm. "Let's get moving before they change their minds," he told Quiller.

"It could still be a trap," Quiller warned as he keyed the repulsorlifts and swiveled the Suwantek toward the atmosphere screen. "They might just be letting us get outside where they can nail us with the heavy stuff."

"I don't think so," Marcross said. "They wouldn't go for a burned-ground endgame without at least trying to take us alive and find out what in blazes we think we're doing."

"I hope you're right," Quiller said. "Here we go . . ."

Seconds later, they were outside. Quiller curved them up the Star Destroyer's flank, swinging them around behind the superstructure as he headed for deep space. A minute after that, as LaRone watched the tactical display for signs of a last-minute change of heart, the *Reprisal* flickered with pseudomotion and vanished again into hyperspace.

"Whew," Quiller exhaled with a huff. "It's so nice when ISB's cloak-and-blade nonsense works against them."

"Though that doesn't mean we should sit here and wait for them to wake up," Marcross warned. "Any thoughts as to where we go from here?"

"I was thinking Drunost might be a good first stop," Quiller said, keying in an overhead display. "It's about three hours away, a nice little back-world place that happens to have a Consolidated Shipping hub and outlet, which means it'll have all the fuel and supplies we'll need. It's a long way to the edge of the Empire, you know."

"*If* we decide we really have to go that far," Marcross said. "There are any number of closer systems where we could hide."

"We can hash that over later," LaRone said. "Go ahead and get us started for Drunost."

Quiller nodded and keyed his board, and the stars outside flashed into starlines. "Of course, one question we're going to have to answer before we get there is what we're going to do for money," he pointed out.

There was a beep from the intercom. "Quiller?" Brightwater's voice came. "We clear?"

"Clear and free, and the *Reprisal*'s gone," Quiller assured him.

"Great," Brightwater said. "You might want to set it on auto and come back to the number two crew cabin—second on your right, just aft of the lounge. Got something interesting to show you."

Brightwater and Grave were waiting when LaRone, Marcross, and Quiller arrived. Like the crew lounge itself, the cabin was designed with the kind of care LaRone would have expected of men running on an ISB budget. Furnishings included a narrow but comfortable-looking bed, a wall locker, a small computer desk, a repeater display over the desk that showed the ship's current heading and overall flight status, and even a small private refresher station.

"Nice," Quiller commented, looking around approvingly. "This one must be the pilot's."

"It's mine, actually," Grave told him. "But don't worry—they're all like this."

"And if you think *this* is nice, hang on to your bucket," Brightwater added. Stepping to the repeater display, he ran his finger along the underside of the frame. With a quiet *snick*, a section of the bulkhead at the end of the bed popped ajar, and Brightwater swung it open to reveal a hidden walk-in closet.

Or rather, a hidden walk-in arsenal.

There were a dozen blasters racked together on one sidewall, everything from fleet-issue BlasTech DH-17 pistols to standard stormtrooper E-11 rifles to a pair of hold-out blasters of a make and model LaRone didn't recognize. Beneath the racked weapons were rows of power packs and gas cartridges, plus several small bins of assorted replacement parts. On the other sidewall was one of Grave's favored T-28 sniper rifles plus a selection of vibroblades, grenades, stun cuffs, and a couple of Arakyd hunter/seeker remotes.

And filling the center of the space were two complete sets of gleaming stormtrooper armor.

"The number one cabin's got a slightly different selection," Grave said into the stunned silence. "We haven't checked the others yet, but it's a fair bet they're all tricked out the same way."

"There are two Aratech 74-Z speeder bikes in one of the cargo holds, so I figure one of the cabins must have a set or two of scout trooper armor," Brightwater added. "*That* one will be mine."

"These guys sure came prepared," Marcross commented. "I don't suppose they also happened to leave some cash lying around?"

"If they didn't, we can always rob a bank," Quiller put in drily, gesturing at the weaponry.

"We haven't found any credits yet," Brightwater told Marcross. "On the other hand, it was pure dumb luck that we found *this*. We were looking for stowaways, not buried treasure."

"I think we should remedy that," Marcross suggested.

"Absolutely," LaRone agreed. "We've got three hours to planetfall, stormtroopers. Spread out and let's see what else the ISB was kind enough to put aboard our new ship."

The final tally was impressive. There were fifteen sets of stormtrooper armor, eight standard, six specialized, and a full spacetrooper rig; fifty blasters of various sorts; a hundred grenades, including shock and explosive and even a pair of thermal detonators; thirty-five changes of civilian clothing; two landspeeders; two speeder bikes; a three-seat, six-passenger speeder truck; and numerous bits of tracking, combat, and detention gear, including a small machine for turning out personal identity tags. There was also the rack of false ship transponder codes Quiller had predicted.

And there was cash. More than half a million credits.

"What in the worlds were they planning that they needed all this?" Brightwater muttered as they sat in the lounge comparing their lists.

"My guess is that they're going for a jab at the Rebellion's throat," Marcross said. "Disguised freighters would be perfect for infiltrating enemy supply convoys."

"Or for posing as renegades who want to join up," LaRone said.

"Well, whatever they had in mind, it sure puts us in a good position," Grave said. "So where exactly on the Outer Rim are we heading?"

"We could try Hutt space," Quiller suggested. "The Empire keeps a pretty low profile there, and we could easily pick up a little enforcer or bodyguard work."

"We're not working for criminals," Brightwater said stiffly.

"I just meant—"

"No, he's right," LaRone seconded. "We're Imperial stormtroopers, not thugs for hire."

"We're not Imperial stormtroopers anymore," Quiller muttered, tossing his datapad onto the hologame table.

"We're still not working for criminals," Brightwater insisted.

"There's another possibility," Marcross offered. "Instead of running for the Outer Rim like frightened Toong, why not stay right here in Shelsha sector?"

"I don't know," Quiller said doubtfully. "I looked over the system list earlier, and there aren't a lot of places we could go to ground without someone eventually noticing us."

"Unless we kept moving," Brightwater suggested. "We've got enough credits to do that, at least for a while."

Marcross cleared his throat. "Actually, I was thinking we might try someplace on Shelkonwa."

LaRone frowned in surprise. From the looks on the others' faces, they were having the same reaction. "You want us to hide on Shelsha's *capital*?" Quiller asked.

"It *is* the last place ISB would think to look for wanted fugitives," Marcross pointed out. "And I know people there who could help us."

"If you have friends there, it's the *last* place we want to go," Grave countered. "You remember the name of the first girl you ever kissed?"

Marcross snorted. "Of course."

"How about the second?"

"Well . . . no, not really," Marcross conceded.

"Well, ISB *does*," Grave said. "Or they'll know soon enough. We're *fugitives*, Marcross. That means we can never again make contact with anyone we ever knew. Ever."

"Let's go a little easy on the long-term planning here," LaRone put in. "First thing is to get in and out of Drunost without tripping any alerts. Once we've got full tanks and a full pantry, we can talk more about our options."

Marcross still didn't look convinced, but he nodded. "Fine," he said. "But I still want a chance later to make the case for Shelkonwa."

"You'll have it," LaRone promised. "We'll all have our say, and we'll make the decision together. Like Grave said, the five of us are all we've got."

Brightwater shook his head. "Why," he said, "does that not exactly fill me with confidence?"

Chapter Four

"So," Emperor Palpatine said, his eyes glinting from the shadows beneath the peak of his hood. "It is as I suspected. Moff Glovstoak is a traitor."

"He's at least an embezzler, my lord," Mara said. "I don't yet know whether or not he's committed actual treason."

"I consider theft of Imperial funds to be treason," the Emperor countered. "Your part in this is now ended, my child—others will carry on from here. You have done well."

"Thank you," Mara said, feeling the warmth of his approval flow through her. "Then unless there's something more urgent pending, I'd like permission to do an investigation of the six artworks I found in Glovstoak's safe. The ones I examined appear to be from a batch of ten that were stolen from a gallery five years ago during an attack on a Rebel cell on Krintrino."

The Emperor's face darkened. "So as well as being an embezzler, Glovstoak may also be connected with the Rebel Alliance?"

"Or he may have a connection with the Imperial forces who carried out the attack," Mara pointed out, a little cautiously. The Emperor was a wise and good man, but he had an odd tendency sometimes to see Rebels and Rebel conspiracies where they might not actually exist. "Or it could have been pirates or thieves who simply took advantage of the attack's chaos to grab and run. The interesting point is that Glovstoak apparently bought them through an auction house, which suggests he and the seller wanted a stamp of legitimacy put on the transfer."

"You said ten were stolen," the Emperor said. "Yet only six were in Glovstoak's safe?"

"Yes," Mara confirmed. "*And* all six were apparently bought at the same time about eighteen months ago."

"Where are the other four?"

"As far as I know, they're still missing," Mara said. "That's one of the questions I'd like an answer to. Another is why the original owner suddenly decided he needed such a large influx of cash a year and a half ago."

For a minute the Emperor remained silent, and Mara felt a flicker of satisfaction. Private transfers of valuable objects happened all the time across the Empire, for any number of legitimate or borderline-shady reasons. Such questions coming from many of the Emperor's other advisers and assistants would likely have been dismissed out of hand as irrelevant.

But Mara was the Emperor's Hand, recruited and trained personally by him, and he trusted her instincts. "The loss of the Death Star was a great shock to even my strongest supporters," he said at last. "Some, perhaps, might be wondering if my Empire is indeed the likely winner in this conflict with the Rebel Alliance."

"Of course it is," Mara said automatically.

The Emperor gave her another thin smile. "Indeed," he agreed. "But not everyone sees things as clearly as you and I. If Glovstoak is not connected to the Rebellion, perhaps one of our wealthier citizens has decided to play both sides. Tell me, what is the current Rebel presence in Shelsha sector?"

"I don't know yet," Mara said. "I was planning to comm Shelkonwa and ask Governor Choard's office to prepare a summary for me."

"Don't," the Emperor said, the corners of his lips turning down with contempt. "Barshnis Choard is a competent administrator, but he has far too many ties with the wealthy and powerful of his sector. He might leak news of your investigation to the very people you seek. No, you will instead use my personal library for your research."

Mara bowed her head. "Thank you, my lord."

The Emperor held out his hand to her. "Go," he said.

Mara stepped forward and took his outstretched hand, feeling a fresh wave of warmth and strength flow into her, then stepped back again. "One other thing, my lord," she said. "When you have Moff Glovstoak and his administration arrested, I would ask that a member of his staff, General Deerian, be exempted from punishment."

The Emperor regarded her thoughtfully. "You believe him to be innocent of Glovstoak's treason?"

"I'm certain of it," Mara said. "He's also an honest and honorable man. I don't wish to see the Empire deprived of his service."

The other's lip may have twitched slightly at the word *honorable*. But he merely nodded. "As you wish, my child," he said. "I will have General Deerian transferred immediately to a position here on Imperial Center, where he will remain untouched by Glovstoak's imminent destruction."

"Thank you," Mara said. Turning, she strode across the expanse of the throne room, passed between the silent red-robed Royal Guards, and stepped into the turbolift.

The Emperor's library was a large and very private place, used only by a few of his top people, and only with his express permission. Normally, there were a handful of attendants on hand to assist, but as Mara walked between the tall stacks of data card file cabinets toward the retrieval stations at the center she was struck by the unusual silence. Apparently all the attendants had suddenly found a need to be elsewhere.

As she rounded the last cabinet she discovered the reason for their absence. Seated alone at one of the three computer stations was Darth Vader.

"Lord Vader," she said politely as she stepped past, her eyes flicking automatically to the display screen in front of him.

His arm came up, just high enough to block her view. "Emperor's Hand," he greeted her in turn, his voice deep and stiff and darker even than usual. "What do you want?"

"I was given permission to do some research," Mara said, continuing past him and seating herself at one of the other stations.

But even as she turned on the console and started keying for her data search, she could sense his brooding attention switch from his research to Mara herself. Vader had always been polite enough, but even without

Mara's Force sensitivity it would have been abundantly clear that he didn't like her.

She'd never figured out why that was. Certainly their goals were the same: service to the Emperor and his New Order. Perhaps he thought her training had taken too much of the Emperor's time and attention, or perhaps he suspected her of trying to supplant him in the great man's eyes.

Both thoughts were ridiculous, of course. Mara had her work to do, and Vader had his, and there was no point trying to second-guess the Emperor's wisdom in the way he employed either of them.

But she had yet to find a way to get that message through to Vader.

"You seek information on the Rebels," Vader said.

"Don't we all?" Mara said drily. "Specifically, I'm interested in the ones in Shelsha sector. Would you happen to know anything about that?"

"There are no known or suspected bases in the sector," the Dark Lord rumbled. "The single major listening post was raided and destroyed a few days ago. I suspect there to also be some important supply lines running through the sector, but that has yet to be verified."

"Any important sympathizers?"

The sense of coldness around him deepened. "There are sympathizers everywhere," he said. "As well as others who conspire to overthrow their superiors."

Mara felt an unpleasant trickle run through her. "Lord Vader, rest assured that I have no intention—"

"Good day, Emperor's Hand," Vader cut her off. With a swirl of black cloak, he stood, turning off the console as he did so. Turning his back, he strode away.

"Thank you for your assistance, Lord Vader," Mara called after him.

The other didn't reply, the sense of coldness fading as he departed. The door slid open at his gesture, and he strode from the library.

Mara took a deep breath, let it out in a weary sigh. What *was* he worried about, anyway? Loyalty was, after all, one of the Emperor's greatest qualities; loyalty to all who were loyal to him. How could Vader even think his Master would push him aside for anyone else? Especially for someone as young and inexperienced as Mara?

Shaking her head, she turned back to her console, forcing her mind back to her job. So the Rebels had supply lines through Shelsha sector. That was good to know. She finished keying in her request for general Rebel data, then added a search for major and minor traffic lanes, out-of-the-way spaceports, and any known centers of smuggling or other criminal activity.

The computer set to work, and Mara sat back to wait . . . and as she hunched her tired shoulders, her eyes drifted over to Vader's console. The Dark Lord was never very pleasant, but as she thought back on their brief encounter it seemed to her that he'd been even more on edge than usual.

Maybe she could find out why.

She glanced toward the exit as she stood up and went to the other console, wondering briefly what Vader would do if he caught her at this. But it was too good an opportunity to pass up. Sitting down, she turned on the machine. There was a computer trick the Dark Lord might not know how to block . . .

He didn't. Punching in the proper code, Mara pulled up the last file that had been accessed from that terminal.

It was a search program. A highly sophisticated one, too, that had been busily sifting through the personnel records of hundreds of star systems when Vader had interrupted its work and shut it down.

And not just the personnel records, but also movement and sighting reports, financial profiles, travel permits, and every other means the Empire had at its disposal for locating or tracking one of its citizens.

She scrolled up to the top, looking for the target list of names. If Vader was trying to track down Prince Xizor's Black Sun connections again, the Emperor was going to be very annoyed with him.

But to her mild surprise, there was only one name on the list.

Luke Skywalker.

Mara frowned, searching her memory. Had she ever heard that name before?

She didn't think so. But then, she was barely eighteen, and new to the Imperial court.

In the meantime, she had her own work to do. Filing away the name for future reference, she shut down the console and returned to her own search.

*   *   *

To Han's complete lack of surprise, the rendezvous turned out to be like all the rest of the little hidey-holes General Rieekan seemed to have stashed around the Empire. It was quiet, reasonably private, and about as sorry an excuse for a military base as he'd ever seen.

Still, it did have one redeeming value. Leia was there.

"Han," she greeted him with her usual official smile as he strode down the *Falcon*'s ramp. "Sounds like you had something of a close call."

"Not really," he assured her, smiling back. The cool formality of her smile didn't fool him for a minute, of course. "Everyone else get through okay?"

"Mostly," she said, a hint of a frown crossing her face. "Chivkyrie still hasn't shown up."

Han glanced over his shoulder to where Luke and Chewbacca were helping the techs pull their equipment out of the *Falcon*'s holds. "You want Chewie and me to go find him?"

"I'm afraid it's not that kind of problem," she said ruefully. "We're hav-ing some problems with his whole organization."

"Ah — politics," Han said, nodding. "In that case, you can leave me out of it."

"Yes, I thought as much," Leia said. "By the way, Mon Mothma wants to see all of us — you, Luke, and me — in the command center."

"Who?"

"Mon Mothma?" Leia repeated patiently. "The Alliance Supreme Commander?"

"Oh," Han said as the memory of the name finally surfaced. "Her."

"Yes, *her*," Leia said. "She has a job for us."

Han suppressed a grimace. There it was again: everyone just assuming he and Chewbacca were officially aboard this leaky ship. "Fine," he said. "We'll be there when we're finished."

Leia raised her eyebrows slightly, and for a second he thought she was going to remind him of his place. But maybe she remembered in time that he didn't really have one. "We'll see you then," she said, and moved off.

"Trouble?" Luke asked from behind him.

Han turned to see the kid walking toward him. "No more than usual," he said. "Why?"

"Leia looked like she was worried."

"Her Royal Highness is *always* worried," Han growled, annoyed in spite of himself. Ever since they'd pulled the Princess off the Death Star, Luke had been mooning over her, and ever since Yavin he'd fancied they had the kind of deep spiritual connection where he could sense her moods and feelings.

Or maybe it was part of this whole Jedi Knight kick he'd gotten on. Sometimes it was hard for Han to figure out which part of Luke's personality was the most annoying.

Still, the kid was mostly okay. Better than a lot of the people Han had had to deal with over the years.

"She's got a lot of responsibility," Luke reminded him quietly. "And Alderaan wasn't all that long ago."

Han grimaced. The kid was right, of course. Leia had been too busy right then to react much, but ever since Yavin she'd had more than enough time for the grief and horror of her world's destruction to start weighing in.

And if it came to that, Luke had had a couple of recent kicks in the teeth, too, what with first losing his aunt and uncle and then watching old man Kenobi get killed right in front of him. The least Han could do was cut them some slack. Both of them. "Yeah, I know," he said. "By the way, our glorious Supreme Commander wants us in the command center when we have time."

"Great," Luke said, visibly brightening at the prospect of another assignment. "Let's go. Chewie can direct the rest of the unloading."

Jump when ordered. The old military adage ran through Han's mind. *Ask "how high?" on the way up.* Whatever reservations Han might still have about this Rebellion, Luke had clearly jumped in with both feet.

Had jumped, was on his way up, and wasn't even bothering to ask how high.

Cut them some slack, Han reminded himself firmly. *Lots of slack.* "Sure," he said. "Let's see what Her Highest Highness wants."

∗   ∗   ∗

Mon Mothma was a regal-looking woman with short auburn hair and pale greenish blue eyes. She wore a simple white robe decorated only by a medallion of some sort around her neck. Seated at the head of the plotting table, flanked by General Rieekan on her right and Leia on her left, she was exactly what Luke would expect to find as the head of the Rebel Alliance: warm, strong, and determined.

"Thank you for your time here today, Captain Solo; Master Skywalker," she said, nodding gravely to each of them in turn. "Both of you have served the Rebellion bravely, and the entire galaxy owes you a great debt. Now I've come here to ask you to perform yet another service for us."

Glancing at Han, Luke saw the wary look in his eye and the slight curl to his lip. "We'd be delighted—" he began.

"We're listening," Han cut him off.

Luke winced. But Mon Mothma either didn't notice the brusqueness or else chose to ignore it. "As you know, the Rebel Alliance is made up of many groups that once fought their own individual wars against Emperor Palpatine's tyranny," she said. "It was only when we began uniting and coordinating our efforts—"

"We know the history," Han interrupted again. "What's the mission?"

Beside Mon Mothma, Leia stirred in her chair, glaring at Han in silent warning. But again, if Mon Mothma was irritated or insulted, she gave no sign.

"One of our member groups, the Republic Redux, is led by an Adarian named Yeeru Chivkyrie," the older woman said. "He has a proposal that he believes will give a strong boost to the Rebellion."

"Boosts are good," Han said. "What's the problem?"

"The problem," Mon Mothma said, "is that the leaders of two of the sector's other groups are as strongly opposed to the project as Chivkyrie is in favor of it."

"How strongly?" Han asked.

Mon Mothma's lips compressed briefly. "They're threatening to pull out if Chivkyrie's plan is accepted."

"Are they worth keeping?" Han asked.

Luke looked at him in disbelief. "What kind of question is that?"

"A perfectly good one," Han said, sounding a little defensive. "I thought the reason we pulled the Teardrop listening post out was because the Alliance didn't have much of anything going on in Shelsha."

"Actually, Skywalker, it *is* a good question," Rieekan said. "We've had trouble getting a real foothold in the sector, partly because of cultural problems, partly because of infighting like this."

"If you go strictly by numbers, Chivkyrie's group is the smallest of the three we're discussing here," Leia added. "Adarians have a strict social tier system, which means Chivkyrie's recruited almost exclusively from second-tier people like himself. The rest of the populace doesn't seem interested in fighting against the Empire."

"I thought everyone was supposed to give up this kind of infighting when they joined the Alliance," Luke said.

"That was the agreement," Rieekan said. "But Adarians are a stubborn people. Once they've made up their minds, it's almost impossible to change them." He shifted his gaze to Leia. "*Unless* whoever has the alternative idea is from a higher tier, which is why we're sending Princess Leia to try to mediate."

"I take it you don't think much of Chivkyrie's scheme?" Luke asked.

"Actually, we have no idea what it is," Rieekan said. "He refuses to discuss the matter via HoloNet, not even with encrypted transmissions. The only way we're going to find out about it is for you to go to Shelsha sector and talk to him."

It took Luke a second to notice the pronoun. Han, typically, caught it right away. "For *us* to go?" he asked pointedly.

"Yes," Rieekan said, looking him square in the eye. "I'd like you and Skywalker to accompany the Princess."

Luke felt his heartbeat pick up a little. Another mission for the Rebellion—and he'd get to spend time with Leia, too?

"We want to keep the whole thing as low-profile as possible," Leia explained. "That means no Alliance ships, and no obvious Alliance personnel."

"No *obvious* Alliance personnel?" Han echoed.

Luke frowned at him. What was eating Han, anyway? "She just means we don't have any official rank or status yet," he explained, trying to be helpful.

It was, apparently, the wrong thing to say. Han flashed him an almost glare, then turned back to Rieekan. "Where exactly would we be going?"

"As the Princess said, we all want to keep it low-key, Chivkyrie included," the general said. "He lives in Makrin City, the government seat on the capital world of Shelkonwa, but you'll actually be rendezvousing in an uninhabited system a few hours' flight time away."

"We don't know if the Empire's monitoring his movements," Leia added, "but if so, he should be able to sneak away that long without triggering any alerts."

"Assuming you can sort out the infighting without a week of discussion," Han said.

"She'll sort it out," Mon Mothma said, quietly confident. "Are you willing to accompany her?"

"I am," Luke said firmly, daring to send a small smile in Leia's direction. His reward was an equally subtle smile in return.

"Yeah, I suppose," Han said, his tone far more reluctant. "When do we leave?"

"Not for another few days," Rieekan said. "We need to get some details arranged first with Chivkyrie and the other leaders."

"Like what shape the conference table should be?" Han suggested.

Leia and Rieekan exchanged glances. "We'll let you know the schedule as soon as we have it," the general said. "Thank you for coming."

"And once again, the Alliance is in your debt," Mon Mothma said.

"Right," Han said. Standing up, he strode out of the room. Luke watched him go, wondering what exactly was going on.

It was, apparently, a universal question. "What's bothering *him?*" Rieekan asked.

"I don't know," Luke said. "He was like this on the way back from Teardrop, too."

"I'll go talk to him," Leia volunteered, standing up. "Thank you for your time, Mon Mothma; General Rieekan."

"Thank *you,*" Mon Mothma said gravely.

"Let me know if there's anything I can do regarding Solo," Rieekan said. "We need all the good people we can get."

"You really think there's a good person under all that?" Leia asked drily.

"Of course there is." Rieekan shrugged. "Somewhere."

Leia caught up with Han at the *Falcon* just as the techs were carting off the last of the Teardrop equipment. "Han," she greeted him gravely.

"Your Worshipfulness," he countered, inclining his head to her.

With an effort, she bit down on the retort that wanted to come out. Why did he *do* that? He *knew* she hated that kind of sarcasm.

Or maybe that was why he did it. "You were a little abrupt in there," she said instead. "*And* disrespectful."

Han's lip twitched. "I didn't mean it that way," he said. "I *don't* disrespect them. Well, not Rieekan, anyway—I've seen enough bad officers to know a good one when I see him."

"Well, if it wasn't disrespect, it was a pretty good imitation," Leia said.

Han turned his back on her and started fiddling with a piece of equipment on the *Falcon*'s underside. "I just don't like politics," he said over his shoulder.

"This isn't about politics, Han," she said. "This is about survival against—"

"Of course it's about politics," he interrupted, turning back to glare at her. "It's *always* about politics. One Rebel leader pushes to get what he wants, the other leaders try to keep him from grabbing all the credit, and you and Mon Mothma and Rieekan try to soothe everyone's ruffled feathers. That's not survival, Princess. That's politics."

"Is *that* what's bothering you?" Leia asked, sifting rapidly through his tirade as she hunted for clues. "You're not getting enough credit?"

"Of course I'm getting enough credit," he said. "Don't you remember that shiny medal you hung around my neck?"

Leia felt her cheeks burning. "My apologies, Captain Solo," she ground out with more acid than she'd really intended. "I'm just trying to understand you."

For the briefest fraction of a second she thought she saw something almost vulnerable in his eyes. But the moment passed, and the mask of cynical indifference dropped back into place. "Don't bother," he advised. "Even if you did, you wouldn't believe it."

He turned away again, his hands and eyes pretending to busy themselves with random bits of the *Falcon*'s equipment. Leia remained where
she was for a few seconds, until it was clear the conversation was over.
Spinning around, she strode back across the hangar floor, her cheeks still
warm. Never in her life had she met a man whose strengths she so admired
while at the same time wanting to strangle him with her bare hands.

Luke was waiting just outside the hangar door. "Anything?" he asked.

"Just the usual bluster," Leia said with a sigh. "Maybe you can get
something out of him."

Luke's eyes flicked over her shoulder. "Probably better to wait until he
cools down."

"I just wish I knew what had stirred him up in the first place," Leia said.
"He talked about politics, but I know that's not the whole story."

"Meanwhile, we have to get to Shelsha sector," Luke said. "I hope
General Rieekan's got a backup plan for transport."

"I'm sure he does," Leia said. "But we've got a few days. Maybe we can
bring Han around."

"Yeah," Luke said doubtfully. "Maybe."

Chapter Five

From the air, the Drunost hub of Consolidated Shipping looked exactly like its familiar star-in-swirl corporate logo. Standing behind Marcross, peering over his shoulder, LaRone could see a dozen large transports parked at various points around its edges, with several small landing/service areas forming a loose ring a few kilometers farther out. A couple of kilometers southeast of the hub, a medium-sized city pressed up against the edge of a swift-flowing river.

"See all the transports?" Quiller said, pointing at the hub building. "A convoy must have just come in. That's good—means lots of people and vehicles and ships moving around picking up their stuff."

"A crowd we can lose ourselves in?" Marcross suggested.

"Exactly."

"What are all those little landing areas around the hub's edges?" LaRone asked.

"Privately owned service fields," Quiller told him. "They're for people who want to come and pick up shipments or buy directly from Consolidated's outlet center."

"We're not going to the hub itself, are we?" Grave asked from the shield/sensor station behind Quiller.

"We're not even waving at it," Quiller assured him. "Consolidated has their own security force, and they're not a group you want to tangle with.

But these transfer fields have their own shopping areas. Actually, once I put down we shouldn't have to go more than a couple hundred meters from the ship to find all the food and gear we need."

"What about Imperials?" Brightwater asked from the astrogation/comm seat behind LaRone. "They're bound to have a presence here."

"Actually, probably not," Marcross told him. "Consolidated doesn't like having government flunkies underfoot, and they're big enough that Imperial Center usually cuts them some slack."

"Which is one reason I chose this spot in the first place," Quiller confirmed.

"We still might want to warm up the lasers," Brightwater warned. "Even if we don't see any Imperials, raiders like to hang around transfer stations, too."

"Especially when *they* don't see any Imperials, either," Grave said drily.

"Good point," LaRone agreed. "Why don't you and Brightwater go ahead and fire up the cannons?"

"Sure," Grave said. He gestured, and he and Brightwater left the cockpit. LaRone glanced back to see them circle past the life support and ship computer stations on either side in the anteroom and slip through the small blast doors into the two gunwells flanking the ship's nose.

"Those lasers are going to be a nasty surprise to anyone we have to fire at," Quiller commented as he flipped on the gunwell intercoms. "I took a quick look earlier, and they've been seriously upgraded from anything that's standard for this class of ship."

"Figures," LaRone said, studying the ring of landing areas as they dropped toward the ground. "Quiller, what do you say we take that medium-crowded field due east of the hub?"

"Sounds good to me," Quiller said. "I'll put her down near those two Barloz freighters at the northern end."

"So how do we work this?" Marcross asked. "We spread out with shopping lists?"

"I don't think we should split up quite that much," LaRone said. "I was thinking Grave and I would do the shopping while the rest of you stay here. We'll buy a few days' worth of supplies, bring them back to the ship, then go to a different shop and buy a little more. That way it'll be less obvious that we're stocking up for a long trip."

"Sounds reasonable," Marcross said. "I presume the rest of us can at least put in special requests?"

"Hey, this is on the ISB," LaRone reminded him. "Just give me your lists."

The landing field was rough and aged, its permacrete surface crisscrossed with cracks and dips and ridges, its nav markings faded or nonexistent. Despite all that, they settled almost gently onto the surface, with far less bumping than even the typical stormtrooper drop ship. Either Quiller was a better pilot than LaRone had realized, or else the Suwantek's landing gear had been as lovingly upgraded as everything else on the ship.

"Keep an eye out for trouble," LaRone told the others as Grave maneuvered one of the two landspeeders onto the cargo lift.

"You, too," Marcross said. "If they've got an alert out, this whole place could be plastered with our pictures by now."

"I hope not," Grave said, patting the sport blaster belted at his side. "For their sake."

Either Drunost had been left out of the loop or else Captain Ozzel and the ISB were still trying to figure out how to word a wanted posting for stormtrooper deserters. LaRone watched the shopkeepers closely as he and Grave filled their baskets, but there was no hint of recognition or even interest in the two strangers.

They paid for their purchases with ISB credits and headed back outside. To the west a wave of loaded airspeeders flew out from the Consolidated complex with freshly obtained cargoes, and a line of speeder trucks and landspeeders shimmered their way down the road or across the hardened ground on either side of it. Plodding along among them were half a dozen men and women in threadbare farmers' garb, leading a pair of animal-drawn wagons loaded with large plastic crates.

"The nearest farmland looked to be a good fifteen kilometers away," Grave commented quietly, nodding toward the latter procession as he and LaRone loaded their packages into the landspeeder. "Going to be a long walk."

"Maybe they'll get to ride some of it," LaRone said.

"I doubt it," Grave said. "The crates are full of farming gear—I recognize the Johder company logo. Low-tech, and as heavy as a moff's private vault. They won't risk straining their animals by making them haul passengers, too."

LaRone grimaced, his mind flashing back to the dirt-poor farmers back on Copperline. "This is the sort of life I joined the Fleet to escape," he murmured.

"You want to offer them a lift?" Grave suggested. "We could put their cargo into one of the Suwantek's holds and the animals and carts in the other."

"And have ISB come knocking on their doors someday?" LaRone countered. "No. They've got enough trouble already."

Grave exhaled loudly. "I suppose."

From somewhere behind LaRone came a soft whooshing sound. Frowning, he turned—

And dropped reflexively into a crouch beside the landspeeder as a pair of swoops shot past half a meter over his head. "Grave!" he snapped as half a dozen more followed hard on the exhaust vents of the first two, all of them heading straight toward the farmers and their wagons.

LaRone yanked out his blaster, his eyes and mind automatically assessing the situation. The two lead swoops had split formation now and were making tight circles above and around the two wagons as they waited for their comrades to catch up. The riders were little more than a blur, but from their garish outfits and the highly illegal underslung blaster cannons spitting a warning circle into the dust around the wagons it was obvious they were some sort of gang. The other speeder trucks on the road were scattering like smoke in the wind, leaving the farmers to stand alone.

"They're coming from that freighter," Grave called. LaRone turned and saw a pair of open-topped speeder trucks loaded with rough-looking humans and aliens sliding down the ramp of one of the two Barloz freighters parked near the Suwantek.

Which meant this wasn't just some group of delinquents here for the twisted fun of terrorizing helpless locals. They were bandits or raiders, intending to steal the farmer's new equipment.

LaRone felt a snarl catch in his throat. Pulling out his comlink, he flicked it on. "Quiller?"

"We're here," Quiller's voice was tight and professional. "You want a pickup?"

"I want firepower," LaRone retorted. "We're taking them down."

There was just the briefest pause. "You sure you want to do that?"

"We're sure," Grave cut in. "LaRone and I will handle the swoops— you see what you can do about that freighter."

"Acknowledged," Quiller said. "Stand by."

LaRone slipped the comlink back onto his belt and braced his gun hand along the side of the landspeeder. At the raiders' distance, this was going to be a tricky shot, especially with them running an encirclement pattern around their prey while they waited for their speeder trucks to arrive. Even more especially with the unfamiliar sport pistol he'd brought from the Suwantek's collection.

But he would just have to make do with what he had. Lining up the muzzle on the nearest swoop rider, he squinted along the barrel.

"Heads up!" a faint voice called from his belted comlink. He frowned, looking up—

To see Brightwater in full scout trooper armor flash past on his speeder bike, his own underslung blaster cannon spitting death at the distant swoops.

LaRone barely had time to goggle at the sight when a second rapidly moving object caught the edge of his vision. He twisted his head that direction to see Marcross roaring toward them in the Suwantek's other landspeeder. "Here!" the other called, lobbing a pair of large, dark objects toward him. LaRone dropped his blaster and stood upright, his eyes tracking, his arms outstretched.

A second later the familiar bulk of Grave's BlasTech T-28 sniper rifle dropped neatly into his right hand, while his own BlasTech E-11 landed in his left. "Grave!" he called.

Grave glanced over, quick-holstering his own pistol as LaRone tossed him the T-28. He spun back around, lifted it to his shoulder, and began adding his own deadly sniper attack to the rapid fire spitting from Brightwater's speeder bike.

The raiders never had a chance. The last thing they could have expected this far from the hub's private security was serious resistance, and the *very* last thing they could have expected was resistance from Imperial stormtroopers. Brightwater spiraled around the raiders, running deft rings around the more amateur swoopers, keeping them herded together as Grave picked them off one by one. The backup troops in the speeder trucks fared no better, with Marcross in his landspeeder blocking any escape as he and LaRone rained blasterfire on them.

The speeder trucks were on the ground, their occupants out of the fight for good, and Brightwater and Grave had just tagged the last swoop when there was a violent explosion from the direction of the raiders' freighter.

LaRone turned to look. The Barloz's entire engine section had disappeared, blown into a cloud of blazing smoke, taking the freighter's lone gunwell with it. The Suwantek's starboard laser was already shifting aim as Quiller stitched a line of fire across the Barloz's boarding ramp, discouraging any raiders still inside from joining the party.

LaRone pulled out his comlink. "Quiller, shift the lasers to auto and get the engines started," he ordered. "Everyone else, pull back to the ship."

"Wait a minute," Grave objected, lifting the muzzle of his T-28 into rest position. "We don't have all our supplies yet."

"We'll get them somewhere else," LaRone said. "Right now, we need to get out of here before someone from Consolidated arrives and starts asking awkward questions."

Grave made a face but obediently loaded his rifle into the landspeeder's cargo bay and hopped up into the driver's seat. LaRone paused long enough to make sure Brightwater and Marcross were also on their way back, then got in beside him.

Five minutes later they were once again in the air, heading for space.

"We're clear," Quiller announced, giving his displays a final look. "No sign of pursuit."

"Well, I can't say that it wasn't fun," Brightwater commented. "But we really ought to try to avoid that sort of thing in the future."

"I agree," Grave said. "What in the *worlds* possessed you two to come charging out that way?"

"Oh, I don't know," Marcross said with a hint of sarcasm. "We thought maybe you could use a little help."

"No, no, the help was much appreciated," Grave assured him. "Especially the part where you brought me a blaster I could actually shoot with. I was referring to the fact that you came charging out in full armor."

"That was my idea," Brightwater said. "I thought there was a chance we might need to throw a little bluster around, and there's nothing like a stormtrooper presence to persuade nosy locals *and* corporate hirelings to back off."

"Plus, once the blaster bolts started flying, it seemed like a good idea to have the extra protection," Marcross added. "Not that we had time to change anyway."

"Yes, but—"

"It's all right, Grave," LaRone said. "We got away with it, and we helped some farmers out of a jam. That's the important thing."

"Besides, there isn't one person in a billion outside the corps who can tell one stormtrooper from another in their armor," Quiller reminded him. "They'll never know who we were. So what's the new plan?"

"Same as the old one," LaRone said. "We head somewhere else and finish collecting fuel and supplies. Pull up a map and let's see what our choices are."

"Just a second," Marcross said, lifting a finger. "Before we go any farther, I'd like to know how exactly we ended up with LaRone making all the decisions."

"You have a problem with it?" Grave asked, an edge of challenge in his tone.

"In principle, yes," Marcross said calmly. "As far as I know, we're all the same rank here."

Brightwater snorted. "I think the standard Table of Organization's a little irrelevant at the moment," he said. "We're not exactly an official fighting unit anymore."

"I thought we did okay back there," Grave said.

"I said we weren't an *official* unit," Brightwater said. "What's wrong with us just discussing our plans and coming to a consensus?"

"Nothing, assuming we can come to one," Marcross said. "Unfortunately, that isn't always possible."

"Translation: you're still pushing for us to go hide on Shelkonwa?" Grave asked.

"I still think it's our best bet," Marcross said.

"Regardless, he's right about us needing to have a clearly defined chain of command," LaRone said. "Discussion and agreement are fine, but in crisis or combat you need one man giving orders and everyone else obeying them."

"So again, what's wrong with LaRone taking point?" Grave asked.

"For one thing, he's the one who got us into this mess," Brightwater muttered.

"What's *that* supposed to mean?" Grave growled.

"Just what it said," Brightwater said. "If he hadn't killed Drelfin, we'd still be aboard the *Reprisal*."

"Doing what?" Grave shot back. "Slaughtering more civilians like we did on Teardrop?"

"Maybe they were all Rebels," Brightwater insisted. "*We* don't know. Anyway, I think I just heard someone say that someone had to give orders and someone else had to follow them."

"When those orders are for the legitimate protection of the Empire and its citizens," Grave said.

"Do you want to go back?" LaRone asked.

The argument broke off. "What do you mean?" Grave asked, frowning.

"It's not a trick question," LaRone told him. "If you want to go back, Brightwater—if *any* of you want to—you're welcome to do so. Just drop me off somewhere and go."

"You'd be dead in a week," Grave said flatly. "They'd drag your location out of our minds and nail you to the wall."

"Maybe that would be enough to calm them down," LaRone said. "As Brightwater pointed out, *I'm* the one who killed Drelfin. Maybe they'll let you go back to the unit."

"Of course, as Grave pointed out, Palpatine's Empire may not be worth serving anymore," Quiller said quietly. "I was under the impression we'd already been wondering about that when all the rest of this went down."

"Well, *I'm* not going back," Grave said emphatically. "Brightwater?"

The other made a face. "No," he said reluctantly. "Even if we *could* . . . never mind. We can't, and we won't."

"Which brings us back to the question of command," Marcross said.

"And for the record," he added, looking at Brightwater, "let me remind everyone that it was *Drelfin* who precipitated this, not LaRone."

"Maybe we should start from the other direction," Quiller suggested. "Does anyone here particularly *want* to be in charge?"

"Personally, I see no reason not to let LaRone hang on to the job," Marcross said. "At least, for now."

"I thought you were the one who didn't want him giving the orders," Quiller said, frowning.

"I said I disagreed in principle," Marcross reminded him. "I don't necessarily disagree in practice."

"I've seen LaRone in plenty of combat situations," Grave said. "He's got my vote."

"*I* sure don't want the job," Quiller said, half turning to face Brightwater. "That just leaves you, Brightwater."

The scout trooper grimaced, but nodded. "No, it makes sense," he said. "I presume this isn't a lifetime appointment?"

"Not at all," LaRone assured him. "Furthermore, if and when anyone has any objections or suggestions about anything we're proposing or doing, you're to let me know immediately. It's us against the universe now, and the last thing we can afford is private doubts or resentments."

"Then that's settled," Marcross said, climbing out of the copilot's seat. "I'm going to go check the landspeeders, see if either of them picked up any damage. You four go ahead and pick us a target planet—anywhere is fine with me."

Marcross was stretched out flat on his back beneath one of the landspeeders when LaRone caught up with him. "How's it look?"

"It's got a few dings," Marcross said, squirming back and forth on his shoulders as he wiggled his way out from under the vehicle. "But they all seem to be superficial. Incidentally, if you've got that shopping list handy, you could add a mechanic's crawler to it."

"Got it," LaRone said, offering his hand. Marcross reached up and took it, and LaRone hauled him back to his feet. "I'm surprised ISB didn't include one in the ship's equipment."

"If they did, it's nowhere obvious," Marcross said, reaching awkwardly around to brush off his back where he'd been lying on the deck. "Besides, everybody knows the easiest way to find a missing item is to buy a replacement. Quiller find us a commerce center?"

LaRone nodded. "We're going to try Ranklinge," he said. "It's about two days' flight away."

"Isn't there an Incom Corporation starfighter plant there?" Marcross asked, frowning. "Turns out I-7 Howlrunners, as I recall."

"Good memory," LaRone complimented him. "Yes, it's on the outskirts of Ranklinge City. Quiller thought a medium-high-profile place like that would put the planet lower on ISB's list of places we might go."

"Provided we don't land right next to all those I-7s," Marcross said. "*And* provided we don't plan on making it our permanent home." He cocked an eyebrow. "We *aren't* planning to make it our permanent home, are we?"

"No, that discussion's still for the future." LaRone hesitated. "I wanted to ask you a question."

"After raising the whole leadership issue in the first place, why did I suddenly support you for the job?"

LaRone pursed his lips. "Basically."

Marcross shrugged and crossed to one of the tool and equipment racks along the cargo bay's rear wall. "The short answer is that you seem to have some abilities in that direction." He glanced over his shoulder as he pulled out a tube of sealant. "I gather you don't see that?"

LaRone shook his head. "Not really."

"True leaders often don't," Marcross told him. He checked the label on the tube, put it back, and selected a different one. "But I was watching you during our little discussion up there. You stood quietly by and let everyone voice their opinions, even blow off a little steam. But then you stepped in and calmed everything down before it could degenerate into a full-fledged argument."

LaRone thought back. Was that really what he'd done? It certainly hadn't been nearly as deliberate as Marcross seemed to think. "What about you?" he countered. "You could have done it as well as I could."

Marcross shook his head as he returned to the landspeeder. "I've had some experience watching leaders in action," he said. "But knowing the theory doesn't mean I can actually do it. Besides, even if I could, I don't think the others would really support me." He smiled wryly. "I get the feeling they find me stiff and a little overbearing."

"They just don't know you as well as I do," LaRone said.

"Which is another part of leadership: knowing and understanding the men of your command," Marcross said. "*And* trusting them." His lips tightened. "Besides, you're the one who refused to fire on unresisting civilians. That gives you the high moral ground, one of the most important assets a leader can have."

LaRone swallowed, the scene of that horror flashing again across his mind. "The rest of you would have done the same."

"Maybe," Marcross said. "Maybe not. Grave and Brightwater were in positions where they didn't have to make that decision. I don't know about Quiller."

"And you?"

Marcross looked him straight in the eye. "I obeyed my orders."

For a long, taut moment, neither man spoke. Then Marcross turned and knelt down beside the landspeeder. "You might mention to Brightwater that his speeder bike took a couple of dings, too," he said as he opened the sealant tube and started brushing the paste over the blaster marks.

"Right," LaRone said, keeping his voice steady. *I obeyed my orders . . .* "I'll tell him."

The sky had turned into a magnificent star-sprinkled blackness, and the animals pulling the heavy carts were puffing heavily with the strain when the man who called himself Porter and his team finally reached the edge of the woods and the rendezvous point. "Casement?" Porter called softly, his hand slipping beneath his coarse farmer's robe and getting a grip on his blaster.

"Over here, Porter," the expected voice called back. In the starlight he saw a lanky figure unfold itself from the base of one of the trees and stand up. Behind him, a deeper shadow among the trees, was the bulk of the familiar Surronian heavy freighter. "You're late. What'd you do, stop to catch some butterbugs?"

With a quiet sigh of relief, Porter pulled his hand back out of his robe. With a job like this, there was always the chance of discovery, even right at the very end. But the *butterbug* code word meant all was well. "That little relabeling stunt meant the crates weren't where they were supposed to be," he explained as he stepped over to the other man. More shadowy figures were emerging from the forest now, some of them pulling repulsorlift transfer dollies behind them. "It took them awhile to track them."

"I hope they didn't get too curious about why they were misplaced," Casement said.

"No, they were mostly just annoyed at whoever's incompetence had landed them in the wrong stack," Porter assured him. "Anyway, I had a cover story all set in case they looked inside."

"I'll bet."

"No, really," Porter insisted. "I was going to tell them that the ground here is so rocky that heavy blasters are officially classed as agricultural equipment."

Casement chuckled. "That would have been a conversation worth sitting in on."

"Speaking of things worth sitting in on, you missed a doozy," Porter said, digging into his pocket as Casement's people began transferring the precious cargo onto the dollies. "Ever seen anything like this?"

He handed over a shoulder patch he'd cut from the shirt of one of the dead swoop riders. Casement produced a small glow rod, and for a moment he studied the patch. "Never seen the whole thing before," he said at last. "But this twisted-thorn cluster at the base sure looks like the Blood-Scar pirate logo."

"That's what I thought," Porter agreed. "Only this was a swoop gang working out of an old Barloz freighter."

"Could be they're affiliated with the BloodScars," Casement said, rubbing his jaw. "Maybe the pirates are taking a file line from the Hutts and are trying to expand their operations."

"Which is worrisome enough in its own right," Porter said. "More troubling is the fact the swoopers ignored everyone else in the area and came straight for us, as if they already knew we were carrying something more interesting than farming equipment."

"Terrific," Casement growled. "Like we didn't have enough trouble with pirates already. Especially with the Imperials now pretty much ignoring them."

"Maybe not," Porter said. "The swoopers were shot off us by a pair of stormtroopers."

He couldn't make out Casement's expression in the starlight, but the abrupt stiffening of the other's stance was almost as impressive. "*What?*"

"You heard me," Porter said. "A scout on an Aratech speeder bike and a regular trooper in a landspeeder, working out of an old freighter—I didn't recognize the make. They also had a pair of plainclothesmen already on the ground and at least one more running backup inside the ship."

"Plainclothes?" Casement repeated thoughtfully. "Not fleet or army fatigues?"

"One hundred percent pure civilian," Porter confirmed. "I'm thinking ISB or maybe some special commando squad."

"Then why did they let you go?" Casement looked up suddenly at the sky. "Unless this is a trap."

"If it was, they should have sprung it by now," Porter said. "No, I don't think they had the faintest idea who or what we were. I think all they were after was the swoopers." He grimaced. "I just wish I knew what that meant."

"Nothing good for us, that's for sure," Casement said, tucking the gang patch into his pocket. "I'll send a report to Targeter. She'll know the right people to kick it on to."

"Good," Porter said, gesturing toward the working shadows. "Meanwhile, we've got cargo to load."

"And suddenly this rock doesn't seem quite so cozy anymore," Casement agreed grimly. "Let's get this done."

Chapter Six

THE MANAGER OF THE PEVEN AUCTION HOUSE ON CROVNA WASN'T much help. Both the seller and the buyer of Glovstoak's private art objects had been anonymous, and neither the manager nor any of his employees had recognized either of the representatives who'd been sent to the auction. The house had no records or indication of how the objects had come to Crovna; nor had the manager any idea what kind of vessel they'd left on.

He did, however, remember that he'd had to bring the artworks in for appraisal on two separate occasions before the actual sale took place. Both times they'd been in his office less than an hour after he'd contacted the seller's agent. Furthermore, he recalled that they'd been brought by landspeeder, not airspeeder.

They could have been stored before the auction in a private home, Mara knew. But with thieves routinely slicing into auction house records in the hope of finding a good target, that would have been both dangerous and stupid. The seller would more likely have kept them in a vault somewhere in the area, someplace secure, private, and easily accessible.

A little research turned up just over fifty storage businesses within an hour's drive of the auction house. Most of them were small facilities, however—adequate for storing spare furniture or business papers but hardly up to the task of protecting half a billion credits' worth of artworks.

There was, in fact, only one facility Mara could find that fit all the parameters she was looking for.

It was called Birtraub Brothers Storage and Reclamation Center, a sprawling complex of interconnected gray buildings not far from the city's main spaceport. With thirty or forty ships parked in its docking bays at any given time and several thousand workers buzzing about like hive insects as they accepted and dispersed and stored hundreds of thousands of crates and lockboxes a day, she could well believe its claim to be one of the largest such facilities in Shelsha sector.

But there was something else about the place, something that sent her senses tingling. Perhaps it was the grim-faced guards she could see from her table at the tapcafe across the street from the facility, guards who carried the unmistakable stamp of the Fringe in their expressions and body language. Perhaps it was the fact that many of the ships she could see moving cargoes in and out of the docking bays had clearly forged markings on them.

Or perhaps it was the fact that Mara's very presence here at this window table had set off quiet alarm bells all the way to the tapcafe's back room.

Lifting her glass, she took a sip, surreptitiously glancing at her chrono as she did so. She'd been here since just after the lunchtime rush, and in the past three hours had nursed her way through two small drinks and an appetizer plate of tomo-spice ribenes, watching the traffic going in and out of the facility. For those same three hours the tapcafe's staff had been watching her, their quiet vigilance punctuated by numerous comlink calls to party or parties unknown. The calls had become increasingly intense in the past hour, and though Mara was too far away to overhear any of the conversations she could sense a growing nervousness.

Which wasn't really surprising. If the higher-ups at Birtraub Brothers had guilty consciences, they would immediately have checked all the nearby spaceports for her ship, pulled every record that might possibly pertain to her, probably even contacted people familiar with a wide range of law enforcement personnel in the hope of identifying her.

None of it would have done them the slightest bit of good. The name on her identity tag was complete fiction, her ship was unregistered, and neither face, prints, nor DNA pattern was recorded in any file or computer or surveillance droid memory anywhere in the Empire. As far as an inquiry would determine, she simply didn't exist.

Out of the corner of her eye she saw the tapcafe manager walking toward her through the sea of tables, and stretched out with the Force for a quick assessment. He was as nervous as ever, but there was a determination that hadn't been there earlier. Apparently they were finally ready to make their move. "Excuse me, miss?" the manager said tentatively.

Mara looked up at him. "Yes?"

"I'm sorry, but we need this table," he said. "I'm afraid you'll have to leave."

"Oh?" Mara said, looking around. In point of fact the place *had* gotten more crowded in the past half hour, with nearly all the tables now hosting at least one occupant. However, since most of them appeared to be hired thugs pressed from the same mold as the Birtraub Brothers' door guards, it didn't seem a particularly relevant argument.

"I'm afraid so," the manager said, gesturing toward the bar. On cue, one of the waiters started toward them, balancing a drink on a tray. "One final drink—on the house, of course—and you'll have to leave."

The waiter arrived and set the drink in front of her. "I've got a better idea," Mara said, lifting the glass and sniffing once. The odor was well hidden, but her sensory enhancement techniques were more than equal to the challenge. "Instead of trying to drug me," she went on, giving the liquid a swirl and setting it back onto the table, "why don't we just go across to the facility and have a chat with the brothers Birtraub?"

The manager blinked. Clearly, this sort of thing wasn't in his usual job profile. "Ah . . . I don't understand."

"Never mind," Mara said, looking around the room again. Her eyes settled on a man a couple of tables away, a few years older than the rest of the toughs, with a watchful look in his eyes as he pretended to ignore the conversation. "You," Mara said, gesturing to him. "Shall we end this nonsense and go see your boss?"

The other smiled in a carefully tailored attempt to show amusement as he glanced over at her, noting her plain gray jumpsuit and lack of weapons. "What makes you think he'd be interested in anything you have to say?" he countered.

"Trust me," Mara said, letting her expression and tone harden as she looked him straight in the eye.

He hesitated a moment, then gave a small shrug. "As you wish," he said, rising from his chair and gesturing to the door. "This way."

Mara stood up and reached for the satchel she'd placed on the seat beside her. The crew leader was quicker, his hand darting forward to grasp the handles. "Allow me," he said, picking it up.

Mara inclined her head in acknowledgment, and together they crossed the room. As they reached the door two of the bigger thugs silently fell into step behind them.

A long landspeeder was waiting for them at the curb. Mara and the crew leader took the backseat while the two thugs unfolded jump seats across from them. "Master Birtraub's office," the crew leader instructed the driver, and they pulled out into the street.

"You have a name?" Mara asked.

His lip quirked. "Pirtonna," he said. "You?"

"Call me Claria," Mara said.

"Nice name." Pirtonna gestured to her satchel, resting on his lap. "May I?"

Mara nodded. All her weapons and other gear were in there, but the more incriminating ones were hidden inside various pieces of electronic equipment, and she doubted Pirtonna would bother with more than a cursory examination until they reached their destination.

He didn't. He spent probably a minute going through the spare clothing and electronics, then sealed the bag again and set it on the seat beside him. "Happy?" Mara asked.

"I was never anything but," he replied, smiling back.

A few minutes later the driver pulled up beside a nondescript entrance tucked out of the way between a pair of empty docking bays. Pirtonna led Mara inside and down a brightly lit corridor, the two toughs again trailing behind. In contrast with all the activity Mara had observed earlier outside the facility, this particular area seemed completely deserted.

A couple of turns later they reached an unmarked door. "In here," Pirtonna said, palming the release plate and gesturing Mara forward.

It was indeed an office, but it obviously didn't belong to either of the

Birtraub brothers, or to anyone else with a scrap of real authority. The desk was old and stained, the chairs plain and unpadded, the lighting simple and bright and functional. From the rows of file cabinets along the side-walls, she tentatively tagged it as a record keeper's office.

But it was just as obvious that the man standing glowering at her from beside the desk was no minor executive. "*This* is her?" he demanded, look-ing Mara up and down. "This—this—*girl* is the one that has you all wor-ried?"

"This is her," Pirtonna confirmed stiffly. "And a person who doesn't show up on any records is well worth worrying about."

"Really?" the man asked acidly.

"Really," Mara confirmed. On the back of her neck she felt a whisper of air currents as the two thugs came in behind her and closed the door. "Which Birtraub brother you are?"

He smiled thinly. "The nastier one."

"Fair enough," Mara said. "To business, then. I want the name of the person who rented the space where six valuable artworks were being stored a year and a half ago."

Birtraub's eyes widened. "You want *what*?" he demanded, his air of hostility momentarily eclipsed by bewilderment. "*Artworks?*"

"Fine," Mara said, hiding a grimace. To her Force-enhanced senses, it was clear that Birtraub wasn't lying; he really *didn't* know anything about the artworks or their sale. Too bad; that would have made things so much easier. "In that case I'll settle for a list of everyone who had spaces here at that time."

Birtraub's bewilderment vanished, his face darkening. "You're either insane or joking."

"Then how about just telling me why strangers watching your facility make you so nervous?" Mara offered.

Birtraub's face settled into hard lines, his eyes flicking to Pirtonna. The other nodded and stepped around behind Mara, and she felt the pressure as his blaster muzzle was pressed against her back between the shoulder blades.

Mentally, she shook her head. *Amateurs.* The first thing a professional learned was that touching an opponent with a weapon did nothing but show the opponent exactly where the weapon was. "That would be an extremely bad idea," she warned Birtraub. "The penalties for assaulting an Imperial agent are fairly gruesome."

Birtraub snorted, but Mara could sense a flicker of uncertainty. "You're no Imperial agent. *You?*"

"I'm sure your men hope you're right," Mara said calmly.

The uncertainty winked out again. "Find out who she's working for," Birtraub ordered. "Then kill—"

And right in the middle of his order, Mara turned 180 degrees to her left in a dancer's spin, swinging her left arm up to catch Pirtonna's and knocking the blaster away from her back. He fired, a fraction of a second too late, sizzling the blue fire of a stun blast into one of the file cabinets. Mara slid her left hand to his wrist, grabbing it as she snapped her right hand around his arm at the elbow. Shoving against that pivot point, she twisted his forearm over his shoulder and lined up his blaster on the first of the two thugs.

Pirtonna's finger was still filling the trigger guard, blocking access to the trigger itself. But that was all right. Stretching to the Force, Mara reached beneath his finger and flicked the trigger to send a blue sizzle into the thug, then shifted her aim and stunned the second man. A quick torque against Pirtonna's wrist and the blaster came free into her left hand, and she fired a final burst directly into his torso.

She tossed the gun across to her right hand and had it lined up on Birtraub's face before the first of the thugs even hit the floor.

"Stun settings," she commented approvingly as the triple thud of falling bodies faded away. "So Pirtonna wasn't nearly as ready to play all-or-nothing with me as you are. Smart man. Means he gets to live through the night." She lifted the blaster slightly. "What do you think *your* odds are?"

Birtraub was staring at her, his body rigid, his face gone a pasty white. His mouth opened, but nothing came out. "So, now," Mara continued. "You were going to explain why you were ready to kill me just for being in your neighborhood."

Birtraub's throat worked, and his face sagged subtly in defeat. "There's a man," he said, the words coming out with difficulty. "Name's Caaldra. He works with a pirate gang—a big one. They store a lot of their loot here. They . . . don't like people watching them."

"I don't blame them," Mara said. So perhaps Glovstoak's artworks hadn't come from Rebels after all. "Where do I find him?"

Birtraub's face went even whiter. "No," be breathed. "Please. He'll kill me if he finds out I told you about him."

"He won't ever know," Mara assured him. "Where is he?"

"You don't understand," Birtraub said, his voice thickening with desperation. "A couple of hours after they grab you, they'll know everything."

"A couple of hours after they grab me, they'll be dead," Mara corrected. "Where is he?"

Birtraub took a deep breath and folded his arms across his chest. "No," he said. The pleading was gone, replaced by the defiance of a man with nothing left to lose. "Whatever you're going to do to me, it can't possibly be as bad as what Caaldra would do."

Mara felt her lip twist. The Emperor had often warned her that she was far too young for most people to take her threats seriously. "Fine, if that's how you want it," she said. "I'll just have to find him myself." She gestured toward the door with her blaster. "After you."

The look of relief that had started to cross Birtraub's face abruptly reversed itself. "What?" he asked.

"I'm certainly not going to go wandering around this place all by myself," Mara said reasonably. "Besides, this way when we find Caaldra, I expect he'll be polite enough to stop and say hello and ask who your new friend is. Then he and I can be properly introduced."

Birtraub's face had gone white again. "You *are* insane," he hissed. "Forget it. I won't go."

"You don't have a choice," Mara said.

"I have armed people all over the facility."

"You had armed people in here, too," Mara pointed out as she started walking toward him. "But we're wasting time. Come on."

In his eyes and body language she saw the subtle clues that he was going to try something stupid. She kept going, preparing herself; and as she came within reach, he threw a punch at her throat with everything he had.

But speed, power, and desperation were no match for Force-driven awareness and reflexes. Mara merely leaned slightly to the side, allowing the fist to shoot harmlessly past. The clean miss threw Birtraub completely off balance, and as he half lunged, half fell toward her Mara swiveled on her right foot, moving out of his way.

Some people would have figured it out at that point. Birtraub wasn't one of them. Even as he lurched past, cursing, he snapped a kick backward toward her. Mara sidestepped it and, almost as an afterthought, swept his other leg out from under him.

He hit the floor flat; and with that, the last bit of fight was finally out of him. "Whenever you're ready," Mara said calmly, nudging him in the ribs with her foot.

Grimacing with pain, Birtraub pushed himself up on one hand, half turning to look up at her. "Warehouse Fourteen," he managed, wincing as if the words hurt to say. Considering how he'd landed, they probably did. "East side of the complex." His gaze drifted to his unconscious men. "If they get you, tell them it was Pirtonna who told you."

Mara smiled cynically. Typical. "Thank you," she said, lifting her borrowed blaster. "If he's not there, I'll be back for another chat."

She fired, and he collapsed beneath the blue stun blast. Retrieving her satchel, she headed back along the deserted corridors to the exit.

The driver was still waiting in the long landspeeder. Mara stunned him, dragged his unconscious form out of sight, and drove away.

Warehouse 14 was located conveniently next to Docking Bay 14, currently occupied by a nicely polished Hyrotii *Crescent*-class freighter, a model that mostly saw service as a rich-kid toy. But once again, appearances were deceiving. Mara studied the ship as she drove a leisurely circle along the complex's outer drive, noting the hidden laser and torpedo ports, the forged markings, and the neatly dressed but rough-looking men walking guard duty around both the vessel and the wide cargo doors leading into the warehouse. Beside the doors, tucked out of the way, were three landspeeders with the Birtraub Brothers logo on their sides. Through the warehouse doors she could see a group of men loading crates onto repulsor carts and maneuvering them out to the ship's ramp. The warehouse itself seemed well stocked, with multiple stacks of crates scattered throughout. She took special notice of the placement of the stacks along the back wall, and continued her drive.

The back of Warehouse 14 butted up against another warehouse-sized building, this one subdivided into smaller storage units, with a narrow service corridor running between the two. Mara found the entrance to the corridor and headed to a spot where her memory told her a stack of crates would shield her from view from inside. Stretching out to the Force, confirming there was no one nearby who might walk in on her, she opened her satchel and got to work.

Her first task was to retrieve her lightsaber, hidden inside a long data analysis unit. The unit had three hidden catches, positioned far enough apart that a single person couldn't hit all three. Mara squeezed two with her hands and used the Force to pop the third. Pulling out the lightsaber, she tucked it into her belt, then freed the sleeve gun and holster from one of her two datapads and strapped the weapon to her left forearm. Checking a final time for possible observers, she stepped back from the warehouse wall and ignited her lightsaber.

With a *snap-hiss* the magenta blade flashed into existence. It was a unique color, the Emperor had told her when he'd given her the bit of starter she'd used to grow the crystal for the weapon, one that had been seen only once in the last hundred years. He hadn't said where he'd gotten the crystal; probably it was from one of the collections of weapons and artwork and historical artifacts he had scattered around the Empire.

For a moment she held the lightsaber motionless, gazing at the blade and letting the feel of the weapon flow into her mind and back again into her hands. Then, setting her feet, she lowered the blade and eased its tip delicately into the wall in front of her.

The wall was thick and heavily armored, and it took three careful cuts to establish its actual thickness. But once she did that the rest of the task went quickly. Positioning the blade so that it would slice completely through the wall without letting through any of the telltale glow that might be noticed among the shadows, she carved out a narrow upside-down triangle just big enough for her to slip through. Closing down the lightsaber, she got a Force grip on the cut section and pushed.

It broke free with a muffled crunch. Straining with the effort—the section was even heavier than it looked—Mara floated it forward half a meter and cautiously looked in.

Once again, the Emperor's memory training had served her well. Her new private entrance was behind the exact center of the stack of crates she'd been aiming for.

She retrieved her satchel as she pushed the triangular plug another half a meter forward. Making sure she was unobserved, she slipped through the opening, then used the Force to slide the plug back in place. She tucked her satchel out of sight between two of the crates, returned the lightsaber to her belt, and made her way to the edge of the stack.

Her first thought when she'd seen all the cartloads of crates being delivered to the ship was that the pirates had gotten wind of her investigation and were pulling out. But now she realized that wasn't the case. The men and aliens with the carts weren't simply loading at random, but were taking crates only from two specific stacks near the doors, stacks that were by now nearly depleted. Even more interestingly, there were two different styles and classes of clothing being worn: one set by those handling the carts, the other by half a dozen men and aliens who were mostly lounging around keeping a watchful eye on the first batch. Apparently some kind of goods redistribution was going on.

She stretched out to the Force, trying to get a feel for the two groups. The ones with the carts had the low-level rebelliousness and slight paranoia of career criminals, but none of the underlying viciousness she could usually sense in habitual killers. Smugglers, she tentatively identified them, or else receivers of stolen goods.

The loungers, in contrast, not only had the killer edge but were insolently proud of it. Each of them also had a long, prominent scar along his left cheek, or whatever passed for a cheek in the case of the nonhumans. That, combined with their shoulder patches and a warehouse full of loot, tagged them as the pirates Birtraub had mentioned.

But one figure was still missing from the mix. Mara continued her visual and mental sweep of the room; and there, standing alone by a stack of crates off to her left, she saw him.

He wasn't much to look at, at least not on the surface. A human of medium height and build, he was dressed in a plain dark red tunic, with black trousers and boots. He carried no obvious weapon, and had a bland, utterly forgettable face.

But Mara's training and Force sensitivity told a different story. The eyes in that bland face were alert and probing, the tunic and boots concealed weaponry exotic and deadly, and even in a relaxed state his unremarkable build had the sense of a watchful predator. Unlike Pirtonna and his thugs, unlike even the brutal pirates around him, this man was a warrior.

Caaldra.

She studied him another minute, watching the way his eyes moved around the room, noting how his hands stayed close to the weapons whose positions she could read in the subtle folds of cloth and slight bulges of boot leather, sensing the automatic flow of contingency combat plans through his mind as the other inhabitants of the warehouse moved about their tasks.

One of the pirates watching the procedure turned and started in Caaldra's direction. From his age and the number of souvenir trinkets Mara could see glittering on his chest, she guessed he was high up in the organization. Keeping a wary eye on the rest of the room, staying in the shadows behind the stacks of crates, she moved closer.

She had reached a spot two stacks away from Caaldra when the pirate arrived. Sinking into a crouch, she eased an eye around the edge of the lowest crate and stretched out with her sensory enhancement techniques.

"—almost done," the pirate was saying. "Be glad to get those furs out of here."

"Not much profit in it," Caaldra commented.

"*Any* profit's fine with me," the pirate countered. "Floogy things take up way more room than they're worth." He gestured to Caaldra. "So you got our next targets?"

"Right here," Caaldra said, pulling out a data card and handing it over. "Ten ships, the first and third for me." He paused. "That's *everything* in the first and third, Shakko. Make sure the Commodore explains to your people what'll happen if there's any, shall we say, leakage this time."

Commodore. Mara's lip twisted in contempt. Pirate chieftains did so enjoy taking on pseudo-military titles and airs.

"Yeah, yeah, I'll tell him," Shakko growled. "Don't worry—I'll take the first target myself."

"Fine," Caaldra said. "It leaves port in three days, with your optimal ambush point in five. Plenty of time. And the other targets should be in easy range of your other ships."

"Plenty of time if we can get these flanked smugglers hoofing, anyway," Shakko muttered, turning back. "Hey! Tannis!"

One of the other pirates detached himself from the section of wall he'd been leaning on and strode over. "Yes?"

"Take Vickers and one of the speeders back to the ship and send this list to the Commodore," Shakko ordered, handing him the data card. "Then comm Bisc and tell him he's got half an hour to finish picking up the supplies and get them stowed."

"Want me to start engine prep?"

"Might as well wait till we're finished here," Shakko said. "I'll comm and tell you when."

"Okay." Tannis headed for the warehouse door, grabbing one of the other men along the way.

Mara didn't wait to hear any more, but quickly retraced her steps through the shadows toward her satchel and her private entrance. It was clear that the smugglers, the pirates, and Caaldra would soon be going their separate ways, and even the Emperor's Hand couldn't follow three quarries at once.

She could, of course, return to her ship and call it in. But even if there were Imperial forces in the area who could react quickly enough, it was unlikely they would be set up for the kind of subtle tracking and surveillance work that was called for here. For all intents and purposes, Mara was on her own.

Fortunately, there wasn't any real question about which way she should go on this one. Intriguing though Caaldra might be, it was clear the pirates were about to head off on a frenzy of attack and murder. That was where the immediate danger to the Empire and its citizens lay, so that was where Mara would go.

Besides, Caaldra had told Shakko that the first and third targets were his. It would be interesting to find out what those targets were.

Three minutes later she was back in her borrowed landspeeder, following the two pirates at a discreet distance as they drove along the storage facility's outer drive.

Shakko's ship was parked in a docking bay on the west side of the storage complex, close enough to the warehouse for easy access but far enough away that a casual observer wouldn't immediately make the connection between it and the smugglers. It was a Corellian HT-2200 medium freighter: almost sixty meters long with four climate-adjustable cargo holds, a solid pack beast of a ship. As with the smugglers' vehicle, though, appearances were undoubtedly not to be trusted.

The pirates hadn't left any guards on outside duty, but it was quickly clear that there was at least one man still inside. Even before Tannis coasted the landspeeder to a stop by the leftmost of the two forward-jutting cargo arms a boarding ramp had lowered to meet them. Parking the landspeeder, the two pirates hopped out and trotted up the ramp, which immediately lifted shut behind them. There was another ramp on this model, Mara knew, over on the right cargo arm, probably as vigilantly watched as the other one.

But then, she hadn't really planned on using any of the usual entrances.

Her landspeeder's present vector would take her past the ship's stern, with her nearest approach being about twenty meters away. Adjusting her direction slightly, she aimed the vehicle past the edge of the next section of the storage complex, where it would be out of view of the pirate ship when it either coasted to a halt or crashed. Getting a grip on her satchel, she gunned the vehicle; as it passed directly behind the freighter she tossed out the satchel and leapt out after it.

She hit the ground, rolled twice to kill her momentum, then rolled back to her feet. Satchel in hand, she sprinted to the pirate ship's stern, pausing beneath the four large drive nozzles for a final check of the area. Then, heaving the satchel up into the lower-rightmost nozzle, she reached to the Force for strength and leapt up beside it.

The nozzle wasn't big enough for her to stand upright, but there was plenty of room for her to crouch. For a moment she looked around, stretching out with her senses and trying to determine whether she'd been spotted. There wouldn't be any out-hull visual sensors back here, she knew—the high radiation level during flight would fry them in double-quick time. But she could have been wrong about the pirates having posted outside guards.

Still, if anyone had noticed her unorthodox arrival, they were being quiet about it. Moving the satchel out of her way, she pulled out her lightsaber and set to work enlarging the opening between the nozzle and the reaction chamber.

It was a tricky operation, one she'd practiced only a few times and never actually performed in the field. The key was to cut away some of the extra sideward insulation and shielding—which would reduce the operating lifetime of the engine but not endanger anyone inside—while leaving the flow, coolant, and sensor lines intact.

Fortunately, with engines this big there was plenty of extra room to play with. She'd whittled away no more than a quarter of the shielding before she had an opening big enough to squeeze through. Closing down the lightsaber, she wriggled her way through and found herself in the engine's reaction chamber.

With some engines there would be at least one more stage to go before she could get to the ship's interior. But the Corellian Engineering Corporation had thoughtfully included a human-sized circular access hatchway into the reaction chamber along with the more standard hopper holes suitable only for maintenance and cleaning droids.

The hatch was several centimeters thick, of course, and sealed from the other side, but that wouldn't be a problem. Again igniting her lightsaber, Mara slipped the glowing blade between the hatch and frame, trying to damage the material as little as possible, until she felt the blade poke through the far end. She eased the tip up and down until she felt the brief resistance that indicated she'd found and cut through the catch. Closing down the weapon, she drew her sleeve blaster and cautiously pushed the hatch open.

It opened into a small, cramped, and surprisingly clean engineering area. No one was visible, but with Tannis already here and Shakko and the rest of the gang soon to be on their way she knew the solitude wouldn't last.

Her first task was to reseal the hatch. Borrowing a welding torch from a compact machine shop tucked away in one corner, she carefully reconnected the sections of the hatch she'd cut. The weld was far from perfect, but it should stand up to anything but a close examination.

More importantly, it would also hold the hatch closed against the pressures of the reaction chamber behind it. It would be of small comfort for her to successfully infiltrate the pirates, only to have their ship blow up beneath her.

The engineering section opened forward into the crew common room, a comfortable, relatively open area flanked by the galley, medical bay, and eight sets of crew quarters. Directly forward was the blast door into the step-up cockpit; angling past it to right and left were twin corridors leading to the starboard and portside cargo arms. Satchel in one hand, sleeve blaster in the other, Mara took the right-hand corridor, passing the cockpit area and heading into the starboard cargo arm. She could hear muffled voices now, along with the faint sounds of movement, and picked up her pace. Directly ahead, the corridor narrowed and curved around what appeared to be another crew cabin snuggled up against the cargo arm's inner wall. She started toward it—

The sudden tingle of the Force was her only warning. Half a second later, the cabin door gave a soft *snick* and slid open.

And she found herself face-to-face with Tannis.

He hadn't seen her yet, his eyes focused downward on the data card in his hand as he started out of the cabin. But discovery was as imminent as it was inevitable. There was no way for Mara to get past him around the side of the cabin and down the corridor, not without him spotting her, and it would be equally impossible to back up and duck around the side of the cargo hold before he looked up.

Which left her only one option. Reaching out with the Force, she slammed the side of his head against the edge of the doorway.

He went down without a sound, collapsing into a heap on the floor. Mara crouched beside him, automatically checking his pulse as she looked around for inspiration. Her move had bought her a little time, but only a little, and at the additional cost of now having to come up with a plausible explanation for Tannis's accident. She peered into the cabin, glanced again around the corridor, and then looked up.

There was the answer: a group of five pipes running together along the upper corridor wall, curving to follow the bulge of Tannis's cabin and then continuing around it into the cargo arm. If the colored rings on the pipes followed standard shipboard code, two of the conduits carried water, one had cryo fluid for the cargo bays' temperature controls, one contained laser coolant, presumably for whatever concealed weaponry the pirates had up there, and the last carried backup hydraulic fluid for the boarding ramp.

And everyone who flew the galaxy knew that hydraulic fluid plus water made for a dangerously slippery combination.

There was an attachment clamp right at the corner by Tannis's cabin where the pipes started their bend. Igniting her lightsaber, Mara worked the tip of the blade behind the clamp where vibration might possibly have worn a hole, scratching delicately at the metal of one of the water pipes until a trickle appeared and began dribbling down the wall. Another careful scratch, and it was joined by an equally small trickle of hydraulic fluid. Stepping over the dribbles now beginning to inch their way across the deck, she twisted Tannis's legs around and gave the soles of his boots a good coating with the stuff.

As deceptions went, it was a pretty weak one. If the pirates decided to be suspicious, they could probably tear the whole scenario apart in ten minutes.

But Shakko hadn't struck her as having that much imagination. Besides, she was pretty sure she would eventually end up killing them all anyway. If they figured it out, that judgment would simply be administered a few days early. Making sure not to touch the fluid herself, she continued down the corridor to the forward-most of the two cargo holds in this arm.

As she'd already surmised from the coolant line, the pirates had installed some extra weaponry aboard their ship. What she hadn't expected was the sheer scope of the refitting that had been done. The entire forward hold had been turned into a weapons bay, with two sets of quad lasers, a small ion cannon, and a highly illegal Krupx MG7 proton torpedo launcher. Most of the remaining space was taken up by a boxy Cygnus 5 short-range transport standing ready to deliver boarders once the prey was pounded into submission. In one rear corner was a small armory with grenades and blaster rifles; along the back wall was a wardrobe containing vac suits, helmets, and oxygen tanks. Apparently the drill was to swing down the entire front bulkhead for attack, opening the cargo bay to space and bringing the full range of weaponry to bear.

There was no place in the weapons bay with enough concealment for her to safely set up housekeeping. Fortunately, the cargo hold directly aft of the weapons bay was another story. A quarter of its volume was filled with crates and barrels of stolen plunder, some of them bearing the scars and burns of close-in blasterfire. A few minutes' rearrangement, and she had constructed herself a snug little burrow inside one of the stacks.

Her gray jumpsuit had been rather badly stained and rumpled by her trip through the engine nozzle. She had another in her satchel, plus a set of business wear that could be converted into something more formal should the need arise.

But for the situation at hand, she had an even more appropriate outfit.

A few minutes later she was in her combat suit: skintight black, with high boots, a weapons belt, and knee pads for the kind of violent exercise she tended to get into in these situations. A compact BlasTech K-14 blaster was holstered against her right hip, her lightsaber rode her left, and a pair of small knives waited hidden in the sides of her boots.

It probably wasn't as impressive an arsenal as Caaldra's, but it should be adequate for her needs. She removed the outfit's detachable sleeves, anticipating the extra heat that freighters this size usually produced, and left the cloak in the satchel as well. Aboard ship, people seldom fought in the kind of near-complete darkness where the cloak would help obscure her outline, and unless the pirates had weapons with autotargeting systems the material's passive sensor confusers wouldn't be necessary.

And with that, her preparations were complete. According to Caaldra, the pirates had five days until their attack. Somewhere in that time, she needed to find and get a look at the data card he'd given Shakko. After that, she could decide what her own move would be.

The mission had started out as a search for a possible connection between Moff Glovstoak and the Rebellion. Now it had taken on a different flavor entirely. Idly, she wondered if there would be any more twists before it was resolved.

Stretching out on the deck inside her new burrow, her head pillowed comfortably on her satchel, she unwrapped a ration bar and settled down to wait.

Chapter Seven

"THE FORCE," LEIA COMMENTED DRILY, "DOES INDEED HAVE A SENSE OF humor."

"Or at least a sense of irony," General Rieekan said, frowning at his datapad. "Are we sure these stormtroopers didn't know who it was they were rescuing?"

"Wouldn't they have arrested Porter's group if they had?" Luke asked.

"They might have let them go in order to leave the supply line open," Leia told him, studying the farm boy's face. There was something bothering him, she could see, something beyond this mission they were preparing for. Beyond even the strange stormtrooper rescue of the Rebel group on Drunost. "Leaving them on the vine in the hope of finding bigger fruit."

"Still, Casement said no one tracked his ship," Rieekan pointed out. "And Porter has been in touch with Targeter since then and didn't indicate any trouble at his end."

"It still might be a good idea to shut down that entire supply line," Leia said. "At least for now."

"I'm not sure we can," Rieekan warned. "There's a lot of pirate and raider activity going on right now in Shelsha sector. If we shut down this line, we may not be able to open another one."

"*That'll* put Chivkyrie in a good mood for the negotiations," Luke murmured.

Leia made a face. He was right. Chivkyrie was already feeling slighted by the Alliance leadership, and the last thing they needed was an additional grievance to deal with. "Which just means we need to have a solution ready before we tell him about the problem," she said. "What do we know about these pirates?"

"For starters, they seem to be pretty much everywhere," Rieekan said. "Casement mentioned a group called BloodScar, but a single group can't possibly be big enough to be doing this much damage across the sector. My guess is that we've got several groups who've carved up the sector into individual territories."

"Sounds like the first thing we need is better intel," Leia said. "Someone needs to go out there, talk to our supply people directly, and see if we can get a handle on what exactly is going on."

"And it should be someone who knows more about fringe types than the rest of us," Luke added.

Leia frowned at him with sudden understanding. "Are you talking about Han?"

Luke shrugged uncomfortably. "Mostly," he admitted. "I mean, I don't like the idea of throwing him into danger like this—"

"It shouldn't be that dangerous," Rieekan put in. "He'd be there to gather intel, not take on the pirates single-handed."

"I know," Luke agreed, looking only marginally relieved. "The point is—he just doesn't seem to fit in anywhere around here. If we can't make him feel useful, I think we're going to lose him." He looked at Rieekan. "I don't think we want that to happen."

"In that case, we definitely want to give him this," Rieekan said.

"I agree," Leia said, bracing herself. Over the short period of time that she'd known Luke, she'd developed a pretty good feel for him, and she was quite sure he wasn't going to like what she was about to say. "And if he accepts, I think Luke should go with him."

Luke's jaw dropped a few millimeters, his eyes widening by roughly the same amount. "I thought I was going with *you*."

"I'm meeting with trusted Alliance leaders in the safety of deep space," Leia reminded him. "Han will be rubbing shoulders with criminals and possibly ducking Imperials and local government patrols. He'll need you more than I do."

"But he'll have Chewie," Luke protested. "That's all he's ever needed before."

"He wasn't on Imperial watch lists before," Rieekan said. "I agree with Princess Leia. If Solo goes, someone needs to go with him."

"But—" Luke broke off, grimacing. "You're right," he said with a sigh. "You want me to go tell him?"

Rieekan caught Leia's eye and raised his eyebrows. "No, I'll do it," she said, getting to her feet.

"Meanwhile, you'll need contact information," Rieekan said, swiveling around to his terminal and punching keys. "Let me pull up some names and locations for you."

They were sitting together at the display, Rieekan in private optimism, Luke in private disappointment, when Leia slipped out of the room.

She found Han in the hangar, crouching on top of the *Falcon*'s starboard arm, his arms buried to their elbows in one of the maintenance access bays. "Han?" she called up to him.

"Hang on a second," he said, straightening up and craning his neck to look across the hull at the cockpit. "Chewie? Give it a try."

Faintly through the transparisteel canopy Leia heard the Wookiee's answering bellow. For a moment nothing happened. Then, with a muffled *thunk*, a thin wisp of smoke drifted up from the access bay. "Okay, great," Han called. "Go ahead and shut 'er down."

There was another acknowledgment, and Han coiled his welder and slid off the arm onto the deck. "*Okay, great?*" Leia echoed, raising her eyebrows.

"Sure," he said blandly. "Why?"

"I don't remember smoke usually being part of *okay great* starship repair work."

"Oh, that." He waved a hand. "Extra soldering compound. No problem."

"If you say so," she said, part of her just as glad she wasn't going to have to ride this thing to her rendezvous. "Something's come up that General Rieekan would like you to look into."

His lip twisted. "Is this before or after I take you to this Grand Royal Elite Privileged Ball?"

With an effort, Leia forced herself to stay calm. In their brief acquaintanceship Han had somehow managed to learn exactly where all her irritation keys were, and took great satisfaction in flipping them. "Actually, you're off the hook on that one," she said.

"What?" he said in a tone of wounded outrage. "You mean I had the *Falcon* fumigated for *nothing?*"

"Don't worry, I'm sure it needed it," Leia said, determined for once not to let him goad her.

"I ordered new carpet, too."

Leia clenched her teeth. "You want to hear this, or don't you?"

"Sure."

She gave him a quick rundown of the situation in Shelsha sector. "So this is a send-the-scum-to-catch-the-scum sort of thing?" he asked when she'd finished.

"You're not going out there to catch anything," she told him. "All we want is information and maybe some ideas on how to rearrange our supply lines so pirates can't hit them."

"That *is* the trick," he agreed, frowning in thought. "People trying to fly under the scanners make good targets, and every pirate in the galaxy knows it."

"True," she said. "And since you've probably been in that situation once or twice, we thought you might know ways to avoid it."

Han shrugged. "Mostly, you try real hard to have the faster ship," he said. But Leia could see he was becoming intrigued by the mission. That, or he was simply relieved that he wasn't going to have to go to the meeting with Chivkyrie.

Or perhaps he was relieved he wouldn't have to spend so much time with Leia herself.

"So it'll just be you and Luke at your little finger-sandwich party?" he asked casually.

"What?" Leia yanked herself back to the conversation, annoyed at having let her mind wander. Especially over something like *that*. "No. No, we're asking Luke to go with you instead."

Han raised his eyebrows. "*We're* asking?" he echoed, a slight edge to his voice.

"General Rieekan and I made the decision," Leia told him. Too late, she realized she should have phrased the statement so as to give Rieekan all the responsibility. Knowing Han, he was bound to jump to the conclusion that Leia didn't want Luke along, or at least didn't want him there without Han. Not only was that completely wrong, but it made her feel—

Actually, she wasn't exactly sure *how* it made her feel. But she knew she didn't like it.

"Ah," Han said, nodding. "Makes sense."

He was playing it cool, but Leia could hear the mocking amusement in his voice. The amusement, and *definitely* the wrong conclusion. "It's not like that," she insisted.

"Not like what?" he asked innocently.

"Never mind," she said between clenched teeth. He'd done it again. How did he *always* manage to do this to her? "The general's giving Luke the names and locations of your contacts. You can leave whenever you're ready."

"Absolutely, Your Worshipfulness," he said. "Your simplest wish is my—"

"Good luck, and try not to get yourselves killed," Leia cut him off.

"Sure," he said, mock-solemnly. "You, too."

She turned and, with all the dignity she could manage, made her escape from the hangar.

But she could feel his eyes on her back the whole, long way.

LaRone was running an integrity check on one of the sets of armor in his hidden closet when Quiller pinged him. "We're here," the pilot announced.

"On my way."

The others were already gathered when he reached the cockpit. "How's it look?" he asked as he came up behind them.

"The northern continent's our best bet," Quiller said, pointing to the map of Ranklinge he'd pulled up. "If we avoid Ranklinge City and the Incom fighter plant, we've got a choice between one major city with a decent-sized port and about a hundred hole-in-the-ground regional fields scattered around the ranching and mining areas."

"How big is the city?" Grave asked.

"Not very," Quiller said. "Maybe a hundred thousand. More like a big town, really."

"There's nothing on the southern continent?" Brightwater asked.

"Nothing but a civil war," Marcross told him grimly. "Been going on for the past ten years."

"Let's definitely skip that," LaRone said, wincing. In the aftermath of the Clone Wars, the newly declared Empire had made a strong effort to clamp down on these planetary and regional conflicts as it tried to reestablish order. But there had been too many of them, and eventually Palpatine had given up and turned to other matters. "Any suggestions?"

"We tried the small-field approach on Drunost and ended up having to dust a swoop gang," Grave said. "I vote we try something with a decent patroller presence this time."

"Patrollers who might have our pictures plastered across their datapads?" Brightwater asked pointedly.

"If the big-city group has them, so will the smaller ones," Quiller replied.

"But it's easier to shoot your way out of a small port."

"We're not shooting our way out of anywhere," LaRone said firmly. "Not against patrollers who are just trying to protect Imperial citizens. Besides, we've got all these new identity tags that ISB's magic machine cranked out for us. We'll be fine."

"If you say so," Brightwater said, still sounding unconvinced. "What's the name of this town-sized city?"

"Janusar," Quiller said. "It's got decent port facilities, a good air-defense system to discourage raiders, and all the supply shops we should need."

"Sounds good," LaRone said. "Give port guidance a shout and get us a bay."

Quiller nodded and keyed the comm. "Janusar Port Guidance, this is freighter *Ville Brok*," he called. "Requesting a docking bay assignment."

"Freighter *Ville Brok*, this is Janusar Guidance," a voice came back. "What's your cargo?"

Quiller threw a frown over his shoulder at LaRone as he tapped the MUTE key. "Should they be asking that?"

"I don't know," LaRone said, an odd sensation starting to tickle the back of his mind. "I've never heard of a port asking that question before a freighter's even landed."

"Maybe it's some local regulation," Grave suggested.

"So what do I tell him?" Quiller asked.

"Tell him we're picking something up," Marcross said.

Quiller nodded and keyed the microphone again. "No cargo yet, Janusar. We're hoping to pick up something there."

"From who?"

"We don't know yet," Quiller said. "Like I said, we're hoping. If it's the docking fees you're worried about, that won't be a problem."

There was a brief silence. "Fine," port guidance said. "Docking Bay Twenty-two."

On Quiller's map display an indicator flicked on, marking the landing site. "Bay Twenty-two, acknowledged," Quiller said.

"By the way, you have any weapons aboard?"

LaRone smiled grimly. If they only knew. "Nothing to speak of," he said. "Why?"

"Just asking," the other said. "Janusar Guidance out."

Quiller switched off the comm. "Curious types, aren't they?" he commented.

"Oddly curious," Marcross seconded. "I wonder why they wanted to know about weapons."

"I don't know," LaRone said. "But I think the question all by itself means we definitely go in armed. Hold-outs only, though, and we keep them out of sight until and unless they're needed."

The Janusar spaceport consisted of a basic core region, well laid out but showing its age, surrounded by a patchwork of newer areas that had been added on over the years. The add-ons, LaRone noted, seemed to be further divided into high-class and low-class sections.

Bay 22 turned out to be in one of the low-class areas.

"I'm guessing freighters that come sniffing around for on-spec cargoes usually don't get much business from the upper-class merchants," Quiller commented as he shut down the Suwantek's systems.

"That, or you need a secret password to get into the nice side of town," Grave said.

"Doesn't matter," LaRone said. "All we want is food and fuel, and we can get those anywhere. Same duties as last time: Grave will go with me, the rest of you stay here—"

"Hold it," Marcross interrupted, leaning toward the right-hand side of the canopy and frowning aft toward the starboard boarding ramp. "We've got company: five patrollers plus an officer. Look's like sergeant's insignia."

"There are five more over here," Quiller said, looking out his side of the canopy. "No officers."

Brightwater muttered something under his breath and started aft. "Come on, Grave, let's hit the turrets. What was that someone said about not having to shoot our way out?"

"Wait a second," Marcross said, still looking out the canopy as he caught Grave's arm. "This is way too small a crowd to be facing down military fugitives."

"He's right," Quiller agreed. "Nothing but hand blasters, still holstered. They're probably just here to collect our docking fees."

"They need a whole squad for that?" Brightwater asked suspiciously.

"Maybe incoming freighters with no cargo kick up a warning flag," LaRone said.

From the direction of the starboard boarding ramp came the sound of a fist hammering on metal. "Well, if we *don't* answer it really *will* kick up a flag," Marcross pointed out, getting up from his seat. "Come on, LaRone."

The visitors had resumed their pounding by the time LaRone and Marcross reached the boarding ramp. LaRone slapped the release, and the ramp lowered to reveal six scowling faces.

"About time," the sergeant growled as he stalked his way up into the ship. "Go let in my men on the other side and get me your registry and cargo manifest."

"Registry's right here," LaRone said, handing over a data card as Marcross walked across the anteroom and lowered the other ramp. "As we told port guidance, we don't have any cargo."

The five men on the Suwantek's other side trooped up the portside ramp and joined the others. "Crew?" the sergeant asked, plugging the card into his datapad and glancing at it.

"Us, plus three in the cockpit," LaRone said, pulling out his freshly minted identity tag.

The sergeant didn't even glance at it. "Fine," he said, handing back the registry card. "We'll start with two hundred for the docking fee." Gesturing to his squad, he started aft toward the crew lounge.

"Wait a second," LaRone said, frowning. Even given his lack of experience with the financial end of these things, two hundred credits for a third-rate docking bay seemed a little high. "We'll *start* at two hundred?"

"No, we'll start at two fifty," the sergeant retorted, his eyes narrowing. "You want to argue some more about it?"

I wasn't arguing, LaRone thought, annoyed. He was opening his mouth to say so when Marcross's warning touch on his arm stopped him.

"That's right—listen to your friend," the sergeant said sarcastically. "Where's the cargo hold on this flying nerf trap?"

"Straight aft, left, and right, just before you reach engineering," Marcross told him.

"Thank you," the sergeant said with exaggerated politeness. He started to turn, then cocked an eyebrow. "By the way, I trust you're not carrying any weapons aboard?"

"Just the two laser cannons mounted in front of the boarding ramps," Marcross said.

The sergeant grunted. "Good," he said. "That's another hundred fifty each." For a moment he stared at LaRone, his eyes daring him to argue the point. But LaRone had learned his lesson. He remained silent, and with another grunt the sergeant gestured again to his men and turned aft. Touching the door release, he led them into the lounge.

LaRone waited until the whole squad had passed through and the door was closed before saying the word that best described his feelings. "What kind of gleening shakedown *is* this?" he muttered.

"Probably the usual kind," Marcross said. His voice was even, but it was clear that he was already well beyond annoyed himself. "You didn't have this sort of thing at your home spaceport?"

"If we did, I never knew about it," LaRone said. "Still, I suppose whatever they want to gouge from us, we can afford it."

"That's the spirit," Marcross said approvingly. "Nice and low-profile, and we can spit the dust of this world back into the wind on our way out."

"I suppose," LaRone said. "Come on—let's make sure they're not stealing the galley flatware."

The lounge was deserted when they entered. So was the crew section when they passed through the lounge's aft door. LaRone opened the first cabin—Quiller's—but there was no one inside. "Must have decided to go straight to the cargo holds," Marcross commented as he checked Grave's cabin across the corridor.

"Good," LaRone said, closing the cabin door and continuing aft. "Maybe this'll go quicker than I thought."

They were passing the galley when two of the patrollers stepped into view through the starboard hold door. They caught sight of LaRone and Marcross and beckoned. "Come on, kleegs," one of them called. "Whisteer wants you."

The rest of the patrollers were standing silently around the hold; their eyes turned to LaRone and Marcross as they stepped inside. In the center of the group was the sergeant, a tight smile on his face, his left elbow resting casually on the handgrip of one of the two speeder bikes. "So much for *no cargo*," he said. "You have a permit for these things?"

LaRone stifled a curse. He'd lived around military hardware for so long that it had never even occurred to him that civilians would see it in an entirely different way. "We bought them at a surplus sale," he improvised. "Banged-up and wrecked equipment."

"They don't look very banged up to me."

"We've been working on them."

"Ah." Whisteer patted the saddle. "And of course, before they sold them to you they would have removed—" He craned his neck to look at the underside. "Why, look at that," he said in mock surprise. "Someone forgot to take off the blaster cannon." He cocked an eyebrow at LaRone. "And someone else forgot to list them among their weapons."

"I forgot about them," LaRone admitted. "But it was purely accidental—you can see we made no effort to hide them."

"True," Whisteer agreed, his voice going silky smooth. "But with contraband, that doesn't much matter, does it? Purposeful or not, the stuff gets confiscated."

LaRone looked sideways at Marcross. The other's expression was mirroring his own thoughts: Brightwater would flay them both alive if they let some ground-hugger walk off with his precious speeder bikes. "Is there any way to appeal that?" he asked, looking back at Whisteer. "I mean, if we file the proper forms and pay the necessary fees, of course."

Whisteer smiled again, his eyes glittering. "There might be a way," he allowed. "Could be expensive, though."

"We understand," Marcross put in. "What's the procedure?"

"Come to Patroller Central at eight tonight," the other said. "Market Street at Fifth. I'll have the forms ready for you to fill out."

"We'll be there," LaRone said. "I don't suppose you'd have some idea of what the filing fees might run?"

Whisteer shrugged. "Won't know till I look up the regs."

Translation: it would depend on how many more people he had to cut in on the deal. "But it *will* be expensive, you think?"

"Could happen," Whisteer said. He jerked a thumb at one of the other patrollers. "Speaking of expensive, Chavers has the rest of your list. You can pay him while we get these things out of here."

LaRone took a deep breath. "I'll go open the safe."

Ten minutes later LaRone and the others stood at the foot of the port-side ramp and watched as the patrollers drove away in a pair of repulsor-sleds, the speeder bikes strapped carefully to the rear storage racks. "You should have called us in," Brightwater said, his voice dark and menacing. "We could have taken them."

"You would have gotten your heads blown off," a voice said from behind them.

LaRone spun around, his hand darting automatically toward his hidden blaster. A man in a dirty coversuit was walking toward them beneath the Suwantek's belly, dragging a thick fuel hose behind him. "Who are you?" he demanded.

"Name's Krinkins," the man said, clearly startled by the reaction. "Fuel service. You *did* call for a fill, right?"

"Yes, we did," Quiller confirmed.

"And we *wouldn't* have gotten our heads blown off," Brightwater added stiffly.

"Sure you would." Krinkins paused, measuring them with his eyes. "Well, maybe not you," he conceded. "At least, not right away. But sooner or later they'd have gotten you. There's way too many of them to fight."

"You saying Whisteer's squad isn't running this alone?" LaRone asked.

Krinkins snorted. "Whisteer's not the one running it at all. That plum-merine goes to Patroller Chief Cav'Saran."

"The *chief*?" Marcross echoed disbelievingly.

"What, that surprises you?" Krinkins asked.

"Yes, it does," Marcross said. "The sector government's supposed to screen the credentials of people appointed to high-ranking law enforce-ment positions."

Krinkins snorted. "Yeah. Right."

"I mean it," Marcross insisted. "There are bureaucrats all over Shel-konwa whose only job is to watch out for this sort of thing."

"Well, the one in charge of Ranklinge apparently takes long naps at his desk," Krinkins said bitterly. "We complained plenty in the early days. Didn't do a scrap of good. Now, of course, Cav'Saran makes sure messages like that never make it onto the HoloNet."

"What about the Empire?" Quiller asked.

Krinkins laughed, a short, derisive bark. "The *Empire*? We've had *one* Imperial ship come by Ranklinge in the past eight years, and *that* was an old Republic cruiser picking up a couple of diplomats who'd given up try-ing to mediate South Cont's civil war. The Empire doesn't even know we exist. Or care."

"What about you and the other locals?" LaRone asked. "Or don't the citizens of Janusar care if their officials shake down visitors?"

"The rest of Janusar hates it," Krinkins said bluntly. "And it's not just visitors, either—they lean pretty hard on all of us. But it's blamed hard to fight blasters with your bare fists."

"I *thought* everyone seemed way too interested in our weapons," Mar-cross murmured.

"Yours and everyone else's," Krinkins said. "Eight months ago, right after Cav'Saran took over, they went through every house for two hundred kilometers and confiscated all the weapons they could find. Probably no more than a dozen slug rifles left anywhere in the whole four districts, and most of those are out on ranches where they need 'em to protect the herds from predators." He glanced furtively around. "I don't suppose . . . no— never mind."

"We don't have any weapons for sale, if that's what you were wondering," LaRone said, flicking a warning glance at the others. They had no way of knowing whether or not Krinkins was really what he seemed. "How many men does Cav'Saran have?"

"About three hundred," the fueler said. "All the uniformed patrollers—he fired or squeezed out the honest ones after he took over—plus a few plainclothesmen who wander around watching for troublemakers."

"Aren't you worried about talking to *us* this way?" Grave asked. "How do you know we're not informers?"

Krinkins snorted and started attaching the hose to the Suwantek's intake port. "I don't," he growled. "But I'm at the point where I don't even care anymore. You want to call Cav'Saran and have me locked up for sedition, go right ahead."

"I admire your courage," LaRone said. "Any more like you who are sick enough of this to take a chance?"

Krinkins frowned at him, an odd look on his face. "What do you mean?" he asked carefully.

"I just thought that anybody ready for a change might want to gather together outside Patroller Central tonight," LaRone said. "Say, about seven o'clock."

Krinkins snorted. "If you're talking about a protest, forget it," he said. "They just ignore things like that. At least, until they get tired enough of the crowds to break 'em up with a little scattered blasterfire."

"You just get them there," LaRone told the fueler, sternly forcing back his rising anger. There was no room for emotion here. "And make sure you invite all those honest ex-patrollers you mentioned."

Two minutes later the five stormtroopers were gathered in the crew lounge. It was Brightwater who stated what LaRone knew the others were thinking. "You realize, of course," he said, "that doing anything at all here would be totally insane."

"Agreed," Grave seconded. "We haven't got the manpower *or* the support system."

"Not to mention the authority," Quiller murmured.

"I disagree," LaRone said. "We took an oath of allegiance to serve the Empire. These people are citizens of that Empire."

"And Cav'Saran is clearly violating his own oath," Grave said. "I agree the man's a scum sorter. That doesn't change the fact that we can't take on three hundred armed men all by ourselves."

"It won't be all by ourselves," LaRone said. "If I'm reading Krinkins right, we should have a good-sized crowd waiting when we pull up to Patroller Central tonight."

"All of them unarmed," Brightwater reminded him.

"Not for long," LaRone said. "We're talking a patroller station. There should be plenty of blasters sitting in racks inside."

"And you're going to hand them over to an angry mob?" Quiller countered.

"No, that's why I asked Krinkins to bring the ex-patrollers," LaRone said. "Hopefully, they'll have both the training and the moral authority to take charge."

"It's still insane," Brightwater insisted. "Marcross? You're being awfully quiet."

"Of course it's insane," Marcross agreed. "My only question is how exactly we want to put it together."

Brightwater looked at Quiller and Grave, a stunned look on his face. "You're kidding," he said, looking back at Marcross. "*You*, of all people, want to do this?"

"You *do* remember we're on the run, right?" Grave asked.

"And we're on the run ultimately because we didn't like being ordered to abuse our authority," Marcross countered. "Are we going to be selective as to which abuses we stand up to and which we turn our backs on?"

"Are you sure you're not just mad at people like this running around your own sector?" Quiller asked pointedly.

"I'll admit there's some of that," Marcross conceded. "But my personal feelings don't change the reality of the situation." He gestured to LaRone. "A minute ago LaRone mentioned moral authority. If we as representatives of the Empire don't have that, who does?"

"Except that we *aren't* representatives of the Empire," Quiller reminded him. "Not anymore."

"Cav'Saran won't know that," LaRone said. "And if we do this right, he also won't know we don't have a whole legion behind us."

For a long moment the lounge was silent. Then Grave shrugged. "As long as we all agree it's insane, I don't mind going along. Besides, we have to get Brightwater's speeder bikes back."

"There is that," Brightwater said reluctantly.

Quiller shook his head, expelling his breath in a soft huff. "Oh, sure, why not," he said. "Assuming we can come up with a halfway workable plan."

"Don't worry about that," LaRone assured him grimly. "The only real question is how much damage we want to inflict on Cav'Saran's people. Here's what I had in mind . . ."

Chapter Eight

THEY SPENT THE REST OF THE DAY BUYING THEIR SUPPLIES, DOING SOME quiet reconnaissance in the Patroller Central area, and preparing and fine-tuning their plan.

By the appointed time, they were ready.

There was a surprisingly good crowd waiting outside Patroller Central as LaRone maneuvered the speeder truck along the road. At least four hundred of them, he estimated, three to four times more than he'd expected. Apparently the citizens of Janusar really were serious about dealing with their oppressors.

The stormtroopers hadn't tried to get inside the headquarters on their earlier probes, but from the building's design they'd concluded it had probably started life as a regional assembly center, with a large domed gathering room in the center and a single-story ring of offices and smaller meeting rooms wrapped around it. The protesters were gathered on a small grassy park area just in front of the building, the park separated from the building itself by a wide passenger-drop drive. From the building side of the drive a wide flight of stone steps led up to a set of ornate double doors.

Standing in a line in front of those doors, scowling and fingering their holstered blasters as they gazed out across the gathered citizenry, were six uniformed patrollers.

The crowd had spilled from the grass onto the drive, but they moved aside with only scattered hesitation as LaRone eased the speeder truck slowly through the mass toward the building. A few peered intently in at him, or tried with shaded eyes to pierce the rear windows' privacy tint and see who might seated on the two bench seats behind him, and LaRone found himself wondering what exactly Krinkins had told them about the strangers.

He reached the front of the building, but instead of parking alongside the curb he gave the vehicle a hard ninety-degree turn, leaving it straddled across the drive with its nose pointed toward the scowling guards at the top of the stairway. "Hey!" one of them called as LaRone lifted the swing-wing door and got out. "Get that bantha dropping out of there!"

"Yeah, yeah, just a second," LaRone called back, waving vaguely at them as he closed the door again.

He'd expected Krinkins to be close at hand, and he wasn't disappointed. Even as he turned to survey the silent crowd the fueler detached himself from the front line and walked over to him. His face was grim but with an edge of cautious hope. "You came," he said, his eyes flicking to the privacy-tinted windows. "I wasn't sure you would."

"Did you get any of the ex-patrollers?" LaRone asked.

Krinkins nodded back over his shoulder. "I found eight. They're all here."

"Good," LaRone said. "When I signal you, bring them forward."

"Wait a second," Krinkins said. "What are you—"

Without waiting for him to finish, LaRone turned and strode up the steps.

"You deaf, sluggy?" one of the patrollers growled as LaRone reached the wide landing. The man had a single-ear headset with a wire mike curving along his cheek and wore a lieutenant's insignia on his shoulders. "I told you to move that thing."

"Don't worry, I will," LaRone assured him, taking another step to close the gap between them. "I'm just here about some property your people seized earlier today."

"Oh, you're Whisteer's guy," the man said, eyeing him with contemptuous curiosity. He gestured over LaRone's shoulder with his blaster. "You the one responsible for this, too?"

LaRone half turned to look at the crowd. "You mean them?" he asked, his left hand waving out toward the assembly. Under cover of the movement, his right hand dipped into his side tunic pocket.

"Yeah, them," the man said. " 'Cause if you are—"

And in a single simultaneous motion all four of the speeder truck's rear doors swung up and the other stormtroopers stepped out, their armor gleaming in the streetlight, their BlasTech E-11s pointed at the line of patrollers.

The lieutenant's threat broke off in midword as a startled gasp rippled through the crowd. "No noise, please," LaRone said quietly, pressing his hold-out blaster into the notch at the base of the other's throat. With his other hand he pulled off the headset, shutting it off as he did so. "No sudden movements, either," he added.

From the expressions on the patrollers' faces, it didn't look like any of them had the slightest intention of making trouble. They stood as stiff as six hardwood trees, their hands frozen well clear of their holsters, as the four stormtroopers marched up the steps. Catching Krinkins's eye, LaRone gestured him forward. The fueler nodded and made a gesture of his own, and with five men and three women behind him he headed up the steps behind the stormtroopers. "These your patrollers?" LaRone asked as he pulled the white-faced lieutenant's blaster from its holster.

"Yes, sir," Krinkins said, his voice crisp and vibrant with a sudden new hope as he nodded to a middle-aged man with streaks of gray through his hair. "This is Colonel Atmino, senior officer."

"Forcibly retired," Atmino added, a glint in his eye as he looked at the patrollers.

"Consider yourself reinstated," LaRone told him, handing him the lieutenant's weapon. "I hereby deputize you and your squad. Disarm these men, and put them under arrest pending prosecution for any crimes they may have committed."

"Yes, sir," Atmino said, straightening up to full parade attention as he waved three of his people forward. "Other orders?"

"Just stay here and guard the prisoners," LaRone said. "We'll take care of Cav'Saran." He looked over Atmino's shoulder. "And keep the crowd under control. When you inform the governor's office about this, you won't want your claim muddied by charges of disorder or rioting."

"Understood," Atmino said, getting a firm grip on the lieutenant's arm. "We'll take care of it."

LaRone gestured to the other stormtroopers. "Let's go."

The double doors opened on a wide, marble-floored lobby area that stretched fifteen meters ahead to a curved wall and a second set of double doors. To the right and left the lobby narrowed into a pair of corridors that curved around the central core, their elaborately frescoed walls interrupted at intervals by the doors of private offices.

At this hour, LaRone guessed, most of the outer offices would be vacant. Leaving them for later, he strode to the double doors, dropping his hold-out blaster back into his side pocket. He gestured to the other stormtroopers to stay out of sight, then pulled the doors open and stepped inside.

As they had surmised earlier, the inner room was indeed a single large chamber, which the patrollers had converted from a meeting hall into a squad room. Packed onto the main floor and the ring of small balconies set into the upper wall beneath the dome were almost two hundred desks and workstations. Nearly all the desks were occupied, LaRone noted, though only a few of the patrollers seemed to be actually working. The rest were just sitting there, fiddling with data cards or their blasters, or conversing in low tones with the other fifty or so patrollers who were standing or wandering around the room. In response to the protest outside, Chief Cav'Saran had apparently pulled in most of his force.

Perfect.

LaRone made no effort to downplay his grand entrance, but even if he had, he doubted it would have made any difference. The patrollers were on hair-trigger, and even before he'd made it all the way into the room all heads had snapped around.

"What do you want?" a bulky patroller demanded from his perch atop a tall reception desk just to the right of the door.

"I'm here to see Whisteer," LaRone said, putting enough air behind the words to make sure they carried all the way across the room. "And Chief Cav'Saran."

"You're early," Whisteer's voice growled back, and LaRone saw him straighten up from a conversation by one of the desks. "The forms aren't ready yet."

"That's okay," LaRone said. "I wasn't going to fill them out anyway. Which one of you is Cav'Saran?"

There was a moment of silence, and then a man with a badly scarred face detached himself from one of the conversation groups. "I'm Chief Cav'Saran," he growled, his tone making it a challenge. "You have a problem?"

"I have a complaint," LaRone said. "Some of your men tried to shake me down this morning."

Cav'Saran's eyebrows lifted. "Really?" he asked in a tone of feigned politeness. "How?"

"They charged excessive fees and stole some of my cargo."

"Did they, now," Cav'Saran said, an amused smile starting to tug at the corners of his mouth. "And who exactly was responsible for this outrage?"

"Sergeant Whisteer, for one," LaRone said, pointing at Whisteer as he let his gaze sweep across the room's occupants. The circular floor plan allowed for no blind corners, and though the desks would provide cover in a gun battle there wasn't nearly enough room behind them for everyone.

More problematic was the high ground being held by the men on the balcony workstations. Most of the ones up there were wearing officers' insignia, though, and seemed more curious or bemused than hair-trigger hostile.

Still, there were plenty of the latter type scattered around the main floor. Mentally tagging their locations, LaRone pointed to three of the others who'd been aboard the Suwantek that morning. "Those three were there, too," he added, "plus seven more."

"And what exactly would you like me to do about it?" the chief asked, still playing along.

"I want them arrested," LaRone said. "They're to be charged with extortion, theft, and abuse of power."

"And if I refuse?"

LaRone looked around the room again. The sense of hostility was starting to grow as the novelty of the confrontation faded, but so far none of the patrollers seemed to have considered it worth drawing their blasters. "Then I'll have to find someone else to do the job," he said.

"Like that losers' mob outside?" Cav'Saran asked acidly; and with that, all traces of levity were gone from his face. "Good; because along with the fines already levied, you're now under arrest for sedition and incitement and unlawful assembly." He raised his eyebrows. "And for *that*, I think we'll confiscate your ship." He gestured contemptuously. "Whisteer, dump him in a cell."

"Fine with me," LaRone said calmly. "A public trial would be most enlightening."

"Good point," Cav'Saran agreed as Whisteer strode forward. "You're not worth that kind of risk. Whisteer? Dump him in a swamp instead." He smiled maliciously. "Thanks for pointing that out."

"And thank *you* for confirming the charges I'd already heard from some of the citizens," LaRone said. "I hereby place you and your entire patroller contingent under arrest."

Cav'Saran smiled. "Really. You and who else?"

It was the perfect opening, and Marcross had the flair to take him up on it. From behind LaRone came the soft clicking of armored boots on marble—but even without the sound he would have known the other stormtroopers had made their grand entrance. The sharply inhaled breaths, the jerking of heads and bodies, and the sudden widening of eyes were all the clues he needed. "In the name of the Empire," he said formally into the brittle silence as he drew his hold-out blaster, "you and your men are ordered to surrender your weapons."

With a muttered curse, Whisteer yanked his blaster from its holster.

Or rather, yanked it halfway out. Brightwater's shot caught him squarely in the chest, dropping him before he could so much as gasp.

Across the room to the right, three of the men LaRone had pegged as possible troublemakers went for their own weapons. LaRone was ready, dropping two of them as Marcross took out the third. There was a quick double shot from LaRone's left, and he looked up to see the two officers in one of the balconies fold themselves limply over the railing, their blasters dropping from limp fingers to clatter onto the floor below.

And with that another, even more brittle silence descended on the room.

"That's six who've chosen to opt out of the legal system," LaRone said. "Any others?"

For a moment no one moved. Then, without warning, Cav'Saran grabbed the arm of the closest patroller with his right hand, pulling the man in front of him. Hooking his left arm around the other's throat to keep him there, he drew his blaster.

Without even appearing to aim, Grave shifted his blaster slightly and sent a shot sizzling past the living shield's ear to blow a hole in Cav'Saran's face.

LaRone waited until the body had finished clattering its way across one of the desks and onto the floor. "Anyone else?" he called.

There wasn't. An hour later, it was over.

"We've collected the ones who were out on patrol," Atmino reported as the last of the former patrollers were escorted to the bulging holding cells. "Weren't too many of them, as it turned out. I guess Cav'Saran was more interested in being ready to grind our protest into the dirt than he was in actually protecting the city."

"You'll want to mention that in your report," LaRone said. "You have enough former patrollers on duty now to handle things?"

"I think so," Atmino said. "Though I'm a little confused as to why we need them. Aren't you taking over security duty?"

"No, that's your responsibility now," LaRone told him. "We're not in the business of taking over from the locals unless there aren't any other options. The mayor and city council *are* backing you, aren't they?"

"Oh, sure, now that Cav'Saran and his thugs are safely locked up," Atmino said, an edge of contempt in his voice. "Though to be fair, I don't suppose any of the rest of us have been showing much backbone lately, either."

"Then you should be all set," LaRone said. "All the council needs to do is send official word to Shelkonwa about what's happened. They'll either approve it directly or suggest some modifications."

"As long as the modifications don't involve putting Cav'Saran back in," Atmino said. "You get back your bait all right?"

"Our what?"

"The speeder bikes," Atmino said. "You *were* just dangling them out there so that Cav'Saran would pull that illegal confiscation, right?"

"Of course," LaRone said. It was amazing sometimes how hindsight enabled people to jump to such incredibly wrong conclusions. "Yes, they're in the speeder truck."

"Good," Atmino said. "Incidentally, I don't know if you're interested, but we've dug up an odd connection between Cav'Saran and some big pirate gang called the BloodScars. Had you heard about that?"

"No, we hadn't," LaRone said, frowning. A corrupt patroller chief and a *pirate* gang? "What kind of connection?"

"We don't have that exactly nailed down yet," Atmino admitted. "But we found a data card in his office with contact information for one of their message drops and an encryption system for him to use." He dug a data card out of his pocket. "I made you a copy in case you wanted to follow up on it."

"Thank you," LaRone said, taking the card and tucking it away. Offhand, he couldn't think of anything lower on their priority list than chasing down a group of pirates, unless it was going on a tour of the Imperial Palace. "Seems to me this falls more within the sector government's purview, though."

"Oh, I'll be sending them a copy, too," Atmino assured him.

"Good," LaRone said, holding out his hand. "At any rate, we need to get going. Congratulations on taking back your city."

"We couldn't have done it without you," Atmino said, taking the proffered hand in a brief but firm handshake. He looked at the four armored men as if wondering if he should offer his hand to them, apparently decided against it. "Incidentally, I never did get your unit number."

LaRone felt his throat tighten. For the past few hours, in the rush of defeating Cav'Saran's men and bringing justice back to Janusar's people, he'd almost been able to forget their situation. Now Atmino's comment had brought it flooding back. "What do you need it for?" he hedged.

"So I can file an appreciation with your superiors," Atmino said, sounding puzzled that LaRone would even have to ask.

"Ah," LaRone said. "Actually, we're on special assignment and don't have an official unit number."

"Oh," Atmino said, a little taken aback. "But you must have *some* designation."

"Of course," LaRone said, trying to kick his brain into gear. But nothing was coming. Nothing except— "We're known as the Hand of Judgment."

"Ah," Atmino said, his eyes flicking to the other stormtroopers. "That's . . . different. Definitely suits you, though."

"We like it," LaRone said, trying to sound casual and relieved that the relative darkness would cover up any reddening of his face. What a *lame* thing to say. "Well, we're off. Good luck."

They'd driven two blocks, and none of the others had said a word, when LaRone finally couldn't stand it anymore. "All right, I give up," he said. "Somebody *say* it."

The others let the silence drag on another few seconds before Grave finally spoke up. "Okay," he said agreeably. "The *Hand of Judgment?*"

LaRone winced. It sounded even worse coming from Grave than it had when he'd said it. "I know, and I'm sorry," he growled. "My brain froze up."

"You could have just picked a unit number at random," Quiller pointed out. "It's not like he could have checked before we got offplanet."

"Fine," LaRone said, his embarrassment spilling over into grumpiness. "Next time *you* can be the officer and group spokesman."

"Great," Quiller said blandly. "Does that mean you're promoting me from finger to thumb?"

"No fair," Grave said, in the exaggerated tone LaRone remembered all too well from growing up with two younger brothers. "*I* want to be the thumb."

"All joking aside, LaRone, there'd better not *be* a next time," Brightwater put in. "I know we needed to get our speeder bikes back, but we were pushing our luck *way* too far on this one."

"Actually, I don't think we were," LaRone said.

"Trust me," Brightwater said. "Stormtrooper armor may carry a psychological edge, but even at that five against three hundred shouldn't have worked."

"Except that it never *is* only five of us," LaRone reminded him. "That's the point. The presence of even a single stormtrooper always implies an organization of men and weaponry lurking somewhere in the shadows behind him. They saw five of us and assumed there were hundreds more."

"Which only works up to the point where someone calls our bluff," Quiller warned.

"At which point they die," Grave countered.

"Maybe," Quiller said. "By all rights, though, we still should have had our skins handed to us. The sooner we leave this whole sector behind us, the better."

Marcross stirred in his seat. "What's your hurry?" he asked.

"What's our *hurry*?" Quiller retorted.

"He still wants us to go to Shelkonwa," Grave reminded him.

"Actually, I was thinking more about this connection between Cav'Saran and the BloodScar pirates," Marcross said.

"What about it?" LaRone asked.

"Remember that swoop gang we dusted on Drunost?" Marcross asked. "I thought those shoulder patches they were wearing looked a little too classy for that kind of lowlife, so I did some checking after we got back to the ship. Turns out the lower section of the patch is basically the Blood-Scars' twisted-thorn insignia."

"Small galaxy," Quiller murmured.

"Or maybe not so small," Marcross said. "The BloodScars may be trying to branch out."

"What, into swoops and law enforcement?" Grave asked.

"Go ahead and laugh," Marcross said darkly. "But look at where both these groups were positioned. The swoopers were sitting on top of a Consolidated Shipping hub, which is a perfect carrier for small to medium quantities of valuable or sensitive material. Cav'Saran set up shop in a city only a few hundred kilometers from an Incom plant turning out I-7 attack starfighters. Anyone else noticing a pattern?"

There was a moment of silence. "Hiring three hundred thugs is an expensive proposition," Brightwater said at last. "I doubt swoop gangs come cheap, either, even ones as amateurish as that lot were. If the BloodScars are expanding, they must be doing *very* good business."

"Or are being funded from the outside," Quiller said quietly.

"Exactly," Marcross said. "And who's the most obvious money source that would also have an interest in fighters and clandestine shipping?"

"The Rebellion?" Grave asked.

"Who else?" Marcross said.

"I don't know," Brightwater said, sounding doubtful. "Pirates are an awfully low form of life to associate with. Even for Rebels."

"They're trying to destroy the Empire and tear down the New Order," Grave reminded him.

"Sure, but hitting military targets is a far cry from piracy against civilians," Brightwater countered.

"Which is why we're trying so hard to stop them," Marcross said, a little tartly. "Or maybe the BloodScars aren't a real pirate gang at all. The name and reputation could be a cover label for a Rebel cell."

"I think Marcross is right," LaRone said. "It's something that should be looked into."

"So send an anonymous note to the nearest Imperial garrison and let *them* handle it," Grave suggested.

"A nice thought, but impractical," Marcross said. "You heard what Krinkins said—it's been eight years since they even had Imperial visitors here, and that was almost by accident. In fact, as far as I know the *Reprisal* is the only Star Destroyer in the entire sector. Shelsha is pretty low on everyone's priority list."

"It didn't sound like Shelkonwa was all that interested in this part of their territory, either," Grave said.

"No, it didn't," LaRone agreed. "Maybe that's why the BloodScars have decided to set up shop here."

"We, on the other hand, happen to have some time on our hands," Marcross said. "At the least we could see if we can find a connection between the BloodScars and the Rebellion. At best we might be able to follow the links and give Shelkonwa and Imperial Center an actual military target to aim at."

"Which brings up the point that we're something of a target ourselves," Quiller reminded him. "I thought we were supposed to be looking for a place to hide."

"I'm not talking anything high-profile," Marcross assured him. "Just a little soft probe into enemy territory. No matter what our current circumstances, we're still Imperial stormtroopers."

"Who other Imperial stormtroopers are currently hunting," Quiller persisted.

"We took an oath to protect the people of the Empire," Marcross said doggedly. "Rooting out a Rebel cell is well within that job description."

"How do you suggest we start?" LaRone asked.

"We go back to Drunost," Marcross said. "Cav'Saran was stupid enough to leave an incriminating data card behind. I doubt those swoopers were any brighter than he was."

"Of course, the people of Drunost have already seen us *and* the Suwantek," Quiller reminded him.

"No, the people of *one* store saw us," Grave corrected him. "And even that group only saw LaRone and me."

"As for the ship, we can certainly afford to burn another of the fake IDs that ISB left us," Marcross said. "LaRone?"

LaRone waited a moment before answering, as if he were carefully thinking it through. It was all for show, though—he'd already made up his mind. "It's worth the risk," he said. "Even if someone actually recognized us and called it in—which I think is unlikely—we'd still have several hours to poke around before anyone could make trouble."

"And if the trail's already cold?" Quiller asked.

LaRone shrugged. "We can leave for the Outer Rim from Drunost as easily as we can from here." They had reached the docking bay, and he let the speeder truck roll to a halt by the Suwantek's starboard cargo lift. "Are we in agreement?"

"I'm in," Quiller said.

"Me, too," Grave said. "If the Rebels are consorting with pirates, I want them *and* the pirates nailed to the wall. Brightwater?"

"I still don't like it," Brightwater said heavily. "But I don't like shredded grum on flatcake, either, and I learned to eat it. If you really think we'll find something useful, I'm game."

"Then we're on," LaRone said. Pushing up the swing-wing door, he climbed out and stepped to the turbolift control. "Let's stow this thing and get moving."

"Drunost," Han said flatly.

"Oh, come on, Han," Luke cajoled. "It can't be *that* bad."

Standing a little way off at the foot of the *Falcon*'s entry ramp, Chewbacca made a soft urfing sound. "Sure it can," Han growled, sending a warning glare at the Wookiee. "I was there once. It's all farms and ranches and mines and a few company towns. A few very well-organized company towns."

"We'll stay as clear of the towns and companies as we can," Luke soothed with that irritating farm-boy cheerfulness.

"Sure," Han said, knowing full well it wouldn't happen. "Why can't we just meet this Porter guy out in deep space like Leia's doing?"

"Because Porter hasn't got a ship of his own," Luke said patiently. "Drunost is where he lives, that's where his team is, and that's where he wants to meet."

"It's also where those stormtroopers of his popped up out of nowhere," Han reminded him.

"And then left."

"According to *him.*"

Luke cocked his head in a look of strained patience that was almost as irritating as his cheerfulness. "If you don't want to do this, I can go alone," he offered. He looked sideways at Chewbacca. "Or Chewie and I could do it."

"Just get in the ship," Han growled. When he'd agreed to this whole thing, the plan had been to take a quick trip out to Shelsha sector, nose around a few cantinas and pick up a few leads, then head for home.

But after Luke and Rieekan and Her Royal Plush Gowns And Hair Fashions had gotten through with it, the mission was looking to turn into a major diplomatic tour, complete with talks with the local Rebel leader.

In other words, politics. Exactly what he'd backed out of Leia's trip to avoid.

Except that on this one Leia wouldn't be along to at least keep things fun.

A movement at the far end of the hangar caught his eye, and he grimaced. Typical. The minute he started thinking about her, there she was.

She was dressed in a practical tan jumpsuit, apparently getting ready for her own departure. For a moment their eyes seemed to meet, though it was hard to be sure at that distance. She stirred, her shoulders moving as if she was thinking of coming over to him—

"Hey, guy," a cheerful female voice came from the other direction.

Han turned. It was one of the new X-wing pilots—Stacy something, he vaguely remembered. "Hey," he said, watching Leia out of the corner of his eye as he walked over to the pilot. Leia's shoulders weren't moving anymore, and she seemed to be standing stock-still as she gazed across the hangar at him.

"You and the big guy off again?" Stacy said brightly as she strolled over toward him.

Han suppressed another grimace, forcing it into a friendly grin instead. And he thought *Luke's* cheerfulness was irritating. "You know how it is," he said. "There's a problem, and they need someone to fix it."

"So they call you," she said with a knowing smile. "Well, have fun."

"Everywhere I go," he assured her, flicking a finger through the edge of the girl's hair. If Leia wanted a show, she was going to get one. "You hold things down here, okay?"

"Sure," she said. With another smile, she sauntered away.

Han watched her go, then turned around again.

Leia was definitely no longer thinking about coming over to him. Leia, in fact, had disappeared completely.

He smiled tightly at the empty chunk of deck space. *That* would teach her to maneuver him around. Giving the *Falcon's* undercarriage a final glance, he headed up the ramp.

And tried to ignore the nagging little pang of guilt.

Chapter Nine

BARSHNIS CHOARD, GOVERNOR OF SHELSHA SECTOR, WAS A BIG RANCOR of a man: tall and broad-shouldered, with wild black hair and a bushy beard that made him look more like a pirate than the governor of a sizable chunk of Imperial territory. He invariably paced around his office when he was angry, striding back and forth across the thick carpet, his expression daring anyone to get in his way or even to breathe very loudly.

And he was angry now. As angry as Chief Administrator Vilim Disra had ever seen him.

"I don't want excuses," Choard snarled. "I want results. You understand me, Disra? *Results*."

"Yes, Your Excellency," Disra said, bowing his head in the half-groveling attitude that was the best way to steer clear of these outbursts. "I'll see to it at once."

"Then don't just stand here," Choard growled. "Get going and *do* it."

"Yes, Your Excellency." Bowing again, Disra made his escape.

His own office was two doors down the corridor from the governor's far more expansive reception chamber. Humble though it might be, it was still connected to the same warren of secret passageways as the governor's own working and living areas. That meant Disra's private visitors could slip into the palace unannounced just as easily as Choard's could.

And sure enough, the visitor he was expecting was waiting in one of the comfortable chairs in the office's conversation circle. "You're late," Caaldra told him.

"I was busy," Disra said, making sure the door was privacy-locked. "The governor is unhappy."

"The governor's always unhappy about something," Caaldra said contemptuously as Disra came over to the circle. "What was it this time? Soup too cold? Wrong flatware pattern for the next big dinner party?"

"Let's talk about something a little more interesting, shall we?" Disra suggested. "Starting with the Bargleg swoop gang. Did you send them to Drunost to intercept a shipment of heavy blaster rifles?"

"The BloodScars sent them, yes," Caaldra said. "What happened? The Rebel couriers put up a fight?"

"The Rebels didn't have to lift a finger," Disra said coldly. "The stormtroopers handled it all by themselves."

Caaldra's eyes narrowed. "*Stormtroopers?*"

"If they weren't, they were a very good imitation," Disra said. "You assured me that most of the Imperial presence had been pulled out of Shelsha sector."

"It has been," Caaldra said, frowning. "There's the *Reprisal* and a few antique Dreadnaughts on patrol, the two remaining army garrisons on Minkring and Chaastern Four, and that's it."

"Then maybe you'll explain to me where all the stormtroopers came from," Disra countered. "The *Reprisal*?"

"The *Reprisal* never gets within fifty light-years of Drunost," Caaldra said, wrinkling his nose in disgust. "Captain Ozzel likes simple, comfortable routines. The man is excruciatingly predictable."

"Well, they came from *somewhere*," Disra snapped. "The Commodore says the surviving Barglegs read it as at least three squads, plus heavy-weapons support."

"Called to cry on his shoulder, did they?" Caaldra asked snidely. "I hope they at least used one of the message drops."

"It didn't sound like it," Disra said. "Besides, screaming works so much better when it's done face-to-face."

Caaldra's face went rigid. "They called Gepparin *directly?*" he demanded. "Those stupid *idiots.*"

"Those stupid idiots are mostly dead," Disra reminded him. "Taking their million-credit recruitment money with them, I might add."

"Forget the money," Caaldra snapped. "Are you blind *and* stupid? A direct call leaves a record in the HoloNet system that can be traced."

"Traced by whom?" Disra countered. "And to where? There must be a hundred thousand HoloNet transmissions going out from Drunost every hour. No one's going to be able to figure out which one was theirs."

"It's still sloppy," Caaldra insisted, calming down a little. "But then, what do you expect from a swoop gang?"

"I personally expected to at least get our money's worth out of them," Disra said. "Incidentally, the surviving Barglegs want off Drunost, and the Commodore wants compensation for the Barloz freighter they used to get there."

"The ship got impounded?"

"The ship got demolished," Disra corrected. "That's where the heavy-weapons support comes in."

Caaldra made a face. "All right, I'll check it out," he said. "Maybe the damage isn't as bad as the Barglegs think."

"And if it is?"

"Consolidated Shipping has a nice little bank repository near their hub," Caaldra said. "I'll organize some people and we'll go collect the Commodore's compensation."

"Well, while you're out that way, you might also take a moment to look in on Ranklinge," Disra suggested. "I got word a few hours ago that the man you set up as patroller chief in Janusar has been deposed. By force."

"Now, that one *is* impossible," Caaldra said flatly. "Cav'Saran knows his business. The first thing he would have done was confiscate every weapon in the district."

"I'm sure he was very thorough," Disra said. "Unfortunately for him, the stormtroopers were thoughtful enough to bring their own."

A muscle tightened in Caaldra's cheek. "*More* stormtroopers?"

"Yes, *more* stormtroopers," Disra retorted. "And given that you told me Cav'Saran had three hundred hardened men on his side, there must have been at least *five* squads on this one."

Caaldra's gaze defocused slightly. "Yes, well, his men probably weren't all *that* hardened," he mused. "He wouldn't have hired anyone expensive, not to intimidate a small city full of unarmed civilians. He was always cheap with a credit."

"He'll never learn his lesson now," Disra said. "He's dead, along with six of his men. The stormtrooper squad commander identified his group as the Hand of Judgment, by the way."

"Interesting designation," Caaldra said thoughtfully. "Not really standard format."

"You can file a complaint with Stormtrooper Command," Disra said acidly. "I'm still waiting for your explanation of where this Hand of Judgment came from."

"They're certainly not official forces," Caaldra said slowly. "The governor's office is supposed to be informed whenever Imperial military units are operating in his sector, and my own taps into the intelligence system haven't mentioned any extra stormtroopers being assigned to the area."

"Are you suggesting the Barglegs and half of Janusar were hallucinating?"

"Hardly," Caaldra said, his voice turning suddenly grim. "I'm suggesting we may have an Imperial agent in our sector."

Disra felt his mouth go dry. "An Imperial *agent*? You mean Imperial Center's on to us?"

"Not necessarily," Caaldra said. "He might just be going after the BloodScars."

"I thought you said Imperial Center wasn't interested in pirates anymore."

"In general, they're not," Caaldra agreed. "But we *have* taken eight military transports in the past eighteen months. Maybe Imperial Center finally noticed."

"Wonderful," Disra growled. "Those military targets were supposed to be masked by all the civilian targets we were hitting. That *was* one of the reasons you gave for shelling out all that money to those other pirate and raider groups, wasn't it?"

"Trust me, when the time comes you'll be glad to have all that extra firepower under a central control," Caaldra said.

"If we *get* that far," Disra warned. "So what about this Imperial agent?"

"What about him?" Caaldra said. "Imperial Center doesn't know anything—if they did, we'd have a dozen Star Destroyers in the sector instead of an agent and a few squads of stormtroopers. We can afford to let them poke around the edges for a while."

"And if they start poking closer to the center?"

"They have to find it first," Caaldra said. "Assuming no one else does anything stupid—like not using the message drops—there's no way even an Imperial agent can tag either the BloodScars or us. Not before we're ready to move."

Disra grimaced. But Caaldra was the one with the military training. He presumably knew what he was talking about. "What about Ranklinge?" he asked. "With Cav'Saran gone, we don't have anyone in easy striking distance of that I-7 plant anymore."

"Not a problem," Caaldra assured him. "It would have been nice to hit the plant from the ground, but we can take it from the sky almost as easily. I'll ask the Commodore to recommend someone to handle that."

"Someone fierce, competent, and expendable?"

"Basically," Caaldra said. "As to the blaster rifles the Barglegs lost, it turns out that's going to be completely irrelevant. I've got a cargo in my sights now that'll work even better to neutralize the Minkring and Chaastern Four garrisons."

"More E-Web repeaters?"

"No, we have plenty of those already," Caaldra assured him. "I'll tell you after we see if the BloodScars can pull it off—their best ship and crew are on the way right now." He stood up. "But the Commodore might not want to turn it over to us if I don't have their compensation for the lost Barloz in hand. I'd better get that operation rolling."

"Just be careful," Disra said. "With an Imperial agent on the loose, we can't afford any slip-ups."

"There won't be," Caaldra assured him. "Relax, Disra. Your governor's about to go down in history. Remember?" With a tight smile, he crossed the room to the hidden door and disappeared back into the secret passages.

Only then did Disra permit himself a smile of his own. Yes, Governor Choard was indeed going to go down in history.

But not under the heading anyone was expecting.

*   *   *

Pirate captains, one of Mara's instructors had taught her, seldom ran their ships on a standard military three-shift, down-the-chrono system. More typically they used a single-day cycle, with everyone except a duty pilot retiring to their cabins to sleep during ship's night.

Shakko, as it turned out, was a typical pirate captain.

Mara spent the first two nights roaming freely about the ship, searching everywhere except the cabins and the cockpit for Caaldra's data card. The cabins were a trickier proposition, but after a couple of days of studying the pirates' movements she discovered they spent most of their nonmeal waking hours away from the cabin area, either on duty in the cockpit or engineering room, or else working on the various weapons in the forward hold. With stealth and the prescience provided by the Force, she was able to find opportunities to slip into and search each of the cabins.

Unfortunately, none of the skulking did her any good. Either Shakko had filed the data card in the cockpit, the one place she hadn't yet had a chance to search, or else he was carrying it with him.

And she was starting to run low on time. The search had already cost her nearly four days, with only one left until their scheduled attack. So far she had avoided any further contact with the crew, knowing that two unexplained blackout accidents on the same trip would be something even the stupidest pirate would start to wonder about. But if there was no other way, she would just have to do it.

The fourth ship's day had ended, and she was waiting in her cargo hold burrow for everyone to retire for the night, when she heard the quiet footsteps.

She sat up a little straighter, stretching out with her senses. There had been occasional visitors to the cargo bay over the previous four days, but on those occasions the footsteps had been casual and unconcerned, their owners making straight paths to one or another of the crates and then retreating just as casually. Now, in contrast, the intruders were coming in a group, and clearly trying not to be heard.

And they were headed directly toward the stack of crates where Mara was hiding.

She rose silently into a crouch, making sure her blaster and lightsaber were near at hand. Pressing her back against the wide barrel that held up the center of her burrow's ceiling, she prepared herself for combat. Their first move would probably be some sort of grenade . . .

And sure enough, a second later a small concussion grenade dropped neatly through one of the air gaps she'd left between the crates and clattered to the deck directly in front of her.

Instantly she twisted to her right, rolling backward onto her shoulders and kicking her legs into a tightly curled tuck over her head. Halfway through the backward somersault she twisted again, this time to her left, bringing her legs down and shoving off the deck with her left shoulder and forearm.

She had just rolled up into a new crouch on the far side of the barrel when the grenade went off.

The blast was deafening, the impact lifting the crates of her roof a few centimeters and driving the supporting barrel hard against her back. The shock was too much for the delicate equilibrium she'd set up, and even as she pushed herself away from the barrel the whole burrow collapsed. The two crates directly above her tipped off their supports and toppled toward her head; stretching out to the Force, she deflected them to either side past her shoulders.

It would have been simpler to use the Force right from the beginning, to grab the grenade and throw it back out of her burrow. But that would have alerted her attackers to the fact that their prey was on to them. Now they would come in less cautiously, expecting to find their victim helpless or dead. Drawing her blaster, Mara stood.

There were four pirates in the attack group, spread out in a semicircle around her, their eyes goggling at her sudden appearance, their blasters still in hand but pointed carelessly at the deck. Raising her own weapon, Mara opened fire.

She dropped the two in the middle before any of them could get their weapons back up to firing position. The man on the far left was the fastest, and Mara had to bend out of the way as his first shot sizzled past her head. She stretched toward him with the Force, and his second shot, to his clearly stunned consternation, took out his fellow pirate on the far right as Mara twisted his gun hand in that direction.

He was still wearing an expression of disbelief at what he'd done when Mara's final shot ended all his expressions forever.

She was working her way out of the ruins of her hiding place when, beneath her feet, she felt a *thunk* through the hull, a tremor without accompanying sound, followed immediately by a more subtle and stretched-out vibration. She frowned, wondering what the pirates were up to now.

And then, with a rush of adrenaline, she understood. The *thunk* had been the lowering of the weapons bay's front hull section, the longer vibration the firing of the quad lasers and ion cannon, and the total lack of sound due to the total lack of air in the bay.

A day ahead of schedule, the pirates had launched their attack.

Mara was halfway to the weapons bay before it suddenly occurred to her that there was nothing she could do there to stop them. With the area already open to space, breaking in would merely drain the air from the rest of the ship, killing Mara along with everyone else aboard. There were spare vac suits in the engine section, but it would cost her precious minutes to get into one of them.

If she couldn't stop the attack directly, though, maybe she could do so indirectly.

She had expected the blast door leading into the cockpit to be sealed, and she was right. She'd also expected her lightsaber to have no problem slicing it open, and was right again. With the blazing magenta blade held in guard position in front of her, she leapt inside.

There were four pirates in the cockpit, including both Shakko and Tannis, all four with blasters drawn and ready. But instead of firing in volley, which might have given her trouble, they opened up more or less at random, their bolts ricocheting off her lightsaber blade to sizzle their way into deck or bulkhead or ceiling. Slowly, Mara moved forward, keeping the blade moving, taking care to keep the deflected shots from hitting any of the controls or, worse, the transparisteel canopy. "Surrender!" she ordered, the word coming out with difficulty as she shifted just enough of her attention away from her defense to work her mouth.

"Go crink yourself," Shakko snarled back. "Crinking Imper—"

The curse collapsed into a gurgle as Mara sent one of his own shots backward into his throat.

The other three pirates redoubled their efforts, the first hint of fear starting to show through their rage. But neither fear nor rage could help them now. Mara had the timing and the distance, and the next two shots sent two more of the pirates to join their captain in death. The last one, Tannis, hesitated a split second, then lifted his blaster high and fired defiantly straight at Mara's face.

With only one opponent left, Mara could afford a little finesse. Instead of returning his shot to head or torso, she deflected it into his right thigh.

He gasped with pain, stumbling as his leg collapsed beneath him. His blaster wavered out of line; taking a step forward, Mara twirled her lightsaber in a tight cone spiral and sliced the weapon neatly in half. Holding her left hand toward him, palm outward, she gave him a Force shove that staggered him back into the copilot's seat.

"Stay there," she ordered, stepping up beside him and peering out the canopy. The target ship was a large Rendili freighter, something high-class by the looks of it. Or at least, it had been high-class once. With the pirate ship's lasers pounding at its hull and engine section, it was rapidly losing that new-ship luster. Lowering her gaze to the board, she located the acceleration compensator control.

There were fail-safes built into the system to prevent anyone from easily turning it off, so she didn't bother trying. Instead she stabbed her lightsaber into that part of the board, fusing the controls and sending a feedback surge through the system that she hoped would knock out everything in its path.

The compensator indicators went solid red. Closing down her lightsaber, Mara put it away. "Better strap in," she advised Tannis as she sat down in the pilot's seat and fastened her own restraints. Peripherally, she noted that Tannis had stopped clutching his wounded leg and was doing likewise. A survivor type, clearly, and Mara tucked that bit of data away for future reference. Keying in the main drive, she fired a short forward burst.

An invisible hand shoved her hard against her seat back. Tannis gave a strangled gasp, a reaction Mara could completely sympathize with. No one flew without compensators, and even though tight maneuvers could strain them enough to let a little of the acceleration through, even Mara hadn't been entirely prepared for what their complete absence would feel like.

She keyed off the drive, and the backward weight vanished as abruptly as it had appeared. Bracing herself, she keyed the forward thrusters and fired again.

The invisible hand reversed direction, this time pushing her forward against her restraints. With the forward thrusters still firing she keyed in the starboard maneuvering jets, pressing her right hip against the seat's armrest.

The firing from the weapons bay had ceased, replaced by howls and curses of protest from the comm speaker. Ignoring the complaints, Mara shut down all the thrusters, then fired the portside jets, followed by the forward thrusters, then the starboard jets, then the main thrusters, then the forward and starboard jets together. Then, shutting everything down again, she leaned forward and looked out the canopy.

There they were: ten vac-suited bodies, shaken or rattled or bounced straight out the front of the open weapons bay by Mara's maneuvering, now floating and twisting and squirming helplessly through the void outside the ship.

Most of the complaints coming from the comm had ceased, replaced by a complete spectrum of somewhat dazed-sounding curses. Shutting off the chatter, Mara rekeyed the system. "Rendili freighter, this is the Corellian HT-2200 that's been shooting at you," she announced. "I've taken command and stopped the attack. Please identify yourself, your ship, and your cargo."

There was a short pause. "Who is this?" a voice demanded suspiciously.

"The new master of this ship," Mara countered. "Right now, that's all you need to know. Identify yourself, your ship, and your cargo."

There was another pause, a longer one this time. Clearly, the man at the other end was trying to figure out what this new trick was his attackers were trying to pull. Just as clearly, he couldn't figure out how it could possibly gain them anything. "I'm Captain Norello, commanding the *Happer's Way*," he said at last. "We're a private freighter contracted out of Chandrila by the Imperial Army."

So the cargo Caaldra had claimed as his was Imperial military supplies. Interesting. "And your cargo?"

There was another short pause. "Fifty AT-STs bound for the garrison on Llorkan."

Mara felt her stomach tighten. The All Terrain Scout Transport was one of the army's most versatile combat vehicles, suitable for use on nearly any terrain from rolling forest to crowded inner city. Properly deployed, fifty of them could lay waste to an entire district, or conceivably even capture and hold a small colony world.

What in *space* was Caaldra up to? "How bad is your damage?" she asked.

There was a snort. "We're not going anywhere for a while."

"I need a better estimate than that," Mara said tartly. "Do you have any command-rank military personnel aboard?"

"We don't have any military personnel at all," Norello said. "We're a civilian transport."

"Yes, you told me," Mara said, thinking hard. As Emperor's Hand she theoretically had access to any personnel or resources she chose to commandeer. But as a practical matter such access required her to find someone she could prove her identity to. "Where's the nearest Imperial capital ship?" she asked.

"How should *I* know?"

"You're carrying a military cargo," Mara countered. "That means you have an emergency call list."

There was a moment of silence, and when Norello spoke again there was a subtle new respect in his voice. "Yes, ma'am, I do," he said. "Nearest capital ship is the Star Destroyer *Reprisal*. I can give you the contact information."

"I'd rather you call them," Mara said. "Pirate ships are sometimes gimmicked to copy long-range communications to the main base."

"Yes, ma'am," Norello said. "What should I tell them?"

"Tell them I want to speak to the captain," Mara said. "And *only* to the captain."

"Understood," Norello said.

The comm went silent, and Mara turned to Tannis. "Where were the AT-STs to be delivered?"

He measured her coolly, the pain from his injured leg a background simmering in his eyes. "What's in it for me?"

"Your life?" Mara suggested.

Tannis shook his head. "Good start, but I think you can do better than that."

Mara looked around the cockpit. The only obvious data cards were a set in a rack by her knee. Reaching down, she pulled them out.

"It's not there," Tannis said.

"What's not here?" Mara asked, shuffling through them.

"The card with the attack data," Tannis told her, a note of dour enjoyment in his voice. "Shakko never left stuff like that lying around where someone could find it. He transmitted the list to the Commodore, memorized our own target data, then destroyed it."

"Then I suppose I'd better talk to the Commodore," Mara said. "Where do I find him?"

"What's in it for me?" Tannis repeated.

Mara stretched out to the Force. Even through all the pain and fear she could sense a rock-solid defiance. Tannis knew he had something she wanted, and he was ready and willing to put in all his chips on the chance that she needed it badly enough to deal. "You attacked a ship carrying Imperial cargo," she said. "The penalty for that is death."

"I know. And?"

"I can commute it to twenty years on a penal colony."

He pursed his lips thoughtfully, then shook his head. "No," he said. "No prison time."

Mara raised her eyebrows. "You must be joking. Even if I could make that kind of deal, what makes you think your information is worth it?"

"Oh, you can make the deal, all right," he said. "See, we got a message from one of our contacts—"

"You mean Caaldra?"

Tannis's lip twitched. "Yeah, Caaldra," he said, his eyes taking on a wary look. He'd probably hoped to deal her that name. "He told us there might be an Imperial agent sniffing around." His eyes flicked to the bodies of his three dead comrades, lying in twisted heaps where Mara's violent ship maneuvering had thrown them. "I'm guessing that's you. So either you deal, or the trail evaporates."

"A Star Destroyer carries a full set of interrogation equipment," Mara reminded him.

Tannis swallowed. "That'll take time," he said, apparently not yet ready to give up on the bluster approach. "If we don't deliver on schedule, the Commodore will know something's wrong and pull out."

He could be bluffing, Mara knew—his pain and overall nervousness made an accurate reading impossible. But if he wasn't, and if the Commodore did indeed pull out, she could end up right back where she'd started.

And this mission was already way too interesting for her to risk that.

"Ma'am?" Captain Norello's voice came from the speaker. "I have the *Reprisal* on comm."

"Link me through, then turn off your speaker," Mara instructed him. "I'll flash my landing lights when you can come back on."

"Yes, ma'am."

There was a click. "This is Captain Ozzel of the Imperial Star Destroyer *Reprisal*," a gruff voice said through the speaker. "Who in blazes is *this*?"

"The recognition code is Hapspir, Barrini, Corbolan, Triaxis," Mara said. "Do you need me to repeat that?"

"No," Ozzel said, his brusqueness suddenly gone. "What is your—that is, what shall I call you?"

"Emperor's Hand," Mara told him. "You have our current coordinates?"

"We do," Ozzel confirmed.

"Then break off your current activity and come here at your best speed," Mara ordered.

"Acknowledged," Ozzel said, stiffly formal now. "We'll be there in approximately ten standard hours."

"Good. Emperor's Hand out."

She waited for the click that meant the *Reprisal* had broken the transmission, then flashed her landing lights twice. "Norello," Norello's voice returned instantly.

"Do you have an estimate yet on repair time?"

"It looks like it's going to take about thirty hours to get the engines back online," the other said. "There are some bad hull breaches we need to fix first."

"Get busy on the breaches," Mara ordered. "The *Reprisal's* on its way—I'll get their engineers to assist when they arrive. What's the smallest crew your ship can manage with?"

"Four," Norello said, a fresh note of caution creeping into his voice. "Why?"

"I'll let you know when the *Reprisal* gets here," Mara told him. "And you might send out a boat to pick up those ten pirates floating around out there. I presume you have a secure place you can stash them?"

"We'll find a place," Norello assured her grimly. "You want them alive?"

Mara looked over at Tannis. He was staring at her as if he were seeing a ghost. Apparently rumors about the Emperor's Hand had reached even into the Fringe. "Only," she told Norello, "until we see whether we'll need any of them."

Captain Ozzel switched off his office comm and looked at the man seated on the other side of his desk. "The Emperor's Hand," he said, a shiver running through him.

"Calm yourself, Captain," Imperial Security Bureau Colonel Vak Somoril replied sternly. "I heard nothing in that conversation that indicated she knows about our deserters."

And if she did, Ozzel reflected bitterly, Somoril would certainly find a way to shove it off onto the *Reprisal's* captain and not himself. "We should have reported it," he growled. "I should never have let you talk me into holding it back."

"Do you really want your superiors to know you allowed five stormtroopers to escape?" Somoril asked. "Especially with that one stormtrooper in particular among them? *And* that you even dropped out of hyperspace for their convenience?"

"It wasn't *my* reputation you were worried about," Ozzel countered tartly. "Your own second in command, murdered with his own gun? I'd love to be at the next budget session when the ISB reps start talking about their oh-so-professional personnel."

For a long second, he was afraid he'd overstepped his bounds. Somoril's face hardened, a look of death in his eyes. Then, slowly, the look faded. "I think we both understand the situation, Captain," Somoril said. "There's plenty of potential damage here for both our careers. The question is what precisely we're going to do about it."

"For starters, we're not letting her aboard the *Reprisal*," Ozzel said. "This whole freighter-under-attack thing may be nothing but a pretext for an investigation."

"I was thinking along the lines of a more permanent solution," Somoril said. "How many people know about Major Drelfin's death?"

"Too many," Ozzel said heavily. "Commander Brillstow and some of the bridge crew during his shift, the entire stormtrooper contingent—"

"I said Drelfin's death, not the desertion," Somoril interrupted.

"Oh." Ozzel thought a moment. "That would be the crewer who found the body, the medic who examined him, a couple of medical droids, Commander Brillstow, you, and me. Plus any of your group you may have told."

"I told no one," Somoril said, tapping his chin absently as he gazed toward a spot past Ozzel's shoulder. "So: three others aside from us. How certain are you that the tech and medic didn't tell anyone else?"

"Reasonably certain," Ozzel said, wondering where the colonel was going with this. "I warned them to keep quiet, as per your instructions."

"I *know* what I instructed," Somoril said acidly. "I was asking how well those instructions had been carried out." He took a deep breath, let it out in a carefully measured huff. "Very well. Captain, you are hereby authorized to add to your log the fact that the hitherto unexplained departure of the freighter *Gillia* was in fact a secret ISB mission undertaken by Major Drelfin and five stormtroopers whom he commandeered from your shipboard contingent."

Ozzel stared at him. "Are you *insane*?" he demanded. "We have Drelfin's *body* down there!"

"Which will be gone within the hour," Somoril said evenly. "Certainly before we arrive at our rendezvous with the *Happer's Way*."

"What about the tech and medic?"

Somoril's lips compressed briefly. "You'll also log the fact that Drelfin subsequently sent private word to you to have a tech and medic join the team."

Ozzel felt the blood draining from his face. "You can't be serious."

"Come now," Somoril asked sardonically. "Squeamishness hardly befits a senior Imperial officer."

"I won't be a party to this," Ozzel insisted. "You're talking about deliberate murder—"

"This is war, Captain," Somoril cut him off harshly. "Men die all the time in war. It's a minuscule price to pay for keeping two experienced senior officers in the service." He raised his eyebrows. "Or would you rather be stripped of your rank and sent home in disgrace?"

Ozzel grimaced, those admiral's bars shimmering in his mind's eye. "No, of course not," he muttered. "Do whatever you want."

"*Thank* you," Somoril grunted, getting to his feet. "Have the tech and medic report to me, then get your ship ready to fly." He smiled grimly. "Our glorious Emperor's Hand is waiting."

Chapter Ten

"HERE'S THE TRANSMISSION LOG YOU ASKED FOR, INSPECTOR," THE woman at the Conso City HoloNet center said, pulling a data card from her computer. "But I'm afraid I'll need a tri-authorized judicial request to give you access to the sender name files."

"I'll have it for you by tomorrow," LaRone promised, taking the data card from her. "In the meantime I can start with this. Thank you."

A minute later he was back out in Drunost's late-afternoon sunlight, the data card snugged securely away in an inside pocket. He hadn't really expected Consolidated's privacy policy to let him dig into more detail without first jumping through a set of nested legal hoops, but it had been worth a try.

Still, he had the transmission log. Maybe that would be enough.

There was a lot of traffic on the streets around the HoloNet center, he noted as he walked along. A block down the street was the likely reason: a large white building with Consolidated Shipping's logo and the words REPOSITORY AND CURRENCY EXCHANGE above the door. As the day's business activities wound down, the various merchants and service area managers would be bringing in their take, mostly Imperial credits, but also a smattering of local and regional currencies that some of the people of this backworld region still weren't quite ready to give up. Idly wondering how much the repository took in every day, LaRone looked around for Grave.

The other was nowhere to be seen. Frowning, LaRone keyed his comlink. "Grave?"

"Here," the other's voice came back promptly, with none of the code words that would mean there was trouble. "I'm in the tapcafe down the block on your right, across the street from the repository. I think you'll want to join me."

"On my way," LaRone said, picking up his pace. "Anything from the others?"

"Quiller called," Grave said. "Consolidated has what's left of the Barloz locked away and isn't inclined to let strangers look at it. He didn't want to press the point until we could compare notes and see what else we had to work with. Marcross and Brightwater are in the same situation vis-à-vis the autopsy reports."

And meanwhile, Grave had taken up residence in a tapcafe.

"So are we celebrating or drowning our sorrows?" LaRone asked.

"Neither," Grave said. "Come in quietly—I'm at a back table to the right of the door."

The tapcafe was like hundreds LaRone had seen across the Empire: low lighting, large serving bar against the back wall, four- and six-person tables filling most of the rest of the space, a wild mix of humans and various types of aliens. Grave was at one of the smaller tables along the right-hand wall. "So what's the big secret?" LaRone asked as he sat down to the other's left.

"Table over there," Grave said nodding ahead and to his right. "Three humans and a Wookiee. Any of the humans look familiar?"

LaRone reached up to scratch his cheek, looking casually over at the table as he did so. One of the humans was a kid, late teens at the oldest, with that indefinable but distinctive air of someone seeing the big city for the first time. The second was a somewhat older man with the equally distinctive worlds-weary look of someone who'd already seen it all. The broken red line of a Corellian Bloodstripe caught LaRone's eye; apparently the man was some kind of hero. The third man—

He frowned. "Is that one of the farmers we shot the swoop gang off of?"

"Sure looks like him," Grave agreed. "He seems to have upgraded his wardrobe a bit."

LaRone nodded. Instead of the grubby robe the man had been wearing the day of the swooper attack, he was now dressed in the same style of edge-embroidered tunic and trousers the rest of the tapcafe's customers sported. "Interesting," he murmured.

"I spotted him as he was coming down the street," Grave said. "He seemed okay until he turned to come in. Then he suddenly got this furtive look as he did a quick scan of the area. I thought it might be worth checking out."

"Any idea who the other three are?"

"No, but they were already here when he arrived."

A prearranged meeting, then. "I'll send Quiller back to the ship and have him run any known human–human–Wookiee teams," he said, reaching for his comlink.

"Not so fast," Grave said, putting a hand on his arm. "First tell me what you think of the two humans and the Rodian by the door."

The kid and Corellian at the first table had carried the stamp of known types. The two humans and Rodian were just as recognizable. Violent criminals, all three of them. "Uh-oh," LaRone murmured.

"They were also here when our gentleman farmer showed up," Grave said. "They have that settled look, like they've been here awhile, but they're way too alert to have been drinking very much."

"Casing the place?" LaRone suggested. But even as he spoke he realized that wasn't precisely it. The three had the look of criminals; but more than that, they had the look of criminals already in the middle of a scheme.

And they weren't watching the bar or the bartender or the cash box. Their attention was focused instead on the far side of the tapcafe. Tracking their eyes, LaRone found himself looking at a group of seven men seated around a pair of tables.

Men with broad shoulders and short hair and alert eyes. Men very much like LaRone and Grave themselves, in fact. "Security?" he hazarded.

"Or mercs or off-duty military," Grave said. "Could be some business feud."

"No," LaRone said as it suddenly clicked into place. "Someone's about to hit the repository."

"Oh, *shunfa*," Grave murmured. "With the three dirt-singers at the door here to watch for off-duty wild cards?"

"That's my guess," LaRone said, surreptitiously lifting his comlink and keying it on. "Quiller, where are you?"

"On my way back to the Suwantek," Quiller's voice came back. "I wasn't able to—"

"I know—Grave told me," LaRone cut in. "Get back fast—we're going to need some airpower."

"Wait a second," Grave said, frowning suddenly. "LaRone—"

"On my way," Quiller said, his voice suddenly tight and professional. "Where and how much?"

"The Consolidated repository on Newmark at the northern edge of the city," LaRone told him. "Looks like someone's planning a hit."

There was a short pause. "And we're getting involved why?"

"Because helping Consolidated nail the raiders may help lube the wheels to get us the HoloNet and autopsy data they're still sitting on," LaRone said. "Better comm Marcross and Brightwater and have them get back to the ship, too—we may want an official stormtrooper appearance before this is over. Grave and I will stay here on the scene where we can feed you intel and targeting data."

"Got it," Quiller said. "Ship'll be fired up in ten minutes. Let me know where you want me."

LaRone clicked off the comlink. "How soon?" Grave asked.

"He said ten minutes," LaRone told him.

Grave grunted. "Let's hope that's soon enough."

"What do you mean?"

"Well, it just occurred to me that those Consolidated Security guys look a lot like us," Grave said. "Or to put it another way, *we* look a lot like *them*."

LaRone glanced casually over at the door. The two humans, he saw, were still watching the security men in the back.

The Rodian, on the other hand, was now watching him and Grave. "Terrific," he muttered.

"So what now?" Grave asked.

"We sit tight," LaRone told him. "For the moment."

*   *   *

"And you think they were with the BloodScar pirates?" Han asked when Porter had finished his description of the swoop attack.

"That's my read from their shoulder patch design," Porter said. "In fact, the shoulder patches themselves are a pointer that direction—the Blood-Scars fancy themselves a military sort of group."

"Have you had run-ins with them before?" Luke asked, sniffing carefully at the drink Porter had ordered for him. It smelled a lot like engine cleaning fluid, and he wasn't at all sure he wanted to let it anywhere near his stomach.

"Not really," Porter said. "Most of our trouble's been from smaller pirate groups, especially off Purnham and Chekria. The only time we ran into actual BloodScar ships was a couple of months back when Casement was with a convoy that was attacked off Ashkas-kov."

"So what makes you think they're that big a group?" Han asked.

"Because they had ten ships on that Ashkas-kov attack," Porter retorted. "If they can afford that much juice to hit a single trade route, they must have one blazing number of ships."

Chewbacca warbled softly.

"Good question," Han agreed. "How many ships of that convoy did the pirates actually hit?"

"I think just four of them," Porter said, crinkling his nose in concentration. "But Casement said they fired on everyone—blew 'em pretty much to shreds. Only reason he survived was he had an armored inner hull and could play dead until they left. They blew the other four away after they'd stripped 'em, too."

"So maybe they already knew which ones had stuff they wanted?" Han suggested.

"I suppose, maybe," Porter conceded reluctantly. "But they'd have to have a blazing good intel service for that. A thousand guys in a thousand different dispatch offices."

"Or just two or three in the right ones," Han said.

"That'd be just as hard as building a really big fleet," Porter argued. "Maybe even harder. Why are you arguing so hard on this?"

"Hey, pal, don't jump on *me*," Han protested. "I just want to figure out what's going on. You've either got a big fleet hitting everything, or you've got a small one with good intel. You want to fix the right problem, or the one you happen to like?"

Porter took a deep breath, exhaled it between clenched teeth. "The right one," he growled. "But if the BloodScars are eating up a lot of other gangs, then we've got ourselves an entirely different problem." He scowled at Chewbacca. "*Especially* if what they've done up to now is because of good intel."

"Let's get back to the swoopers," Han said. "Any idea where they came from?"

"Somewhere off Drunost, anyway—they came in on a Barloz freighter." Porter lifted a finger. "But there were at least a few survivors. I saw a couple of landspeeders take off after the stormtroopers wrecked the ship."

Stormtroopers. Luke shivered. He'd grown up tangling with Sand People and had some idea how to deal with them. But Imperial stormtroopers were something else entirely. He and the others had survived a couple of brief encounters with them aboard the Death Star, but even at the time he'd had the feeling the Imperials had been taken by surprise and weren't operating at full efficiency.

Now, of course, he knew that Tarkin and Vader had deliberately allowed the *Falcon* and its crew to escape so they could track it to Yavin 4. Their next encounter with the Empire's elite, Luke suspected, would be very different.

"Survivors are a good thing," Han said approvingly. "Means there's someone you can talk to. Where did they go?"

"Last anyone saw, they were burning dust for here," Porter said, gesturing around them. "No surprise—this is the only population center anywhere around where you could go to ground."

"You sure they haven't left?"

Porter shrugged. "They sure didn't leave in what was left of their ship," he said. "Or anything else that they might have left inside. Consolidated would have gotten all of that when they impounded their ship."

"*Consolidated* has it?" Luke asked.

"Who else?" Porter said, looking puzzled.

"I thought the port authority would have it," Luke said. "Or the local patrollers."

Porter shook his head. "Don't have either here."

"I told you Drunost was all company towns," Han reminded him. "That means the whole planet's been carved into corporate territories."

"Like the Corporate Sector, only on a smaller scale," Porter added. "Also not nearly as bad."

"Debatable," Han muttered.

"No, really, they're okay," Porter insisted. "They keep law and order pretty good. Beats dealing with the Empire, anyway."

Luke.

Luke started, his eyes flicking around before he recognized the voice. It was Ben Kenobi, speaking in his mind as he had during the attack on the Death Star. *There is danger, Luke. Stretch out to the Force.*

"What kind of danger?" Luke muttered under his breath.

The voice didn't answer. Luke hunched over his drink, his eyes darting around the tapcafe. Everything looked all right to him.

But Ben hadn't said to *look*. He'd said to use the Force. Setting his jaw, Luke stretched out with his mind.

The images and voices around him seemed to fade into a distant background hum. He looked around again, trying to see through the faces to the emotions and basic overall impressions of the tapcafe's patrons.

But he didn't sense anything. For that matter, he wasn't even sure what exactly he was seeking.

And then, abruptly, an image flashed into his mind: a picture of a hungry, shaggy-furred predator, coiled to spring onto its prey.

He caught his breath as the image faded. What in the worlds—?

He smiled tightly. Of course—it was a hint. He let his eyes and mind drift around the tapcafe again, this time holding the image of the predator in his mind and trying to match the sensation that image had evoked with the emotions of the people in the room.

There it was: two men and a Rodian, seated at a table near the door, all three with the same coiled-spring anticipation he'd sensed in Ben's predator image.

And not just anticipation, but simmering evil.

"Kid?"

Luke snapped his attention back. "What?"

"We're not boring you with this strategy stuff, are we?" Han asked.

"No," Luke said distractedly, turning and searching across the tapcafe in the direction the two human predators were looking. There were seven men back there, seated around a pair of tables. "You know those men?" he asked, pointing at the latter group.

Porter glanced over his shoulder. "Off-duty Consolidated Security," he said. "They get their drinks half price here—encourages them to hang out in the neighborhood. Why?"

"They're being watched," Luke said. "The two men and the Rodian by the door."

"Ridiculous," Porter said with a snort. "No one makes trouble *here*."

"Those swoopers did," Han reminded him, looking sideways at the table Luke had indicated.

"That was way outside town," Porter countered. "Not counting the hub, this is the main part of Consolidated's local operation. It's got their HoloNet center, their main administration offices—"

"And a bank repository right across the street," Han interrupted.

"That's it," Luke said as the pieces suddenly fell into place. "They're going to rob it."

"Terrific," Han growled. "This place got a back door?"

"Right through there," Porter said, pointing at a curtained doorway at the side of the bar.

"Good," Han said, starting to get up. "Nice and easy."

"Wait a second," Luke objected. "We're going to *run*?"

"From a bank robbery?" Han countered. "You bet."

"But we have to help."

"Which side?" Han retorted. "Robbers against a big corporation? Big choice."

"That's not fair," Luke objected.

"He's right, kid," Porter put in nervously. "Besides, we're trying to keep a low profile, remember?"

Luke grimaced. His words to Ben on Tatooine whispered through his mind: *I can't get involved.* Yet if he hadn't, Tarkin and the Death Star would have won, and Leia and Rieekan and hundreds of others would now be dead. "Fine—you keep your low profile," he said. "I'll do it myself."

Across the table Chewbacca rumbled a protest, his massive paw batting at Han's arm.

"Oh, for—" Han broke off, glaring up at his partner. "Chewie—oh, all *right*. You two stay put—Chewie and me'll handle it."

"Solo—" Porter began.

"Or go ahead and run," Han cut him off. "I don't care which."

"But I want to help," Luke objected.

"Then find a way to distract them," Han said, standing. "Come on, Chewie. Let's get it over with."

"There they go," Grave murmured as the Corellian and Wookiee stood and headed unconcernedly toward the door. "Think they're with whoever's outside?"

"Could be," LaRone said, watching the kid. He and the farmer were still sitting at the table, the boy fingering something inside his tunic. Getting ready to draw a blaster? The Corellian and Wookiee walked past the trio at the table, the Corellian's hand dropping casually toward his holstered blaster.

And then from the street outside came the sound of a muffled explosion. The murmur of conversation in the tapcafe abruptly cut off as everyone froze, listening.

Everyone, that was, except the threesome at the table. Even as a second blast rumbled, all three abruptly stood, one of the humans pointing a large blaster at LaRone and Grave, the other targeting the two tables of security men at the back, the Rodian turning to cover the Corellian and Wookiee. "So much for taking them by surprise," Grave muttered.

"Right," LaRone murmured back. The would-be ambushers had turned to face the Rodian now, the Corellian with feigned bewilderment on his face, the Wookiee just looking dangerous. Out of the corner of his eye LaRone saw the kid stand up beside his table and raise his arm over his head.

And with a sizzling *snap-hiss* a blue-edged blade blazed into existence.

The distinctive sound of a lightsaber probably hadn't been heard on Drunost since the Clone Wars. But it wasn't an easy sound to forget. Instantly, magically, every eye in the tapcafe turned to look at the lightsaber the kid was holding over his head like a war banner. Even the Rodian half turned before he remembered he was supposed to be on guard and spun back.

But that half second of inattention was all it took. The Corellian took a long step forward and grabbed the end of the Rodian's blaster, twisting it to point toward the ceiling as he yanked out his own weapon. The Wookiee's approach was even more straightforward: grabbing the front of the Rodian's shirt, he lifted the alien straight off his feet and hurled him over the table into his two companions. All three went down, crashing into both their own table and the one next to them and disappearing from LaRone's view into a confused snarl of arms and legs.

The Rodian was quick. Even as LaRone drew his hold-out blaster the alien rolled back up into view, chattering curses at everyone within range. Dragging his blaster out of the tangle, he lifted it toward his attackers.

LaRone was lining up his blaster on the Rodian's back when the Corellian fired a single shot. This time the Rodian went down for good.

And then the security men from the back tables were there, three of them swarming over the two men on the floor with binders at the ready, the rest brushing past the Corellian and the Wookiee. The security man in front threw open the door, paused there a moment to assess the situation, then charged through with the others close behind. As the door swung closed again LaRone could hear the sounds of blasterfire beginning to fill the street.

The Corellian and Wookiee didn't follow. Their job apparently done, they turned and headed back to their table. The kid with the lightsaber closed it down and tucked it away as their farmer friend got to his feet, and all four of them made for a curtained door beside the bar. As the others passed through the curtain and a hidden door behind it, the kid with the lightsaber paused and turned around.

And looked directly at LaRone and Grave.

For a moment he held that pose. Then, turning back, he disappeared through the door with the others.

"Well, *that* was different," Grave commented, fingering his hold-out blaster as he stood up. "We joining the party?"

"I don't know," LaRone said, getting out his comlink. There had been something in the kid's look that had set his skin tingling. "Quiller?"

"On our way," the other's voice came back. "ETA, about ninety seconds."

"Does Consolidated have anything in the air yet?"

"Oh, they've got *everything* in the air," Quiller said. "Patrol boats, high-cover skimmers, even a couple of small gunboats. Give them full points for preparedness."

LaRone looked back toward the curtained back door. "In that case, break off and swing up and over the line of buildings east of the repository. I want you to find and track a group of four people: three humans and a Wookiee."

"Hang on."

The comlink went silent. "You thinking maybe our farmer may be mixed up in something a little more complicated than dirt scratching?" Grave asked.

"Dirt scratching is complicated enough," LaRone told him. "But yes, I was wondering that. If he was a loot-sniffer on that swooper raid, it could be he and his three friends are associated with the BloodScars."

"Who wanted to prevent the bank robbery and why?" Grave asked.

"Maybe the raiders are from a rival gang," LaRone said. "I just think they're worth keeping an eye on."

"Got 'em," Quiller's voice announced. "Two different landspeeders—one with one of the humans, the other with the other two and the Wookiee . . . the singleton's splitting off."

LaRone made a fast decision. "Stay with the threesome."

"Acknowledged," Quiller said. "Looks like they're heading for one of the service yards."

Did that mean their mission was over? "We'll pick up trail behind them," LaRone said, standing up and gesturing Grave toward the back door. "Let me know when they mark their ship. And set up a track—we're going to want to follow them."

"We are?" Grave asked. "Why?"

"Because they're connected to this," LaRone said. "I don't know exactly how, but they are. And at the moment, they're our *only* solid connection."

"Doesn't sound all that solid to me," Grave said doubtfully.

"It may be a little loose," LaRone conceded. "But it won't cost us anything to at least see where they're going."

Grave shrugged. "Nothing but time and fuel."

"We've got the time, and ISB's providing the fuel," LaRone pointed out as they slipped into the tapcafe's back room and headed for the exit. "Let's go before they spot Quiller."

"No, *Purnham*," Han repeated. "The *Purnham* system. Where Porter said you got hit once by pirates?"

"Are you crazy?" Casement's voice demanded over the *Falcon*'s comm. "We're trying to *avoid* pirates, remember?"

"No, we're trying to lock down this BloodScar thing," Han said.

"But the Purnham attack wasn't *from* the BloodScars," Casement objected.

Han rolled his eyes as, beside him, Chewbacca warbled a softly contemptuous growl. Couldn't these idiots *see* it? "Look," Han said, pitching his voice as if he were talking to a small child or a midlevel bureaucrat. "We don't know where the BloodScars are, but you and Porter think they're trying to snap up other fringe groups. Maybe they're also trying to recruit the Purnham gang; and we *do* know where *that* group hangs out. If we can catch a couple of them, maybe they can tell us where to find the BloodScars."

"Well . . . maybe," Casement conceded. "But getting them to talk won't be easy."

Han looked at the glowering Wookiee beside him. "Let me worry about that," he said. "You just get a cargo ship there—let's make it three days from now. Be sure you route the manifest the same way you did before, in case someone's slicing the dispatch records for good targets."

"Fine," Casement said, a heavy layer of resignation in his voice. "Whatever you say. But I've got to tell you, I've got a bad fe—"

"Three days," Han said, and cut off the comm. He turned a glare toward

Luke, sitting quietly behind Chewbacca. "Or are there other objections?" he challenged.

"No, no, I like it," Luke assured him hastily. "The last thing they'll expect is an ambush."

"Good," Han said, turning back to the controls. "Then we're all agreed. Wonderful."

Keying on the repulsorlifts, he lifted the *Falcon* off the pad. *Go and talk to the supply people*, Rieekan had said. *That's all. Just go and talk to them.*

Yeah. Right.

"My engineers say everything will be up and running in four more hours," Captain Ozzel said, taking a hasty step backward as a long shielding plate on its way across the *Happer's Way* engine room swung dangerously in their direction. Mara, her eyes and brain automatically making quick size and distance calculations, didn't bother to move as the metal plate passed no closer than five centimeters from her face. "Is there any other way we can serve you?"

"I'll need two of your crewers," she told him. "Men who can both fight and handle a ship this size."

"You mean close-in fighting?" Ozzel asked doubtfully. "That won't be easy."

"Maybe you can pull them from your stormtrooper contingent," Mara suggested.

There was a flicker of something in Ozzel's face and sense. "That may be possible," he said carefully. "I'll check with the group commander."

"Don't bother—I'll meet with him myself," Mara said. "Tell him to report to the bay duty office."

"Right away," Ozzel said, pulling out his comlink.

Maneuvering her way along the *Happer's Way*'s narrow corridors, Mara stepped out through the hatch into the *Reprisal*'s hangar bay, where the freighter had been brought for repairs. As per her orders, the purely cosmetic damage Shakko's men had inflicted on the outer hull hadn't been touched. She glanced over it, satisfied herself that there was nothing to show that the repairs hadn't been made in deep space by the *Happer's Way*'s own crew, and headed for the duty office.

A smooth-faced man wearing colonel's insignia was waiting when she arrived. "Emperor's Hand," he greeted her gravely. "I'm Colonel Vak Somoril. I understand you wished to see me?"

"You're the stormtrooper group commander?" Mara asked.

"Not the overall commander, but I head a specialized contingent," Somoril explained. "Captain Ozzel thought my unit would be more likely to have the sort of men you're looking for."

"I need two warriors who also know their way around a Rendili heavy freighter," Mara told him. "Can you supply them?"

"I think so," Somoril said. "When do you want them?"

"Immediately," Mara said. "Have them collect civilian gear and report to the *Happer's Way*. Captain Norello will meet them there for a quick orientation to the ship and its systems. We'll be leaving the *Reprisal* in four hours."

"As you wish," Somoril said briskly. "They'll be aboard in twenty minutes."

"Good. Dismissed."

Somoril left. For a few seconds Mara gazed at the closed door, allowing him time to get across the hangar bay. Then, stepping over to the duty office computer terminal, she punched in her special override password and keyed for a search of the *Reprisal*'s personnel roster.

There was no Colonel Vak Somoril listed.

Pursing her lips, Mara keyed for the bridge log and repeated her search. Again, nothing. Switching to the flight log, she searched for arrivals and departures.

There, finally, she found something. There were still no names, Somoril's or anyone else's, but a little over two standard weeks earlier eight nonmilitary vessels had arrived aboard the *Reprisal* and been given berths in Hangar Bay 5. One of the ships had left three days later, though under odd circumstances and with some apparent contradictions in the sequence of log reports. The other ships were still aboard.

Put together, the pattern was obvious. Colonel Somoril and his specialized stormtrooper contingent were Imperial Security Bureau.

Mara wrinkled her nose in disgust. ISB was a necessary evil, she knew, though to her mind there was too much evil and not enough necessity in the mix. Her own limited experience had found them to be generally arrogant, heavy-handed, and overly proud of their elite status.

And if there was prestige or political advantage to be had, they could be trusted to be first in line. Probably why Somoril had maneuvered himself ahead of the *Reprisal*'s official stormtrooper commander to offer a combat force to the Emperor's Hand.

Odd, though, that he hadn't then made a point of identifying himself as ISB. Perhaps he planned that revelation for just before Mara's departure.

Shutting down the terminal, Mara left the office and crossed the bay to the pilots' briefing room. Two troopers stood on guard, and at her gesture one of them unlocked the door and opened it.

Sitting at the conference table, securely shackled to one of the legs by two sets of binders, was the pirate Tannis. "About time," he growled. "When do I get something to eat?"

"Shut up and listen," Mara said, pulling out a data card and holding it up for his inspection. "I've prepared a list of charges against you. Added together, the total package reads out as anywhere from thirty standard years in a penal colony all the way up to the death penalty."

Tannis's mouth twisted. "This is your idea of a deal?"

"I'm not finished," Mara told him. "So far you've had a pretty easy ride, you and the rest of your friends down in the brig. You've been nicely anonymous, given that the only people who could finger you for piracy were always dead before you left the scene with their cargoes. As long as you weren't stupid enough to wear your BloodScar patches, you could stroll down any street in the Empire without anyone being the wiser as to who you really were."

She tapped the card with one fingertip. "But that's all over now. Along with the charges, this card also details your face, your fingerprints, your biometrics, and your full DNA profile. Once this is in the Imperial data bank, any law enforcement officer curious enough to punch you in will have your entire criminal history in the time it takes to comm to Imperial Center and back." She raised her eyebrows. "Which means you're going to either spend the next thirty-plus years in prison or else spend it hiding in sewers and dark holes."

Tannis's face was under good control, but Mara could sense the fear starting to tug at him as he looked ahead to the bleak future she had sketched out. "Unless?" he asked carefully.

"The data's already in the system," Mara said. "But at the moment it's in one of my private files, isolated from everything else, with a thirty-day release timer on it. That means that anytime in the next thirty days I can go in and erase it, and no one will ever even know it was there."

"So what we're talking about here is sort of like a blanket pardon?"

"Basically," Mara said. "Interested?"

The tip of Tannis's tongue slipped across the center of his upper lip. "What do I have to do?"

"We're taking the *Happer's Way* to your base," Mara told him. "After suffering damage to his hyperdrive and comm system in the battle, your friend Captain Shakko decided to send you home with the prize while he and the rest of the crew stayed behind to make repairs."

"And where did *you* come from?"

"My men and I were hijackers who'd sneaked aboard the *Happer's Way*," Mara said. "We were making our move when you showed up, which is why you were able to capture the ship without having to first blast it into a worthless hulk. We'd heard about the BloodScars and made a deal with Shakko for you to take us to the Commodore to discuss our joining up."

"What if he asks what group you're with?" Tannis asked. "He knows a lot about the people in this sector."

"Trust me," Mara said. "I'll make it work."

Tannis grimaced. "You're asking me to betray my comrades."

"You're a pirate," Mara countered. "Your comrades are acquaintances of convenience, any of whom would stab you in the back for an extra ten percent."

She gave that a moment to sink in before continuing. "As it happens, though, you're not really going to betray them. You're a local problem, to be dealt with by the local authorities. The only person I'm interested in right now is whoever it is who's currently pulling your strings."

Tannis frowned. "You mean Caaldra?"

"I mean the one behind Caaldra," Mara said. "Impressive though he might look, he's only a high-priced errand boy. I want access to the Commodore's records so I can find out who's making the decisions, who's giving the orders—" She paused, just briefly. "—*and* who's handing out the money."

Once again Tannis's face gave nothing away, but the sudden emotional ripple showed Mara she'd hit the target directly on the crossmark. Tannis might be a few steps down the chain of command, but he knew how to follow a money trail.

So she'd been right. At least some of the money from Glovstoak's artworks had apparently found its way to the BloodScars.

"What happens if the Commodore tumbles to you?" Tannis asked.

"You'll try very hard not to let that happen."

"And if you krong up and end up getting yourself killed?"

"You'll try even harder not to let *that* happen. Are you in?"

Tannis snorted. "Do I have a choice?"

"Sure—you can start your sentence today," Mara said.

"No thanks," he said, and in his eyes and altered tone Mara knew he'd suddenly realized that he had a third option: to betray her to the rest of the BloodScars and use his thirty-day grace period to find a place to hide. "I'm in."

"Good," Mara said, stepping over to stand in front of him. "And just so we're clear what exactly it is you're agreeing to—" Dropping her gaze to his binders, she reached out with the Force and unfastened them, letting them drop clattering to the deck.

For a handful of heartbeats Tannis stared down at them, the muscles in his neck suddenly taut. Then, slowly, he lifted his eyes to hers again.

And whatever thoughts he might have had about betrayal were suddenly gone. "Vader," he whispered. "You're like Vader."

"Only better," she said coolly, a part of her mind wondering what Vader would do if he ever heard her talk that way. But what the Sith Lord didn't know wouldn't hurt him. "We have a deal?"

Tannis swallowed hard. "Yes," he managed. "Absolutely."

"Good," she said, taking a step back and stretching out again, this time to call the binders to her hand. Tannis followed them with his eyes the entire way. "I'll have a guard take you to your ship to pick out some clothing and anything else you want to take with you. Then you'll report to the *Happer's Way* for an equipment orientation. I'll make sure there's enough bacta in the medical capsule to get that leg of yours back in shape before we arrive at your base."

"Right." Slowly, Tannis stood up, his eyes still on the binders. He looked back up at Mara, and managed a taut smile. "Welcome to the BloodScars, Emperor's Hand. You're going to love it."

"Thank you," Mara said. "I'd better."

Captain Ozzel leaned back in his chair, staring at his computer display with a bitter sense of defeat. All of it—all the work, all the sweat, all the struggling—gone.

The admiral's bars. Gone.

Across the office the door slid open and Colonel Somoril stepped in. "They've just made the jump to lightspeed," he told Ozzel.

"It doesn't matter," Ozzel muttered, gesturing to the display. "We're finished."

"What in space are you talking about?" Somoril demanded, stepping to the desk and swiveling the display around to face him.

"Our clever little Emperor's Hand found her way into the ship's computer," Ozzel said bitterly. "She accessed the personnel files, the bridge log, *and* the flight log."

Somoril's face had gone stiff, his eyes darting back and forth as he skimmed the file on the display. Ozzel watched; then, to the captain's amazement, he saw some of the other's tension drain away. "Fine," Somoril said, sitting down. "So she knows the *Gillia* left a couple of weeks ago. So what? As far as she knows, that could have been a perfectly legitimate ISB operation."

"Oh, really?" Ozzel snarled. "You really think she maneuvered herself aboard this ship and into the computer without already knowing what she was looking for?"

Somoril lifted his eyebrows. "She *maneuvered* herself aboard? Including setting up a pirate attack on an Imperial-chartered freighter?"

"Special Imperial agents don't bother with anything as trivial as pirates," Ozzel shot back. "And the Emperor's Hand *certainly* doesn't. If she happened to foil a pirate attack, it was purely incidental to her main mission."

Somoril shook his head. "I'm not convinced."

"Then be convinced," Ozzel said acidly, keying for a new file. "I pulled up these items from planetary news services. We have two separate reports of Imperial stormtroopers in action."

Somoril's eyes narrowed. "What sort of action?"

"The first wasn't too bad," Ozzel said. "All they did was engage and destroy a swoop gang who were harassing a group of farmers. But the second action ended up tearing down a city's entire patroller structure."

"They took over a *city*?"

"No, apparently just reinstated the last group who'd been in charge," Ozzel said. "I haven't been able to get any more details. Not that it matters. The point is that our Emperor's Hand now knows where those stormtroopers came from."

"*If* she's made the connection," Somoril said. "She may not have. More to the point, even if she has it won't matter if she's never able to tell anyone else."

Ozzel stared at him, something unpleasant starting to gnaw at his gut. "What exactly are you suggesting?"

"I'm saying that she sent no transmissions from the *Reprisal*, and that she won't be sending any from the *Happer's Way*," Somoril said. "Brock and Gilling will make sure of that. That just leaves the transmitters at her destination point." He paused. "Which, from our track of their departure vector, is almost certainly the mining operation on Gepparin."

"You *tracked* them?"

"How else would we know where to find her?" Somoril replied reasonably. "So now, Captain, you have a decision to make."

"You realize what you're suggesting," Ozzel said, his voice sounding strange in his ears. "You're talking about killing an *Imperial agent*. A woman who gets her orders from Palpatine himself."

"A *girl* who gets those orders," Somoril corrected. "She's barely had time to finish her training, let alone build up any real field experience."

"She's an *Imperial agent*."

"Stop *saying* that," Somoril growled. "This is a dangerous life she's chosen for herself. Agents in the field die all the time."

"So why didn't you deal with her when she was here?" Ozzel demanded.

"What, in front of potentially hundreds of witnesses?" Somoril countered contemptuously. "Besides, at the time I didn't know how close to the trail she was sniffing. Now we do."

Ozzel exhaled noisily. But the colonel was right. Terribly, horribly right. "How do you propose we proceed?"

"As I said, an agent's life is dangerous," Somoril said. "You never know when you might get caught up at the wrong end of a military action." He lifted his eyebrows. "The sort of action that might occur if a patrolling Star Destroyer happened on data pointing to a suspected pirate nest."

For a long minute the two men gazed across the desk at each other. Then, slowly, Ozzel reached to his intercom. "This is the captain," he announced grimly. "Set course for the Gepparin system. Get us under way as soon as the hyperdrive's up to full power."

He got an acknowledgment and keyed off. "I presume you've also calculated how far behind her we'll be?"

"No more than a few hours," Somoril assured him. "Brock and Gilling can easily keep her away from any HoloNet transmitters that long." He stood up. "With your permission, Captain, I'll go see if I can search out any further details on what our five deserters have been doing."

He gave a slight bow and turned to the door. "What would you have done if I'd said no?" Ozzel called after him.

Somoril didn't turn around. "I'd have sent one of my own ships to deal with her," he said. "And I would have had utter contempt for you for the rest of your days."

Ozzel snorted. "Don't you mean for the rest of *your* days?"

"Not at all," Somoril said quietly. "I have the feeling your life would have ended up being significantly shorter than mine."

Chapter Eleven

CHIVKYRIE'S SHIP, BY PREARRANGEMENT, WAS ALREADY WAITING WHEN Leia's courier ship dropped out of hyperspace over the uninhabited rendezvous planet. Two other vessels were also in sight, running in parallel orbits: the two Rebellion leaders who had come to argue against whatever this plan was Chivkyrie had come up with. Gazing out her viewport, taking deep, steadying breaths the way her father had taught her, Leia watched as her pilot eased them alongside Chivkyrie's ship. *It's just another negotiation*, she told herself firmly. Like hundreds she'd participated in during her career.

But there was something ominous about this one, an odd uneasiness that refused to go away. Distantly, she wished Luke was with her. Or even Han.

She hadn't had much occasion to deal with Adarians when she was in the Imperial Senate—their interests and those of Alderaan had seldom coincided. But since joining the Rebellion she'd been forced by necessity to learn more about their customs and psychology. Living through a war, her father had once said, forced one to learn geography. Participating in a war, Leia had discovered, forced one to learn people.

The welcoming ritual aboard Chivkyrie's ship was short but densely layered with history and custom and significance, and Leia was exceedingly glad she'd made a point of studying the ceremony ahead of time. She made it through with only a few small errors, all of them due to the fact that her human vocal apparatus couldn't quite hit some of the Adarese words.

"You grace my ship and my company with your courtesy," Chivkyrie said when the ceremony was over, his Adarian mouth mangling the Basic words almost as badly as Leia had done with his language. "Allow me to present the other leaders who seek your wisdom." He gestured to a Mungra with piercing orange eyes standing to his left. "This is Ydor Vokkoli, leader of the Freedonna Kaisu."

"Leader Vokkoli," Leia said, nodding a greeting to him. Mungras were one of the two species native to Shelsha sector, a people who had already created a realm of a dozen interstellar colonies when the Great Exploration of the galaxy had begun millennia ago.

"Princess Organa," Vokkoli said, bowing his shaggy maned head in return.

"And this is Thillis Slanni of the Shining Hope," Chivkyrie continued, gesturing to a tall Ishi Tib to his right.

[Though I am not the leader, but merely the director of planning,] Slanni corrected in the complex series of squeals, honks, and beak-clicks that made up the Tibranese language.

"I understand," Leia said, nodding. "The organizational skill of your people is well known. I'm pleased to have both you and Leader Vokkoli here to help guide my decision."

"A decision that may mean life or death for us all," Vokkoli rumbled.

So much for small talk. "Then let's sit down and discuss it," Leia said. "Leader Chivkyrie, if you'll show us the way?"

The conference room was down the corridor from the entryway and featured the stepped floor and multilevel tiered conference table typical of Adarian design. Chivkyrie escorted Leia to the highest part of the table, then took a seat at the next level down. Vokkoli took the chair opposite him, at the same table level, while Slanni sat one level below Vokkoli on his side.

It was an odd setup, Leia had often thought, and in long meetings tended to give the participants vertigo and stiff necks. Still, she had to admit that it made it abundantly clear where everyone stood on the issue at hand.

"First of all," she said after Chivkyrie's servants had laid out drinks and plates of nibblings on each of the occupied tiers, "I need to know from you, Leader Chivkyrie, the details of this plan you're proposing."

"It is simplicity itself," Chivkyrie said. "I do not understand how anyone cannot see the vast potential for benefit—"

"We'll discuss the benefits in a moment," Leia interrupted him smoothly. "First, I need to know about the plan itself."

Chivkyrie looked across the table at his fellow Rebels, the light peeking through the aeration hole in his elongated skull as he did so. "I propose to bring Shelsha sector to the side of the Rebellion." He looked at Leia. "The *entire* sector."

"Interesting," Leia said, keeping her diplomat's face firmly in place. "How exactly would this be achieved?"

"That is the most delicious part of the plan," Chivkyrie said. "We—the Rebel Alliance—would need do very little. It is Governor Choard himself who has proposed this."

"He's said as much to you?" Leia asked.

"Not the governor personally," Chivkyrie said "But I've spoken at length with his assistant, Chief Administrator Vilim Disra. He assures me Governor Choard has already set in motion a plan for Shelsha to withdraw from the Empire and declare its independence."

[Which is not the same as stating Shelkonwa will in fact join the Rebellion as an active member,] Slanni pointed out.

"Chief Administrator Disra has assured me that will be the next step," Chivkyrie said. "Governor Choard has become increasingly appalled by the horrors of Imperial Center's rule and understands that joining the Rebellion is the only answer."

"*If* Imperial Center actually allows such open defiance to occur," Vokkoli rumbled, the subsonics from his deep voice sending vibrations through the table. "The Freedonna Kaisu believe that Palpatine would respond instead by turning the full might of the Imperial Fleet against Shelkonwa."

"Which is precisely why an alliance with the Rebellion is vital to Choard's success," Chivkyrie countered. "Simultaneous attacks by our forces elsewhere across the galaxy would tie down many of the Imperial forces that would otherwise be used against Shelsha sector."

[The Shining Hope agrees with Leader Chivkyrie that the political and psychological gains of such a move would be immense,] Slanni said. [But we do not agree that Choard intends to actually join the Alliance.] He gestured to Vokkoli. [Nor do we believe, as Leader Vokkoli has suggested, that the Alliance possesses the military strength to sufficiently dilute Palpatine's response.]

"Whether or not our actions would be sufficient depends directly on the extent of Governor Choard's preparations," Chivkyrie pointed out.

"I agree," Leia said, trying to sort through the implications of this unexpected bombshell. Slanni was right—the news that an entire sector had seceded from the Empire would be devastating to the illusion of unity that Palpatine had so carefully constructed around his New Order. It would create a natural rallying point for discontent, and give the Rebellion a legitimacy the Alliance could never hope to achieve by itself. In fact, a breakaway sector could very well prove to be the beginning of the end for Palpatine's rule.

On the other, darker hand, it had been precisely the same sort of Separatist movement a generation earlier that had torn the Republic to bloody pieces. The last thing she and the other Alliance leaders wanted was a repeat of that era's mass chaos and death. "Do we know anything about Choard's own plans?" she asked Chivkyrie.

"I know he is preparing and positioning forces to take control of key installations," Chivkyrie said. "Beyond that, I have no specifics."

"Specifics that are of primary importance," Vokkoli said.

"Indeed," Chivkyrie agreed, nodding to the Mungra. "That is precisely why I asked Princess Leia Organa to join us."

Leia felt her breath catch as she suddenly understood where the conversation was heading. Of course Chivkyrie hadn't talked directly to Choard—a sector governor was vastly above him in tier rank, and for an Adarian that made a one-on-one conversation unthinkable. But Leia was a Princess of royal Alderaanian blood, even if the world that had granted her that title no longer existed. "Do you know whether or not the governor would be willing to speak with me?" she asked.

"Chief Administrator Disra has assured me the governor would speak with anyone of his own tier," Chivkyrie assured her. "With your permission, we will leave immediately for Shelkonwa."

"You haven't given him my name, have you?" Leia asked.

"Of course not," Chivkyrie said, looking rather scandalized. "For one thing, I was not certain whom the Rebel Alliance would send. For another, I would never have brought any name to him without permission." He looked across the table again. "But Chief Administrator Disra has warned me that the governor's preparations are nearly complete," he added. "If we are to be a part of this, we must move quickly."

"I understand the need for haste," Leia said. "Yet Leader Vokkoli and Planning Director Slanni are also correct in their concerns. This would involve great risk for the Rebel Alliance, yet might come to nothing."

"All of life involves risks that may come to nothing," Chivkyrie said, some impatience creeping into his tone. "You of the Alliance leadership claim you seek to draw all enemies of the Empire beneath one roof. If you are unwilling to accept Governor Choard to that gathering, perhaps it is not truly unity that you seek."

[But is it *our* victory Governor Choard seeks?] Slanni countered. [Or would he gain his independence only to turn and banish us from his territory?]

Thus turning Shelsha sector into a neutral zone, perhaps as part of a deal with Palpatine to allow Shelkonwa more freedom from Imperial rule? Similar things had been done in the past, Leia knew, in the Corporate Sector and other places. If Choard's new freedom was accompanied by public pronouncements of his loyalty to Imperial Center, Palpatine might be willing to play along, especially if the alternative was to divert the military resources necessary to bring Shelkonwa back into line. The end result would be that Choard would gain the limited independence he apparently wanted, and the Alliance would have fought and died for nothing.

Or it could be worse. Choard could be a completely loyal Imperial, with all of this nothing more than an elaborate attempt to lure a few Alliance leaders into a trap.

"If we let this opportunity slip past unhindered, Governor Choard will surely be defeated," Chivkyrie said into her thoughts. "His bid for freedom will become nothing more than a footnote to the dark history of Palpatine's rule." He cocked his head toward her. "And the Republic Redux will need to consider whether the Rebel Alliance is truly the proper home for us."

So there it was. Mon Mothma had warned Leia that Vokkoli and Slanni had threatened to pull out of the Alliance if Chivkyrie's plan was accepted. Now Chivkyrie was delivering the same ultimatum.

One way or the other, it seemed, the unity of Rebel forces in Shelsha sector was doomed.

But maybe she could postpone that doom, at least for a while. "I will not give in to blackmail," she warned Chivkyrie, putting a double helping of royal displeasure into her voice. "But neither will I dismiss out of hand any possibility of bringing about our ultimate victory against the Empire. I will return to my ship and communicate with my fellow Alliance leaders. If they agree, I will come with you to Shelkonwa to assess the situation."

She looked over at Vokkoli and Slanni. "I would also ask for your presence and counsel on this journey," she added.

Chivkyrie stirred in his seat, but remained silent. Vokkoli looked down at Slanni, then back up at Leia. "We would be honored to accompany you, Princess," the Mungra said gravely. "May the Force be with you and your decisions."

"Thank you," Leia said, suppressing a grimace as she stood up. The Force. If only she had the Jedi ability to tap into that source of power and wisdom. But she didn't. "I'll be back within the hour."

"I will await your return," Chivkyrie said gravely. "But be warned: within that same hour I return to my home. With you, or without."

Luke was playing lightsaber games with the practice remote when Han arrived from the cockpit. "What, *again*?" he growled to Chewbacca, who was watching from just inside the room.

The Wookiee rumbled the logical question.

"No, I don't know where else he would practice," Han admitted. "But who says he has to practice aboard the *Falcon* at all? What happens if he slices through a wiring conduit or hydraulic line, or cuts off his own arm?"

Still, he had to admit that Luke was getting better with the ridiculous weapon. Those first few times old Kenobi had run him through the drill, the kid had blocked maybe one attack in ten. Now, as Han watched, the remote launched a six-shot attack, only one of which got through. "He could still cut off an arm," he muttered.

Chewbacca warbled a reminder of Luke's ambitions and responsibilities.

"Yeah, and I'll bet that if he practices every day he'll grow up to be a terrific Jedi Knight," Han said with only a little sarcasm. "Luke? Hey— Luke."

There was a slight pause, as if the kid had to readjust his attention to something besides the remote. "What is it?" he asked, turning to look at Han. "Oh—hi, Chewie. Didn't see you there."

Mentally, Han shook his head. Some all-seeing, all-knowing Jedi Knight Luke was. Simple tricks and nonsense, just like he'd always said. "We're coming up on the Purnham system," he told Luke. "Need to fire up the quads."

"Right." Closing down his lightsaber, Luke stepped around the still-humming remote and touched a switch on the engineering control panel, sending the hovering ball scooting back to its charging station.

As he did so, the familiar two-tone approach warning sounded. "Come on—move it," Han said, crossing to the ladder and heading down. "Casement's going to be real unhappy if the pirates make it to the party before we do."

"There," Marcross said, pointing ahead out the canopy. "One freighter, dead ahead."

"Got it," Quiller confirmed, his fingers tapping their way across his board as he keyed for an ID. "It's . . . not our Corellian. Looks like a Surronian of some kind—not familiar with the particular model."

"You reading any weaponry?" LaRone asked.

"Couple of blaster cannons," Quiller said. "Nothing unusual for this class."

"Easy pickings, in other words," Marcross muttered. "When exactly is the Corellian due?"

"Assuming he stayed with the speed he was doing when he jumped, he could be here anytime," Quiller said. "If he really pushed it, he might conceivably have come and gone already."

"I didn't know YT-1300s could go that fast," Brightwater said.

"*They* can't; *this* one can," Quiller told him. "I was reading all sorts of interesting upgrades and modifications before they jumped. If these guys aren't pirates, I'm betting they're either smugglers or blockade runners."

There was a trill from the board. "Company," Quiller announced, peering at his displays. "Coming out from that cluster of asteroids to starboard."

"I see them," LaRone said grimly. There were two ships swinging into view, patrol boats of some sort, sleek and fast and heavily armed. The Corellian ship they'd been tracking might or might not be a pirate, but these two definitely were.

And they were on the hunt. Swinging their bows around, they accelerated toward the distant freighter. "Intercept in about ninety seconds," Quiller warned. "LaRone?"

LaRone pursed his lips. "Well, if all we want is a few random pirates to interrogate—"

"Whoa—there he is!" Grave said suddenly, pointing ahead and to the left. "There's our Corellian."

"Son-of-a-drabble," Brightwater breathed. "They *did* get here ahead of us."

"And there they go," Marcross added as the YT-1300 put on a burst of speed. "Looks like he's targeting our pirates."

"Nothing like having a full buffet to choose from," Quiller commented. "You have any preferences as to which ships live through the next few minutes?"

LaRone studied the situation unfolding in front of them. Standard military procedure would call for disabling all three suspect ships if possible and sorting out friend from foe later. But until he'd worked through his own vague feelings and impressions of the Corellian and his friends— "Go for the two patrol ships," he ordered. "We *know* they're pirates. Target their engines first, and try to disable at least one without blasting it to rubble."

"What about the Corellian?" Grave asked.

"Leave him alone for now," LaRone said. "Don't fire on him unless he fires on us first."

Brightwater tapped Grave's shoulder. "That's our cue," he said. "Let's go find out how accurate these cannons are at long range."

*   *   *

The pirate ships were looming ever larger as Chewie closed the distance, and Luke was settling his mind into Jedi combat mode when he heard the familiar voice again whispering into his mind. *Luke.*

"Yes, I know," Luke muttered, focusing his thoughts on the pirates.

Don't focus, Ben's voice admonished. *Not yet. First seek out and identify all possible threats, wherever they may lurk.*

Luke frowned. Wherever they may lurk? What was *that* supposed to mean?

Stretch out to the Force, Luke. In all directions.

Grimacing, Luke emptied his mind, forcing himself to ignore the obvious targets directly ahead of him, and sent his awareness flowing outward. Though where any other danger could possibly be coming from—

The sense of distant minds suddenly touched his own. He looked around quickly, trying to locate the source.

And caught his breath. Swinging into view around the side of one of the nearby asteroids was another ship, turning onto an intercept course behind the *Falcon.* "Han!" he called.

"Yeah, I see it," Han's voice growled through his headset. "Should have expected they'd have backup. Chewie, evasive course to Casement. Luke, you take the party crasher. Keep him back, or bring him down."

"Got it," Luke said. Coming in low on their stern, the trailing ship was barely within his fire arc.

But he could only do what he could do. The *Falcon* was starting to roll like a drunken dewback as Chewbacca threw them into a series of twists and turns, and off the edge of the hull he could see multiple red flashes as Han opened fire on the two pirate ships they were chasing. Swinging his fire-control yoke all the way over, Luke aimed his quads as far aft as he could and waited for Chewbacca's evasive maneuvering to roll him into position for a clear shot.

Luke, focus your thoughts.

Luke grimaced again. *Now* Ben wanted him to focus his thoughts. He took a deep breath, turning his mind toward the newcomers.

And paused. With his thoughts focused, and with the other ship starting to close the distance, the overall sense of the men aboard was becoming clearer.

But it wasn't the same coiled-spring predator feeling he'd sensed back at the Conso City tapcafe. It had some of the same strength and anticipation, but there was definitely something different about it. Something less angry, or less vicious. Less evil.

The Force will guide you, if you let it.

The closing ship was almost in range. Luke peered out at it, wondering how he was supposed to get this guidance.

Maybe the way he let the Force control his movements when he practiced with the remote? Taking a deep breath, painfully aware of the risk he was taking, he settled his hands on the yoke and allowed the Force to flow into him.

And to his amazement, his fingers lifted off the firing controls.

Very good, Ben's voice came again, and Luke thought he could sense approval in the tone. *Not all strangers are enemies.*

Luke had to smile at the obviousness of that one. Still, it was a lesson he would do well to keep in mind. Throwing one last look at the oncoming ship, he swiveled the quads around and settled the sights onto the pirate ships ahead of him. Once again he let the Force's guidance flow into him, and once again his fingers moved of their own accord.

Only this time, it was to settle themselves firmly onto the firing controls.

The message was clear. Instead of taking out the new ship, Luke was to join Han's attack on the known pirates.

He just hoped the Force knew what it was doing.

"Will you look at that?" Quiller muttered as the Suwantek drove hard toward the battle. "Twin quad lasers. That's, what, a three-year prison sentence right there?"

"Probably, but it beats getting blown out of the sky," Marcross said, the sides of his face momentarily lighting up green as the Suwantek's own laser cannons sent another volley at the two patrol boats. "I'm wondering when the pirates are going to start looking for alternatives of their own."

"Actually, they haven't got any," Quiller said. "With the Corellian riding their portside flank and us hammering their sterns, they're pouring every bit of power they can spare into those two deflectors. Any direction they veer now will open up another flank to attack, and they can't afford that. They can't even separate and try to split our fire."

"Couldn't the one on the right at least ride up a little so he could bring his guns against the Corellian?" Marcross asked.

"Sure he could," Quiller confirmed. "But then he'd be in range of the Corellian's quads, too. Ten to one that's the ship the attack commander's riding."

LaRone felt his lip twist. Typical. Hitting defenseless freighters was fine, but when it came to a real fight pirates generally showed themselves to be cowards at heart. "So what *are* they doing?"

"The only thing they can," Quiller said. "They're trying to catch up to the target freighter and use it for cover."

"That assumes any of us care if the freighter gets blown to bits, of course," Marcross murmured.

"True, but like I said, it's all they've got," Quiller said. "Actually, at this range and with his firepower the Corellian could be doing a lot more damage than he is. Looks like he's trying to take them alive, too."

"Handy for us," Marcross said. He threw a look at LaRone. "Though I missed the part where they and we started working together on this."

"Allies of convenience," LaRone told him. "We'll just have to wait and see how long that convenience lasts."

"We may be about to find out," Quiller said. "Looks like he's about to make some kind of move."

LaRone peered out the canopy. He didn't see anything different, but he was willing to take Quiller's word for it. "Okay," he said. "Grave, Brightwater: hold your fire a minute. Let's see what the Corellian's up to."

"Chewie?" Han called. "You ready?"

There was a growled acknowledgment through the headphone. Han resettled his grip on his firing yoke, trying to ignore the uncertainties fluttering through his gut. He'd personally trained Chewbacca in this sort of lunatic maneuver, after all, and the big Wookiee was nearly as good at it as Han was.

But there was still that Suwantek-shaped question mark back there, a question mark with a *lot* more firepower than a freighter that size had any business carrying. So far the party crasher had concentrated his attention on the two pirate ships and ignored the *Falcon*, but that could change at any time.

And if they were just waiting for the right moment to switch targets, this would sure give it to them. "Luke?"

"Ready."

"Okay," Han said, bracing himself. "Chewie . . . *go.*"

There was another acknowledgment from the cockpit, and suddenly the *Falcon* was on the move, breaking from its parallel course to lunge sideways toward the two pirates. The hull dipped as Chewbacca sent them skidding laterally beneath the other ships, cutting off Han's view. From above him he could hear the upper quads firing as Luke sent a salvo upward into their bellies, and the teeth-aching screeches of laser against deflector as the pirates returned fire. The sideways momentum sent the *Falcon* shooting past the second pirate; with a corkscrewing twist that sent the stars spinning dizzyingly across Han's canopy, Chewbacca brought them around the pirate's flank and over its upper surface.

With a final drop and thud, the Wookiee slammed them down onto the other ship, locking them solidly together with the *Falcon*'s landing claw.

The pirate's dorsal laser turret was directly aft, no more than three meters away from Han's own gunwell. Point-blank range for both of them, except that Han was ready for the trick and the pirate gunner wasn't. The turret had barely begun to swing around when Han blew it to metal scraps. "Okay, Chewie."

There was a click as Chewbacca keyed the comm over to him. "First and last chance," Han called into his mike. "Surrender or die."

The flanking pirate ship swung wide in reply, raising itself from its original defensive position where it could bring the entire flank's worth of weaponry to bear on this incredibly impudent hitchhiker. Han swung his quads around, stitching a line across its flank as Luke did the same.

The pirate's turrets were still lining up for their own salvo when the Suwantek coming up from behind blew it to dust.

Han peered out at the other ship. If there'd been any doubt that the Suwantek wasn't with these other pirates, that pretty well ended the question. But they could still be a rival gang . . . and with one ship down and the *Falcon* locked sitting-avian on the other, they'd reached the moment of truth. "Unidentified Suwantek freighter—"

"Hold your fire, Corellian freighter," a voice cut him off. "Do not, repeat do *not* destroy the patrol boat you're sitting on. We want some of them alive."

"Understood, Suwantek," Han said carefully. The speaker hadn't identified himself, but his tone had sounded awfully military.

The remaining pirates apparently thought so, too. There was a lurch as the pirate ship poured power to its sublight engines, clearly trying to shake the *Falcon* off. There was an answering flash of red, a brilliant explosion from somewhere aft—

"There," the military voice said again as the pirate's drive shut down. "Again, Corellian, please hold your fire."

At least this time he'd said *please.* "No problem," Han assured him. "Actually, we want to talk to these guys, too."

"Excellent," the other said. "Wait there. We'll go aboard first."

"Sure," Han said. "Be my guest."

Chapter Twelve

THERE WERE TWO SURVIVORS ON THE REMAINING PIRATE SHIP. BOTH were young, both were terrified, and both were anxious to cooperate. Unfortunately, they had very little to cooperate with.

"I don't *know* where he came from," the slightly older of the two, Badji, insisted nervously. He started to gesture, but the motion was cut short by the binders fastening his arms to the cargo hold restraint ring. "One day he was just *there*, telling Captain Andel that the BloodScars wanted to bring all of us together into one big gang."

"What did Andel say?" Brightwater asked.

"He told Caaldra we'd think it over," Badji said. "But I don't think he was going to. I heard him say that it would be a cold day on—" He broke off, his eyes going suddenly wide. "Wait a minute. You're not—I mean—?"

"No, we're not the BloodScars," LaRone assured him. "Did this Caaldra leave Andel any contact information?"

Badji shook his head. "No, nothing."

"You're lying," Brightwater accused sharply. "He wouldn't have left without giving you a way to get in touch with him."

"But he didn't—I swear he didn't," Badji said, his whole body starting to shake. "He said he'd be back in a couple of weeks for Captain Andel's answer."

"And this was when?"

"Maybe a week ago," Badji said. "No, no — it was eight standard days. I remember because—"

"So you're telling me that if we want to talk to Caaldra, we're going to have to sit on you for another *week*?" Brightwater cut in.

"I don't *know* when he'll be back," Badji said, pleading now. "I'm not trying to pull anything—I swear I'm not."

"Of course not," LaRone said. He caught Brightwater's eye and nodded over his shoulder. Brightwater nodded back, and they left.

Marcross and Grave were waiting in the lounge, talking together in low voices. "Anything?" LaRone asked as he and Brightwater joined them.

"Nothing useful," Marcross said. "The BloodScars were definitely trying to recruit them, though—some merc type named Caaldra came by about a week ago, ready to lean on their chief."

"That's basically what we got," LaRone confirmed, feeling more than a little disgusted. They'd gone to all this effort hoping to track the Corellian to the BloodScars, and all they had to show for it was a couple of teenagers who'd thought it would be fun to join a gang and play pirate.

"What about the Corellian and his friends?" Brightwater asked. "Did we ever get anything on them?"

LaRone leaned over to touch the intercom. "Quiller, did anything come up on that team search?"

"The human–human–Wookiee one came up negative," Quiller's voice came back. "You want me to try human–Wookiee? Could be they picked up a friend."

"Let's hold off on that for now," LaRone said. Dipping into Imperial databases on this had been pushing it, and he didn't want to risk a second search too soon. "What are they doing?"

"Sitting quietly where we told them to," Quiller said. "The Surronian freighter hasn't tried to run, either."

"Cool customers," Brightwater commented.

"They were the same way back on Drunost," Grave reminded him. "I just wish I knew what their angle was."

"Maybe they were delivering a message," Brightwater suggested. "If this Caaldra character got the impression Andel was going to turn him down, he might have decided to show them why that would be a bad idea."

"Or maybe the Corellian *is* Caaldra," Marcross said suddenly. "He *did* tell us he wanted to talk to the survivors."

"Let's see if we can find out," LaRone said. "Quiller, give them a call and invite them aboard."

Han was up to his elbows in hyperdrive guts when the invitation came. "I appreciate the offer," he said as Luke held the headset to his ear. "But we're kind of busy right now—took a little feed-through damage in that last jolt."

"Sorry to hear that," the voice in his ear said. "Need any assistance?"

Han scowled. If the Suwantek's sensors had been as upgraded as its weapons, odds were they already knew what his hyperdrive was looking like. Not good even at the best of times, and this definitely wasn't one of those. "No, we can handle it," he said. "Just going to take a little time."

"Understood," the other said. "But I believe you expressed some interest in speaking to the pirates. We have two prisoners, but we also have limited time to spend in this system. If you're interested, you need to come over now."

Han looked at Luke. The other shrugged, but nodded. "Fine—we'll be right over," Han said. "You have a transfer tunnel that can lock with any of our hatches?"

"Even better—our ventral hatch has a universal collar," the other said. "We'll come up over you and lock to your upper hatch."

Han had already noted that the voice that had spoken to him had sounded military. Now, as he and Luke climbed the ladder from the Suwantek's lower hatch, he found that the two men waiting for them looked every bit as military as they had sounded.

"Welcome aboard," one of them said as Luke finished the climb and stepped to Han's side.

"Thanks," Han said, looking around. They were in a relatively wide corridor with six doors on either side and one in the forward bulkhead directly behind their two hosts. Crew cabins along the sides, probably, and either the bridge or a crew lounge forward. Glancing over his shoulder, he saw that the corridor widened briefly toward twin escape pod berths, then narrowed again to doors leading to cargo bays and engineering. "Nice ship."

"Thanks," the first man said. "My name's LaRone. This is Grave."

"Solo," Han introduced himself, feeling a twinge as he did so. There were any number of ways, legit and otherwise, for someone to check up on his identity, and lying about it would just make him look more suspicious. Besides, aside from the thing with Jabba and a couple of other minor problems, he wasn't in any particular trouble with anyone at the moment. At least, not if you didn't count that whole Death Star thing, which nobody could prove. "This is Luke."

LaRone nodded a greeting. "Who do you fly for?"

"We're independents," Han told him. "Pick up cargo where we can."

"Anyone else aboard your ship?"

"My first mate, Chewbacca," Han said.

"That's the Wookiee you saw on Drunost," Luke added.

Han threw the kid a warning look. But LaRone merely smiled. "Good—you remember us," he said. "We certainly remember *you*." He gestured toward the lightsaber hanging from Luke's belt. "You actually know how to use that thing?"

"A little," Luke said. "I'm still learning."

"Where'd you get it?"

"He stole it from a guy named Tooni," Han said impatiently. "What do you care where he got it from? You said we could talk to your prisoners?"

"In a minute," LaRone said. "First, I'd like to know what you were doing in that tapcafe in Conso City."

Han shrugged. "Having a quiet drink."

"Who was the fourth person at the table?"

"A friend," Luke said.

"One of the locals," Han put in before Luke could say anything else. "Is there some problem with him?"

"Could be," LaRone said. "Let me lay it out for you. You were on Drunost when a raider attack went down. The man you were sitting with had also been present at another attack a few days earlier, that one by a swoop gang. And now we find you here at Purnham at the scene of yet *another* attack."

"We're just doing a friend a favor," Han said, feeling sweat gathering under his collar. There were several directions LaRone could be going with this conversation, none of them good. "He told us a friend of his was having trouble with pirates on the Purnham run. We weren't especially busy, so we said we'd see if we could clear 'em out for him."

"We appreciate your help on that, by the way," Luke added.

"You're welcome," LaRone said. "We don't like pirates much, either. Can you tell us why this friend of yours was also present at both Drunost attacks?"

"For one thing, that's where he lives," Han said. "Besides, the hard part these days is *avoiding* trouble like that. The locals don't have the resources to chase down these raiders, and the Imperials seem to have dropped out of the fight completely."

"So you're saying it was pure coincidence?"

"Not entirely," Luke said.

Han twisted his head around, forcing back a curse. What was the kid *doing*? "Luke—"

"Explain," LaRone said, his eyes still on Han.

Luke flashed Han a slightly guilty look. But his voice was firm enough. "There's a pirate gang working this sector called the BloodScars," he said. "We understand they're trying to make deals with all the other local pirates and raiders."

"You have any basis for that besides rumors?" LaRone asked.

"The swoop gang you mentioned had shoulder patches with the Blood-Scar emblem," Luke said. "When we heard about the pirates here at Purnham, we thought we might be able to find out from them what the BloodScars are up to."

"Why do you care what a gang of pirates is doing?" Grave asked.

"Why do you think?" Han countered. "So we can figure out how to avoid them."

"Not because you want to join them?" LaRone countered, his voice suddenly sharp.

"No, we want to avoid them," Han repeated, a terrible thought icing its way through him. Up to now he'd been assuming LaRone was connected to Purnham law enforcement somehow, possibly a mercenary hired by the locals. But what if he was with the BloodScars? "But you guys seem to be on top of it," he added, taking a casual half step back toward the ladder. "Like Luke said, thanks for the help."

"What's your hurry?" LaRone asked. "I thought you wanted to talk to our prisoners."

"No, that's okay," Han said, taking another step toward the open hatch. Neither LaRone nor Grave seemed to be armed; if he could get Luke clued in on this, they might be able to duck down the ladder to the lower hatch before the rest of the Suwantek's crew could react.

Only Luke seemed to have missed the cue completely. He was still standing there, his head cocked a little to the side like he was listening to voices in his brain.

"I think you ought to hear what they have to say," LaRone persisted. He and Grave hadn't moved, either. Was Han the only one who was picking up on trouble here? He took another half step—

And then, abruptly, Luke's hand snaked out to grab his left arm. "It's all right, Han," he said, staring at LaRone. "They're not with the BloodScars."

"Who said they were?" Han protested, stifling another curse. That tore it. Swinging his left arm in a wide movement designed to shake off Luke's hand and simultaneously draw LaRone's and Grave's eyes in that direction, he dropped his right hand to his side—

"Don't," a voice advised from behind him.

Han froze, his hand bare centimeters from his blaster, and looked carefully over his shoulder.

Two men stood there, cut from the same ex-military cloth as LaRone and Grave, their blasters leveled at him and Luke.

And Han hadn't even heard any of the doors open. These guys were smooth, all right. "Okay," he said as calmly as he could as he turned back to LaRone. "Now what?"

"That depends," LaRone said, stepping forward and relieving Han of his blaster. With only a slight hesitation, he took Luke's lightsaber, as well. "Let's start with exactly who—and what—you and your friends are."

"Like I said, we're independent shippers," Han told him.

"With dual quad lasers on your ship?" LaRone asked pointedly. "Try again."

"We need those for protection."

"I'm sure you do," LaRone said. "Tell me, if we searched your holds right now, would we find anything that shouldn't be there?"

"Absolutely not," Han assured him. For a change, it was even true. "We're not smugglers."

"Of course not," LaRone said. "Back to the BloodScars. You genuinely think they're trying to create their own little copy of the Rebel Alliance here in Shelsha sector?"

"I'd call it more like a Hutt pyramid," Han said, a small part of his mind wondering why he found LaRone's comparison so irritating. Certainly that *was* what the Rebel Alliance was, when you boiled it down: a big illegal group of lots of other illegal groups. "But yeah, I think they could be trying something like that."

"Good," LaRone said. "Because that's exactly what they *are* doing. Our prisoners say an agent from the BloodScars came by only a week ago pressuring them to join up. He's supposed to return soon for their answer."

Han frowned as it suddenly hit him. "And you think one of *us* is the agent?"

"The thought *had* crossed our minds," LaRone said. "Rather ironically, since I gather you were wondering the same thing about us."

"Well, we're not," Han said firmly.

"Can you prove that?"

"We helped you blow away these other pirates," Han reminded him. "Not the sort of thing recruiters usually do."

"Maybe the Purnham group had already turned down the BloodScars' invitation," LaRone pointed out. "Our prisoners say their chief was leaning that way. In that case, you might have been sent to create an object lesson."

"Or maybe he *didn't* turn him down," Han said. "In *that* case, we just have to sit here until they send someone back here for his answer."

"What, wait another week?" LaRone shook his head. "We can't afford to sit around here that long."

"Maybe there's another way," Luke spoke up.

LaRone eyed him. "We're listening."

"If they *did* turn down the BloodScars, they probably did it through the HoloNet," Luke said. "If they did, and if we can get the local station's call log, the contact may still be in there."

Han winced. A call log was useless in itself—all it would show was all the planets that had been called in a given time frame, and even a world as small as Purnham put out a *lot* of HoloNet traffic. There was no reason for Luke to even bring it up unless he had something else to add to the mix.

"Let's assume we can get the log," LaRone said, a note of fresh interest in his voice. He'd probably tracked through the logic the same way Han had. "Then what?"

"Then we—"

"What's *your* interest in all this?" Han cut him off. He was pretty sure he knew what Luke had in mind, and there was no way he was going to give that up. Not until he knew what side LaRone and his friends were on.

"The same as yours," LaRone said, frowning at the interruption. "Only instead of just avoiding the BloodScars, we want to wipe them out." Reaching into his pocket, he pulled out an official-looking identity tag. "We're with Consolidated Shipping Security."

"Oh," Han said, the hairs on the back of his neck starting to tingle. "Well. I guess you're all right, then."

"I told you they were," Luke murmured.

Han grimaced. Yes, the kid had said that, all right.

Problem was, the kid was wrong.

"But I believe you were starting to say something?" Grave said, raising his eyebrows at Luke.

"Not really," Han said, giving Luke a warning glance. "He sometimes pops off his mouth before he thinks things through."

"*Enough,*" LaRone snapped.

Han jerked at the sudden flash of fury, his hand dropping automatically to his empty holster.

"No more games," LaRone bit out. "These pirates are a threat to the entire sector. If you have information about them, let's have it. *Now.*"

Han gazed at him, the bitter taste of distant memory welling up on the back of his tongue. He'd had that same noble fervor once, back before the Empire's basic fundamental cruelty had finally gotten through to him.

And it was a righteous passion no pirate or raider could ever counterfeit. Whoever these men were, they weren't with the BloodScars. "Let me use your comm a minute."

LaRone studied his face. "In here," he said, stepping to one side and gesturing to the door behind him.

Beyond the door, as Han had guessed, was a crew lounge. "We can patch you through the intercom," LaRone said, pointing to an entertainment computer desk. "Quiller?"

"Who do you want to talk to?" a voice asked from the speaker.

"Our friend in the freighter out there," Han said, sitting down at the computer. A keyboard lit up, and he punched in Casement's comm frequency. "Casement, it's Solo."

"About time," Casement's voice growled. "Are you all right? Chewbacca said you'd gone aboard the Suwantek—"

"We're fine," Han interrupted. "Porter said you had a brush with the BloodScars off Ashkas-kov a couple months ago. Did you get their vector when they left?"

"Yes," Casement said, sounding puzzled. "But there's no reason to think they were going anywhere in particular."

"I'm betting they were headed home," Han said. "Porter told us everyone was dead except you, and they thought you were, too. No reason for them to hide where they were going."

"I suppose," Casement said. "You want me to send you the vector?"

"If you haven't got anything better to do," Han said, trying hard not to be sarcastic. These Rebel types could be ridiculously slow sometimes.

"Sure," Casement growled. "Just let me put down the hook-point scarf I was working on."

Han rolled his eyes. Slow *and* snippy. "Anytime."

"Here it comes," Casement said.

"Got it," Quiller's voice confirmed.

Han looked at LaRone. "Now what?"

LaRone looked at Grave. "Tell him he can go, with our thanks."

"Our new friends say you can take off," Han relayed. "Good flying."

"You, too," Casement said. "And thanks for your help. You *and* your new friends."

There was a soft click as the contact was broken. "There he goes," Quiller reported.

"So now all we have to do is hit up the HoloNet station and see what kind of messages they sent to systems along that vector," Han said. "That pretty much what you had in mind, Luke?"

"Yes," Luke confirmed.

"Let's hope they like Consolidated Shipping people down there," Han added, eyeing LaRone closely.

The other's face didn't even twitch. "Fortunately, we won't have to find out," he said. "As it happens, we already have the Conso City HoloNet records from just after the swooper attack." He smiled faintly. "That's why *we* were on Drunost. We thought that whatever was left of the gang might have called big brother for help." He gestured to one of the two men who'd played backstop earlier. "Marcross?"

"I'll set up the program," Marcross said, giving Han a speculative look as he brushed past. He went through a door at the forward end of the lounge, and Han caught a glimpse of a cockpit anteroom before the door closed again.

"This is Brightwater, by the way," LaRone added, gesturing to the remaining man.

"Nice to meet you," Han said. "I guess we'll be off, then. If I could have my blaster back?"

"What's your hurry?" Brightwater asked.

"Independent shippers, remember?" Han said. "We've got a schedule to keep."

"What schedule?" Brightwater countered. "You haven't got any cargo."

"*And* you have a damaged hyperdrive," Grave added.

"It's not *that* damaged," Han said.

"Let's cut to the core," LaRone said. "Bottom line is, we're not sure we want to let you out of our sight just yet."

The hairs on the back of Han's neck were starting to tingle again. "We gave you that vector," he pointed out.

"There could be any number of reasons the BloodScars wouldn't mind us having that," LaRone countered. "It could lead to a base they've already abandoned, or into a trap."

"But don't worry," Grave assured him. "I think you'll find the accommodations up to independent shipper standards."

"Great," Han growled. "We're dead."

"If you'll call the Wookiee up here, we'll be off," LaRone said. "He's to come unarmed, of course."

"What about our ship?" Han asked, keeping his expression neutral. *Unarmed Wookiee*—now *there* was a contradiction in terms. "We can't just leave it here."

"Quiller?" LaRone called.

"No problem," the pilot's voice came. "We can lock it to the hatch collar and take it in tow."

"You're kidding," Han said, frowning. "The *Falcon*'s as big as you are."

"It'll work," Quiller assured him. "Trust me—we've got power to spare."

"Call the Wookiee," LaRone said. "Then we'll show you to your quarters."

The cabin door slid shut on the glowering Wookiee. LaRone double-checked the lock, and then he, Brightwater, and Grave returned to the lounge.

Marcross and Quiller were waiting for them there, Marcross still seated at the computer desk. "They all happily snugged in?" Quiller asked.

"As happily as possible, which isn't very," LaRone told him. "Opinions?"

"There's definitely something off key about them," Brightwater said. "I just don't know yet what it is."

"How sure are we they *aren't* with the BloodScars?" Grave asked. "A smart enforcer might have been able to spin that kind of story for us on the fly. Might even have been willing to frost those local pirate ships to throw us off the mark."

"Maybe, but it doesn't explain their work at Conso City," Quiller pointed out. "According to the latest reports, the raiders made off with about fifty thousand in cash, plus a few passengers."

"The BloodScars picking up the swoop gang survivors," Brightwater murmured.

"With the robbery as a diversion or cover," Quiller said, nodding. "And Solo and his friends were definitely working against them."

"Part of a rival gang, then?" Grave suggested.

"Possible," LaRone said. "But they just don't feel like pirates to me."

"You're sure you're not letting that lightsaber influence you?" Grave countered.

LaRone snorted. "Not when the only other person I've ever actually seen carrying one is Lord Vader."

"Interesting you should mention Vader," Marcross said thoughtfully. "There was a rumor making the rounds awhile back about some special Imperial agent called the Emperor's Hand who's popped up onto the scene. Reports directly to Palpatine, outranks practically everyone in the Empire—"

"*And* carries a lightsaber," Brightwater said suddenly. "Yeah, I heard that same rumor."

"Rumors being worth half a credit a truckload, of course," LaRone reminded them.

"But it's definitely the sort of thing Palpatine would do," Marcross pointed out. "Look at how he tried to outflank the regular military establishment with the ISB and the Grand Admirals."

"You think Luke might be this Emperor's Hand?" Grave asked doubtfully. "I don't know. He doesn't seem the type, somehow."

"Maybe that's what he *wants* you to think," Marcross said. There was a beep from the computer, and he swiveled back around. "Got it," he said, peering at the display. "Correlation between Solo's vector and our HoloNet data gives us exactly one system: Gepparin. A few farming settlements, a good-sized mining complex, and not much else."

"Good spot for a pirate hideout," Brightwater commented. "How far out is it?"

"About forty hours," Marcross said. He cocked an eyebrow at LaRone. "I trust you weren't planning to show our guests our shiny white dress outfits?"

"Not to worry," LaRone said. "As long as they're locked in their cabins, we can come and go as we please."

"Speaking of locking, I hope someone remembered to lock down the armories in those three rooms," Quiller warned.

"I did," Brightwater assured him. "There's a simple sequence in the cabin computers that can lock and unlock them. What about the two kids in the hold?"

"Purnham security's going to take them off our hands," Quiller said. "Their brig shuttle's on its way now."

"Good," LaRone said. "Quiller, set course for Gepparin. We'll leave as soon as the prisoners are off."

Chapter Thirteen

MARA'S TRAINING HAD INCLUDED A BASIC OVERVIEW OF STARSHIP OP-
eration, but most of that had been geared to military craft. Fortunately, Tannis seemed to know his way around civilian ships like the
Happer's Way, as did the two men Colonel Somoril had sent with her.

Mara had dealt occasionally with ISB men, and generally found them
to be rather cold fish. But even by that standard Brock and Gilling were ex-
ceptional. They were unbendingly formal, keeping to themselves and
away from both her and Tannis as much as possible. Even when accepting
and carrying out orders, they spoke no more than necessary, often completing a job in complete silence. They asked no questions, made no comments, indulged in no idle chatter. For all their companionship, Ozzel
might as well have given her a pair of maintenance droids.

As a result, Mara focused on Tannis, spending as much free time with
him as possible as she tried to learn everything she could about this nest of
gundarks she was flying into.

The BloodScars had apparently been on Gepparin for only two years,
having taken over the big mining complex at that time. They had set up
their base in one half, Tannis explained, leaving the other half still pulling
out low-grade ore as a cover for their other activities. Most of their loot was
taken directly to the base, where it was sorted and repackaged into ore
crates and sent out either directly to buyers or to various warehouses like
the Birtraub Brothers operation on Crovna.

"But there are a few cargoes that go directly to Caaldra," Tannis added as he sketched out a floor plan of the base. "This ship was supposed to be one of them, actually. Taking it to Gepparin could get us in trouble."

"Blame it on Shakko for dying with that data instead of surrendering like I told him to," Mara said.

"Blame it on anyone you want, but it's going to be trouble," Tannis warned. "I hope your buddies back there are good fighters. *And* that they don't start blasting before they have to."

"Captain Ozzel wouldn't have given us anyone but the best," Mara assured him, wishing she actually believed that. Knowing ISB, it was more likely Somoril had picked a pair of expendables. "How many crew are typically at the base?"

"Depends on whether there are any ships there," Tannis said. "There are only thirty or so full-timers, but a couple of unloading ships could double that."

"Any idea how many ships might be there right now?"

Tannis shook his head. "With all these other gangs Caaldra and the Commodore have been bringing into the nest, your guess is as good as mine."

Mara nodded. Apparently they would have to find out the hard way. "So what's behind all this, anyway? I assume Caaldra is smart enough to realize that creating a huge pirate gang just begs Shelkonwa *and* Imperial Center to come down on you."

"Caaldra is mostly noise," Tannis said contemptuously. "Well, noise and credits."

"Any idea how much he's dropped on the whole operation?"

"Not really," Tannis said. "But it's one to five million straight up front to every group that signs on, plus a bonus if they've got a lot of ships or special skills or something."

And Moff Glovstoak had shelled out a good six to eight hundred million in embezzled money for the artworks Mara had found in his safe. Depending on how much of that Caaldra and the BloodScars had gone through, they could be looking at a coalition of more than a hundred raider gangs.

All of them apparently in this single sector. What was so special about this sector? "Well, I'm sure the Commodore knows all that," she said.

Tannis snorted. "Question is, can you get him to tell you?"

Mara shrugged. "We'll find out."

Gepparin was a cold, dark world circling a red star, one of a trinary system that also included a small yellow star and a brilliant blue-white one. Tannis had threaded them neatly between the two brighter stars and was bringing them in toward the planet when the first challenge came.

It was, not surprisingly, perfectly civil. "Incoming Rendili freighter, this is Gepparin Landing Control," a cultured voice said. "Please identify yourself and your parent transport corporation."

"Hey, Capper, it's Tannis," Tannis said. "Is the Commodore around?"

There was a brief silence. "What are you doing here, Tannis?" Capper asked. He didn't sound nearly so cultured now. "Where's Shakko?"

"Still with the *Cavalcade*—they had some work to do on it," Tannis told him, throwing Mara a sideways look. "We've got some possible new allies aboard."

"*Possible* allies?" Capper said ominously. "You brought them here and they're only *possible* allies?"

"Laser cannons coming online," Brock murmured from the sensor station behind Mara.

"Where?" Mara murmured back.

"Midway up those drill derricks," he said, pointing at the intricate framework of buildings and support structures on the main display.

"Hey, chill out, Capper," Tannis chided. "They want to join—trust me. They just need to work out the details."

"Fine—we'll play," Capper said. "Pad Eight. Don't lower your ramp until the reception committee gets there."

The comm clicked off. "What kind of ships are we reading down there?" Mara asked.

"Aside from five small insystem ore transports, I see two actual freighters," Brock reported. "Probably both are pirates."

"They are," Tannis confirmed tightly. Now that he was no longer having to play a role, the tension was back in his voice. "That size, I'd say fifteen to twenty crewers each. Means there could be as many as seventy pirates total on the ground."

"I'm more interested in this reception committee," Gilling said darkly.

"Were you expecting an open door and the key to the Commodore's quarters?" Tannis growled back. "They don't trust you. I wouldn't, either, if it was me down there."

"Calm it, everyone," Mara ordered. "We go in unarmed and let them convince themselves we're harmless."

"What do you mean, unarmed?" Gilling demanded.

"The word is straightforward enough," Mara told him. "No weapons, no equipment that anyone might think could be weapons, no harmless devices that could be turned into weapons."

"They'd take anything like that away from you anyway," Tannis said.

"Exactly," Mara said. "And above all, relax. We're not here to start a fight. We're here to talk politely with possible allies, pull a little information, and leave." She looked at Tannis. "Peaceably," she added.

Pad 8 was a circle of heavy gridwork mesh surrounded claustrophobically on three sides by derricks and catwalks and connecting support girders. It was a difficult area to get into, and would be even harder to get out of.

Tannis, fortunately, was up to the challenge, easing them through the obstructions without trouble. As he set the freighter down in the center of the grating, Mara could see the promised reception committee emerging from the buildings and maintenance hangars in front of them. There were about two dozen men and aliens total, half of them crowded into a pair of approaching landspeeders, the others spreading out on foot a cautious distance back. All of them were armed with belted sidearms, blaster rifles, or both.

"And they'll have heavier stuff pointed at us from the derricks and catwalk supports," Tannis warned as he shut down the systems. "Try anything, and you'll be slagged where you stand."

"No one's going to try anything," Mara promised, peering out the canopy. The structural maze around them, plus the relatively dim light from Gepparin's red sun, was creating a labyrinth of small shadows that stretched all the way across the mining area to the pirate base half of the complex. "As soon as you finish shutting down, get to the ramp," she ordered Tannis as she headed to the cockpit door. "Brock, Gilling, go with him."

"Where are you going?" Tannis asked suspiciously.

"I'll be there before you have to open up," Mara told him, and left.

The pirates, she knew, would be watching the hatches and access panels for any tricks their visitors might have planned. Fortunately, Mara had something else in mind.

She reached the engine room and popped the maintenance access cover leading to a thermal vent beneath the engines. Pulling a pair of black combat gloves from her dark green jumpsuit, she slipped one over each end of her lightsaber haft, leaving only the middle few centimeters of shiny metal uncovered. In the relative darkness out there, the gloves should adequately shield the weapon from unfriendly eyes. Sliding the weapon into the opening, she used the Force to maneuver it down the narrow passageway and around the corner toward the outlet.

The others were waiting at the hatchway when she arrived. "Anything?" she asked as she quickly gathered her hair into a ponytail where it would be out of the way and secured it with a decorative fan-shaped comb.

"They haven't knocked yet, if that's what you mean," Tannis said. "Probably looking over the hull for anything cute we might have done."

"They're welcome to do so," Mara said calmly. It would take a very close examination of the vent to spot the glove-covered lightsaber, and she wasn't expecting them to be that thorough. At least, not until they'd had a good hard look at the ship's crew.

From outside came the dull thud of a blaster grip against metal. "Here we go," Tannis said, taking a deep breath and keying the release. Motioning Brock and Gilling to bring up the rear, Mara followed him out.

The dozen men from the landspeeders were waiting, spread out in a standard guard semicircle a few paces back from the end of the ramp, their weapons drawn and ready. "Hey, Bobbler," Tannis said, nodding to the large man in the center of the arc. "You guys mind pointing those things somewhere else?"

"That's far enough," Bobbler ordered, his eyes flicking between Mara and the two ISB men. "Tannis, come here. Alone."

Silently, Tannis obeyed. The pirate to Bobbler's right stepped forward with a handheld scanner and ran it quickly over Tannis's body. "Looks clean," he announced.

"Yeah, and looks can get you killed," Bobbler said, his eyes shifting to Mara. "We'll check him inside. You—girl—come here."

"The name's Celina," Mara said as she walked over to him.

"Whatever," Bobbler said, looking her up and down. "What are you, the extra bonus prize?"

"She's part of a gang—" Tannis began.

"Shut up," Bobbler cut him off. "Vinis, Waggral—search her." He grinned evilly. "See if she's got anything interesting in there."

Two of the pirates holstered their blasters and swaggered forward. "Wait a second," Tannis said, his voice rising with alarm. "Jorhim could just scan her—"

"If I have to tell you to shut up again, it'll be with my blaster butt," Bobbler growled. "Is she special to you or something?"

Tannis closed his mouth firmly, but Mara could see his throat working. Turning slightly, she sent warning looks at Brock and Gilling, then turned back to face Bobbler. "You really shouldn't deal with guests this way," she commented.

"Oh?" he countered. "What way is that?"

The two men reached Mara, and the first man's fingers started to close around her right upper arm. Mara moved her arm inward in response, the motion breaking his partial grip even as it pulled him slightly off balance. Cursing under his breath, he lunged toward her, grabbing again for the arm. Mara leaned a little farther out of his reach, then dropped suddenly into a crouch as the second man also tried to grab her. Both sets of hands swept uselessly through the air above her head; snapping her own hands out to both sides, Mara delivered a double punch into their exposed stomachs, then deftly yanked their blasters from their holsters.

The men recovered from the punches and tried again. But again they were a fraction of a second too late. Mara stood upright, swinging the blasters upward as she did so to deliver solid blows to their jaws.

And as they staggered backward, she flipped the weapons around into firing position and pointed both of them at Bobbler.

For a second she held that pose, stretching out with her senses as she gauged the stunned silence around her. Before any of the pirates could recover enough to start wondering if he should try to be a hero, she raised the weapons to point at the sky. "I meant your men should disarm themselves before searching people," she said mildly. Flipping the blasters around again in her hands to grip the barrels, she stepped forward and offered them to Bobbler.

He ignored the weapons, his eyes hard on her. "Was that supposed to impress us?" he demanded.

"I certainly hope so," she said. "Shakko said you pay sign-up bonuses to people with special talents."

Bobbler snorted derisively. Still, Mara could see a new level of respect in his eyes. "Nothing special I can see," he said with a sneer as he finally took the blasters from her. "And you're still not getting in without a search."

Silently, Mara held her arms out to the sides. Bobbler hesitated, then caught the eye of the man with the scanner and gestured him forward. Mara held her pose as he quickly and a little gingerly ran the scanner over her body. "She's clean," the man said. "You want me to do the others?"

Bobbler sent a speculative look at Brock and Gilling. "You two also feeling like trouble today?" he challenged as he motioned Vinis and Waggral over and handed them back their blasters.

"They do nothing without my orders," Mara said before either could answer. "If you want to search them the old-style way, be my guest."

She'd half expected Bobbler to back down. Instead he nodded and gestured, and four more men left the line. This time, one of each pair handed his blaster to his partner first. The partners, for their part, made sure to stay back out of reach.

The searches were quick and thorough. Mara tried to read the two Imperials as the pirates ran rough hands through their clothing, but if either of them was angry or discomfited she couldn't sense it. "Tannis, you go with Rer'chof," Bobbler ordered when they were finished. "Jorhim, take a squad and check out the ship, and I mean all the way down to the rivets. You"—he pointed at Mara and the Imperials—"come with me."

He led them to one of the two landspeeders, motioning Mara, Brock, and Gilling into the backseat as he climbed into the driver's seat. One of the other pirates got in beside him, turning around and resting the muzzle of his blaster warningly on the seat cushion. Vinis and Waggral climbed up onto the back, blasters in hand. Tannis and one of the other pirates got into the second landspeeder, and they were off.

Mara let them get about twenty meters, then half turned in her seat to look back at the *Happer's Way*. "I hope they know how to properly search a ship," she commented to no one in particular. Shifting her eyes aft, she stretched out with the Force and slid her glove-covered lightsaber out from the thermal vent.

Bobbler grunted. "Don't worry, they won't wreck anything."

There were no shouts of reaction at the lightsaber's appearance. Lowering the weapon nearly to the mesh of the pad, Mara sent it speeding silently to a nearby gantry and along its side, keeping it in shadow as much as she could.

"Unless it *needs* wrecking," Vinis added, jabbing his blaster into her shoulder for emphasis.

"Glad to hear it," Mara said. The lightsaber was nearly to the gantry operator's station; shifting direction, she ran it over to one of the horizontal support girders and began paralleling the landspeeders' own course.

Bobbler drove them around one of the support buildings, between a pair of separator towers, and across an arched bridge to the other half of the complex. Through it all Mara kept the lightsaber pacing them, the small section of uncovered metal just visible. As they pulled away from the taller structures and machinery she sent the weapon into the shadow of a guy cable, and as the cable angled off toward a section of cliff face she jumped it finally across a short stretch of empty air to the cluster of linked two- and three-story buildings Bobbler was driving toward. Many of the windows showed lights; picking a dark section on the top floor of one of the taller buildings, she eased the lightsaber into concealment in the rain catcher running along the roof just above the window.

Bobbler parked outside one of the doors and led the way inside to what had probably once been a miners' prep room. It had been converted into a pirate-style welcoming center, complete with scanners, wall restraints, and a dozen more armed pirates. Under their watchful eyes Mara and her companions were run through each of the scanners in a sequence designed to progressively study them, from clothing and skin down to the near-molecular level. The pirates took special care with her hair comb, taking it away for its own set of scans.

"Looks good," Bobbler said when they were finished. "You—Celina— come with me."

"What about my men?" Mara asked.

"They're going somewhere else," Bobbler said, handing her back her comb and waiting while she fixed it into her hair again. Then, picking out a four-man escort, he led her through an armored door into a maze of rooms and corridors and connection tubes. Finally, two buildings over, they reached a large, hot, humid room. In the center of the floor was a large sunken oval pool, which seemed to be generating most of the heat and all of the humidity. Four large armed men stood around the head of the pool, their faces and clothing damp as they watched Mara and her escort approach.

Floating in the pool was a man.

A smallish, slender, clean-shaven man, Mara noted as Bobbler led her toward the pool. He was dressed in a plain white floater suit, his arms and legs splayed slightly apart as he drifted on the gently rippling water. A soft blindfold mask, also white, covered his face from forehead to nose. At each side of the room, apparently taking advantage of the heat and steam, were five more men dressed in thick white robes with towels over their heads. The backup bodyguards, undoubtedly.

"Come in," the man in the pool called as they approached. "Is this our audacious little ship thief?"

"It is, Commodore," Bobbler confirmed, motioning Mara to step to the end of the pool. "She calls herself Celina."

"A nice name," the Commodore said approvingly. "You have a voice, Celina?"

"I do, Commodore," Mara said.

"Excellent," the Commodore said. "Describe yourself for me."

Frowning, Mara looked at Bobbler. The other nodded and gestured for her to proceed. "I'm about medium height—" she began.

"How tall exactly?" the Commodore interrupted.

"One point six meters," Mara told him. "I have a slender build, red-gold hair, and green eyes."

"How is your hair arranged?"

"At the moment, it's in a ponytail fastened with a fan comb," Mara said.

"I prefer a woman's hair to be down," the Commodore said. "You sound quite attractive. Are you?"

Mara looked at Bobbler, who merely shrugged. "Various acquaintances have said so on occasion," she said.

"Good," the Commodore said. "Please don't dismiss me as an eccentric or, worse, insane. What I am doing here is silencing all my other senses, the better to hear your voice and judge your honesty. Does that worry you?"

"Not really," Mara said, not entirely candidly. Some members of the Emperor's court had experimented with similar sense-deadening tricks for the same purpose, and a few of them had gotten quite adept at it. Depending on the Commodore's skill, he might even be able to sniff out the lies of a trained Imperial agent.

Or, at least, those of a normal Imperial agent. For Mara, there were tricks of equal subtlety she could use against him. Reaching out with the Force, she began to gently stir the water.

"So: to business," the Commodore said. "I understand you like to hijack ships."

"We don't necessarily *like* it," Mara said. "But yes, it *is* our job."

The Commodore's mouth hardened. "I understand you like to hijack *my* ships."

"My apologies," Mara said, starting to stir some of the water in the other direction. The gentle ripples took on an equally gentle crosshatch appearance as the new pattern collided with the old. "In my defense, let me remind you that it wasn't yet *your* ship when we started our operation. Certainly if we'd known the BloodScars were interested, we'd have kept our hands off."

"What were you planning to do with the cargo?"

"Sell it, of course," Mara said, letting her eyes drift. There were a handful of louvered vents spaced around the room where the walls and ceiling intersected. Stretching out again, she opened two of the louvers a little farther than the others. "We ourselves certainly have no use for AT-STs."

"Who was your buyer?"

"We didn't have one yet," Mara said. A light breeze drifted across her face; hastily she closed the vents down a bit. The idea was to add a little distraction to the Commodore's other senses, but at a low-enough level that even he wouldn't be aware of it. "But we would probably have tried the Hutts first."

"A highly valuable cargo," the Commodore said. "Yet Shakko allowed you to simply fly away with it?"

Mara shrugged. "The *Happer's Way* was flyable; the *Cavalcade* wasn't. Shakko and I discussed the situation and decided you'd probably prefer having a freighter and cargo to having the cargo alone."

"Yet Shakko allowed you to simply fly away with it?" the Commodore repeated.

Mara suppressed a grimace. Either he'd heard something in her voice just then, or else the distractions were starting to get to him and he wanted a second take on her answer. "He *did* put Tannis aboard to make sure we behaved ourselves," she reminded him.

"As if Tannis could have stopped you," the Commodore said contemptuously.

"Well . . . probably not," Mara conceded. "Still, we *did* deliver it intact."

"Wise of you," the Commodore said. "Did Shakko happen to mention that the cargo is not mine, but belongs to our patron?"

"Yes, we discussed that aspect," Mara confirmed, feeling her heartbeat pick up a little. *Patron.* Now if she could just get him to mention a name . . . "We concluded that—"

"You're lying."

Mara froze. Had he sensed the sudden heightened interest beneath the words? "I'm not lying," she protested, trying to buy a little time. The four nearest bodyguards would have to be taken out first, and she'd have to make sure to get hold of at least one blaster in the process.

"You are," the Commodore shot back. "Shakko would never have mentioned our patron."

And with that, Mara felt her tension wash away. So he hadn't heard anything incriminating, but was simply using supposition and logic against her. "Well, he did," she insisted. "He told us someone named Caaldra was waiting for the goods."

"*Caaldra?*" Abruptly, the Commodore laughed, the suspicion vanishing even as the movement sent small waves through the water. "Oh, no, no. Caaldra isn't our patron. He merely works for him."

"Oh," Mara said, putting a little chagrinned embarrassment into her voice. As a general rule, whenever an opponent found a way to feel superior to her, in even the smallest way, she'd found it wise to nurture that misconception. "Well, the way Shakko talked, he sure *sounded* like a patron."

"I'm sure he did," the Commodore said, the brief flicker of humor gone. "Tell me how you hijacked the freighter."

"It wasn't difficult," Mara said. "We overpowered the crew—"

"*How* did you overpower them?" the Commodore cut in. "Which rooms and stations did you take first? Which of you did which job? I want details."

Were Brock and Gilling being separately asked the same questions so that the three sets of answers could be compared? Probably. Fortunately, Mara had anticipated this one. "I'm sorry," she said. "Those details are what give us our edge in this business. We don't reveal them to anyone."

"Even if I order all of you killed as a consequence?"

"If you order us killed, then we die," Mara countered. "But that would end any chance of our organizations ever working together, which would mean you'd continue to waste your victims' ships instead of capturing them intact."

She raised her eyes to the four sweating men standing at the far end of the pool. "And trying to kill us would also cost you more of your men than I think you really want to lose," she added.

"Is that a threat?"

Mara shook her head. "Merely stating a fact."

"Of course," the Commodore said, his voice darkening. "Facts. Truth, in neatly packaged form. Perhaps I should give *your* neatly packaged body to my patron. It was his cargo you stole, after all." He raised his voice. "What do you think, Caaldra? Would he like a pretty young ship thief to play with?"

"I'm sure he'd find her fascinating," a familiar voice said from the right side of the room.

Mara turned her head. The five robed men sitting there had thrown off the towels that had been hiding their faces. The one in the middle was Caaldra, flanked by two large men she didn't recognize. At Caaldra's far right, staring at her from a taut and heat-reddened face, was Tannis. "Who are you?" Mara asked.

"Why, this is Caaldra," the Commodore said as Caaldra and two of the men came toward the pool. "The man your stolen cargo belongs to . . . and the man who came here to warn us about you, Celina Ship Thief." He paused dramatically, and something in the half of his face Mara could see warned her that he was suddenly listening very hard. "Or should I say, Celina *Imperial Agent?*"

Silently, without any obvious orders, the four men at the head of the pool drew their blasters. With a supreme effort, Mara kept her face expressionless as she looked again at Tannis's pinched expression. So all her instincts, not to mention her threats and bribes, had been for nothing. Tannis had betrayed her. "Oh, so now I'm an Imperial agent?" she retorted, putting some contempt into her voice. There was certainly no point in making this easy for them. "How very convenient. For someone."

"What are you talking about?" the Commodore demanded.

"I'm talking about how convenient it is that there's a stranger in town whom your friend can point fingers at." She eyed Caaldra as he came to a stop a couple of meters from her. "Let me guess. Things aren't going too well at his end?"

Caaldra's face hardened. "Nice try, Imperial, but you're wasting your time," he growled. "The Commodore knows who *I* am."

"I never said he didn't," Mara countered, intrigued by the intensity of his retort. Did that mean things really *weren't* going well for him and his patron? "I'm just pointing out that shifting blame is a time-honored way of trying to wriggle out of trouble."

She had hoped to goad him into continuing his rant and perhaps saying something useful. But the moment had passed, and he was back on balance. "Sounds just like what *you're* trying to do right now," he countered calmly.

"I'm just trying to keep the Commodore from making a mistake that will cost him potential allies, and possibly cost *me* my life," Mara said. "So let's stop the posturing and snarl-words and figure out how I can prove who I am."

"You could tell us exactly how you gained possession of the *Happer's Way*, as the Commodore asked," Caaldra said. "Or you could take me to your alleged base to talk to your alleged chief."

"Not until we have a deal," Mara said firmly, part of her wondering why she was still playing this game. Tannis's betrayal made the whole thing rather ridiculous.

And then, suddenly, it struck her. Caaldra and the Commodore both had referred to her as simply an Imperial agent.

But Tannis knew that her actual title was Emperor's Hand.

She looked again at Tannis, realizing now that the tension in his face was not due to betrayal, but to the knowledge that his head was on the execution block right beside Mara's.

And with that, she suddenly had her way out.

"Look, you can just ask Tannis," she offered, gesturing toward him. "He was there—he saw how the *Happer's Way*'s defenses crumbled practically before their attack got going. Ask *him* how an Imperial agent could possibly have known you were going to hit that particular freighter." She looked back at Caaldra. "Unless you're also suggesting Shakko or one of his men leaked that information."

Caaldra glared at her. But he clearly had no answer. "Tannis?" the Commodore invited.

Tannis shot Mara a hooded look, and it didn't require the Force to recognize that he was in a quiet panic at the thought of trying to lie to the Commodore, especially here in his private truth-detection chamber.

But there was, in fact, no need to worry. Mara was back on balance, and with balance came control of the situation. Reaching out with the Force, she gave a slight tap to one of the bodyguards' blasters, knocking the weapon from his hand.

He tried to get it back. He really did. But the heat in the room had left both his hands and the blaster itself sweaty, and there had been no hint of anything beforehand to warn his reflexes, and there simply wasn't enough time. The weapon slipped through his desperate attempts to grab it, bounced with an echoing clank off the tiled floor, and landed with a resounding splash in the pool.

Mara half expected the Commodore to bellow with surprise or anger. But he didn't make a sound as he bounced across the fresh wave pattern, the echoes fading away. In some ways, Mara thought, his lack of reaction was more unnerving than any outburst would have been.

Certainly the offender seemed to think so. He froze, his face going pale behind the sheen of sweat. The Commodore let the silence drag out another five or six seconds, then took a careful breath. "You may retrieve your weapon, Nirsh," he said, his voice almost calm.

Nirsh's face went a little paler. "Yes, sir," he said, dropping down on his knees and burying his right arm up to the shoulder into the pool. A little scrabbling around, and he pulled out the dripping blaster. "And you will now put yourself on report," the Commodore said. "Tannis?"

"Yes, sir?" Tannis said. His expression hadn't changed, but Mara could sense the relief behind his eyes. "Oh—yes, sir. I don't really know how they did it, sir. But she's right. They were putting up a real good fight—had already blown a nasty line across the comm antenna, in fact—when suddenly they just stopped."

"Or maybe they just decided to let you live so they could find this base," Caaldra suggested darkly.

"Why bother?" Mara countered. "Any Imperial agent worth the title would know how to pull a data dump from the nav computer of a wrecked ship." She raised her eyebrows. "*And* an Imperial agent wouldn't have come here alone. He'd have brought a stormtrooper legion and some serious air support."

"Maybe they got lost along the way," Caaldra shot back.

"Careless of them," Mara said sarcastically. "When they catch up, do let me know." She turned back to the Commodore. "So are you interested in working with us, Commodore, or aren't you?"

For a moment, he didn't reply. Then, carefully, he paddled his way to the edge of the pool and got a hand on it, letting his legs dip down out of sight into the water. "You intrigue me, Celina Ship Thief," he said. "We will speak again after the evening meal."

He pulled off his half mask and blinked up at her. "Your acquaintances are quite correct," he said, running his eyes up and down her body. "You are indeed attractive."

"Thank you, Commodore," Mara said, her mouth going a little dry. Now, as she gazed for the first time into his eyes, she realized that he hadn't been entirely correct earlier when explaining about his pool.

The Commodore might not be eccentric. But he *was* most certainly insane.

Chapter Fourteen

ACCORDING TO THE TRAVEL DATA CARD LEIA HAD BROUGHT ALONG, Makrin City billed itself as the Second City of Spires. It was an obvious allusion to one of Imperial Center's former titles in the days when it was known as Coruscant, before the Republic had gradually built up the planet to the point that most of the old spires had been either obscured by taller buildings or quietly torn down. Leia had seen pictures of what Imperial Center had looked like back then, and Makrin City was definitely a poor-waif's version of the ancient grandeur.

"You will enjoy my home, I think," Chivkyrie commented as his pilot settled the ship onto the approach path to the city's main spaceport. "It is large and well appointed. Of course," he added with sudden uncertainty, "it has not been furnished with humans in mind."

"That's all right," Leia said. "Actually, I don't think staying in your home would be the best idea."

[I agree with Princess Leia,] Slanni said. [If Governor Choard plans treachery, we do not wish him to know where precisely to find us.]

"He does not plan treachery," Chivkyrie insisted. "I trust him with my life."

"Perhaps we do not yet trust him with *ours*," Vokkoli said. "That is, after all, part of what we have come here to establish."

"Your fears are misplaced," Chivkyrie said crossly. "But if Princess Leia so desires, we will find a different habitation for you."

"Thank you," Leia said, feeling a flicker of relief. "I suggest a quiet hotel that caters to multiple species, where a human, a Mungra, and an Ishi Tib wouldn't be too noticeable." She tapped a key on her datapad and offered it to him. "This one, perhaps."

Chivkyrie recoiled in obvious horror. "This place is unfit for even fifth-tier Adarians," he objected. "If you insist on a hotel, let me select a place more suitable for first- and second-tier guests such as yourselves."

[I believe the lower-tier status of the establishment was purposeful in Princess Leia's mind,] Slanni suggested.

"Director Slanni is correct," Leia confirmed, hoping all these shocks weren't coming too fast for Chivkyrie to handle. "Knowing that a proper second-tier Adarian such as yourself is our host, a searcher would naturally begin with the finest accommodations."

"Which is therefore where we would prefer not to be," Vokkoli said.

Chivkyrie sighed. "Though it pains me to do so in this instance, I must accede to my guests' wishes," he said. "Very well. I will instruct my servants to make the arrangements."

"That won't be necessary," Leia said, striving for patience. What part of *secretive* did Chivkyrie not understand? "We'll get a transport at the spaceport and just go there."

"But—"

"It would honor us greatly for you to allow this," Leia said.

Chivkyrie looked like he'd just eaten a bad gruffle, but he reluctantly nodded. "Very well," he said again. "Then I shall take a room there with you, as well. It would be a breach of honor for me to live more highly than guests of a higher tier." He nodded to Slanni. "Or even those one tier lower."

"We appreciate your willingness to serve in this way," Leia said. "As soon as we're settled, you can call Chief Administrator Disra and set up a meeting."

The hotel Leia had chosen wasn't nearly as bad as Chivkyrie seemed to expect. It consisted of three tall buildings spaced around a courtyard that, though small, nevertheless managed to include a pair of sculpted gardens within it. The rooms themselves were large and comfortably furnished.

Of course, there were no private health or full-spectrum food services in the rooms, and not even a single personal droid assigned to each of them, deficiencies Chivkyrie pointed out with clear disapproval. But Leia and the others assured him they would manage.

When they had finished unpacking, they gathered in Leia's room and Chivkyrie made the comlink call.

The conversation was short and veiled and included no names. "He will meet us in one hour at the northern edge of the flower market," Chivkyrie reported as he put the comlink away. "An air taxi can have us there in five minutes."

"What if we walk?" Leia asked.

Chivkyrie's face puckered with more disapproval. But he'd apparently learned there was no point in arguing matters of proper tier status with his troublemaking human guest. "Forty minutes. Perhaps less."

[He will come alone?] Slanni asked.

"Yes, as always," Chivkyrie assured him.

"Then let's go," Leia said, trying to push back the feeling of imminent danger weighing on her mind. After all, even if Governor Choard was playing games, there was no reason for him or Disra to change the pattern on this particular contact. "I'd like a few minutes to look around the area before Disra arrives."

It had been a rotten day already, and Disra was glowering silently to himself as he paid the air taxi fare and stepped out into the crowded streets of downtown Makrin City. A miserable day, full of frustrations and setbacks; and with yet another of these interminable meetings with Chivkyrie and his stuffed-vest Adarian etiquette waiting for him, things weren't going to get better anytime soon. As far as Disra was concerned, the sooner this whole thing was over, the better.

Suddenly everything was going wrong. Caaldra's taps into the Imperial databases hadn't come up with anything on this alleged Imperial agent of his, the stormtrooper squads that had hit Drunost and Ranklinge had disappeared without a trace, and now the cargo ship Caaldra had been counting on to fill in for the missing blaster rifles had also apparently vanished, taking one of the BloodScars' ships with it.

Something was happening out there, something bad. They needed a handle on it, and they needed it fast.

Lost in thought, he didn't even notice Chivkyrie until the Adarian fell into step beside him. "Admin—Friend Seeker," Chivkyrie said, stumbling as always over his natural tendency to greet Disra with his proper title. "We are honored with your presence. This way, please."

Disra frowned as Chivkyrie angled off to the left. *We?* Had the idiot brought some of his Rebel underlings or, worse, a few of his servants? All the day needed to be a complete and total disaster would be for his name to be leaked in public where a wandering Imperial spy could catch it.

They rounded a cluster of miniature mii trees and came in sight of one of the negotiation tables scattered strategically throughout the flower market. Seated around it, looking alert and tense, were a shaggy-maned Mungra, a typically ugly Ishi Tib—

And Princess Leia Organa, of the late and unlamented world of Alderaan.

Disra felt his breath catch like burning coals in his throat. One of the most wanted fugitives in the galaxy, sitting not five meters away from him.

In Disra's own city.

Momentum kept his feet moving; years of political maneuvering kept his face from revealing the thoughts behind it. By the time he seated himself in one of the two empty chairs at the table his brain was back under control. "Greetings to you all," he said as Chivkyrie sat down beside him. "My friend didn't mention he was bringing guests."

"These are Aurek, Besh, and Cresh," Chivkyrie said, gesturing to Organa, the Mungra, and the Ishi Tib in turn.

The first three letters of the alphabet. How terribly original. "Honored," Disra said, remembering to add a little caution to his smile, as befit a man who was supposedly conspiring to commit high treason. "Colleagues of my friend Seeker, I presume?"

"That's what we're here to find out," Organa said evenly. Her face, trained in the same schools as Disra's, was giving nothing away.

Disra glanced around. No one was paying any particular attention to them, and the tables in the market had built-in sonic damper fields to allow for private haggling. "I'm sure you have questions," he said. "Please; ask them."

"We'll skip over for now the issue of whether Governor Choard is actually serious about this," Organa said. She paused briefly, and Disra noted with private amusement that she was watching him closely for any reaction to the question she had just stated she wasn't going to ask. "So let's cut to the core," she went on. "How can even a sector governor possibly muster the resources necessary to defy the Empire?"

"Without the aid of allies, we obviously can't," Disra said. "You and your friends will be those allies, if you're willing. If you're not, there are others."

"Who are these others?"

Disra shook his head. "Like you, they prefer anonymity."

"I'll settle for a few raw numbers of their strength."

Disra pursed his lips, pretending to consider the request. The statistics on the BloodScars and their pirate-raider coalition were right in his pocket, in suitably disguised files on his datapad. But if he simply gave all that to her here, she and her friends might be offworld within the hour. "Yes, I can do that," he said at last. "But it'll take me a couple of hours in my office to pull them together." He looked at Chivkyrie. "I presume you're staying at my friend's home?"

"No, we've made other arrangements," Organa said.

"A wise idea," Disra said. "How do I get in touch with you?"

"We'll call you tomorrow morning," Organa said, standing.

Disra frowned up at her. "No other questions?"

"Let's see first what you have in the way of allies," she said as the others also rose to their feet. "Then perhaps we'll have more questions." She nodded, and the four of them walked off.

Disra swiveled around, scowling at their backs as they rounded the mii trees and disappeared into the crowds. That had been quick. Too quick. He'd had a dozen questions of his own to ask, questions dealing with the Rebel leadership and whether or not Organa might have brought any of them with her.

Instead she'd cut off the discussion practically before it had started. Had she somehow sniffed out his game?

Or maybe she was already way ahead of him. Maybe everything he and Caaldra had assumed was the work of an Imperial agent was actually some kind of insane Rebel operation.

Well, if it was, Organa herself was going to get very cold comfort from it. Pulling out his comlink, he keyed for spaceport control. "This is Chief Administrator Disra," he told the controller. "I want an immediate lock-down of all ships carrying human crew or passengers."

"Excuse me, sir?" the controller asked, sounding stunned.

"You heard me," Disra said coldly as he stood up and headed toward the air taxi station. "As of this moment you're on fugitive watch. And put the order on the 'Net to all other spaceports and planetary transport systems."

"But, sir, we can't just—"

"You can and you will," Disra cut him off. "I'll have the fugitive's description and biometrics to you within the hour; after that you'll be able to let everyone else through. But for now, no human is to leave this planet. Understood?"

The controller's grimace was clearly audible in his voice. "Yes, sir."

Disra broke the connection and keyed for an air taxi. It would take twenty minutes to get back to his office, and probably another ten to put together a fugitive sheet with Organa's face and biometric profile. Thirty minutes from now, and they would have her trapped.

And then he would finally be able to make the HoloNet call he'd been waiting on for so long. The call that would set him on his rise to Imperial power.

"If you will forgive my impertinence, that was extremely impolite," Chivkyrie chided Leia as they traveled the twisty path between the market's booths and plant stands. "He was a guest at my table."

"And I had questions I wished to ask," Vokkoli added, his tone more puzzled than angry.

Leia ignored both of them, her full attention on the people around them, the instincts she'd built up over her years of quiet treason screaming at her to get out *now*.

"Perhaps if I called and apologized—"

"You're not to call him," Leia cut him off. "You're never to call him again."

[What is it?] Slanni asked, the increased pitch of his beak-clicks indicating sudden nervousness. [What is wrong?]

"I don't know exactly," Leia told him. "But there was something terribly wrong about him."

"You are imagining things," Chivkyrie insisted. His tone was starting to change, too, though. "He has never given me cause for concern."

"Because you've never had *me* here before," Leia said; and with that, her vague sense of dread suddenly dropped into clear focus. The Empire had kept her role in the Rebellion reasonably quiet, probably fearing that she would become a rallying point for disaffected citizens. But Disra had clearly recognized her, and the sense she'd gotten from him was not one of respect or awe. He was planning to turn her in.

And if *he* wasn't the Rebel sympathizer he pretended to be, then Governor Choard probably wasn't, either.

She'd been right the first time. This whole bid for independence was nothing but a trap.

"We have to get out of here," she told Chivkyrie. "Off the planet, out of the sector, as quickly as possible."

"You're overreacting, Princess," Chivkyrie said, frowning in puzzlement. "I admit Administrator Disra's manner takes a little getting used to—"

"We're leaving," Leia cut him off. "If you're smart, you'll come with us."

"Do not be ridiculous," the Adarian said huffily, apparently forgetting for the moment that Leia was his tier-superior. "This is my home."

"As you wish," Leia said, looking around for an air taxi station. "Please call your pilot immediately and have the ship prepped for us."

Silently Chivkyrie pulled out his comlink and keyed it on. It was answered, and he launched into a chatter of Adarese.

Leia grimaced. Even with her limited knowledge of Adarian culture she knew that holding a conversation in a language a tier-superior guest didn't understand was a violation of etiquette. Apparently Chivkyrie's estimation of her status had dropped at least two levels in the past few minutes.

Which meant he was no longer going to listen to what she had to say. Against her advice, he would continue with this plan, pulling his group out of the Rebel Alliance. And if he left, others would follow, until perhaps their fragile coalition ceased to exist.

Chivkyrie keyed off and returned the comlink to his belt.

[How soon may we leave?] Slanni asked.

"You may not," Chivkyrie said, his voice grim. "Humans have been forbidden to leave Shelkonwa."

Vokkoli stopped abruptly. "What do you say?"

"It appears Princess Leia was correct," Chivkyrie said, bowing his head to her in a gesture of humility and remorse. "Administrator Disra has betrayed us."

"Maybe not all of us," Leia said, trying to think. She was undoubtedly Disra's main target, but it wouldn't be long before he also closed the port to Mungras and Ishi Tib. Still, there might yet be a small window of opportunity for them. "You said the ban only applied to humans," she went on. "If you three can get to the ship fast enough, maybe you can slip out before he tightens the ring."

"Yes, you must go," Chivkyrie seconded before the others could answer, pulling out his comlink again. "I will have my pilot—"

"No," Vokkoli said flatly. "We will not leave a comrade in danger."

"Even if your presence increases that danger?" Leia countered. "Don't forget, Disra has seen all three of us. It'll be easier for a single human to hide than for a human, a Mungra, and an Ishi Tib together."

[She unfortunately does make sense,] Slanni said reluctantly.

"And you should go, too," Leia said, turning to Chivkyrie. "But not by your own ship—Disra probably has people watching it by now. Get on the next transport and get out."

They had reached an air taxi station now, and Leia could see one of the brightly colored vehicles dropping toward them. "The others will go," Chivkyrie said firmly. "But I will stay. You are my guest, and this is my home."

"Chivkyrie—"

"You are my guest, and this is my home," the Adarian repeated in a tone that offered no room for argument. He looked at Vokkoli and Slanni. "You: go at once. Serve the Alliance, and the cause of freedom." His face hardened. "And live in the knowledge that you and your organizations were indeed right."

"We will leave, for the sake of our people," Vokkoli said gravely. "And

we will pray that your error does not cost you your life." He reached out a
hand and touched Chivkyrie's fingertips. "May Fortune smile her protection upon you."

Slanni bowed silently. A few seconds later they were in the sky, headed
for the spaceport.

"And upon you, as well," Chivkyrie murmured as he and Leia watched
the taxi disappear over the city's spires. "Come," he said, taking her arm.
"We will return to the hotel to retrieve your effects."

He gave her a tight, shamefaced smile. "And then an Adarian will show
you the true meaning of secrecy."

The palace was a hive of fresh chaos when Disra arrived. He strode
through the milling employees, paying no attention to the questions and
demands being hurled at him from all directions, concentrating on the
quickest way to his office.

Waiting there, unfortunately, was the one person in Makrin City he
couldn't ignore. "What in blazes is going on?" Governor Choard demanded, the expression behind his bushy beard a combination of appre-
hension and anger. "They tell me you've shut down all the *spaceports*?"

"Just to humans," Disra soothed, starting to circle around him. "I have
good reason."

The other apparently wasn't in the mood to be brushed off. Reaching
out a massive hand, he closed it around the collar of Disra's jacket. "Tell
me this good reason."

Disra ground his teeth, sorting quickly through a list of the possible
lies. "I received a tip that someone's planning to rob the Nightowk Repository," he said. "I only have a description of the team's female—"

"The *Nightowk*?" Choard cut him off, his beard bristling.

"—and the obvious conclusion was that they're after the artworks you
have stored in there," Disra continued impatiently. "I'd like to get the female's description to the port authorities so that we can focus the search on
her and reopen departures to everyone else."

"Yes, of course," Choard murmured, his eyes going distant as he let go
of Disra's collar. "Order extra security for the Nightowk, too."

"I was planning to," Disra said, straightening his jacket as he made it the rest of the way around the desk and sat down. "But I'm sure you have other matters to attend to?"

For another moment Choard didn't move. Disra pulled out his datapad and shuffled through the files, wondering impatiently if the governor was going to simply stand there and watch the entire operation. Then, as if his administrator's words had suddenly penetrated his concern over his precious stolen artworks, the governor spun around and stalked across the office to the door.

Disra watched him go, his mind flashing back for some reason to his first meeting with the governor three years ago. Even then it had been obvious the man had buttons that were easily pushed, and Disra had spent patient hours locating those buttons.

He might very well need to use every one of them in the next few days.

It took only a few minutes for him to give the spaceport controller Organa's description. The conversation would have gone even quicker if he could have simply given the man her name, since her full description was undoubtedly somewhere in the Empire's official wanted files. But for the moment, at least, he needed to keep that crucial bit of data his own little secret. Switching to a HoloNet connection, he punched in the special governors' access number for the Imperial Palace.

"This is Chief Administrator Vilim Disra, Shelkonwa, Shelsha sector," Disra said when the responder appeared in the holofield. "I have an urgent message for the Emperor and Lord Vader."

"State your message," the responder said, her face expressionless, her voice the flat monotone of someone who has spent half her life listening to official pronouncements, complaints, and other drivel.

"Tell them I've located Princess Leia Organa of Alderaan," Disra said. "And that I have her trapped."

He had the satisfaction of seeing the woman's dulled eyes actually widen. "One moment," she said, her voice suddenly brisk and professional. "Let me transfer you directly to Lord Vader's command ship."

Chapter Fifteen

Mara had expected the BloodScars' evening meal to be bland and simple, a step or two above ships' rations but no higher. To her surprise, it turned out to be a small feast more along the lines of a Harvest Day banquet. Apparently one of the Commodore's men fancied himself a gourmet chef.

The reason for the pirates to expend such effort grew clear the minute the Commodore dug into the first course. The harsh lines in his face began to smooth out, the glistening look of madness in his eyes faded away, and by the time the second course arrived he seemed almost normal.

Mara sat at the middle of the Commodore's table, wedged in between one of his lieutenants and one of the visiting ship captains. Vinis, his chin bruising up nicely where Mara had hit him, stood silently behind her as her private server and, no doubt, less-than-private watchdog. Brock and Gilling had been put at two of the other tables, with server/guards of their own standing at the ready. Tannis was at a fourth table, and while he appeared to be joining in the general conversation around him, Mara could tell that a lot of his attention was on her. Caaldra, to her mild surprise, was absent.

There was no interrogation during the meal; clearly, the Commodore loved his food too much to mix it with business. Whether through direct order or merely instinctive caution, the pirates seated around Mara were careful not to talk about their current plans, the BloodScars' ship strength, or anything else related to the organization. The result was a dinner conversation made up almost entirely of chitchat, the sort Mara had heard at formal and informal dinners all across the galaxy. It made for an interesting contrast with the pirates' casually blistering language.

After dinner the Commodore led Mara and the two ISB men to a small conference room, and the negotiations began in earnest.

Mara could remember the first time she'd done something like this, discussing matters that weren't real with someone who was firmly convinced they were. In those early days the procedure had felt eerie and surrealistic, almost as if Mara herself were the one with the warped sense of reality. Now it was simply one more tool in her arsenal.

"We would want a seventy–thirty split, the seventy going to us," Mara said. "All you need to do is tell us which ship or kind of ship you want, and we'll do the rest."

"And what would you get out of the arrangement that would make it worth our taking thirty percent?" the Commodore asked.

"Protection from rival groups or the authorities, for one thing," Mara said. "Safe places to bring the ships once we have them. You might occasionally provide extra personnel if we needed it."

"Sounds to me more like a sixty–forty split, with the sixty going to us," the Commodore suggested.

"That seems a little steep, considering that we're doing all the work."

"Not when you consider the fact that you'd have the BloodScars and our patron as allies." The Commodore's eyes glittered. "And *not* as enemies."

"Point," Mara conceded. "Unfortunately, I'm not authorized to go that far outside my chief's parameters. Would it be possible for me to use your HoloNet link to discuss it with him?"

Out of the corner of her eye she saw Brock shift in his seat. But the Commodore merely smiled. "Tomorrow will be soon enough for that," he said. "I always like to give future allies the chance to sleep on such things. You *will* stay the night, of course?"

"We would be honored," Mara said. "But we don't wish to be a burden. If you'd prefer, we could sleep aboard the *Happer's Way*."

"I wouldn't think of it," the Commodore said firmly. "Vinis will show you to your quarters."

The room Vinis took her to was on the top floor of one of the three-story sections of the complex. It had a single window looking out on the mining complex in the distance; a scattering of old building rubble on the ground directly below the window would discourage any attempt to climb down.

Fortunately, that wasn't the direction Mara was planning to go.

She waited three hours, until all the window lights she could see had gone out and all sounds of life on her floor had ceased. All sounds, that is, except for the occasional shuffling of the guards the Commodore had stationed outside her door.

Like most of Mara's civilian outfits, her green jumpsuit had been designed for double duty. Taking it off, she reversed it to its night-fighter gray-black side and put it back on. The decorative comb that the pirates had been so suspicious of earlier was next; disassembling it like the wirework puzzle that it was, she reassembled it into a pair of palm grippers. Opening the window, she eased herself out into the cold night air and started to climb.

It was one of the trickier ascents she'd ever had to deal with. The wall was reasonably smooth, with no decorative facings or texturing that could be exploited. Fortunately, there'd been enough erosion over the years to create small cracks she could get the grippers into. Still, she was just as glad she didn't have very far to go.

She paused at roof level, stretching out with her senses for any guards or other watchers the Commodore might have stationed up there. But there was no one. Rolling over onto the roof and pocketing the grippers, she headed silently across the building to the spot where she'd hidden her lightsaber.

To find that it was gone.

She moved back and forth along the rain catcher, her pulse thudding in her throat, wondering if she could have gotten herself turned around somehow. But no. This was the place, all right—she could see the marks in the dust where she'd lowered the weapon into concealment. Someone had found and removed it.

Which meant they were on to her.

She dropped into a low crouch, forcing calmness into herself as she tried to think. All right. The Commodore knew now that one of his visitors was more than he or she seemed. But would he necessarily zero in on Mara for that role?

For that matter, would he necessarily zero in on any of them? With the big recruitment drive Caaldra was orchestrating, the BloodScars had probably hosted dozens of visitors over the past few weeks. Couldn't it as easily have been one of them who'd stashed the weapon for future use? That might explain why she and the others had been invited to dinner instead of to a fully equipped interrogation cell.

But it was still hardly a license to linger. She had to get to the command center and try to dig out the name of the Commodore's mysterious patron, then collect Brock and Gilling and get the blazes off this rock.

There was an unlocked access stairway near the center of the roof. Mara slipped inside and headed down. The stairway itself was deserted, as were the hallways she moved down, as was the connecting passageway to the next building over, where the command center was located. The only minds she could sense anywhere around her carried the distinctive vagueness of deep sleep. Whatever the Commodore was up to, he was playing it very cool.

She was on her final approach to the command center door when she finally sensed human presence ahead. She pressed herself into the side of an equipment rack that had been parked at the side of the hallway and stretched out to the Force. There were two, she decided, both of them fully awake and fully alert. Far more alert, in fact, than the usual night watch crew. Perhaps this was where the Commodore had decided to make his move.

If so, hesitation wouldn't gain Mara anything. Looking quickly over the equipment rack for impromptu weapons, she unfastened a pair of fist-sized power couplings and got one in each hand. Stepping to the door, she keyed the release, and as the door slid open she ducked inside and to the right.

The lights were on low, standard procedure for nighttime operations. There were a dozen consoles arranged in rows, each with one or two chairs in front of it. At the far side of the room, through a wide transparisteel viewport, she could see the starlit mining complex stretching across the landscape.

All the chairs were empty. So, apparently, was the room.

But she *had* sensed someone in here, hadn't she? She frowned, stretching out to the Force to check the next room over.

The moment of inattention nearly cost her her life. There was a flicker of warning, and even as she threw herself toward the center of the room a blaster bolt blazed from her left and shattered a piece of the wall where she'd been crouching. She caught a glimpse of a face peering around the side of one of the consoles and hurled one of her power couplings toward it.

Her assailant tried to duck back, but he was a shade too slow. The coupling bounced hard off his forehead, and with a snarled curse the face disappeared.

A curse delivered by a familiar voice. "Brock?" Mara called, pausing midway through her escape roll.

Once again, the momentary hesitation nearly proved fatal. From her right a second blaster spat fire, and a flash of pain lanced across her shoulder. "Don't shoot—it's me!" she snapped, clamping down on the pain as she dived toward the nearest console. Her words were punctuated by another shot, this one going wide as she hit the console chest first and rolled over the top. Two more blaster bolts sizzled through the air from opposite sides of the room, both of them missing, as she landed behind the console.

And found herself crouching in the middle of a group of three dead bodies lying on the floor where they'd been dragged and dropped. The pirates, undoubtedly, who'd been unlucky enough to pull nighttime watch duty.

"I said hold your fire," she called again, twisting her neck to peer over her shoulder at her wound. It didn't look too bad. "Are you deaf?"

"No, we heard you just fine," Gilling said. "Why don't you come out and make this easy on yourself?"

"What do you think you're doing?" Mara demanded. "I'm an Imperial officer."

"No, you're an arrogant little girl who knows more than is good for her," Brock said. "Sorry, kid, but we have our orders. Orders from a *real* Imperial officer."

"What officer?" Mara asked. "Captain Ozzel?"

"That idiot?" Gilling scoffed. "Hardly."

"Shut up, Gilling," Brock said. "He's right, you know. You're just prolonging the agony."

"That's okay—I didn't have anything else planned for the evening," Mara told him, pressing her back against the console and looking around. Besides the chairs and consoles, the room didn't offer anything in the way of cover, and aside from her remaining power coupling the only available throwing weapons were the chairs themselves. Not a good situation. "What exactly do I know that has Colonel Somoril so hot and bothered?"

She sensed the subtle change in their emotions. "You're a cute one, I'll give you that," Brock said. From the sound of his voice, Mara could tell he was starting to move around the left side of the room toward her position. "Just out of curiosity, did you already know about the deserters, or is that what you were looking for in the *Reprisal*'s computer?"

Mara frowned. Deserters? "I don't know anything about any deserters," she said. "And I wouldn't care if I did. That's for the Fleet to deal with, not someone like me."

"No, of course not," Brock said, heavily sarcastic. "The Emperor doesn't care if a few stormtroopers run away from their posts. Not a bit."

"*Stormtroopers?*" Mara said, listening hard. This was an old, old trick: one half of a flanking duo babbled nonstop in order to cover up any sounds while the other half of the team snuck up on the victim.

Generally speaking, though, the talker wasn't supposed to pepper his diversion with genuinely useful information. Either Brock was simply stupid—not impossible with an ISB man—or else he and Gilling were very sure of themselves. "This isn't going to work, you know," Mara called, stretching out to the Force and getting a grip on one of the chairs near where she estimated Gilling was about to make his dramatically lethal appearance. "Even together you two can't take me."

"Oh, I think we can," Brock said. "If not, there'll be others along to finish the job. Probably any minute now, actually."

And then, beneath the chatter, she caught the subtle sound of the room door sliding open.

Brock was still blathering away when the room erupted into a thunderstorm of blasterfire.

Mara crouched low behind the console, squinting against the smoke and flying splinters of ceramic and metal as the barrage continued, cutting into Brock's and Gilling's positions as it first demolished their cover and then demolished them. She heard a wordless shout over the noise, and the assault cut off as abruptly as it had begun. "Come out, Celina," the Commodore's voice said coldly into the silence. "Hands open and empty."

"All right," Mara called back. "Don't shoot. I've got a deal to offer you." Setting the power coupling on the floor beside her, her senses and mind alert, she lifted her open hands into view over the top of the console. No one tried to shoot them off. Keeping them visible, she stood up and turned around.

There were a dozen pirates crowded into the back part of the room, all of them hastily dressed, all of them with blasters pointed at Mara. Vinis and Waggral were among them, their fingers especially tight on their triggers. The Commodore stood in the center of the group, his blaster still holstered, his arms folded across his chest. Beside Waggral at the group's far left end stood a grim-faced Tannis, his blaster also pointed at Mara. "*Another* deal?" the Commodore asked mildly.

"A real one this time," Mara said. "I came here for some information. That's all, just a little information. You let me have that, and I'll leave peaceably."

"What makes you think you'll be leaving at all?" the Commodore countered. "Peaceably or otherwise?"

"Because it would be in your best interests," Mara said. "I have powerful friends."

The Commodore sniffed, his eyes flicking momentarily to Brock's charred body. "They weren't all that powerful."

"They weren't exactly friends, either," Mara said. "It was them trying to kill me that I presume woke all of you up. I was referring to other friends."

The Commodore pursed his lips, measuring her with his gaze. "What exactly is this information you want?"

"You mentioned a patron earlier," Mara said. "I want his name."

She reached out with the Force, knowing the question would automatically bring the name to the Commodore's mind and hoping to pluck it from his thoughts. But his mind was too dark, swirling with too much anger and hatred and insanity, and she got nothing.

"You're a brazen one, I'll give you that," the Commodore commented, his calm voice a stark contrast with the agitation of his mind. "At any rate, your deal is far too one-sided."

"I can fix that," Mara offered. "Just tell me what you want in return. If it's in my power to get it for you—and I have far more power than you think—I will."

The Commodore's smile vanished. "I'm sure you will," he assured her. "Because what I want is you. Dead." He unfolded his arms and lifted a finger toward the ceiling.

"Wait a minute," Tannis put in, his voice tight. "Sir—Commodore— she's not going to do us any good dead."

The Commodore looked at him, his finger still pointed toward the ceiling. "You think she'll do us some good alive, Master Tannis?" he asked. "You who brought her among us in the first place?"

Tannis winced. "I admit she fooled me," he said. "But she fooled Captain Shakko, too. We could at least—"

"*If* Captain Shakko was indeed fooled," the Commodore retorted. "*If* Captain Shakko is even still alive." Abruptly, his face contorted into something nonhuman. "Only he isn't, is he? He's dead, like the rest of your crew."

"No, of course not," Tannis protested, his face going a little paler. "I mean, as far as I know they're all fine. But if we hold her for ransom, we might at least get some money out of her."

"An interesting idea." The Commodore looked back at Mara, his face smoothing back to almost sane. "Well, spy? Are you worth ransoming?"

"There are people who would pay to have me back," Mara agreed. Stretching out with the Force, she lifted the power coupling by her feet to the top of the console, holding it just out of the pirates' sight. "I can give you a couple of HoloNet connections you can call."

"I'm sure you could." The Commodore nodded toward Tannis. "What about him?"

"What about him?" Mara countered. This was an old trick, too. "He's been a useful tool. Not quite as gullible as Shakko, but adequate for our needs."

"As I thought," the Commodore said. "Waggral, kill him."

Without hesitation, Waggral reached over and grabbed the muzzle of Tannis's blaster, twisting the weapon out of his grip. "Wait a minute," Tannis said, his voice cracking with tension. "Commodore—"

His protest was cut off as Waggral slammed the blaster grip across his face, staggering him backward. Flipping the weapon around, Waggral brought both it and his own blaster up to point at Tannis's face.

Lifting the power coupling the last two centimeters, Mara sent it burning across the room to slam into the side of Waggral's head. Before anyone could react, she stretched out to the blasters in his suddenly limp hands, swung them around toward the row of pirates, and opened fire.

The man standing next to Waggral caught the full brunt of that first salvo, collapsing to the floor without even a gurgle. An instant later the rest of the neat line disintegrated as the pirates dived for cover, all eyes and blasters swiveling automatically toward this new and unexpected threat.

All eyes, that is, except those of the Commodore. "Not him, you fools!" he shouted over the noise, his glare burning into Mara as he grabbed for his own blaster. "Her! She's a *Jedi!*"

There was no way the pirates could grasp such a concept, Mara knew, not with the Jedi long gone, certainly not in the heat of battle. But the more important military concept of instant obedience they clearly *did* understand. Even as their faces clouded over in bewilderment, they abandoned their counterattack on Waggral and swung their blasters back toward Mara.

Taking a step away from her console, she picked up one of the chairs with the Force and hurled it at a pair of pirates who'd been careless enough to stand too close together. They crashed to the floor, and Mara sent another chair flying into a different part of the group.

And as she did so, her peripheral vision caught a glimpse of silvery metal arcing toward her from the left. Her hand darted up to intercept, wondering which of the pirates had really been stupid enough to throw a grenade in such close quarters.

But it wasn't a grenade . . . and as her mind belatedly caught up with the evidence of her eyes, she twisted her hand around, shifting it from block to catch—

And her lightsaber dropped with a resounding *slap* into her grip.

For an instant her eyes focused on Tannis as he dived sideways toward the cover of one of the other consoles, his hand still swinging in follow-through from the throw. Then her thumb found the lightsaber's activation stud, and the magenta blade *snap-hiss*ed into existence.

It was as Mara killed the third to the last of the pirates with his own blaster bolt that the Commodore suddenly seemed to wake up to what had happened to his force. With a hoarse shout, he dodged behind the last pirate still standing, a Rodian, firing at Mara over the alien's shoulder as he backed hastily toward the door. Even as Mara dropped the Rodian, the Commodore made his escape.

"Tannis?" Mara called, closing down her lightsaber and circling through the consoles to where the other had gone to ground. "You all right?"

"Mostly," he said between clenched teeth as he pushed himself into a sitting position and peered at the mass of bodies. "And I thought you'd been good on the *Cavalcade*. How in *space* did they wipe out you Jedi in the first place?"

"Strictly speaking, I'm not a Jedi," Mara said, looking around. The once pristine command room was a shambles. "Is there a backup command room somewhere?"

"Yeah, in the emergency bunker," Tannis said. "I suppose you want me to take you there."

"If you don't, all this will have been for nothing."

"Fine," Tannis said with a hissing sigh. "Out the door and to the left." He gave Mara a twisted smile. "I think we'll let you go first."

"I was planning to." Igniting her lightsaber again, Mara palmed the door release and stepped out into the hallway.

There was no one in sight. "You must have some really sound sleepers here," she commented as they headed the direction Tannis had indicated.

"More likely the Commodore's got them prepping the ships for a quick pullout," Tannis said, glancing nervously at each doorway they passed. "I don't suppose you happened to take out Caaldra before you came charging in here."

"Sorry," Mara said. "Actually, I haven't seen him since before dinner. Maybe he left."

"I hope so." Tannis shivered. "The guy scares me."

"Don't worry about him," Mara said. "Thanks for the assist, by the way. How did you get hold of my lightsaber?"

"I went and got it out of the rain catcher where you put it, of course," Tannis said sourly. "Maybe you thought you were being all cute and stealthy, but I could see the thing floating along the towers and guy lines the whole way. Almost gave me a heart attack."

"You only saw it because you knew to look for it," Mara pointed out, nevertheless impressed that he'd caught on to her trick.

"Maybe," Tannis said. "But I sure didn't want to count on everyone else missing it. As soon as I got free I went to the roof—"

"Hold it," Mara said, stopping him with her left hand as she raised the lightsaber to guard position with her right. Directly ahead of them, behind a stack of barrels—

A flurry of blasterfire blazed at her from the edge of the barrels: two men, one low, one high. Mara blocked the bolts with ease, brushing the two attackers back behind their barrier. "Any idea what's in those barrels?" she asked Tannis.

"Not a clue," he said. "I've never seen anything like that stored in the hallway before."

The attackers fired again. Mara responded, catching a faint crunching sound as one of the deflected bolts sizzled into the lower barrel, sending a dark liquid pouring out onto the floor. A second later the blasterfire broke off, and Mara saw a pair of shadowy figures beating a hasty retreat. "Come on," Tannis said, starting forward.

"Easy," Mara warned, again holding him back. Running through her sensory enhancement techniques, she sniffed cautiously at the air.

One sniff was all it took. "Back," she ordered Tannis sharply, taking his arm and pulling him away from the spreading liquid.

They'd gotten three steps when the liquid exploded into brilliant yellow flame.

Mara reacted instantly, pulling Tannis to the floor beside her. A moment later the barrels themselves ignited, sending a fireball in both directions down the hallway. Mara pressed herself against the floor, feeling the heat wash over her legs and back and head. Tannis screamed something; only then, and only dimly, did Mara realize that she'd been burned, too.

The sheet of flame passed over them and continued down the hallway, leaving superheated air in its wake. Blinking back tears, Mara rolled back up into a crouch, using the Force to suppress the pain. Her lightsaber had closed down during the mad scramble, and she ignited it again.

She was barely in time. Even as she brought the weapon up to guard position there was a warning flicker, and she spun thirty degrees to her right as a pair of blaster bolts came at her from a dark alcove that had been shielded from the blast.

The blaster went silent, and Mara heard a soft chuckle. "Impressive," Caaldra's voice came. "Do I have the honor of addressing the Emperor's Hand?"

"The Emperor's Hand is just a rumor," Mara said.

"Of course," Caaldra said. "I'm flattered that the Emperor would send someone like you to stop us."

"Only the best for you and your patron," Mara said, deciding to pass up the fact that she'd happened on this scheme purely by accident. "Nice trap, by the way."

"Only the best for you and your traitor." Caaldra fired again, two widely spaced shots to her head and legs. Mara was ready, blocking both with ease. "You and he must be hurting pretty badly, though."

"We'll manage," Mara assured him. Actually, she had no idea what shape Tannis was in, and she didn't dare risk pulling any of her attention away from her combat focus and her own pain suppression to find out. "It's nothing compared with what a full Imperial interrogation will feel like."

Caaldra snorted contemptuously. "Is this where I'm supposed to spill my secrets and plead for mercy?"

"Spilling your secrets would make things go easier for you," Mara said. "The pleading I can take or leave."

"Ah," Caaldra said. "Sorry to disappoint you, but it's time to go. Give my regards to your friends."

There was a last flicker of thought; and to Mara's surprise, the sensation that had been Caaldra vanished.

Leaving Tannis lying on the corridor floor, Mara took a careful step toward the alcove, stretching out with the Force. Caaldra was gone, all right. Keeping her lightsaber ready, she moved closer, to find that what she'd thought was an alcove was actually a large deep-set doorway. Glancing once around the corridor to make sure no one was trying to sneak up on her, she pushed open the door.

The room beyond was considerably larger than she'd expected, dark and musty, its only light coming from starshine through a large skylight in the middle of the ceiling. In the faint glow she could see rusting ground-moving equipment and dusty stacks of conduit and shoring boards, probably leftovers from when the pirates converted this part of the mining operation into their base.

And near the back of the room, protected by high guardrails, were three wide circular pits.

Mara smiled grimly. Did Caaldra really think he could escape her by ducking down an old survey tunnel? The Force was Mara's servant, and no matter how twisty or tangled the tunnels might be, she would have no trouble tracking Caaldra through them.

She started toward the closest of the pits; and as she did so, out of the corner of her eye she saw a flash of brilliant green through the skylight.

And suddenly the entire building shook as the thunderclap of a distant explosion ripped through the air. Reflexively, Mara threw herself into a crouch beside the nearest ground-mover. Another flash of green fire fell from the sky, and a second explosion scattered the dust around her.

The pirate base was under attack.

Chapter Sixteen

LaRone had just finished suiting up when Quiller came on the intercom. "One hour," he announced. "Starting pre-combat systems check."

"Right," LaRone said. "Grave, Brightwater—get to the gunwells and start your own checks." He got acknowledgments, and with his helmet tucked under his arm he headed for the cockpit.

Predictably, Marcross was there ahead of him, seated in the copilot's seat with his own bucket stashed beneath the control console. "Everything looks good," he reported as LaRone took his usual place at the sensor/shield station behind Quiller. "How are our guests?"

"As of three hours ago they were fine," LaRone told him. "I gave them the updated schedule and suggested they might want to get a little sleep before life gets bumpy."

"I'm betting they asked to join the party," Grave's voice came from the gunwell intercom.

"Actually, they didn't," LaRone said. "Probably didn't think it would do them any good."

"They were right on that one, anyway," Marcross said with a grunt. "Quiller, what's this loop warning I'm getting on the portside sensor?"

"It's nothing," Quiller said. "Let me see if I can clear it."

Listening with half an ear, LaRone watched his own displays and began preparing his mind for combat.

*   *   *

Luke.

Luke startled out of his light doze. "Ben?"

Get up, Ben's voice whispered in his mind, and Luke could sense the urgency behind the words. *Leia's in danger.*

Luke felt his heart freeze. "What kind of danger?" he asked, grabbing for his boots. "Where is she?"

In Makrin City on Shelkonwa. The governor's chief administrator has closed down the spaceport and alerted the Empire to her presence.

Luke felt his throat tighten. He'd been afraid something like this would happen, been worried about it ever since Leia had asked him to go with Han instead of her. "What do I do?" he asked. "I'm trapped here."

There was a moment of silence. *Not as trapped as you think,* Ben's voice came again reluctantly. *Go to the computer.*

Frowning, Luke stepped over to the desk. Was he supposed to figure out how to tap into the ship's comm system and call General Rieekan for help?

Focus on the keypad, Ben instructed. *Focus on the numbers.*

Focus on the keypad? "I don't see anything," Luke said, looking back and forth across the line of numbers. He stretched out to the Force, but there was nothing there.

The first number is seven.

Luke shifted his attention to that key. Was there a lingering sense there? Setting his fingers over the keyboard, he opened himself to the Force, offering it control of his body as he had during the battle with the pirate ships.

But his fingers remained motionless. Without the immediacy and stress of combat to drive his thoughts and emotions, he wasn't getting anything. "I'm not—I can't see it," he said.

There was a whisper in his mind that might have been a sigh. *The numbers are seven seven eight one three one two.*

Luke keyed in the sequence. Nothing happened. "Now what?"

Ben didn't answer. Grimacing, Luke looked around, trying again to listen to the Force. His eyes drifted to the repeater display showing the ship's current position, vector, and systems status. He could almost feel something there, but try as he might he couldn't get the sensation to coalesce into anything clearer.

Run your finger across the underside of the repeater display frame.

Luke obeyed, and this time there was a quiet click from behind him. He turned, and to his surprise saw that a door-sized section of the bulkhead at the end of the bed had popped open a couple of centimeters. Smuggling compartments, maybe? Crossing the cabin, he pulled open the door.

It wasn't a smuggling hole. It was a weapons cache.

A cache that included two sets of Imperial stormtrooper armor.

Luke stared at the gleaming outfits, a ripple of horror running through him. He'd spent the past day wondering if LaRone and his men were pirates or smugglers or bounty hunters or even the Consolidated Security agents that they claimed to be. The possibility that they might be Imperials had somehow never crossed his mind.

Don't be concerned, Ben's voice soothed. *It isn't what you think. At least, not entirely.*

Luke glanced over his shoulder at the cabin door. "That's not a lot of comfort."

Trust me, Luke. Take one of the blasters and load it.

Luke looked at the weapons, hoping fervently that Ben wasn't going to ask him to take on five stormtroopers all by himself, and reached for the biggest blaster on the rack.

Luke, Ben's voice admonished.

He stopped, taking a deep breath and stretching out to the Force. Okay. But if he wasn't supposed to take the biggest blaster . . .

His eye fell on the smallest of the weapons, a tiny hold-out blaster. Still concentrating on the Force, he reached out and took it off the rack. He still couldn't feel any real guidance on the decision. "You know, you could make this whole thing a whole lot easier," he complained as he found the right-sized power pack and gas cartridge and loaded them into the weapon.

Your uncle could have carried you around on his back until you were fifteen, too.

Luke grimaced. It *had* been a stupid thing to say. "Sorry," he apologized.

You've taken your first steps into a larger world, Luke. But there are many, many more steps to go. I cannot carry you along your own personal path. All I can do is guide you, and teach you, and help you to find that path for yourself.

"I understand," Luke said, hefting the blaster in his hand. "I take it I'm supposed to figure out for myself what to do with this?"

You and the Force together will do so, Ben assured him. *Patience. Listen to the Force. When the time is right, you'll know.*

"Here we go," Quiller murmured, getting a grip on the hyperspace levers and pulling. The starlines faded into stars, and stretched out below them LaRone saw the dark shadow that was the planet Gepparin.

He frowned. Directly ahead on the surface, the planet's nighttime darkness had been broken by a tight cluster of brightly glowing reddish yellow spots. "What's that?" he asked, starting to lift a hand to point.

And as he did so, a brilliant flash of green light slashed across his view, stabbing down into the landscape below and adding another glowing spot to the cluster already there. "What the—?" Marcross bit out.

"Oh, *fusst!*" Quiller snarled, throwing the Suwantek up and to the side in a tight spiraling curve, turning them back the way they'd come. From above another cluster of green turbolaser bolts flashed out and downward.

Lit briefly by the reflection of that fire, the wedge shape of an Imperial Star Destroyer appeared in the distance. "It can't be," LaRone breathed.

"It is," Quiller confirmed grimly. "It's the *Reprisal.* They've found us."

Luke was pacing back and forth across his cabin when the Suwantek's sudden turn threw him hard against one of the bulkheads. He caught his balance, rubbing his palms where he'd hit the wall.

As Ben had promised, it was indeed clear that the time was right.

Pulling the hold-out blaster from inside his jacket, he crossed to the door. *Wait,* Ben's voice came as the Suwantek made another sharp turn. *Stretch out to the Force. You'll know when.*

"Got it," Luke said. Pressing the muzzle of the blaster against the door lock, he got a steadying grip on the edge of the computer desk and waited.

*   *   *

"Captain, we have an intruder," someone called from the crew pits. "It just came into the system, and now it's trying to run."

"Get me a reading," Ozzel ordered, turning from his contemplation of the burning pirate base far below and striding down the command walkway toward the sensor station. The freighter's configuration was one he'd never seen before, and he moved to the edge of the walkway for a better look.

"That has to be a meld," Somoril said from his side. "One ship linked to another."

"You're right," Ozzel murmured; and with that, the odd shape suddenly resolved itself. The ship being carried was a Corellian light freighter, probably YT or YR class. The one under power was a—

Somoril inhaled sharply. "That's a Suwantek."

Ozzel felt his mouth drop open. "You don't think—?"

"Tractor officer!" Somoril shouted, spinning around. "Get a lock on that ship. *Now!*"

"Do it," Ozzel confirmed, a sudden hope stirring inside him. They'd come here to silence an Imperial agent who might know their shameful secret—and now, against all odds, they'd been given a chance to bury that secret along with her. "And launch TIE fighters," he added. "That ship is *not* to get away from us."

For a long minute, LaRone thought they were going to make it. Then the Suwantek lurched violently and he was thrown sideways against his restraints. "Quiller?"

"They've got us," the other bit out. "Tractor beam."

"We're still pretty far out," Marcross said. "Maybe we can pendulum our way clear."

"Try it," LaRone ordered.

The roar of the sublight engines changed pitch as Quiller switched direction, driving the Suwantek at right angles to the tractor beam as he tried to break them free. "Anything?" LaRone asked.

"Give it a minute," Quiller said. "We've got some freedom this direction, but for it to work we need to clear the sweep edge before they can lock another projector on us."

There was a sudden screaming thud from the stern. "Or before they can slag our engines," Marcross added tightly.

"Grave, Brightwater—return fire," LaRone ordered as another turbolaser blast shivered across their aft shields.

His answer was a stutter of green light from the Suwantek's laser cannons. "We're way too far away to do any damage," Marcross said.

"I know, but we might be close enough to confuse their sensors a little," LaRone said. "Come on, Quiller—get us loose."

There was a flicker in the Force, exactly the way it felt when Luke was fighting the remote; and as the first laser blast hammered into the stern shield he fired his blaster at the lock.

The door slid open, and he looked cautiously out. The corridor was deserted. Quickly he went to Han's door, staggering with the Suwantek's continued violent maneuvering, and keyed it open.

Han was standing by the computer desk, holding on to it for support, his face carved from stone as he stared at the repeater displays. "You all right?" Luke asked.

Han did a double take. "They let you *out*?"

"Not exactly," Luke said. "Han, Leia's in danger."

"We're in a little of that ourselves," Han said, plucking the blaster from Luke's hand and making a face at it. "Where'd you get this, a krinkle machine?"

"She's trapped in Makrin City on Shelkonwa, and the Empire knows she's there," Luke persisted.

"Later, kid." Brushing past, Han headed out into the corridor.

Luke could hear Chewbacca's bellowing even over the roar of the engines. Han popped the lock and took a quick step back as a hairy Wookiee arm snatched wildly at him through the opening door. "Relax—it's us," Han called.

Chewbacca caught his balance in midlunge, looking both ways down the corridor as he rumbled something.

"I don't know, but whoever it is they've got us locked," Han told him. "Get down to the *Falcon* and get her ready."

"We're leaving?" Luke asked, instinctive relief at escaping a battle fighting with equally instinctive guilt at the thought of abandoning LaRone and the others to whoever or whatever out there was attacking them.

"Not yet," Han growled. "What do you think, Chewie? Bait and switch?"

The Wookiee considered, then warbled a response and headed to the hatch leading down to the Suwantek's ventral hatch. Opening it, he disappeared down the ladder. "What do you want me to do?" Luke asked.

"Stay out of the way," Han said shortly. Hefting the blaster, he headed forward.

The lounge was empty, as was the anteroom beyond it. Slapping the door release to the cockpit, Han strode inside. He got two steps in before he suddenly seemed to notice the stormtrooper armor.

Luke winced. Too late, he realized he should have clued the other in about their captors. But with only the slightest hesitation Han continued forward. "Situation?" he snapped.

"Star Destroyer's got us locked," LaRone said. His face tightened as he saw the blaster in Han's hand, but his voice was crisp and professional. "They may be launching TIEs."

"We're trying a pendulum," the man at the helm—Quiller, presumably—added.

"Any other ships in the area?" Han asked.

"None," Marcross said, gazing darkly at Han from the copilot's seat. "The pirate base also seems to have been effectively neutralized."

"Okay." Han peered up briefly through the canopy at the triangle shape looming in the distance above them, then tapped Marcross on his armored shoulder. "Out," he ordered.

"What?" Marcross asked warningly.

"I said out," Han said, stepping back again to give Marcross room. He started to drop the hold-out blaster into his empty holster, apparently realized the tiny weapon would get lost in there, and instead tucked it into the left side of his belt in cross-draw position. "We've got some tricky maneuvering to do, and I don't have time to explain it to you."

"Look, Solo—"

"Do it," LaRone said.

Glowering, Marcross unstrapped and got out of his seat. He squeezed past Han, who took his place. "Give me comm to the *Falcon*," he ordered, giving the controls a quick look. "Chewie? You ready?"

An answering roar came from the speaker. "Good," Han said. "Somebody get ready to seal the ventral hatch and drop the collar connection."

"Say when," Quiller said.

"Now," Han said. "And give me helm."

Quiller tapped a pair of switches. A moment later the *Falcon* blasted into view from beneath the Suwantek, shooting ahead of them and banking hard to the right.

"LaRone, the Corellian's running," Grave's voice snapped from the intercom.

"It's all right—let him go," LaRone said. "Keep firing at the *Reprisal*. Quiller?"

"Tractor's still holding," Quiller said. "Whatever this trick is, it'd better be good."

"Give it a minute," Han said, sending the Suwantek in a figure eight at the end of its invisible tether. "They've got to notice him first."

Abruptly, a hail of green bolts flashed through the space behind the *Falcon*. "Okay, they've noticed him," Han went on. "Where are those TIEs you said they were launching?"

"Maybe they changed their—no, here they come," LaRone interrupted himself. "Four flights out of the main hangar."

Luke looked up, searching the sky. A moment later he spotted the eight TIE fighters burning their way toward them. Six were definitely heading for the Suwantek, the other two splitting off. "Looks like one flight's heading for the *Falcon*," he warned.

"Good—that's what they're supposed to do," Han told him. He glanced up, then twisted the control yoke hard over and slammed the throttle, swinging the Suwantek back around. "Chewie, we need a shroud."

"You've got a *shroud*?" Marcross asked. "Where?"

"What's a shroud?" Luke asked.

"Tractor beam confuser," Quiller said, sounding puzzled. "A wave-layered bomb containing high-reflectivity particles designed to throw off a lock. But we didn't find anything like that when we searched your ship."

"That's 'cause we don't have one," Han told him as he twisted the Suwantek around again.

"So where are you planning to get one?" LaRone demanded.

"You don't *get* a shroud," Han corrected, looking up again. "You *make* one. Chewie: *go.*"

The *Falcon* cut hard to the left in response, spiraling up toward the two incoming TIE fighters. Shrugging off their laserfire, Chewbacca replied with a quick salvo of his own. The brilliant red bolts caught the lead TIE squarely in the nose, turning it into a ball of smoke and flame.

And small, reflective metallic particles. "*That's* our shroud?" Luke asked.

"You got it," Han confirmed. As the second TIE swerved around its late partner, he threw a burst of power to the Suwantek's drive, sending the ship curving directly beneath the point of destruction and running their tethering tractor beam straight into the expanding cloud of debris.

And with a violent lurch, the Suwantek was free.

"Got it!" Quiller barked. "Go go go!"

"We're clear, Chewie," Han called as he turned the Suwantek away from the Star Destroyer and threw full power to the drive, twisting like a hooked fish to keep the projectors from reestablishing contact. "Get out of there."

There was no reply. "Chewie?" Han called. "*Chewie!*"

"Where is he?" Luke asked, craning his neck to see.

"There," Quiller said, pointing. "He's moving toward the planet."

Han swore as he turned the Suwantek back around. "Hang on, buddy—we're coming," he called.

"What are you doing?" Marcross demanded.

"What do you think?" Han snapped back.

"We go back now and they'll get us for sure," Marcross said.

"Not without a fight they won't."

"Us against a *Star Destroyer*?" Marcross grabbed at Han's shoulder. "Are you *insane*?"

"Let go," Han snarled, trying to shake off his hand. "Luke, get him off me."

"Wait a minute," Luke said, frowning at the drama in the distance. All the remaining TIEs had turned to follow the *Falcon* . . . and unless he was seeing things, so had the Star Destroyer itself. "They're ignoring us," he said. "They're going after the *Falcon*."

"They know they can't get to us before we can jump," LaRone said tensely. "We're as good as gone, so Ozzel's decided to go for the one they *can* catch."

"And they'll blast him out of the sky," Han gritted. "Quiller, what—"

"I'm taking back control," the pilot said as the Suwantek pulled back from its mad drive toward the dodging *Falcon*. "We can't do any good just charging in after him. We need a plan."

"We're going after him," Han insisted, letting go of the controls and reaching across for the blaster in his belt.

But Marcross's hand was closer to it than Han's was, and Marcross himself had obviously been expecting the move. The stormtrooper got there the same time Han did, deftly twisting the weapon out of Han's grip and stepping back out of reach. "Quiller's right," he said firmly. "Instead of arguing, give us a plan that'll work."

"We don't need a plan," Luke interrupted, pointing at the lines of data that had suddenly appeared across the comm display. "Chewie's already got one."

"Transmissions?" Ozzel demanded, glaring down into the crew pit. "What kind of transmissions?"

"I don't know, sir," the communications officer said, peering over his subordinates' shoulders as they worked feverishly at the signal. "They're encrypted, and we were just able to catch the edge of it. But it was definitely aimed at the pirate base and the hills north of it."

Ozzel snorted. "Well, whatever it was, it won't do them any good now," he said. "Fire control: I want that Corellian freighter demolished."

"Not so fast, Captain," Somoril said, his eyes narrowed. "They took a huge risk getting in close enough to make that transmission. I'd rather like to know what it was."

Ozzel clenched his teeth. But Somoril was right. "Belay that order," he called. "Tractor control: get a lock on the Corellian." He glared at that part of the crew pit. "And this time try to hold on to it."

*   *   *

"Looks like your buddy's heading for space again," Marcross said, sounding confused. "Why didn't they didn't hit him while he was still between them and the planet?"

"There must have been something in that transmission that convinced Ozzel they wanted him alive," LaRone said. "Hitting him close in would have splattered him across the landscape."

"Well, they're making up for it now," Quiller said grimly. "There go the TIEs, straight for him. Probably got the tractor beams going, too."

"No problem," Han said, trying to sound more confident than he felt. He and Chewbacca had pulled this sort of flying leap dozens of times, and usually it worked just fine.

Only this time it was just Chewbacca out there, trying to handle both the ship and the quads by himself, and with an iffy hyperdrive to boot. The big Wookiee was good, but Han wasn't sure he was *that* good.

"Nearly far enough out for a jump," Quiller said. "Still no tractor lock."

"There go the TIEs, trying to cut him off," Marcross added. "Looks like Ozzel's finally woken up to the fact that he's going to lose him."

But it was too late, Han saw, with the TIEs too far back for that kind of entrapment. They tried anyway, sending wave after wave of fire spattering off the *Falcon*'s stern shields. One of the bolts punched its way through, and Han winced as the armor picked up yet another dent. "Come on, Chewie, move it," he muttered under his breath.

"Maybe his hyperdrive isn't working," LaRone said soberly.

"He hasn't tried it yet," Han told him. "The lughead's just trying to make sure everyone's on his tail and too far away to come after us."

Quiller whistled under his breath. "Gutsy."

"And stupid," Han growled, wincing as the Star Destroyer belatedly opened up again with its turbolasers.

But once again the captain was too late. With a final quad burst at its pursuers, the *Falcon* flickered with pseudomotion and vanished.

"They're going to be tracking him," Quiller warned. "Trajectory capture, target probability bell—the whole list."

"They can try," Han said, heaving a quiet sigh of relief. Chewbacca could pull the craziest, most self-sacrificing stunts. "The only place he's going is back here."

"What if they leave some ships behind as backstop?" Luke asked. "I mean something bigger than those TIEs, like a patrol boat or two."

"That would be smart," Han agreed. "But I don't think this captain's bright enough for that."

"Definitely not," LaRone confirmed. "Luckily for us."

"Do we have a track on him?" Ozzel bellowed across the bridge. "Sensor officer! Do we have a track on him?"

"We have a track, Captain," a voice called back. "Computing probabilities . . . no."

"No *what?*" Ozzel demanded.

"The bell centers on the Alderaan system," the officer said, sounding confused. "But there's nothing there. Not anymore."

Ozzel smiled tightly. Clever scum. But not clever enough. "Which makes it the perfect place to hide," he told the officer. "Set course to follow."

"What about the pirate base?" Somoril asked, gesturing toward the planet below. "We haven't finished with that yet."

Ozzel peered out at the fires blazing away on the planet's surface. "We've beaten the fight out of them," he said. "The TIEs can finish the demolition."

"But there may still be survivors," Somoril said, lowering his voice. "Particularly . . . you know."

"If she isn't dead already, she will be soon," Ozzel assured him. "The TIEs will see to that. But if you're that worried—" He turned back to the crew pits. "Give me saturation fire on those landing areas to the south and east of the complex," he ordered. "Destroy all the ships. Correction—destroy all of them except the Rendili heavy freighter."

"Sir?" Somoril asked, sounding confused.

"The *Happer's Way* still has fifty of His Excellency's AT-STs aboard," Ozzel reminded him impatiently. Was he the *only* one aboard this ship who could think these things through? "We'll come back for it—and the TIEs—after we deal with this Corellian pirate."

"Sir, I really don't think—"

Deliberately, Ozzel turned his back. Somoril might know more than he did about treachery, assassinations, and lurking in shadows; but he, Ozzel, was the expert here on ships and real, genuine combat.

And that Corellian was *not* going to get away from him. Not after helping those stormtrooper deserters once again slip through his fingers.

Not a chance.

"Course to Alderaan laid in, sir."

Ozzel sent one last look in the direction of the traitors' ship, silently mocking him out there in the distance. He would get them, too, he promised himself. Sooner or later, he'd get them, too. "Go."

The words were barely out of LaRone's mouth when the huge warship flickered and vanished. "And there he goes," Han said, relief and contempt vying for dominance in his brain. This captain really *was* dense. "Didn't even bother to bring his TIEs back aboard first."

"Which just means he's planning to come back," Marcross said. "If we're going to search that pirate nest, we need to get in there before then."

"Not going to be easy with those TIEs standing guard," Luke warned.

But instead of circling outward into a guard formation, the seven remaining fighters turned inward toward the planet. "Only they're not here to keep us away," Quiller said grimly. "Ozzel left them to finish blasting the BloodScar base."

"That tears it," Han said, getting a grip on the yoke again. "We're going in. Quiller, give me control."

Quiller looked over his shoulder. "LaRone?" he asked, an odd edge to his voice. LaRone hesitated.

"What's the problem?" Han demanded, looking back and forth between them. "You want to fly it? Fine. But let's *go*."

LaRone's eyes flicked to Marcross. "I don't know," he said uncertainly.

Han frowned at him—and suddenly he got it. "That was your ship, wasn't it?" he asked quietly. "You know all those TIE pilots."

"We don't exactly *know* them." LaRone seemed to brace himself. "And it isn't our ship. Not anymore."

"That's okay," Han said, trying to keep his voice casual as he looked at Luke. The kid had a sort of pinched expression on his face, but he looked willing enough. "No problem. Luke and me can handle it." It was the easy solution, he knew, but somehow he didn't think these guys would take it that way.

Sure enough, they didn't. "No," LaRone said, a new firmness to his voice. "This was our decision. It's our job."

"Hold it," Luke cut in, pointing out the canopy. "Look."

Han turned, and felt his mouth drop open a little. Where there had been seven TIEs a minute ago, there were now only five . . . and as he watched, a blast of laserfire from somewhere in the hills above the pirate base took out two more. "I guess they *aren't* all dead down there," he commented.

"I guess not," LaRone said grimly. "But if we want any information, we still need to go in. Quiller?"

"Right," the pilot said, bringing the Suwantek around. "Grave, Brightwater—try to get a lock on those laser cannon positions."

"We're on it," Brightwater's voice came back promptly. "Still way out of range, of course."

"Not for long," LaRone said. "Quiller, take us in."

Chapter Seventeen

ABRUPTLY, THE AERIAL BOMBARDMENT FELL SILENT.

Still pressed against the big ground-mover, Mara stretched out with her senses. The air was filled with acrid smoke, and she could hear the crackle of flames coming from at least three places in the near distance. But the turbolaser fire from the sky had definitely ceased.

She didn't know why, but with the respite came the chance to get moving. Stepping carefully over the piles of rubble around her, she headed for the corridor. The firetrap Caaldra had sprung on them had mostly burned itself out, leaving its own contribution of eye-stinging smoke drifting through the air. Blinking a few times, Mara crossed back to where she'd left Tannis.

He was still there, lying motionlessly on the smoking floor. "Tannis?" she said, shoving her lightsaber back into her belt and crouching down beside him.

There was no answer, but at least he was still alive. Mara took a moment to assess the damage—mostly burns from Caaldra's firetrap—then made her way back to the wrecked command center to retrieve the room's emergency medpac.

There was no time to deal with the burns themselves, not with their attackers presumably preparing for Round Two. Selecting a set of military-grade painkillers and stimulants, she injected them into an undamaged section of Tannis's arm. Within half a minute he was awake, blinking up through the smoke at her. "How do you feel?" Mara asked.

"Like I'm dying," Tannis murmured, his voice sounding eerily dream-like. "What happened?"

"Caaldra left us a little surprise," Mara told him, deciding for the moment to skip over the bombardment. "You feel up to a little walk?"

"I don't know," Tannis said. "How far are we going?"

"I thought we'd stop by your emergency bunker for a minute, then head back to the ship and get you to the medical capsule."

"I can try," Tannis said. Grimacing with the effort, he got a hand on the floor and tried to push.

"It's okay," Mara said, stretching out with the Force and raising him up. "All you have to do is point. I can do the heavy lifting."

"I forgot," Tannis said, smiling weakly. "Where are we again?"

"Outside the main control center."

"Right." Tannis peered around. "It's that way," he said, pointing down the corridor in the direction they'd been heading when Caaldra had sprung his trap. Pulling the injured pirate to her side, Mara got a steadying arm around his waist and they set off.

The base was a mess. At least five of the buildings had been completely demolished, a couple of them still burning furiously, the others nothing more than smoldering debris. There were plenty of bodies scattered around, too. Some of the pirates were fully dressed, but others seemed to have been asleep in their bunks when the attack came. At first Mara wondered about their lack of preparedness and sensor protection until it occurred to her that the three men Brock and Gilling had killed in the control center had probably been the ones responsible for spotting trouble and sounding the alert. The two ISB men either hadn't noticed the approaching attackers or else hadn't particularly cared.

Or else had been expecting them. *If not, there'll be others along to finish the job,* Brock had said back in the control room.

"There," Tannis murmured, pointing ahead toward one of the demolished buildings.

Demolished except for a large room in the far corner of the lower floor that was still intact. "Okay," she said, breathing heavily as she eyed the field of broken masonry ahead of them. This wasn't going to be easy.

Tannis had apparently noticed the jagged debris, too. "Just leave me here," he said. "Go get your data and come back for me."

"Forget it," Mara said, resettling her grip around his waist. The barrage could begin again any minute, and there was no way she was going to leave him out here in the open. Especially not with the safest place in the base barely fifty meters away. "Watch your step."

They began picking their way through the rubble. Even with Mara handling most of Tannis's weight, he struggled with the uneven ground, and eventually she had to use the Force again to lift him completely into the air, carrying him over the obstacles like a sack of fruit. She kept her eyes moving, hoping fervently that no one would take a potshot at them while she was too burdened and focused to react.

The corner room Mara had seen turned out to be merely the access air lock to the bunker itself, a much larger complex of rooms two stories underground. Clearly, the Commodore had taken the possibility of enemy attack seriously.

Not that it had ultimately done him any good. His shattered body was there, slumped in a seat by the comm panel. Dead.

"So that's it," Tannis muttered as Mara eased him down into one of the other chairs. "It's gone. It's all gone."

"Looks that way," Mara agreed soberly, looking around. The comm system would be a good place to start, she decided. Unless the Commodore and his shadow ally had been paranoid enough to conduct all their business face-to-face, there should be records of their HoloNet calls to each other. Going to the panel, she gently moved the chair and the Commodore's body aside.

He'd been in the process of setting up a HoloNet communication, she saw, when his broken body had finally given out. The contact number and frequency were meaningless to her, but the destination system was not.

Shelkonwa. Shelsha sector's capital.

"Hand!" Tannis croaked. "Tac display—there."

Mara turned. The visual display was off, but the main tactical display above the defense console was up and running. On it were seven red triangles: enemy fighters, closing rapidly with the base. Round Two, apparently, was about to begin.

Only this time, unlike Round One, there would be *two* sides to the battle.

Mara crossed to the defense console and sat down, a quick glance over the controls showing her options. The main lasers could handle three targets simultaneously, and there were more of the BloodScars' favored proton torpedo launchers waiting in reserve. The lasers were already on standby; bringing them fully active, she got a grip on the firing sticks and waited.

The attackers were nearly to optimal range when they suddenly split formation, fanning out like a Victory Day air show. Mentally, Mara shrugged. Optimal range would have been nice, but then *optimal* merely meant *preferred*. Lining the double crossmarks on two of the attackers, she fired.

The lasers turned the targets into instant clouds of shrapnel. Mara shifted aim, a small corner of her mind wondering about this rival gang whose members were careless enough or overconfident enough to field fighters without even minimal shield capability. She fired again, and another pair of attackers went the way of the first.

Perhaps they were relying on their maneuverability to evade destruction, she decided as she again shifted aim. Certainly they had more than their fair share of nimbleness, twisting around madly as they tried to throw off the lasers' computerized targeting lock. One of the banks of indicators, in fact, went a rapidly flickering red as they succeeded.

But Mara didn't need the help of such technological toys. She had the Force, and all the maneuverability in the universe wouldn't help her attackers now. Shifting the lasers to manual, she continued firing, coolly and methodically destroying the fighters one by one. In the distance she noticed that the sensors were picking up another incoming ship, this one freighter-sized, but the numbers showed it would arrive far too late to assist.

The last two fighters had turned to the attack now, and above her Mara could hear a crackling of laserfire as they made a final desperate strafing run against the bunker. Stretching out again to the Force, she felt the subtle anticipation of their future maneuvers and shifted her aim in response. She fired again, and now only a single attacker was left.

Once again she adjusted her aim . . . and paused. The fire control would be compiling all the relevant tech data on the attackers as the battle progressed, which she could take with her and study at her leisure. But a direct visual contact would be good to have, too. She shifted her attention briefly away from the combat, recognizing as she did so the inherent risk involved in allowing an enemy even a brief breathing space, and activated the visual display.

The sensors had taken a severe beating during the earlier bombardment, and the image that appeared on the screen was dark and grainy and badly distorted. But it was good enough. There was only one fighter anywhere in the galaxy with that profile and architecture.

The pirate base was being attacked by Imperial TIE fighters.

She stared at the image, her mind refusing at first to believe the evidence of her eyes. It was impossible—the Empire's attention was completely absorbed with the Rebellion and domestic instability and alien unrest. By direct order from the Emperor himself, pirates and other raiders had been reclassified as a local and system enforcement problem. This couldn't be any sort of official operation against the BloodScars.

Unless it was against Mara herself.

She felt her face hardening as she turned back to her fire-control stick and blew the last TIE fighter away. So that was how it was. This wasn't just about some grand scheme to unite Shelsha's pirates into a single massive gang. It wasn't even about a link between pirates and the Rebellion. This one went straight into Imperial territory. Straight to the top.

She looked at the tactical display. The unknown freighter was too far out to be a threat, but it was still coming.

Time to go.

Tannis was slumped in his seat, his breathing rapid and shallow. "You up to one more short walk?" Mara asked as she crouched down beside him.

"I can try," Tannis said weakly. "You get what you came for?"

"Oh, yes," she said softly. Stretching out to the Force, she lifted him from the chair as gently as she could. "Just a few more minutes," she said as she carried him toward the door. "We'll get you into the *Happer's Way's* medical capsule—"

She broke off as he groped at her shoulder. "If I don't make it," he rasped, his eyes half closed as he gazed into her face, "bury me in space. You hear me?"

"You're going to make it," Mara said, the lie coming automatically to her lips even as a surge of frustration ran through her. She'd been taught a dozen Force techniques for self-healing, but nothing that could be used on others.

But while there was still life, there was still hope. "Just hang on," she said, heading up the stairs.

They were across the field of rubble and nearly to the shell that had once housed the main command room when Mara heard the distant roar of a sublight drive.

And as she watched, the *Happer's Way* rose from the ruins of the landing area. It turned leisurely around, as if the pilot was surveying the damage around him, then turned again and headed for space.

Mara watched it go, her heart sinking. So that was it. Her freighter was gone; and from the fires she could see burning at that end of the complex it was clear that all the rest of the ships had been destroyed.

She and Tannis were marooned.

But there was still that other freighter-sized ship she'd seen making its cautious way toward the planet. If the pilot was actually foolish enough to land in the middle of all this devastation, she could commandeer the crew and get out of here.

Unless the ship represented Round Three of the attack against her. In that case, she would simply kill everyone aboard.

Beside her, Tannis stirred. "Why've we stopped?" he murmured.

Mara focused on him, his burned face and labored breathing. No, she couldn't wait for the freighter. She had to get help to him *now*.

And then, finally, the obvious answer occurred to her.

Most of the command center building was in ruins, but the entrances to the three survey tunnels where Caaldra had taken refuge were still open. The dust from the attack had obscured any footprints he might have left, but a meter into the left-hand tunnel she found a recent handprint.

There was no lighting, but the floor was smooth enough and the tunnel itself angled down at a reasonably shallow slope. Two gentle turns later, perhaps a hundred meters from the entrance, they reached a dimly lit area and the emergency escape ship she'd hoped to find, a compact Starfeld Z-10 Seeker. The ship was already prepped—clearly, Caaldra had been planning to get out this way until he'd noticed the undamaged *Hap-*

per's Way and decided to take it instead. Getting Tannis into the medical capsule and keying for emergency treatment, Mara engaged the repulsorlifts and sent them moving cautiously down the tunnel.

The fires had mostly burned themselves out as Han and the others picked their way carefully across the rubble-filled base. "Nice to see the Empire taking some interest in pirates again," he commented to no one in particular.

"This wasn't about dealing with pirates, Solo," LaRone said grimly. "This was about covering up a plot."

Han scowled. He hadn't really believed it was that simple, either.

"What kind of plot?" Luke spoke up.

"Someone's been recruiting pirates," Marcross said, his voice even darker than usual. "Someone, as you can see, with high Imperial connections. *Very* high connections."

"Who?" Luke asked.

"That's what we're here to find out," LaRone said. "Quiller?"

"Nothing moving, either above or below," the pilot's voice said from the comlink in Han's belt. "That freighter we saw taking off on our way in must have been carrying the last survivors."

"No sign of the *Falcon*?" Han asked.

"Not yet," Quiller said. "I wouldn't worry, though. He probably just wanted to make sure the *Reprisal* was well on its way before circling back."

Han grimaced. Yes, that was exactly what the big, dumb Wookiee was probably doing. "Let me know the minute you spot him."

"Will do," Quiller promised. "LaRone, I'm reading some deep tunnels ahead of you, survey-sized and fully operational. There might be more people or weaponry down there that I can't scan for."

"As long as it stays down there, it can't hurt us," LaRone said. "Just keep an eye out. We have a hot map yet?"

"Just coming up," Quiller said. "Looks like the only place still drawing power is north and a little east of the attack's epicenter. Single small room on the surface, larger complex beneath it. Some kind of bunker or redoubt, I'm guessing. I'll talk you in."

The underground complex was indeed a bunker, professionally laid out. Narrow stairs led down to a large command room, with side doors leading off three of its walls. There was a single dead body in view, slumped in a chair near the communications console. "Fire control's still on standby," Grave reported, leaning over one of the consoles.

"Duty barracks over here," Brightwater said, looking into one of the side rooms. "Beds don't look slept in, though. The *Reprisal* must have taken them by surprise."

"Sloppy," Grave said.

"They're pirates," Brightwater reminded him.

"What exactly are we looking for?" Han asked, stepping to one of the other doorways and looking inside. This one was a small armory, with racks of blasters and grenades standing ready for whenever an enemy got tired of aerial bombardment and decided to get a little more personal.

"Let's start by finding out who the last person was they were talking to," Marcross said, crossing to the comm panel.

"Good idea," Han said, looking around. The others were gathering around Marcross, their backs to him and Luke. He caught Luke's eye, nodded over his shoulder at the armory, then wandered over toward the group surrounding Marcross. Luke looked puzzled, but nodded back and started edging his way toward the armory. "Find anything?" Han asked as he came up behind LaRone.

"We have their last communications setup," LaRone said, gazing over Marcross's shoulder. His voice sounded odd through the stormtrooper helmet.

"Well?" Han asked, craning his neck to see.

"None of your business," Marcross said, shutting off the display with a quick twitch of his finger.

But not before Han had caught the name of the system. It was Shelkonwa, Shelsha sector's capital. The same place where Luke had said Leia was trapped. "So we're going to Shelkonwa?" he asked as casually as he could.

"*We're* going to Shelkonwa," Marcross said, his voice stiff. "*You're* going wherever you want. In your own ship."

"You can leave as soon as it's back," LaRone added. "Again, thanks for your assistance back there."

"No problem," Han said . . . and with a rush of tangled emotions, he suddenly realized that that was it. If Luke was right about Leia being trapped on Shelkonwa, there was absolutely nothing he and Chewie and the kid could do about it. The Imperials would have the whole planet interdicted by now, and there was no way the *Falcon* could run that kind of blockade. Not every Imperial was as stupid and gullible as Captain Ozzel.

Leia was on her own. But that was all right. She was smart and resourceful, and she had Chivkyrie and his buddies on the ground, and Mon Mothma and Rieekan and their friends on the outside. They'd get her away from Shelkonwa somehow, and then they'd bundle her off to some new hiding place halfway across the galaxy, where Han would probably never see her again.

And once Leia was out of the picture, his last reason for sticking around this crazy Rebellion would be gone.

He was free. Free to drop Luke back with his new friends, free to go square things with Jabba, free to get back to the simpler life he'd had before his meeting with Luke and old Kenobi at that Mos Eisley cantina. There would be no one chasing him; no one expecting him to do anything; no one giving orders except himself. It was over.

If he really wanted it to be.

He looked back around as Luke sidled out of the armory, wearing a studiously casual expression and gripping a blaster, pressed into concealment at the side of his leg.

Han sighed. No, it wasn't over. Not yet. Luke and Leia were his friends . . . and even if he wasn't ready to swear loyalty to Rieekan and this whole Rebellion thing, he still couldn't walk out on his friends. "Actually, we were thinking about going to Shelkonwa, too," he told LaRone. "I don't see any reason why we can't ride together."

"I can think of a dozen of them," Marcross retorted, turning around. His blaster settled down, not *quite* pointing in Han's direction. "What's so urgent on Shelkonwa?"

"And why can't you get there in your own ship?" LaRone added.

There was nothing to do but tell them. Anyway, if it was going to be a problem, it would be better to have it out right here and now instead of on their way to Makrin City. "We have a friend there who's in a little trouble," he said. "Actually, it's more than a *little* trouble. I figure that by now the whole planet's probably been locked down."

"The sector *capital* is locked down?" Brightwater echoed. "What did your friend do, rob the governor's palace?"

"At the moment, she hasn't done much of anything," Han said, hoping it was more or less true. "The point is that you're military—you might be able to get in through that. We can't."

For a long moment the room was silent. Then LaRone stirred. "So that's it," he said, as if some long-standing question had just been answered. "You're Rebels."

"Actually, we're only loosely connected with them," Han corrected.

"So you're only *partial* traitors?" Grave asked acidly.

"Well, *you're* deserters," Luke pointed out.

It was very much the wrong thing to say. All four stormtroopers stiffened, and Han had no trouble imagining what their expressions were like behind those faceplates. "You call us that again, boy," Grave said, his voice like crushed ice, "and you'd better be ready to use that blaster."

"Put it down, Luke," Han ordered. Would the kid *never* learn when to keep his mouth shut? "Anyway, that doesn't matter."

"*Yes* it matters," LaRone retorted as Luke silently set his borrowed blaster down on the nearest console. "No matter what our current situation is, we're still soldiers of the Empire."

"And we swore an oath to defend it against people like you," Brightwater added.

"Yeah, I know the oath you swore," Han said, standing a little straighter himself. "I swore it, too, once."

LaRone's half-aimed blaster seemed to waver a little. "You were in the military?"

"Caridan Academy," Han said, bittersweet memories flooding back. "Graduated with honor. Had a career ahead of me, they said."

"What happened?" LaRone asked.

Han grimaced. "I saw how the Empire treated people," he said. "Especially nonhumans."

This time all four blasters definitely wavered. "So did we," Grave muttered.

"When did you . . . leave?" Brightwater asked.

"I didn't leave," Han said. "I tried to help, my superiors didn't like that, and they threw me out. End of story."

There was another pause. From their stances, Han had the odd feeling this was a discussion they'd already had.

"You Rebels are trying to tear down order and stability," LaRone said at last. "Everything we've worked so hard to build since the Clone Wars."

"We have no problem with order and stability," Han assured him. "No one wants to destroy that. We just want to tear down the parts that are bad."

"Why can't they be fixed from the inside?" Brightwater countered.

"Because the people running things don't want them fixed." Han gestured toward the ceiling. "My partner Chewie was an Imperial slave. A lot of his people still are. You think the governors and Moffs and admirals want that changed?"

"Maybe the Wookiees are the lucky ones," Grave murmured.

"You want to tell Chewie that?"

"No, of course not," Grave said. "I was just pointing out it could be worse. *Has* been worse, sometimes."

"There was an operation on Teardrop just before we parted company with the *Reprisal*," Brightwater said, the words coming out with obvious difficulty. "Part of the reason we left, actually. It was a raid on a suspected Rebel cell in a small town in the hills."

Han looked at Luke. Teardrop. Wasn't that the place where they'd barely skated out from both a pirate gang *and* a Star Destroyer? "The Rebels were all gone," he told the stormtroopers. "Before you ever got there."

The air was suddenly tense again. "You know this for sure?" LaRone asked, his tone that of a man not sure he really wanted the answer.

"Very sure," Han said. "Me and Luke had just pulled the last batch out when your ship showed up."

"Did something bad happen?" Luke asked carefully.

LaRone turned away. "They were . . . *we* . . . were ordered to kill them," he said. "All of them."

"Everyone in town," Grave said. He hesitated. "Starting with the aliens."

"Oh, no," Luke breathed. "But you . . . you didn't. Did you?"

LaRone didn't answer.

Han glanced at Luke, his stomach tightening. Though after Alderaan, what did he expect? What did any of them expect? "And you really think this kind of thing can be fixed from the inside?"

"We're not here to fix the galaxy, Solo," Grave said. "We're just soldiers."

"Not even sure we're *that* anymore," Brightwater muttered.

"I'm not here to fix the galaxy, either," Han assured them, choosing his words carefully. He had a pretty good read on these men now, and the best way to sell them on this would be to echo their own feelings and motives straight back at them. "I just want to fix a corner of it here and there." He waved out toward the stars. "Rescuing our friend is one of those corners."

"Our oath of allegiance was to the Emperor."

"Maybe," Han said. "But if you ask me, a soldier's real job is to protect the people."

"We don't need you to tell us where our duty lies," Marcross said quietly. It was, Han noted with interest, the first comment he'd made since the conversation had turned in this direction. "And we're wasting time."

"You're right," Han agreed. "So what's it to be?"

Han's comlink clicked. "LaRone, he's here," Quiller called. "The *Falcon.* Looks okay to me. You about finished?"

Han looked at LaRone, wishing he could see the man's face. "It's up to you," he said.

LaRone looked at each of the others in turn. Then, almost reluctantly, he turned back to Han. "Quiller, tell the Wookiee we're taking him and his friends to Shelkonwa," he said. "Tell him to hide his ship somewhere in case the *Reprisal* comes back. When he's done that, have him give you the coordinates and we'll come get him."

"Or else Luke and I come with you and Chewie takes the *Falcon* to Shelkonwa on his own," Han suggested. "We can meet at some nice quiet rendezvous point in the system, and he can come aboard then."

"I guess that'll work," LaRone said. "Quiller?"

"I'll let him know," Quiller said. "You find everything you needed?"

LaRone looked at Marcross. "Oh, yes," Marcross said quietly. "Everything."

"We'll be back at the pad in ten minutes." LaRone turned back to Han.

"We'll take you to Shelkonwa," he said. "But once we're there, you're on your own. If we can manage to meet up again, we'll give you a ride back out to wherever you leave the *Falcon*. But that's *all* we'll do for you and your Rebel friend. Understood?"

"Understood," Han said.

"And you can leave that blaster where it is," he added to Luke. "We have better ones aboard the Suwantek." Turning, he headed for the exit.

"Sure," Luke said, throwing Han a look of strained patience.

Han shrugged back. "You heard the man," he said. "Let's go."

The tunnel's exit was ten kilometers farther on, a camouflaged cave north of the base. As Mara lifted the ship above the intervening hills she could see that the incoming freighter had arrived and had landed on Pad 8, the *Happer's Way*'s former home.

For a moment she considered swinging back around and hitting them while they were vulnerable on the ground. But no. She had no real evidence that they were connected to the attack, and anyway she had no time to spare. Keying the nav computer for the nearest system with decent medical facilities, she headed out.

An hour later she dropped the ship back out of hyperspace to carry out Tannis's last request.

The Emperor had little patience with memorials, Mara knew, with extra contempt for the practice of saying words over the fallen. Mara said a few words anyway, half remembered ones from her childhood, before consigning Tannis's body to the emptiness of space.

When she again seated herself at the freighter's helm, it was with a dark and icy anger in her soul. TIE fighters and turbolaser fire together added up to a Star Destroyer, and according to Captain Norello the only one in the sector was the *Reprisal*.

Captain Ozzel almost certainly wasn't in league with the BloodScars directly. The man was ambitious and pompous, but it required a special kind of daring to take that sort of risk, and Ozzel simply didn't have it. Colonel Somoril had both the daring and the utter lack of ethics, but even a senior ISB officer couldn't order a Star Destroyer captain into combat this way. In fact, aside from a few special cases like Mara herself, the only person outside the Fleet chain of command who could do that was the sector governor himself.

And as she'd seen in the bunker, the Commodore's final action had been to call someone in the sector capital.

With a final look at the wrapped body drifting through the void, Mara turned the ship toward Shelkonwa. Governor Choard had sent the *Reprisal* to destroy the BloodScars and cover his tracks. He was a traitor to the Empire.

And Mara was going to take him down.

Chapter Eighteen

LEIA HAD FULLY EXPECTED TO FIND GOVERNOR CHOARD'S TROOPS AL-ready surrounding their hotel by the time she and Chivkyrie arrived. But the hotel and grounds looked just the way they'd left them an hour and a half earlier.

Nevertheless Chivkyrie insisted on entering alone to retrieve their belongings, directing Leia to a tapcafe across the street that catered to off-world personnel. Leia went in, ordered a small drink just for show, and found a table by a window where she could watch.

It seemed like forever before Chivkyrie finally emerged from the hotel, her carrybags looped casually over his shoulders. He looked around, then crossed the street toward her. Dropping some credits on the table, Leia went outside to meet him. "What took you so long?" she asked as she took the bags.

"I thought it would be wise to make a few comlink calls," Chivkyrie said, gesturing her down the street away from the hotel.

"Forgive the impertinence, but that doesn't sound all that wise to me," Leia pointed out. "You could have been tracked and caught."

"If so, better there than in your presence," Chivkyrie said. "At any rate, I believe we may have at least a little breathing space. While the ports have been closed to all female humans of your description, my friends tell me there are no reports of wide-scale patroller activity, at least not in the first-tier areas where any search would naturally begin."

"Or else Choard is smart enough to assume we'll avoid those places."

"Hardly," Chivkyrie said calmly. "There is a large population of Adarians in Makrin City and the surrounding area. Governor Choard is quite familiar with our strengths and weaknesses and way of thinking. Furthermore, Chief Administrator Disra unfortunately knows me all too well. He knows that I could not permit a guest to stay in quarters below her own proper tier."

"Yet you did so," Leia pointed out.

Chivkyrie ducked his head. "No," he said, sounding embarrassed. "I allowed you to check into that hotel, but I never intended for you to actually stay there. I planned to send my servants to pick up your belongings after our meeting and move them to my home."

Leia grimaced. They were indeed an inflexible people. "So where are we going now?"

"Do not worry, Princess Leia," Chivkyrie said, his voice grim but steady. "My tier status will no longer be a problem for us, nor will it cloud my thinking and dictate my actions." He seemed to brace himself. "For you see, my actions have betrayed my guest. I have no choice but to renounce my name, my home, and my tier status."

Leia stared at him in surprise. For an Adarian to do such a thing was the societal equivalent of cutting off his arm. Did he really understand that? She opened her mouth to ask—

And had the grace to shut it again. Of course he understood.

By joining the Rebellion he had tacitly stated he was willing to give his life for freedom. Now he had placed his social standing on the line, as well. For an Adarian, that was a far harder decision to make. "Thank you," Leia murmured. "What now?"

"Now," Chivkyrie said, lengthening his stride, "we find a way to use the brief time we have been given."

Leia picked up her own pace to keep up. Inflexible these people might be, but they were also honorable and brave. It was, she decided, a fair trade.

They walked three blocks, then got onto one of the public air transports heading northwest toward the main spaceport. They got off six blocks later and switched to a transport headed south toward the main interstellar financial district and the third-tier residential areas around it. At the edge of the district they again switched transports, this one heading east toward where Makrin City ended abruptly at a line of craggy cliffs dotted with dark caves.

"The catacombs," Chivkyrie said, pointing at the distant holes visible between the buildings and occasional trees as they walked down a stained walkway. "Over the centuries they have housed the criminals and the exiled, the bringers of war and the bringers of plague. At this time in our history they have become home to the destitute of many species, peoples who came to Shelkonwa looking for a better life but failed to achieve it."

Leia wrinkled her nose, and was immediately ashamed of her reaction. It sounded grim, but no worse than some of the other places she'd found herself in over the years. If Chivkyrie could lower himself to mixing with his society's lowest tier, she certainly could do so.

Besides, the caves could hardly smell any worse than the aromas assaulting her from the packed rows of buildings lining the narrow street. "Sounds like a good place to hide out for a while," she said.

"It is an ideal place," Chivkyrie agreed. "Which is why we are not going there. The caves will be one of the first areas Governor Choard orders searched when he realizes we are not in any of the city's first-tier locations. We will, however, take some of your personal items there later, the better to confuse our pursuers."

"Good idea," Leia said. "If we're not going to the catacombs, where *are* we going?"

Abruptly, Chivkyrie stopped. "Here," he said, pointing to the building beside her.

Leia looked. They were standing by a small tapcafe squeezed in between two secondhand stores, with a faded sign over the door in Adarese and a four-language menu in the tinted window. "*Here?*" she echoed.

"It is sometimes wisest to hide the prize in plain sight, is it not?" Chivkyrie said. He was trying to be decorous, Leia knew, but it was abundantly clear that he was quietly pleased with himself. "I have thus obtained for you a job."

For one of the very few times in her life, Leia found herself at a complete loss for words. "Oh," she said, just to say something.

"I searched the employment ads myself, to eliminate any chance that it could be traced to a servant or friend," Chivkyrie went on. "You can begin immediately."

"Thank you," Leia said, again mostly to say something. The tapcafe, she noted uneasily, seemed to be the source of the majority of the neighborhood's objectionable odors. "What exactly will I be doing?"

"Serving at tables, of course." Chivkyrie frowned. "Unless you would prefer to cook?"

"No, no—serving's fine," Leia assured him. "I don't actually know any Adarian recipes."

"The tapcafe also serves Mungras and other species," Chivkyrie said. "Perhaps later you will be asked to cook for some of them. But we will stay with serving for now. Come—the workers' entrance is around the block and through the back. The manager, Vicria, is expecting you."

Vicria turned out to be a lanky female Mungra with dark red accents in an otherwise tawny mane. "This position requires the lifting of heavy trays," she said doubtfully, her orange eyes measuring Leia's slender form.

"I understand," Leia assured her. "Don't worry, I'm stronger than I look."

"We will soon discover whether that is true," Vicria said. "There are covergowns in that locker. Put one on, then come to my office for an order-pad."

Leia nodded. "Thank you."

On Alderaan all the serving had been done by BD-3000 attendant droids. But Leia had been served often enough by living beings that she'd long since become used to the idea. Indeed, after the first few such experiences she'd hardly even noticed the servers anymore unless there was a mistake or accident of some sort. She'd therefore managed to come away with the impression that such work was both simple and largely effortless.

It took only a standard hour for her to lose the *simple* part of her preconceptions. Serving a table's worth of even these lower-tier Adarians was a subtle minefield of small intra-tier distinctions that required her to take their orders in the proper descending rank succession and not simply by how they were arranged around the table. Since the protocol apparently was for the highest-ranked person to choose his or her preferred seat, followed by the others in their turn, there wasn't even a consistent pattern that repeated itself from group to group, and Leia collected several icy complaints before she figured that out.

The Mungras were less socially rigid, but they presented their own unique set of challenges. It was almost a relief when, late in the afternoon, three humans wandered in. Or it would have been if they hadn't been so obnoxiously falling-down drunk already.

The *effortless* part of the preconceptions took three standard hours to lose.

It was just after midnight when she finally trudged up the stairway to the row of fourth-floor apartments the tapcafe provided its employees. Chivkyrie was waiting, dozing in a large armchair that would have comfortably accommodated an overweight Gamorrean. "Ah," he said, snapping awake and pulling himself upright as she closed the door behind her. "I trust the evening's work went well?"

"It went reasonably well, yes," Leia confirmed, looking around as she took off her covergown and hung it on the rack by the door. The apartment was small and cramped, no bigger than a ship's cabin and only slightly better furnished. But it had a comfortable-looking bed, and that was all she really cared about right now. "The afternoon, on the other hand, was pretty much a disaster," she added. "How about your day?"

"Marginally productive," Chivkyrie said. "The patrollers have begun searching all first- and second-tier hotels, aided by a contingent of Governor Choard's own palace soldiers. There is food in the locker, if you're hungry."

"Thank you." Crossing to the apartment's cooking corner, Leia opened the supply locker. There was some leftover Adarian cuisine in back, a selection of more human-palatable food in front. "Sounds like they're getting serious," she said as she pulled out a meal's worth of the latter and loaded it into the cooker.

"More serious than you realize," Chivkyrie said soberly. "I am told that a message about you has been sent to Imperial Center."

Leia grimaced. She'd hoped that Choard would keep the search local for a while in the hope of reaping whatever political prestige would come of personally turning her over to the Emperor. Apparently he'd decided instead to let the Imperials do some of the heavy work. "Any idea how soon they'll have a force here?"

"It may be here already," Chivkyrie said. "There are two army garrisons in Shelsha sector, one of them only six hours' flight time away. There is also a Star Destroyer on patrol that could be brought in."

"And probably will be," Leia said. "They'll need something with heavy firepower in orbit in case we make a run for it."

Chivkyrie sighed deeply. "I am sorry, Princess. I have failed you. I can see no way out for us."

"I've been in worse places," Leia assured him, fighting against the seductive pull of despair. The only thing at the end of that road was defeat. "All we can do is hold on to freedom as long as we can and watch for an opportunity. Don't forget, if Vokkoli and Slanni made it off Shelkonwa safely, they'll have gotten word to the Alliance leadership."

"Which is too far away to reach us with aid before the Imperials arrive," Chivkyrie pointed out. He took a look at Leia's face and grimaced. "My apologies," he said, ducking his head. "I should not be speaking thus. I know the Alliance will do everything possible to rescue you."

Leia turned her face to the cooker, a memory flashing unexpectedly through her mind. *I'm Luke Skywalker,* the too-short stormtrooper had said eagerly as he pulled off his helmet. *I'm here to rescue you.*

He could have been here beside her now, too, if she'd just kept her mouth shut at that meeting. So could Han, if he weren't so infuriatingly stiff-necked about politics. Instead the two of them were flying madly around the sector trying to figure out how to protect Alliance supply lines from pirates.

A mission that was about to become totally irrelevant, she realized glumly. With Chivkyrie's imminent capture, and with Vokkoli and Slanni now known to Choard and his people, the Rebel presence in Shelsha sector was as good as destroyed. Once it collapsed, there would be precious little need for supply lines.

She shook her head sharply. That was despair talking again. What she needed right now was to put all such thoughts firmly away, and to get herself some food and sleep. The physical inevitably colored the emotional, and she was as physically drained right now as she'd been in a long time.

She was pulling her meal out of the cooker when through the half-open window she heard the faint sound of breaking glass.

Chivkyrie was on his feet in an instant, a blaster in his hand. "Get down," he whispered as he moved cautiously toward the window.

Leia ignored him, crossing instead to the door and flicking off the lights. In the sudden darkness she dug her hold-out blaster from her pocket and joined Chivkyrie at the window.

There were fewer streetlights in this part of town than in the higher-tier areas. But there was enough light to see the two shadowy figures on the roof of the three-story building across the wide back alley, plus a third figure who was even now easing his way through one of the darkened third-floor windows.

"Burglars," Chivkyrie muttered, his voice edged with contempt.

"You suppose anyone's home?" Leia asked.

"Unlikely," Chivkyrie said. "Those will be the homes of the playhouse employees on the next street over, and it does not close for another hour. Typical of coward—"

"Wait," Leia said, straining her eyes. The window two down from the one the burglar had entered—had the curtains there just twitched?

They twitched again; and then, to Leia's horror, they parted and a small Adarian face peered anxiously out into the night.

Stuffing her blaster back into her pocket, Leia pulled the window the rest of the way open. "What are you doing?" Chivkyrie demanded in a startled voice.

"There's a child in there," Leia told him, leaning out the window. Just below her was a narrow decorative ledge extending about twenty centimeters outward from the stone facing that ran the length of the building. Below that was a sheer drop to a ledge beneath the third-floor windows, another to the second-floor ledge, and another finally to the alley below. Above her, similar ledges marked the way up to the tenth-floor windows. The building's stone facing itself was old and crumbling, with plenty of gaps and grooves that an experienced climber with the right tools could probably make good use of.

But Leia wasn't experienced, she had no climbing gear at all, and even if she had, that route wouldn't get her across the twenty-meter gap to where she needed to be.

"You must not interfere," Chivkyrie said urgently, plucking at her sleeve. "If patrollers come—"

"I'm not abandoning that child," Leia cut him off. "I've seen what burglars can do when they run into someone." A meter to the left of her window a thick plastic drainpipe ran from the roof-edge rain catcher to the alley, fastened to the wall at every other floor by a flimsy-looking bracket. Leaning out onto the windowsill, she braced herself on the ledge and gave the pipe a shake. It jiggled in her grip, the brackets not quite flimsy enough for her to simply tear the pipe free by hand. The pipe itself, on the other hand, seemed quite sturdy, more than thick enough to support her weight. Shifting around onto her side, she drew her blaster again and lined it up with the topmost bracket.

"Princess, I implore you," Chivkyrie said, all but begging now. "If the patrollers come, we will be lost. And the intruders, too, may hear."

"I doubt anyone even notices blaster shots in this neighborhood," Leia said tartly. "Or cares." Holding her breath, sighting carefully along the barrel, she squeezed the trigger.

The blaster bolt sounded twice as loud as usual in the relative stillness of the night, its echo from the surrounding buildings almost covering up the soft clatter as the pieces of the shattered bracket skittered across the window ledge. She shifted aim and shot off the next bracket, working her way down to the one on her own fourth-floor level.

She might not be a very good tapcafe server, she thought with a touch of dark satisfaction, but she could play sharpshooter games with the best of them.

Chivkyrie, she'd noticed out of the corner of her eye, had winced at each shot. "Now what?" he demanded as silence again descended on the neighborhood.

Leia frowned. That was, she realized suddenly, a very good question. Her plan had been to shoot off the brackets, push the pipe over from the connection joint just above the fourth-floor ledge to land the end on the other rooftop, and then slide down it to where she could confront the burglars. But now it belatedly occurred to her that as she slid down the pipe she would be presenting herself a perfect target to the two accomplices waiting on the other roof.

And even if they didn't shoot her, then what? If she managed to rescue the child and chase them all away, how would she get back to her room again? Walk her way up the pipe like a darediv stage performer?

In her fatigue she hadn't thought it through. Unfortunately there was no time to think it through any further now. The child was still in danger, and getting over to the other building was still the only way to help. Leaning out the window again, she got a grip on the pipe—

"Wait," Chivkyrie said, grabbing her leg. "Look—they're leaving."

Sure enough, the burglar Leia had seen going into the window had now reappeared, climbing back up his ropes at breakneck speed. Above him, one of his two accomplices was helping to haul him up, while the other was frantically stuffing their gear into a dark shoulder sack. "I guess they *do* notice shots here," Leia commented.

"Your shots will have alerted the entire neighborhood," Chivkyrie said, sounding as if he wasn't sure whether to be pleased or worried. "The intruders have been frightened away."

Leia looked back at the curtained window. Surely the burglar hadn't had time to hurt the youngster.

And then the curtains parted, and the child's face once again peered nervously out.

Leia exhaled in a relieved huff and sent the child an encouraging smile, though she doubted the other would be able to read her expression in the dark. Looking back at the roof, she saw the trio of burglars jump the low parapet to the next building and race out of sight farther down the block.

"Please?" Chivkyrie said, tugging on her leg again. "Before someone else sees you?"

A moment later Leia was back inside the room. "It was a brave and honorable thing you did," he said as he closed the window behind her. "We must hope it will not in turn bring destruction upon us."

"It might," Leia conceded, crossing the room and switching on the lights again. "But it was something I had to do. The reason the Rebel Alliance exists is to free the galaxy from tyranny. The fear of the violent and the lawless is no less a tyranny than the edicts that come from the Emperor's throne."

Returning the blaster to her pocket, she turned back to the cooking corner. "And meanwhile," she added, "even the guardians of freedom have to eat."

*   *   *

Rather to Leia's surprise, the patrollers didn't come that night. They didn't show up in the morning, either, nor were they waiting for her when she reported to the tapcafe just before midday for her shift.

For the first couple of hours she found her heart jumping every time the door opened, followed by an equally quick flash of relief when it turned out to be only another customer. It wasn't until the afternoon lull began to ramp up again toward the pre-dinner hour that she noticed the subtle change in the customers' attitude toward her.

At first she thought they'd simply given up on her; that they'd decided there was no point in expecting her to get the nuances of their culture right and thus no point in berating her, even politely, when she messed up. But while that might explain the regulars' new courtesy, it didn't explain those who hadn't seen her in fumbling action the previous day.

They were midway through the dinner rush when a large but quiet Adarian family arrived . . . a family that included the child whose face she'd seen across from her window the previous night.

And then, finally, she understood. Chivkyrie had been right—her blasterfire had indeed woken up the entire neighborhood. But instead of reporting her to the patrollers, they'd realized it had been an attempt to help, and a successful one at that.

Apparently, their new tolerance for her failings was their way of thanking her.

Leia returned to the apartment later as weary in body as she'd been the night before. But this time, there was no despair to drag her still further down. Perhaps the people of Makrin City weren't yet ready to take a stand against Imperial Center's tyranny. But they were getting closer.

Whether this new determination and respect would survive when Imperial troops were marching through the streets, of course, was another question.

One way or another, Leia would find out soon enough.

Chapter Nineteen

"COMING UP ON SHELKONWA," QUILLER ANNOUNCED. "ARE OUR GUESTS ready to take their leave of us?"

"As far as I know," LaRone said, gazing across the cockpit at Marcross's profile. Even in the flickering hyperspace glow, the tension lines in the other's cheeks and neck were clearly visible. "Grave and Brightwater are keeping an eye on them. Marcross?"

The lines shifted subtly, as if Marcross was coming back from some dark and distant place. "What?" he asked, half turning to face the other.

"Just making sure you're all right," LaRone said. "You've been a little odd ever since Gepparin."

"I'm fine," Marcross said, turning back to face the canopy. "I just want this over with."

"Assuming we can find the BloodScars' contact," Quiller commented. "I know you think you got enough from that HoloNet log—"

"I got enough," Marcross cut him off.

"Fine," Quiller said. "I just meant that Shelkonwa's a big planet—"

"I said I got enough."

"Don't you think it's about time you shared that information with the rest of us?" LaRone suggested. "At least give us the contact number that was on the setup log in case something happens to you and we have to find a way to backtrack it."

The tension lines shifted again. "You won't need to backtrack it," Marcross said. "The traitor's at the palace."

LaRone stared. "The *governor's* palace?"

"That's the only palace down there."

"I know, but—"

"But what?" Marcross snapped. "You don't think traitors come in all sizes and shapes and ranks? Just look at the three we have in the back of our own ship."

"Here we go," Quiller said, and pulled the hyperdrive levers. The stars reappeared—

Quiller stiffened in his seat. "Oh, no," he murmured. "No, no, no."

"Steady," LaRone soothed, his own chest feeling a little tight as he gazed out at the huge command ship floating in high orbit over the planet. "We've got our ID in place. We're all right."

The comm pinged. "*Executor* to incoming Suwantek freighter," a crisp voice said. "We're reading a military ID on you. Please confirm via clearance code."

"Quiller?" LaRone prompted.

There was no response. Quiller was still staring at the huge ship as if he were seeing a ghost. "I've got it," Marcross said, swiveling around and punching the code panel.

For a moment there was silence. "Code confirmed," the voice said. "Destination?"

"Makrin City," Quiller said. "Governor's palace."

"The palace landing area's been temporarily closed down," the voice said. "I can clear you to either Makrin Main or Greencliff Regional. State your preference."

"Why is the palace field closed?" LaRone asked, pulling up a map of the region. Makrin Main was in the heart of the city's northwest quadrant, only a few kilometers from the governor's palace, while Greencliff Regional was a much smaller port tucked between the northeast part of the city and a line of cliffs running down the entire eastern edge.

"There's a military search operation under way in the city," the voice replied. "The palace field's been shut down for security reasons."

"What are they searching for?"

"Classified," the other said, starting to sound annoyed. "State your landing preference."

Marcross looked back at LaRone, raising his eyebrows questioningly. "Makrin Main's closer," he murmured.

"But Greencliff will be less crowded," LaRone murmured back.

Marcross considered, then nodded. "We'll take Greencliff," he said aloud.

"Acknowledged. You're cleared for Greencliff Regional."

"Thank you." Marcross shut down the comm. "Quiller? You all right?"

"Oh, sure, I'm fine," Quiller said, his voice suddenly carrying a grave-yard tone. "I don't suppose either of you happened to notice the name of that ship?"

Marcross glanced a frown back at LaRone. "The *Executor*," Marcross said. "Why?"

"I guess you ground-thumpers don't need to keep up with Fleet news." Quiller took a careful breath. "The *Executor* just happens to be the brand-new flagship of the Lord Darth Vader."

LaRone stared out at the ship, his stomach tightening. *Vader?* "What in the worlds is *he* doing here?"

"At a guess, he's after either our traitor or Solo's Rebel friend," Quiller said tartly. "I guess she must be a little more important than we thought."

"Though he *did* say they'd probably locked down the planet over her," LaRone reminded him.

"I thought he was exaggerating," Quiller bit out. "I don't know about you two, but I don't want to be in the same city as Darth Vader. I don't want to even be in the same star system."

"I don't blame you," Marcross said, his voice sounding tight but deter-mined. "If you want, you can just drop me at the spaceport."

"What are you talking about?" LaRone asked, frowning.

"I'm going after the traitor," Marcross said. "The rest of you don't have to stay. In fact, Quiller's right—with Vader here, it'll be a lot safer for every-one if you don't."

"Forget it," LaRone said. "We're in this together."

"You don't owe me anything," Marcross insisted.

"We owe the people of Shelsha sector," LaRone countered. "Just because one BloodScar base is gone doesn't mean the conspiracy is over. We need to pull this thing out by the root."

"If Vader catches you, you'll wish ISB had found you first," Marcross warned. "Just drop me and go."

"Oh, thanks," Quiller growled. "That makes me feel *so* much better."

"Actually, Vader being here may work out to our advantage," LaRone pointed out. "He'll almost certainly have his private stormtrooper legion on the ground conducting his search. We can just blend into the crowd."

Quiller turned a look of disbelief on him. "You're joking, right? La-Rone, this isn't just some random stormtrooper unit you're talking about infiltrating. This is the *Five-oh-first*."

"So?" LaRone countered, trying to suppress his own private misgivings. "The Five-oh-first puts their armor on one piece at a time just like we do."

Quiller hissed between his teeth. "You're crazy. You know that, right?"

"There've been rumors," LaRone conceded.

"As long as we're all agreed," Quiller said with a sigh. "Fine. If you and Marcross are going to be crazy, we might as well all be crazy together. Next point: what do we do about Solo and Luke and the Wookiee?"

"Good question," Marcross agreed. "If Vader's looking for their friend, we really don't want them running around loose out there. Especially not with what they know about us."

"And it's for fussting sure *they're* not going to blend in with the Five-oh-first," Quiller added. "On the downside hand, I don't see an awful lot of other options. I doubt we're going to be able to keep them aboard. At least not without shooting them, which carries its own set of problems."

"Chief of which would be where exactly you shoot a Wookiee to be sure of bringing him down," LaRone said, an odd thought suddenly striking him. "All right, try this. What if, instead of letting them run free, we give them an escort?"

The suggestion brought the exact reaction LaRone had suspected it would: both Quiller's and Marcross's mouths dropped open. Marcross found his voice first. "Quiller was right," he said. "You *are* crazy."

"Very likely," LaRone said. "But questions of mental health aside, why not? They'd be in the company of legitimate stormtroopers, thereby putting them above suspicion or interrogation by any of the local patrollers. And if we run into flak from Vader's troops, we claim they're our informants."

"Or prisoners we're taking to interrogation?" Quiller suggested.

"That works, too." LaRone hesitated. "And if worse comes to worst and we get caught in a gun battle . . . well, I doubt there'd be anything left for Vader to interrogate."

"Are you saying we'd shoot them?" Marcross asked flatly.

The ghosts of Teardrop flickered in front of LaRone's eyes. "Not us," he said firmly. "Against the Five-oh-first, I doubt we'd have to."

Quiller shook his head. "They'll never go for it, you know."

"Who won't go for it?" LaRone asked. "Solo and Luke, or Grave and Brightwater?"

"*None* of them will."

LaRone shrugged. "Well, we have until we land before we have to make any decisions," he said. "Maybe we'll come up with something better."

The chiming of the ship's proximity alarm, as Mara had prearranged, brought her out of the dreamless sleep of her Force healing trance.

She had arrived at Shelkonwa.

For a moment she lay quietly on the ship's fold-down cot, taking quick inventory. She was hungry and thirsty, a typical side effect of healing trances, but the burns and scrapes she'd received at the BloodScars' base were completely gone.

She headed to the cockpit, snaring a couple of ration bars and a water bottle from the galley locker on the way. She had finished the first bar when the computer prompt pinged, and as she pulled the hyperdrive levers the hazy disk of Shelsha sector's capital world appeared in front of her against the starry blackness.

And floating in space between her and the planet was possibly the last thing in the universe she'd expected to see.

Her comm crackled. "Incoming Z-10 Seeker, this is the Imperial Command Ship *Executor*," a crisp voice said. "State your ID number and your business on Shelkonwa."

Mara felt her teeth grinding together as she keyed for transmission.

What in the stinking fumes of Imperial Center garbage was *Vader* doing here? "*Executor*, this is Z-10 Seeker, ID number unknown," she bit out. "Is Lord Vader aboard?"

There was a moment of silence as the comm operator tried to reset his brain to deal with this thoroughly nonstandard reply. "Uh—"

"Is he there, or isn't he?" Mara demanded.

"Yes, Lord Vader's aboard," the operator said, starting to sound flustered. "Admiral Bentro is in command—"

"Inform Lord Vader that the Emperor's Hand wishes to speak with him," Mara cut him off.

"The—*who?*"

"Lord Vader," Mara snarled. "*Now.*"

There was no answer. Biting back a curse, Mara turned her ship's nose toward the Super Star Destroyer and cut in the drive. The Sith Lord was probably hiding in his personal chamber, or else pacing the command walkway in one of those moods where no one dared to approach him.

But Mara had a job to do. One way or another he *was* going to see her.

She was nearly to the ship's inner defense zone, and the *Executor's* layered arrays of point defenses were swiveling warningly toward her, when the comm finally came to life again. "Emperor's Hand," Vader's familiar voice rumbled. "This is an unexpected pleasure."

"Likewise," Mara said, knowing that neither of them meant a word of it. "Lord Vader, we need to talk."

"As you wish," Vader said. "Come aboard."

The *Executor's* first officer took over, deactivating the ship's defenses and directing Mara to the captain's personal hangar bay. An escort from Vader's own elite 501st Stormtrooper Legion was waiting, and after a short walk they arrived at a small conference room.

Vader was waiting, standing like a brooding storm cloud near the head of the table. "I understand you *demanded* to see me," he said without preamble.

"I apologize for my earlier tone," Mara said, inclining her head toward him in a gesture of humility.

"There is only one person in the Empire who can demand my presence," Vader continued, his voice stiff. Apparently, he wasn't in the mood to accept apologies. "That person is not you. And never will be," he added ominously.

"Then let me make this as brief as possible," Mara said. She wasn't exactly in the best of moods herself. "I'm here on an important mission, and I need some assurance your presence here isn't going to get in the way."

"That *my* presence won't get in *your* way?" Vader demanded, his voice dropping half an octave. "Walk softly, Emperor's Hand."

"I don't walk softly where treason is involved," Mara countered. "I'm on the trail—"

"*No!*" Vader boomed, his voice slamming across the room and straight through Mara's skull. He took a long step around the end of the table toward her, his black cloak billowing, his gloved hand dropping to his lightsaber. "She is the key to finding him. She is *mine!*"

"What?" Mara managed, her own simmering anger vanishing in the realization that she was suddenly in big trouble. "No, I—"

But it was too late. Vader pulled the lightsaber from his belt, and with a *snap-hiss* the blazing red blade appeared. Holding the weapon in attack position, he strode toward her.

Mara took a step backward, snatching out her own lightsaber but leaving it closed down. The last thing she wanted to do was try to match blades with a Sith Lord. She threw a quick look at the door, shifting her weight in preparation for a dash for freedom.

But Vader either spotted the glance or read her body language. Shifting direction, he angled toward the door, blocking any chance of escape.

Grimacing, Mara shifted her weight in the other direction and threw herself sideways onto the conference table. A quick kick-and-roll off her left shoulder, and she had landed in a crouch on the floor on the far side. "Take it easy," she called as soothingly as she could. "What's Governor Choard to you, anyway?"

Raising his lightsaber high, Vader slashed the blade straight through the table.

Mara took a quick step back as the two sections of the bisected table crashed to the floor. With the wall at her back, and Vader between her and the door, there was only one option left. "You want trouble?" she demanded, finally igniting her lightsaber and lifting it to blocking position in front of her. "Fine. Come and get it."

Vader's only reply was to shift his own weapon again into attack position as he stepped into the gap between the two sections of table. Stretching out to the Force, Mara reached to the wall behind him and switched off the lights.

It was a trick she would never have tried with a normal opponent. Their two lightsabers didn't give off a lot of light, but there was more than enough for biological eyes to work with while they adjusted to the gloom.

But Vader's helmet was equipped with optical sensors for use in dim light, with all the strengths and weaknesses inherent in such equipment. There was a chance that for the first crucial second before the contrast adjusted itself all he would see was her glowing lightsaber blade floating in a field of otherwise total darkness.

She was right. With a bellow, the Sith Lord angled his lightsaber and slashed it viciously in a horizontal arc through the air half a meter beneath the glowing magenta blade.

Only Mara wasn't there anymore. Using the Force to hold her lightsaber floating in place, she had dropped to the floor the instant the lights went out and rolled out of sight beneath one of the angled sections of the broken table.

Vader stopped in his tracks, and for a long moment the room was silent except for the hum of the lightsabers. Mara listened carefully, but the steadiness of the sound indicated that he was holding the weapon motionless. Was he finally coming to his senses?

And then, to her relief, she heard the familiar sizzle as he closed down the weapon. A moment later, the room's lights came back on. "What were you saying about Governor Choard?" Vader asked, his voice calm again.

Cautiously, Mara emerged from cover, alert for any last-minute tricks. But Vader had taken a step back from the table, and his lightsaber was again hooked onto his belt. The brief madness was over. "Choard has been recruiting pirate gangs to attack military shipments," she said, calling her own lightsaber back to her hand and closing it down. "A few days ago he sent the *Reprisal* to destroy their base and cover his tracks. They also nearly killed *me* in the process."

"That would have been unfortunate," Vader said. Mara could hear no actual sarcasm in his voice, but she had no doubt it was there. "Still, your information matches my own."

Mara stared at him. "You mean you already *knew*?"

"The knowledge is recent," Vader assured her. "But it is of no interest to me," he added, his voice darkening. "As he denounced his governor, Chief Administrator Disra also claimed that Leia Organa is in Makrin City. *That* is who I seek tonight."

"Really," Mara said, the word *obsession* flashing through her mind as she finally understood the Dark Lord's earlier outburst. She might have guessed it would have had something to do with the former Alderaanian princess and the Rebellion. "What's she doing here?"

"Disra claims she was consulting with local Rebel leaders," Vader said. "He assures me he can supply names."

"Handy," Mara said. "Do we know where this Disra is right now?"

"He has gone to the palace to collect surveillance records that might be of use in our search."

Or perhaps he was there to destroy other, more incriminating records? "I need to get down there right away," Mara said.

"Is someone stopping you?"

Mara felt her lip twist. Even when Vader wasn't being homicidal, he was never pleasant to deal with. "Not at all," she said. "Enjoy your hunt." Nodding to him, she headed for the door.

"Emperor's Hand?"

She turned back, finding his black faceplate turned toward her. "Yes?" she said.

"As you dispense your justice to Governor Choard," he said softly, "take care not to get in *my* way."

The sky had darkened into the hazy starless gray typical of large cities, and Leia had just taken an order for a group of Mungras, when Chivkyrie arrived at the kitchen's back door with the bad news.

"It has begun," he told her, his voice trembling. "Imperial stormtroopers have arrived at the spaceport and are spreading throughout the city."

Leia took a careful breath. So Imperial Center's response had come at last. "I understand," she said.

"No, I don't think you do," Chivkyrie said urgently, glancing furtively both ways down the alley. "It is reported that Darth Vader himself is among them."

That part wasn't exactly unexpected, either, Leia reflected. Vader had always been the type to take things personally, and her role in the Death Star's destruction was about as personal as one could get. Even so, his name sent a shiver through her. "I understand," she said again. "Thank you for the warning. You'd better get moving."

"What is the point?" Chivkyrie said wearily. "No one escapes Lord Vader."

"Of course they do," Leia said firmly. "I suggest you try the catacombs. The local patrollers have probably searched them by now, which means they're not very likely to do so again."

Chivkyrie snorted. "The stormtroopers will not care what the patrollers have or have not done."

"But the stormtroopers aren't looking for *you*," Leia reminded him. "I doubt their orders mention anyone but me. Anyway, you have to try something."

"You are right," Chivkyrie said. "Forgive my moment of despair."

"Everyone has such moments," Leia said, her cheeks warming as she thought back on her own latest battles with that emotion. "The trick is to make sure they stay moments, and don't lengthen into hours or days."

"Or a lifetime," Chivkyrie said.

"We'll win," Leia said quietly. "Someday. I know we will." She leaned out the door, checking the alley. Still empty. "Now get going. And again, thank you for everything."

For a moment the Adarian studied her eyes and face, as if committing them to a final memory. Then, bowing his head, he hurried away.

"Do you need also to leave?"

Leia turned. Vicria, the tapcafe's manager, was standing beside one of the storage lockers, her orange eyes looking even brighter than usual in the dim light. "Not yet," Leia said.

"Because you may go whenever you must," Vicria went on. "You don't belong here—I and all those who have seen you these past days know that."

Leia swallowed. "Then more than ever I am grateful for your discretion."

Vicria shook her head in a Mungran shrug, the movement sending a soft, fluid ripple through her mane. "Many have come to this neighborhood over the years to hide," she said. "But most have been arrogant or hateful or bitter. Few have shown us such honor and courtesy as you have."

She moved to Leia's side, stepping into the doorway Chivkyrie had just vacated and looking up toward the boarded-up third-floor window across the alley. "We have been repaid in full for our discretion," she said quietly. "You are welcome among us anytime, Leia Organa."

Leia felt her throat tighten. So they even knew who she was. "You are a people of great honor, Vicria," she said. "I will do what I can to see that no retribution comes upon you and the neighborhood for your kindness."

"Do not sacrifice yourself for us," Vicria warned, her tone turning gruff. "You are of far higher tier than we."

"I will be certain not to carelessly throw away the gift you have given me," Leia assured her. "But as to our respective tiers, I do not consider them a proper measure of our value as living, thinking beings. They are certainly not an indicator of loyalty or courage."

"A strange way of thinking," Vicria said. "But you *are* an outworlder. Your thoughts and ideas are not those of the Adarian or Mungran peoples."

"Perhaps not," Leia said. "But I have found that the yearning for freedom crosses all such lines and barriers. Not only those between different peoples, but also those between different tiers."

"A strange way of thinking," Vicria said. "Yet you are correct: with foreign soldiers searching the streets, perhaps it would be best for you to stay inside."

"Hiding in plain sight, as my friend first proposed," Leia agreed. The conversation about society and tiers had apparently turned uncomfortable enough for Vicria to change the subject.

But Leia had planted the seeds. Maybe something would eventually grow from them. "Besides," she added, "I couldn't leave yet anyway."

"Why not?"

Leia held up her pad. "I still have two orders to put in."

*   *   *

Disra took the last twenty meters to his office in a dead run, slamming open the door and diving for the secure comm. "Disra here," he panted into the microphone. "Caaldra?"

"Finally," Caaldra said tightly. "Where have you *been*? Never mind that. What the blazes are all these Imperials doing here?"

"Nothing to do with us," Disra assured him. "They're looking for a Rebel leader who was supposedly spotted in Makrin City a few days ago."

"Is that going to be a problem?"

"No, of course not," Disra said, thinking fast. After the broken HoloNet call from the Commodore, and Disra's subsequent failure to raise the BloodScar base again, he'd assumed Caaldra had been killed. Apparently the man had once again cheated death.

Which brought up some interesting possibilities. Disra had all he really needed already, but Caaldra's presence might add a nice extra touch. *If* he could lure him down. "You're on your way in, I assume?"

"I'm on my way to the Greencliff Regional Spaceport," Caaldra said. "The idiot directing traffic from the *Executor* told me no one was allowed to land at the palace."

"You didn't ask for Makrin Main?"

"That's where he wanted to send me," Caaldra said. "I talked him out of it."

Disra frowned. "What on Imperial Center for? Main's both closer and bigger."

"It's also crawling with Imperials," Caaldra retorted. "Considering my cargo consists of fifty AT-STs, I don't think either of us wants me anywhere near the place."

Disra felt his mouth drop open. "Fifty *what*?"

"Remember I said the BloodScars lost my special cargo?" Caaldra reminded him, sounding grimly pleased with himself. "I got it back."

"And you brought it *here*?"

"The *Executor* didn't offer me the option of turning around and running," Caaldra said acidly.

Fifty stolen AT-STs. This just got better and better. "Forget the Imperials *and* Greencliff," Disra told him. "I'll call the *Executor* and get you routed directly here to the palace."

"I already told you, the controller said I couldn't land there."

"Because Governor Choard closed off the grounds," Disra countered. "But what the governor has taken away, he can give back again. Go ahead and change your landing vector—I'll get it fixed."

The comm went silent. Disra slumped back in his chair, wincing as his freshly sweaty back pressed against the cool cloth of his shirt. Fifty AT-STs. No wonder Caaldra had been so upset when they vanished. With those, plus the BloodScars and their allied gangs, they might actually have been able to pull off their grand conspiracy.

Or they could have if Disra had ever really intended to go through with it.

But even though the whole charade was very close to being over, it wasn't there quite yet. Keying the comm again, he signaled for the *Executor.*

Mara was still fuming when, far ahead, she noticed one of the ships heading to the planet below begin to drift out of line.

She frowned, leaning forward as she studied the freighter's new vector. Some kind of malfunction? Her sensors weren't showing any problem, but the equipment on this ship was hardly up to the standards she was accustomed to. Perhaps the other pilot had developed a problem with his attitude system, especially now that they were getting into atmosphere. The distant craft rolled slightly, its aspect shifting toward her—

Mara caught her breath. For a moment she stared, then jabbed at her board, keying for her best magnification.

Her ship's best wasn't particularly good. But it was good enough. The drifting freighter was the *Happer's Way.*

She slapped the comm switch. "*Executor,* I have a ship breaking approach pattern," she said tersely. "Please advise as to its intentions."

Imperial military rigidity being what it was, she fully expected to have to fight uphill to actually get any information. But the controller apparently hadn't forgotten the young woman who had successfully petitioned to speak to Vader and, more important, been allowed to walk away from the meeting. "The freighter *Happer's Way* has been newly authorized to land at the governor's palace," he told her.

The governor's palace. She should have known. "I thought you said no one was being allowed in there."

"Apparently it's been granted an exception."

Mara nodded to herself as she watched the freighter drop ever farther off the Greencliff approach vector. So that was the game. The governor would open his grounds to Caaldra, who would then sneak his stolen AT-STs to safety right past the Imperials' collective nose. "Order it off," she said.

"Excuse me?" the controller asked, sounding startled.

"I said order it off," Mara repeated. "It was cleared to Greencliff, and that's where it's going to land."

"But the governor's office has authorized it to land on his grounds."

"Irrelevant," Mara said. "The governor's office has jurisdiction over the palace and palace grounds, but the freighter's still in open atmosphere." She hesitated, but this was no time for half measures. "Tell him that if he doesn't get back on the Greencliff vector, you'll shoot him down."

There was a pause, and Mara heard the subtle click of a comm switchover. "Emperor's Hand, this is Admiral Bentro," a new and calmer voice said. "I can't threaten a civilian freighter without a reason. Especially not one under the protection of a sector governor."

"I'm giving you an order, Captain," Mara said. "The recognition code is Hapspir, Barrini, Corbolan, Triaxis."

There was another brief pause. "Understood," Bentro said. "But if I could just contact Lord Vader first for—"

"You don't need Lord Vader's permission," Mara cut in. "Besides, we don't have time. Deliver the message, Admiral."

There was a soft hissing of exhaled breath. "Acknowledged," he said. "Commander, order the *Happer's Way* to return to its original course and landing destination."

"Thank you, Admiral," Mara said. "Don't worry—the pilot won't risk getting himself shot down. He's far too confident that he can slip out of any net we can weave."

"Understood," Bentro said doubtfully. "Do you want me to order troops or air support to the Greencliff field?"

Mara hesitated. All the Imperial forces down there were under Vader's direct command, and she had no intention of crowding him twice in one day. "No, I'll handle it," she told Bentro. "Thank you for your assist."

"My pleasure," the admiral said. "Our sensors indicate the *Happer's Way* is returning to its designated course."

"I see," Mara confirmed. "I'll contact you again if I need further assistance."

"Yes, ma'am," Bentro said, and there was no mistaking the quiet relief in his voice. If Mara didn't want to push Vader, a mere fleet admiral certainly didn't.

The comm clicked off. Keeping a wary eye on the *Happer's Way*, Mara keyed her ship for landing sequence. Given the current distance between them, Caaldra would have about ten minutes on the ground before Mara caught up with him.

For a moment she considered leaving her place in line and moving up so that she would be right on top of him when he landed. But if he hadn't already spotted her back here, that would tip him off for sure. Better to let him have his ten minutes to prepare for whoever or whatever had just kicked him away from the safety of the palace.

She was looking forward to seeing what he came up with.

Chapter Twenty

"THIS," HAN SAID, "IS COMPLETELY NUTS."

"That was what *I* said," Quiller commented sourly from beside him. "LaRone didn't listen to *me*, either."

Luke frowned as he gazed out the speeder truck's windscreen. It *was* crazy, he had to admit. Going out alone into a tautly quiet city, just the seven of them, with Vader's stormtroopers all around them and Vader himself somewhere in the city. Even with Chewbacca staying out of sight in the Suwantek—under loud protest, of course—Luke knew he and Han by themselves wouldn't have even made it off the Greencliff Spaceport grounds without being stopped and questioned.

But with five stormtroopers in full armor accompanying them, one of them running escort ahead of the truck on a speeder bike, the local patrollers' questions and suspicions had evaporated like dew off hot sand.

The real question, he knew, would be what would happen if and when they ran into some of the Imperial searchers. To Luke, all stormtroopers looked alike, but from some of the comments the others had made he gathered that there were ways for the stormtroopers themselves to distinguish among one another. If the stormtroopers of the 501st Legion currently combing the city realized that LaRone and his friends weren't part of their unit, there could be some awkward questions.

But the 501st had to spot them first . . . and for that, they had a secret weapon even Vader couldn't anticipate.

There was a subtle nudging from the Force. "Make a left at the next corner," Luke told LaRone, pointing ahead toward the street. LaRone's helmet dipped slightly in a nod as he flipped on the signaler to alert Brightwater to this latest course change.

"I just wish there were a few more vehicles out here we could lose ourselves in," Han muttered, staring out the side window as they took the corner. "Does everyone go to dinner at the same time around here?"

"They're not inside eating," Marcross told him grimly. "They're inside cowering."

"Imperial forces have landed, remember?" Grave added from behind Han. "Or were you expecting the citizenry to line the streets and throw Vader a parade?"

"And then turn right up there," Luke said, pointing ahead.

"You know, this is really starting to weird me out," Grave commented. "How can you possibly know where the other search parties are? I was tapping into their group comm frequency for a while, and even with *that* I couldn't figure out their pattern."

"Don't bother asking," Han said drily. "He'll just tell you it's a Jedi thing."

"Right, from a group of people who were supposed to have been wiped out years ago," Quiller countered. "Gives *me* the creeps a little, too."

"How much farther?" LaRone asked.

"Not very," Luke assured him. "A block or two." And if the stormtroopers were already searching the area, he and the others would have to pull Leia out right from under their noses. That would bring the whole question of stormtrooper identification to the top of the stack again.

There was a sudden whisper across his mind, a mix of the coiled-spring predator image plus the unmistakable urgency that he was learning meant danger. "Stop the truck," he snapped. "Right now."

A second later he was thrown against his restraints as LaRone jammed on the brakes. "What is it?" he asked.

From behind them came the distinctive sound of heavy blaster cannons. Luke spun around in his seat, craning his neck as he looked through the rear window.

He was just in time to see a small ship, its engine section on fire, spiraling toward the street below.

* * *

The *Happer's Way* was sitting silently on the scarred permacrete as Mara eased the Z-10 onto her assigned pad in the uncrowded Greencliff Spaceport. She shut her engines back to standby and studied the freighter. There was no movement she could see, no other indications of life.

Could Caaldra have already made his escape?

There was one way to find out. Lightsaber in hand, she lowered the Z-10's ramp and headed outside. Stretching out with her senses, keeping alert to her peripheral vision in case he was lying in ambush in the shadow of one of the other ships, she started across.

She was halfway there when the freighter's starboard cargo bay blew up.

Force-driven reflexes threw her to the ground, twisting her body around as she fell to take the blast across her back instead of her face. The shock wave rolled over her, tingling against skin only recently healed from the previous burns. She rolled over as bits of debris began falling around her and bounced back to her feet, igniting her lightsaber.

And as she did so, dimly visible through the smoke, the boxy metallic shape of an AT-ST rose into view through the jagged opening. The command module swiveled around to face her, and its twin chin-mounted blaster cannons opened fire.

Mara dived to the side as the salvo blasted a pair of holes in the permacrete where she'd been standing. The module swiveled to follow, the laser cannons firing again. Mara dodged one of the bolts, angling her lightsaber blade to catch the other and try to send it back to its source.

The move nearly ended the battle right there. Mara had never tried to block such a powerful blast before, and instead of successfully returning the shot she nearly had the lightsaber wrenched out of her hands by the concussion. She managed to hang on to the weapon, breaking into a full run as she tried to beat the pursuing bolts to the nearest cover.

She made it, but just barely, diving behind an old and badly corroded ore hauler that looked as if it hadn't been moved in years. The AT-ST's final salvo blew a pair of holes in the hauler's stubby outfoil as Mara quickly made her way to the rear, where the sheer bulk of the hauler's engines would offer her some protection.

But not for long. There was a short pause, and then Mara heard the rhythmic mechanical creaking of the AT-ST's knee joints as it climbed up and out of the hole the explosion had torn in the cargo bay. She listened intently, her eyes studying the semi-haphazard layout of parked ships around her and mapping out two different evasion routes depending on which way Caaldra decided to come around the hauler. There was no way she could outrun an AT-ST in a straight-line path, at least not over any serious distance, but on a twisting obstacle course like this one she was far more maneuverable than the big machine. If she could get in under the guns and cut off part of one of its legs, she could bring it down.

The mechanical clanking started up again, heading right. Mara responded by going left, moving to a spot beside the hauler's nose where she could duck under it and escape out the other side as soon as the AT-ST came into view.

But it didn't come into view, nor did it seem to be coming closer. In fact, as Mara listened, it seemed to her that the AT-ST was actually getting farther away.

And then, suddenly, she understood. Ducking under the hauler's nose, she ran out the other side.

Caaldra was no longer hunting her. Instead, he was driving the big combat machine due south across the landing field. Even as Mara came into sight of it, the AT-ST plowed its way through the low landspeeder fence and headed into the largely deserted city streets.

Mara hissed between her teeth. So Caaldra had recognized her trap and declined to take the bait. On this side of town the streets were fairly narrow but relatively straight, giving the AT-ST that straight-line speed advantage Mara had already noted. All Caaldra had to do was get a few blocks ahead of her and steal a landspeeder, and he'd be away before she could catch up.

Or so he apparently thought. With a final look at the departing AT-ST, Mara turned and sprinted for her Z-10. Two minutes later she was in the air and heading south.

She'd thought Caaldra might try to change direction once he was out of immediate sight of the spaceport, hoping to shake off her pursuit. But while there were a few small clusters of taller structures, most of the buildings in this part of town were only two or three stories high, providing little visual cover for such hide-and-search games. As Mara rose above the parked ships, she could see the AT-ST still plodding its way south in the distance. Kicking her drive to full atmosphere power, she gave chase.

Unfortunately, the same low buildings that provided little cover for the hunted did likewise for the hunter. Moreover, the Z-10's only weapon was a small auto blaster whose fire control was programmed awkwardly into the ship's sensor package. If Mara was going to win this, she would have to get in the first shot, and to get it in from point-blank range.

And with the AT-ST's array of viewports and viewscreens providing a complete 360 view, the only insertion angle that offered her any chance was directly above her target. Climbing into the sky, Mara leveled off; and as she caught up with the AT-ST she rolled the Z-10 over into a nosedive directly above it and started down.

She was lining up the auto blaster's crossmarks on the AT-ST's entry hatch when she saw the light blaster cannon turret riding the command module's left side swivel around to point upward at her. Instantly she swung the control yoke over, wrenching out of her dive and trying to pitch over to the AT-ST's right side where that particular weapons cluster couldn't target her.

But the Z-10's systems hadn't been designed for such a tight maneuver. She was a fatal half second too slow; an instant later the ship bucked beneath her as the engine section took a direct hit.

She was going down.

She fought the crippled ship the whole way, managing to turn what would otherwise have been an instantly fatal nose-first crash into a hull-ripping belly skidder. Her momentum carried her two entire blocks, the grinding of metal against permacrete stabbing into her ears the whole way.

But at last the grinding quieted and the wild bucking slowed to a stop. Breathing hard with reaction, wincing at the acrid smell of smoke and burned metal and leaking fluids, she climbed out of her seat. The ramp had been crushed in the landing, but three quick slashes with her lightsaber provided her an exit through the transparisteel canopy.

Her skid had dropped her about three blocks south of where Caaldra had taken out her engines. Climbing carefully out of the ruined ship, she turned to look north, fully expecting him to have taken the opportunity of her crash to change direction, either back north to the *Happer's Way* or west toward the palace that she knew was his ultimate destination.

But he'd done neither. The AT-ST was still clanking its way toward her, its chin blasters tracking back and forth across the street like an alert sentry walking the line.

Apparently Caaldra had decided to pass up escape in favor of revenge.

The crippled ship disappeared below the level of the buildings around it, and a second later LaRone heard the distant sound of metal skidding along permacrete. "It's down," he bit out, looking around. In the distance to the south he could see a parked landspeeder transport, its complement of stormtroopers probably spread out through the buildings of that neighborhood. No other vehicles or personnel were in sight. Possibly no other vehicles or personnel were in the area.

No one but the Hand of Judgment.

"Out," he snapped to Luke as he swiveled the speeder truck around. "You, too, Solo. Go get your friend—we're going to see if we can help that pilot."

For a wonder, neither Luke nor Solo argued the point. A moment later LaRone was gunning the truck toward the crash site, following Brightwater on his speeder bike.

The crash had been north of them and, it turned out, two blocks farther west. LaRone guided the truck around the final corner, and found himself facing an extraordinary sight. Half a block ahead was the wreckage of the light freighter they'd seen go down, twisted and torn, billows of black smoke pouring out of its burning engines. Moving away from a gaping hole in the cockpit was the pilot, a young woman with red-gold hair.

And two blocks farther north was the towering bulk of an All Terrain Scout Transport, clanking its stiff-legged way down the street toward them all.

"What in the world is *that* doing here?" Quiller muttered.

"Brightwater—check it out," LaRone ordered, gunning the speeder truck toward the wreckage, an odd feeling in the pit of his stomach. The woman up there had to be Luke's and Solo's friend—it was the only reason why anyone would deploy an AT-ST against her. And now that she'd been identified and was on the edge of being caught, Luke's and Solo's own capture wouldn't be far behind.

Clearly Marcross had followed the same line of logic. "We can't get involved," he said urgently from the rear of the speeder truck. "They've got her now."

"What about Luke and Solo?" Grave asked. "We can't let *them* get caught, too."

"We may not have a choice," LaRone said grimly. Still, they had to try. He swung the speeder truck wide in preparation for a U-turn back toward where they'd dropped off the two Rebels, hoping there was still time to get them back to the relative safety of the Suwantek. Ahead, Brightwater was approaching the AT-ST.

Without warning, the walker's chin-mounted blaster cannons swiveled down and opened fire.

The sheer unexpectedness of the attack nearly cost Brightwater his life. He twisted the speeder bike into a tight swerve as the edges of the salvo shattered his right steering vane and then raked along that side. Finishing the turn, he kicked the throttle to full power, the damage to his steering vane making his usually tight evasive maneuvering look more like a drunkard's slalom. The AT-ST's cannons fired two more bursts, both missing, before falling silent again.

But the walker was still coming.

Brightwater made it back to the wreckage just as LaRone brought the speeder truck to a halt and leapt out, bringing his E-11 up to guard position. "Hold it!" he snapped to the red-haired woman. She was young, he could see now, no more than twenty years old.

"I'm an Imperial agent," she snapped back. "Level K-12; recognition code Hapspir Barrini. We've got a bandit in that AT-ST."

LaRone felt his mouth drop open. But years of training instantly took over. "Understood, ma'am," he said. "Orders?"

"Let's start with some air support," the agent said. "Get your group commander on the comlink."

LaRone winced. "Actually, we're not with the main group—"

"Just get them on the comlink," the agent snapped.

"We can't," Marcross said grimly. "The AT-ST's got full jamming going."

"Then we'll have to do it ourselves," the woman said, glacially calm. "You—scout trooper—is your speeder still functional?"

"Functional enough, ma'am," Brightwater said, swiveling back around to face the AT-ST lurching toward them. His armor, LaRone saw, was blistered along his right leg where the blaster cannons' near miss had caught him.

"Do an evasive drive around his left side and try to draw his fire," the agent ordered. "If and when he turns the command module around to track you with his forward cannons, you, sniper, will go for the concussion grenade launcher on his right side."

"Acknowledged," Grave said, dropping the muzzle of his T-28 into firing position.

"If he doesn't turn the module, or when he turns back around again," she continued to Brightwater, "you'll swing around and try for his drive engine radiator and exhaust vents. His transmitter's back there, too—maybe you can knock that out and clear the jamming so we can get some backup. If the sniper was able to take out the grenade launcher, you should be relatively safe on that side, but watch out for the light blaster cannon turret on his left."

"I can stay clear," Brightwater assured her.

"Just remember that if we don't nail the launcher, you'll have that to worry about, as well," the woman reminded him. "If it gets too hot, circle around the block and rejoin us here. You're our only mobile force right now, and I don't want you sacrificing yourself for nothing."

LaRone felt a stirring of surprise. An Imperial agent who actually cared about the troops she had commandeered? That was something new.

"What about the rest of us?" Marcross asked.

"You'll lay down cover fire and try to split his attention," the agent said. "Fall back as he approaches and try to draw him past what's left of my ship. I'll be waiting for him here."

LaRone looked at Grave. Skulking in the middle of burning wreckage in the path of a hunting AT-ST was not a good way to live to pension age. "Ma'am, if I may suggest—"

"Get moving," the young woman cut him off, stepping back beside the wrecked ship and crouching down. "If you can lure him close enough, I should be able to bring him down."

Bring him down? LaRone frowned in disbelief. Then, belatedly, he noticed the slender cylinder gripped in her hand.

A lightsaber.

He looked at her youthful face again, a sudden shiver running through him. An Imperial agent, a lightsaber—the rumors were true after all.

This woman was the Emperor's Hand.

"You have your orders, stormtroopers," he said between suddenly dry lips. "Move it."

There were a dozen stormtroopers visible a block ahead, striding purposefully along the walkway, when Luke came to a sudden stop. "What's wrong?" Han demanded, his eyes on the Imperials.

"Nothing," Luke said. "We're here."

Han frowned, focusing for the first time on the dingy door and faded window menus beside him. A *tapcafe*? "She's hiding *here*?"

"You think maybe we can get inside?" Luke pressed, nodding toward the approaching stormtroopers.

Han shook his head. Her Royal Highclassness, hanging out in a place like this? Luke's mystic Jedi tricks must have popped a circuit breaker.

Still, anywhere out of sight of stormtroopers was a good place to be. Pulling open the door, he stepped inside—

And came to a sudden, disbelieving stop. Across the murky dining room and the clumps of alien heads, he saw her. Not just sitting in a back corner, either, trying to hide with a hood over her head. She was on her feet, moving deftly through the crowded room, serving drinks.

Her Royal Perfectness was actually dressed in a covergown serving drinks.

"There she is!" Luke said excitedly.

"Yeah, I see her," Han said, giving the room another, more careful look. There had been no abrupt silence or turned heads, but the air in the dining room had suddenly taken on a static charge. Everyone had spotted the new arrivals, and they didn't seem at all happy about it.

"Well?" Luke asked impatiently.

Han braced himself. "Nice and easy," he muttered to the kid. Keeping his hand as close to his blaster as he could without being obvious about it, he started threading his way between the tables.

He was halfway there when a pair of Adarians in dusty workers' clothes stood up silently in front of him.

"Easy," Han soothed, holding up both hands, palms forward. "Just dropped in to see a friend."

"Han?" Leia called.

Han looked between the two Adarians to see her coming toward him, surprise and relief on her face. "We interrupting anything?" he asked casually.

"I'm so glad you're here," she breathed, her eyes flicking past his shoulder to Luke. "Both of you. How did you know I was in trouble? Never mind—we have to get out of here."

"Yeah, no kidding," Han said. "This place got a back door?"

"Yes—this way," Leia said, taking Han's arm. The two Adarians stepped aside, and Leia led the way between the tables and into the kitchen.

An orange-eyed Mungran female was waiting by the back door. "Safety in travel to you, Leia Organa," she rumbled. "We will not forget you."

"Neither will I forget you, Vicria," Leia said, bowing her head to the other. "Someday, when the slavery of the Empire is finally over—"

"We'll buy you a drink," Han cut in. Taking Leia by the shoulders, he hustled her through the door. Beyond was an alley, narrow and poorly lit and—for the moment, anyway—deserted. "Come on," he said, shifting his grip to Leia's arm and dragging her toward the alley's north end.

"Han, that was rude," she said accusingly. "These people helped me hide—"

"You want to be standing there thanking her when Vader comes in the front door?" Han interrupted. "*That'll* make good reading at her interrogation. Come on—Chewie's waiting at the spaceport."

They were nearly to the end of the alley when Luke suddenly grabbed Han's arm. "Behind us—someone's coming," he hissed.

Han glanced around. As far as he could see the alley was still deserted.

But the kid had been right way too many times on this trip for Han to start doubting him now. "Over here," he said, drawing his blaster as he pulled Leia toward a stack of trash bins at the side of the alley. Pushing her behind them, he pressed himself against her to give himself some cover as he peered down the alley.

"Han—," Leia began.

"Shh!"

"Han, you're crushing me," Leia complained, the words sounding like they were coming out between clenched teeth.

"You want me to get shot?" Han countered. There was something moving down there in the darkness now, coming up on them fast. They passed beneath a dim light—

"Scout troopers," Han muttered, feeling his stomach tighten. So that was the pattern of the day: the main body of stormtroopers searching the buildings from the main streets, scout troopers on speeder bikes patrolling the back alleys watching for runners. Neat and clean and personnel-efficient.

And Han had about thirty seconds to figure out how to take them out.

At his side, Leia was pushing against his shoulder. "Stay *put*," he growled, looking around for inspiration. There was no other cover he and the others might get to, certainly nothing that would really hide them.

Which meant he would have to shoot the Imperials. Problem was, while he could probably take out one target from ambush without trouble, the second wasn't going to obligingly sit still for his next shot.

But he was just going to have to risk it.

From somewhere in the near distance, a sudden volley of blasterfire drifted across the quiet night air. Setting his teeth, Han lifted his blaster and lined it up on the first scout trooper.

With a final push, Leia shoved her way between him and the trash bins. "What the krink are you *doing*?" he demanded quietly.

"Give me your blaster," she ordered, looking out at the approaching scout troopers.

"*Look*, Your Worship—"

Without another word she reached over and twisted the blaster from his hand. Han started to snatch it back, but she evaded his grasp, pushing him away with her elbow. He looked at Luke, but the kid was frowning down the alley toward the approaching scout troopers, his forehead creased in concentration. The distant blasterfire seemed to be getting worse, and Han saw the two scout troopers glance at each other across their speeders and accelerate.

Leia fired.

Not at either of the troopers, but up along the side of the building across the alley. Han looked up, frowning, and to his surprise saw a twenty-meter length of drainpipe lean ponderously out from the wall four floors up. With a splintering *crack* it broke free and tumbled toward the alley below. It hit the permacrete in front of the speeder bikes and bounced up just in time to catch both troopers squarely across their faceplates.

They flipped backward off the speeders, one of them slamming flat onto the ground, the other managing another quarter rotation before joining him. The speeder bikes, now riderless, coasted to a hovering halt; the scout troopers themselves didn't move at all.

"Let's go," Leia said, thrusting the blaster back into Han's hands. "Which spaceport did you say you were at?"

"Greencliff," Han said, giving the troopers and the mostly shattered drainpipe a final puzzled look. Someday he would have to ask Leia how she'd pulled *that* one off.

"Well, come *on*, then," she repeated impatiently, grabbing at his arm. "Before they miss these two."

"Hang on a second," Han said, eyeing the idling speeder bikes. It was risky, he knew—civilians on military speeders would absolutely catch the eye of any roaming stormtroopers. But the time value might just be worth it, at least for a few blocks. "You ever ride one of these things?" he asked, nudging her toward the nearest bike.

"No," Leia said warily. "Han, I don't think—"

"No, he's right—we can do it," Luke said. He went over to one of the bikes and gingerly climbed on.

"Okay," Leia said, clearly still not convinced. "But I'm driving."

"You said you'd never done it before," Han reminded her.

"Have *you*?" she countered.

"Well, not the military versions—"

"Then I'm driving," she concluded. "Besides, you need your blaster hand free in case we run into trouble."

Han made a face. Female logic.

Still, she had a point. Drainpipe sharpshooter skills notwithstanding, he was still a better shot than she was, especially on the fly. "Absolutely, Your Worshipfulness," he said. "Get on."

They climbed onto the other speeder, Leia taking the saddle while Han balanced himself on the emergency gear storage bag behind her. He wrapped his left arm around her waist, noting with private amusement that she squirmed a little at his touch. This might turn out better than he'd thought.

It took both her and Luke a minute to figure out the controls, and the first twenty meters were pretty jerky going as they tried to fine-tune the throttle settings. But after that both of them seemed to get the hang of it and they were off, sticking to the back alleys. Fortunately, the other scout trooper patrols didn't seem to have gotten this far north yet.

Or else all the stormtroopers in the area had suddenly found more important things to worry about than a Rebel fugitive. The blasterfire coming from the northwest had intensified, with several different models of weapon in play. A major battle was taking place over there, right about the spot where LaRone had kicked him and Luke out of the speeder truck.

But if the stormtroopers were in trouble, they were on their own, at least for the moment. Maybe once he and Luke had Leia safely aboard the Suwantek they could come back and find out what was going on.

They'd made it about three blocks, and Luke and Leia were finally settling into a decent ride rhythm, when out of the corner of his eye Han spotted something flying south just above rooftop level to the west. He looked up—

"Stop!" he barked, squeezing Leia tighter around her waist. "Luke!"

"What is it?" Leia called over her shoulder as she braked to a halt.

"That's our ship," Han told her, pointing toward the spot where the Suwantek had vanished over the cityscape.

"What?" Luke asked, sounding stunned. "Where?"

"Where all the blasterfire's coming from," Han said grimly. "Chewie's headed straight into the middle of it."

"That doesn't sound good," Luke said.

"No kidding," Han snarled, yanking out his comlink and thumbing it on.

Only to instantly shut it off again at the burst of static that erupted.

"They're jamming everything," he bit out, shoving the comlink back into his belt and pointing ahead at the next cross street. "Come on—that way. We need to head him off."

"Right," Leia said, turning the speeder in that direction. Luke was already on the move, heading toward the cross street.

Han grimaced, hanging on tightly as Leia rounded the turn and kicked the speeder bike to full speed. It was LaRone and his friends in trouble, all right—he'd bet the *Falcon's* starboard cargo bay on that. And so naturally Chewie was there, too, charging to the rescue.

If they got out of this one alive, he promised himself darkly, he and Chewie were going to have a long talk about this sort of thing. A *very* long talk.

The scout trooper took off down the street, weaving his sluggishly evasive path as his underslung blaster spit defiant—and useless—fire at the approaching AT-ST. Mara crouched close beside her burning freighter, blinking against the smoke swirling around her as she mentally crossed her fingers. The AT-ST's chin blaster cannons depressed to track toward the trooper, and for a moment she thought Caaldra was going to fall for it.

But then the cannons lifted again, and the side-mounted light cannon turret swiveled around and opened fire. The trooper swerved around the blasts, ducked between the two huge jointed legs, and shot out the other side. The side turret swiveled around, continuing to lay down fire; as the scout veered to Mara's left out of the turret's range, the launcher on the AT-ST's other side hurled a concussion grenade at him.

The grenade hit the permacrete with an explosion that shattered half a block's worth of windows and slammed across Mara's face like a velvety hammer. She peered though the smoke, tensing, but as the air cleared she saw the scout trooper, still on his speeder, disappear around a building and down a side street. Safe, or at least not seriously injured, and coming around for another try.

The other stormtroopers were meanwhile not standing idle, but had settled into a rhythmic fire pattern that was pouring a withering barrage at the AT-ST's joints and sensor clusters and viewports. But the walker had been designed for exactly this kind of combat, and it shrugged off the fire with ease. Indeed, it almost seemed that Caaldra was enjoying the battle, especially the one-sidedness of it. Instead of throttling the AT-ST for top speed, which would have quickly run down his opponents, he had the walker moving almost casually along, daring his opponents to take their best shot.

There was a motion at her side, and Mara saw the squad commander drop into a crouch beside her. "I ordered you to fall back," she said.

"I needed to consult," he said tightly. "We think we may have a way to knock him out."

"Explain."

"The gyro system is layered between the underside of the command module and the leg platform," the commander said. "If I can get my sniper up into one of the buildings ahead of it, he may be able to get a clean shot."

Mara looked back down the street behind the retreating stormtroopers. Yes, there were several buildings back there that should work.

The problem was that the sniper would get exactly one shot. If he missed, or if the gyro was tough enough to survive the attack, Caaldra would simply swivel the command module around and blow both him and the building to rubble.

Which the commander and sniper both knew full well. "Get him set up," Mara ordered. "Let's hope we won't have to use him."

"Right." The commander gathered his feet beneath him, preparing for a sprint.

But before he could move, something suddenly roared past overhead, fire from the AT-ST's entire array of blaster cannons spattering across its underside. Reflexively, Mara ducked, her eyes tracking the intruder. Had Vader's scattered searchers finally decided to investigate all the noise coming from this end of town?

Only it wasn't a stormtrooper transport up there. In fact, it wasn't an Imperial vehicle of any sort. It was some kind of freighter, its features blurred by the smoke and darkness and its own speed. Even as she watched, it veered around and came back again, slowing down on its repulsorlifts as if studying the extraordinary street scene below. "Get him out of here!" Mara ordered.

"The comms are being jammed," the commander reminded her.

"I know that," Mara snapped. "Wave him off, then—do *something*. He's a sitting avian up there."

"I'll try." The commander stood up and lifted his hands high.

And at that moment there was a multiple flicker of blasterfire from somewhere behind the AT-ST.

Luke arrived at the main street and wobbled his speeder bike to a halt at the edge of the building on the corner. Leia stopped behind him and Han jumped off, running the last couple of meters. Blaster ready, he peered around the corner.

Less than half a block away was an Imperial AT-ST, its back to them, striding ponderously southward down the street. A block beyond it was some kind of smoking wreckage, probably the freighter he and the others had seen being shot down. Through the billowing smoke he could see someone standing up in plain sight, apparently unaware of the approaching walker, while beyond him some even vaguer figures seemed to be firing at the AT-ST.

And wheeling around over their heads, looking for all the world like it was thinking about ramming the walker, was Chewbacca in LaRone's Suwantek.

"I guess they're more serious than I thought," Leia said tightly from his side.

"Believe it," Han told her, his mind racing. If he could just warn Chewie off somehow, maybe get him to go back to the spaceport. But with all the comlinks being jammed—

He looked back at the AT-ST, at the gap between the command module and the leg assembly. If the technical readouts he'd seen were correct, that was where all the antennas were located. Including those that handled comm jamming.

It was worth a try. Lining his blaster up on the gap, he opened fire.

"Wave him off, then—do *something*," the Emperor's Hand ordered. "He's a sitting avian up there."

"I'll try," LaRone said, standing up. *Don't fire*, he pleaded silently as he waved his arms in an effort to get Chewbacca's attention. *Please don't fire.* With the upgrades ISB had loaded onto the Suwantek's weapons systems, a single twin burst could probably blow the AT-ST to shredded metal.

Unfortunately, it would also cut straight through the protective armoring on the high-intensity power cells and turn the AT-ST into a fireball that would take out the stormtroopers, most of the buildings on this block, and possibly the Suwantek itself along with it.

Fortunately, Chewbacca seemed to understand that. He was still flying around, but there was no indication that he had even activated the Suwantek's laser cannons. LaRone waved his arms again, trying to get him to pull back.

Then, inexplicably, the low-level static coming from his comlink abruptly vanished. "We have comm," he called to the young woman beside him.

"Someone's taken out the AT-ST's jamming," she said. "Now warn him off."

LaRone nodded and keyed his comlink to their private frequency. "Chewbacca, this is LaRone," he said, lowering his voice. "You need to get out of here. We can handle this."

Apparently he hadn't lowered it enough. "You know that pilot?" the Emperor's Hand demanded.

"He's associated with us," LaRone improvised. "I've told him to go back to the spaceport."

"Good—no, wait a minute," the young woman said. She looked back at the approaching walker, an intense expression on her face. "What kind of armor does that ship have?"

"Reasonably strong," LaRone told her, wondering uneasily what she had in mind. The minute the Suwantek went into serious combat she would surely see it for the disguised special ops craft that it was. Ten minutes after that he and the others would be in custody pending an inquiry. An hour after the inquiry was finished they would be in ISB hands.

"Good, because it's going to have to take a little more fire," the woman said. "Here's the new plan . . ."

✳   ✳   ✳

"LaRone wants you to do *what?*" Han demanded into his comlink, watching as the Suwantek made a wide curve toward the west as if starting to head back toward Greencliff. "That's crazy."

Chewbacca rumbled an answer.

"Yeah, and *he's* crazy, too," Han growled.

"What's he doing?" Luke asked.

"Who's LaRone?" Leia added.

"We don't exactly know who LaRone is," Han said grimly, "and he wants Chewie to be some kind of bait."

"For an *AT-ST?*" Leia asked, sounding stunned.

"Don't worry—that ship's tougher than it looks," Han said. "That's not the problem. The problem is that now that the jamming's gone, this place is going to be crawling with Imperials pretty soon."

"Then shouldn't we go?" Luke prompted.

"Go where?" Han retorted. "Back to the spaceport and pretend we're just shopping? That's our ride up there, remember?"

"*That's* our ride?" Leia put in. "What happened to the *Falcon?*"

"There he goes," Luke said before Han could answer.

The Suwantek was on the move, all right, turning back over the street behind the stormtroopers. Dropping its nose, it threw power to its drive and charged straight for the oncoming AT-ST.

Mara was crouched on the back of the speeder bike, gazing down the narrow alley at the street half a block away, when she heard the scout trooper's muffled comlink acknowledgment. Silently, she counted down the seconds, getting a solid grip on his shoulders as she hunched down behind him—

And as her mental count reached zero, he revved the speeder and they were off.

Mara squinted against the sudden wind rushing across her face, holding tightly to the edges of the trooper's chest plate. Somewhere ahead and to the right the AT-ST was still coming, but with her view blocked by the

building beside her she couldn't see either it or the freighter that was supposedly now flying straight toward it. The squad commander out there was
calling the numbers, and Mara could only trust that he knew what he was
doing.

The speeder was coming up to the end of the alley. Directly in front of
her she caught a blurred glimpse of the freighter as it shot past, climbing
for altitude. Over the roar of its drive she heard the AT-ST open fire; saw
one of its thick-pad feet hit the permacrete directly in front of them. The
speeder shot out of the alley.

And Mara saw that the gamble had worked. Caaldra had pulled out all
the stops as the intruder shot past overhead, his chin blasters elevated as
high as they could go, the light blaster turret on his left side swiveled up,
all the weapons firing at full power. It was the logical response to a large
and unclassified attacker. More to the point, it was exactly the same response Caaldra had shown the first time the freighter had overflown him.

Only what he seemed to have forgotten was that with all its weapons
pointed upward, the ground at his feet was now unprotected. With exqui-
site skill the scout trooper sent his speeder bike straight across the AT-ST's
path, bare centimeters in front of its next step.

As they passed in front of the walker, Mara jumped.

Her outstretched hands caught the base of the chin blasters just in front
of their housing, her momentum swinging her completely around the
weapons and landing her in another crouch on the precarious footing of
the housing itself. Pushing off, she jumped again, this time to the top of
the command module.

With one hand gripping the entry hatch handrail for balance, she
drew and ignited her lightsaber with her other hand and slashed sideways
through the heavy armor, cutting directly through the cockpit's twin seats.

Nothing happened.

For a moment she continued to kneel on top of the hatch, her mind
frozen as the walker continued striding down the street. It was impossible—
an AT-ST's cockpit was nearly as tight as that of a TIE fighter. There was
no way she could have missed the pilot.

Unless there wasn't one.

And then it all fell into place. Swearing under her breath, she stepped back onto the grating of the cockpit cooling system and jabbed her light-saber blade through the entry hatch's locking mechanism. Closing down the weapon, she pulled the hatch open.

The cockpit was empty.

She slid feetfirst through the narrow opening and maneuvered her way through the cramped space into the pilot's seat. The autoguide and sentry-mode sections of the control board glowed a cheerful green; scowling, Mara shut them both down. The ponderous rolling motion stopped as the AT-ST finally came to a halt, the blaster cannons depressing to their off positions.

For another moment Mara sat where she was, glowering at the controls, feeling like a complete fool. An AT-ST's computer could easily handle the uncomplicated terrain of a city street, while its sentry mode could—and would—track and fire at anything that came too close without a properly coded transponder. All Caaldra had had to do was get the machine pointed in the right direction, make sure it was traveling slowly enough that Mara would decide she had a chance of stopping it, and then disappear into the night.

The Emperor would be furious. Vader would never let her hear the end of it.

She took a deep breath, forcing away the images. Neither of them needed to hear about her failure, because she hadn't yet failed. The AT-ST's computer might be competent enough to handle a nice simple city street, but it wasn't nearly sophisticated enough to maneuver itself out of the hole Caaldra had blown in the *Happer's Way*'s cargo bay. That meant Caaldra *had* been with it once, and therefore had been at the Greencliff Spaceport, which meant he couldn't be that far ahead of her. More to the point, she knew where he was going.

She would just have to get there first.

The stream of orders and reports suddenly coming over the general comm frequency had been LaRone's first indication that the Imperial searchers in the area were finally responding. But even he wasn't prepared at how quickly the street began to fill up with stormtroopers. Most of them went for the now quiescent AT-ST while a few headed toward the Suwantek, which had settled down on the street a block north with its nose pointed toward the AT-ST and its left side pressed against the row of buildings.

And some of them—far too many—were coming straight for LaRone and his companions.

A group commander strode ahead of the latter bunch, his faceplate turning to each of the five in turn before settling on LaRone. "You," he said briskly. "Identify and report."

"The AT-ST was stolen and on a rampage," LaRone said, gesturing toward it. "My squad was commandeered to help bring it down."

"Commandeered by whom?" the group commander demanded.

"Commandeered by me," a voice called from above them.

LaRone looked up to see the Emperor's Hand climbing nimbly down the side of the AT-ST, her lightsaber now tucked discreetly away in her belt. "And you are?" the group commander challenged.

"An Imperial agent," the young woman said as she dropped the last three meters to the permacrete. "Recognition code Hapspir Barrini."

The group commander seemed to straighten a little. "Yes, ma'am," he said, his voice suddenly parade-ground formal. "Lord Vader informed us of your presence in Makrin City." He gestured to LaRone. "Are these men with you?"

"For the moment," she said. "Why?"

"I need their unit designation for my report."

"I don't know their designation," the Hand said. "I also don't care." She gestured to LaRone. "Give the freighter pilot my thanks, and tell him he can return to the spaceport. You—scout—is that thing still functional?"

"Yes, ma'am, as long as you don't need anything tricky," Brightwater assured her.

"Then get ready to travel," she said. "The rest of you, back into your speeder truck."

"Just a moment, ma'am," the group commander said, starting to sound a little flustered. Vader was rumored to be a stickler for proper procedure, and this wasn't even coming close. "That freighter needs to be searched before it can leave."

"You can search it at the spaceport," the Emperor's Hand told him. "I don't want it sitting here blocking the street."

"Ma'am—"

"You have your orders, group commander," she cut off the protest, her eyes on LaRone. "Commander?"

"Yes, ma'am," LaRone said, a cold feeling settling into him as he keyed his comm for their private frequency. The Hand hadn't noticed it—she'd been in the AT-ST cockpit at the time—but just as Chewbacca had settled the Suwantek onto the permacrete, its portside ramp had lowered into the mouth of the alley the ship was currently pressed up against. From his angle and distance LaRone hadn't been able to see if anyone had gone aboard, but the Wookiee's carefully casual positioning was way too precise to be an accident. Solo and Luke were almost certainly back aboard, probably with their missing friend in tow.

And if the 501st searchers found them . . .

But there was nothing he could do but obey his orders. "Pilot, you're cleared to return to the Greencliff Spaceport," he called, trying to sound authoritatively casual. "Thanks for your assistance."

He tensed, wondering if the Wookiee's growled response would be loud enough for the others to hear through his helmet. But—"Got it," Solo's voice came instead. "Call us anytime—always glad to help out."

With a slight wobble, the Suwantek lifted from the permacrete, rotated 180 degrees, and headed back toward the spaceport. "He acknowledges and says they were glad to help," LaRone relayed.

"Good," the Emperor's Hand said. "Now get in that truck."

"*After* you identify your unit," the group commander put in, taking a step to put himself between LaRone and the speeder truck. His arms shifted position, bringing his E-11 from its cross-chest rest position to hip aim, pointed at LaRone.

LaRone grimaced. *So this is how it ends,* flickered through his mind. *Not in glorious battle against some enemy of the Empire, but in quiet shame.*

All because he'd seen an air vehicle going down and made the decision to try to help.

Then, to his astonishment, the Emperor's Hand stepped between him and the leveled blaster. "They're with me," she said, her voice calm but edged with permafrost. "Their assignment is to be with me, their unit designation is as assistants to me, their authorization comes from *me*. Are there any other questions?"

"Ma'am—"

"I said, are there any other questions?"

The group commander's chest plate shifted as he took a deep breath. "No, ma'am," he said, bringing his blaster back to rest position.

"Good," the woman said. "Lord Vader told me not to interfere with your search. You'd best get on with it."

"Yes, ma'am." With a final look at LaRone, the commander turned and strode off.

The young woman watched him the first few steps, then turned back to LaRone. "In the truck," she said tartly. "First stop's the spaceport."

A minute later they were heading north, LaRone at the controls. "Where exactly in the spaceport, ma'am?" he asked

"A freighter called the *Happer's Way*," she said. "It's where the rogue AT-ST came from."

"You think the thief went back there?"

"It's possible, but I doubt it," she said. "Mostly I want to lock it down to make sure he *can't* get out that way. I also need to collect some items I left aboard."

LaRone frowned. *She'd* left items aboard the thief's ship? "I see," he said, wishing he actually did.

"And after that," the woman added, "we're heading for the governor's palace."

LaRone felt his muscles tighten. "The palace?" he asked carefully.

"Yes," she said. "You have a problem with that?"

LaRone threw a sideways look at Marcross, seated beside him. Even through the armor he could sense the other's unnatural stiffness. "No, ma'am," LaRone said. "My unit's at your complete disposal."

"Yes," she said softly. "I know."

Chapter Twenty-One

CAALDRA HAD NOT, AS IT TURNED OUT, RETURNED TO THE *HAPPER'S WAY* in Mara's absence. Still, there was no way to know that going in, and there was also no point in taking unnecessary chances. Mara took four of the stormtroopers in with her, sending them out in pairs to search the freighter, leaving the scout trooper outside on guard duty.

Her satchel was exactly where she'd left it, seemingly untouched. But only seemingly. Caaldra had left most of her equipment alone, but had apparently spent a pleasant hour on the way back from Gepparin gimmicking her grenades and the tiny hold-out sleeve blaster. Leaving those items untouched, Mara changed once again into her black combat suit, this time adding the cloak and sleeves for extra protection against prying eyes, targeting sensors, and the dropping air temperatures outside. She fastened her hip-riding K-14 blaster in place, tucked her lightsaber into her belt, and headed back outside.

Ten minutes after arriving at the freighter they were on the road again, heading west along a deserted tree-lined street toward the palace.

"You know where we're going?" Mara called from the rear seat. She'd made a subtle point of creating this seating arrangement when they'd reassembled for the trip: Mara in the back alone, the other stormtroopers seated two by two in the rows in front of her. As usual, the scout trooper ran point on his speeder bike.

"We have a map already loaded," the squad commander confirmed from the driver's seat, pointing to the display. "It has the best route marked."

"Excellent," Mara said. Drawing her lightsaber, she rested the hilt on the seat back in front of her, pointing the weapon forward. "As long as we have a few minutes anyway, let's hear your story."

One of the stormtroopers in the seat in front of her half turned his head. "Excuse me?" he asked. His right shoulder shifted subtly, indicating a movement of his hand toward his holstered E-11.

With a sigh, Mara ignited her lightsaber.

The magenta blade *snap-hiss*ed into existence, running down the center of the truck between the two sets of white helmets. "Just leave your weapons where they are," she advised, in case having a lightsaber blade thirty centimeters from their necks wasn't enough of a hint. "We'll start with your operating numbers, your unit designation, and your current assignment. All the things you tried so hard to avoid telling the group commander back there."

Four helmets tilted as the stormtroopers exchanged glances across the glowing blade. "Shy, are we?" Mara went on conversationally. "Let me get the ball rolling. You and your freighter—*your* freighter, not something belonging to some vague friend or associate—were on Gepparin in the aftermath of the *Reprisal*'s attack on the BloodScars' base. I saw you sitting on the last intact pad when I took off from the Commodore's emergency bolt-hole. All of this sounding familiar?"

"Yes, ma'am, it is," the squad commander said, his voice tight. "But we weren't part of the attack."

"I know that," Mara said. "If you were, you'd have attacked or at least challenged me as I headed out. So why *were* you there?"

"We were tracking the BloodScars," the commander said. "We had evidence that they'd been gathering other criminal organizations in the sector into a single massive pirate group. We went to Gepparin hoping to find out who, if anyone, was funding this operation."

"And did you?"

His helmet shifted as he gave his seat partner a sideways glance. "We think so, yes."

"Good," Mara said. "Because so did I. Whose authority are you operating under?"

"We don't actually . . ." His voice trailed away.

"If you're worried about my clearance, don't be," Mara assured him. "I'm about as high in the ranks as you can get, even if I'm not on anyone's official list." She raised her eyebrows. "I take it *you're* not on any official lists, either?"

"No, we're not," the commander confirmed.

"So what's your unit designation?"

He hesitated again. "Mostly, we're known as the Hand of Judgment."

Mara cocked an eyebrow. "Sounds a little too poetic for Stormtrooper Command," she commented. "And *way* too poetic for ISB."

"We chose it ourselves, actually," one of the others put in.

"And we're not allowed to reveal anything more," the commander continued. "I'm sorry."

Mara pursed her lips. She could force the issue, of course. But with Governor Choard presumably alerted to her presence, it would be difficult and dangerous to try to break into his compound alone. This Hand of Judgment hadn't attacked her as she departed Gepparin; more significantly, they'd come to her aid after Caaldra's gimmicked AT-ST had shot her down.

And with Vader and the 501st completely preoccupied with their search for Leia Organa, this was the most trustworthy help she was likely to find in Makrin City. Reason enough for her to have fended off that nosy group commander. "As you wish," she said. "But whatever your usual chain of command or lack of one, for the next two hours you're working for me. Understood?"

"Yes, ma'am," the commander said.

"Good," Mara said. Closing down the lightsaber, she returned it to her belt. "What are your operating numbers?"

"We usually just use names," the commander said. "It's . . . shorter. Quicker in combat."

Privately, Mara had always thought that, too. But Stormtrooper Command had always loved their fancy number system. "Names, then."

"I'm LaRone." The commander gestured to his right. "This is Marcross. Behind him is Grave; behind me is Quiller. Our scout trooper is Brightwater."

"Call me Jade," Mara told them, stretching out with the Force. She'd never heard of a stormtrooper unit roaming the Empire without a firm chain of command attached. But it could be something the Emperor had set up personally. If he had, they might recognize her name.

There was no reaction that she could sense, however. Apparently the Emperor had chosen to keep her secret from them, as well as vice versa.

"Ma'am?" Grave asked.

"Jade."

"Jade," the other corrected. "May I ask what the plan is once we reach the palace?"

"The plan is for me to break in, and for you to help me do it," Mara said. "That's all you need to know."

"Yes, ma'am," Grave said.

"And be ready for some opposition," Mara added. "I expect we're going to find some."

In the front seat Marcross glanced sideways at LaRone. "Don't worry," he said, his voice grim. "We're ready."

Governor Choard's hastily organized party in the ballroom downstairs had taken up far too much of Disra's precious time this evening. But the guests were finally starting to filter out, and Disra was at last able to slip away to his office. Turning on the lights, he sealed the door behind him and headed for his desk.

He got three steps before his eyes abruptly registered the fact that he had a visitor.

"Why aren't you answering your comlink?" Caaldra demanded as he looked up from Disra's computer.

Disra felt his heart seize up. What in blazes was Caaldra doing with his computer? "The governor threw together a quick reception this evening," he managed. "I had to put in an appearance."

"A reception?" Caaldra repeated. "A *party*? Now?"

"When your city's crawling with stormtroopers, that's exactly what you need to soothe all the top-tier people," Disra said. Unlocking his knees, he started casually toward the desk. There was a hold-out blaster hidden under the chair if he could get to it. "What are *you* doing here?"

Caaldra's face twisted in an almost-smile, and for the first time Disra noticed the rigidly controlled pain lurking behind the other's eyes. "I brought you your AT-STs, of course."

"I meant what are you doing here in this office?" Disra clarified, stepping up to the desk. From his new vantage point he could see Caaldra's torn left sleeve and the rough field bandage wrapped around his forearm. "What happened?"

"Small accident," Caaldra said, lifting the arm slightly. "I had to blow the freighter's hold." His lips twisted. "I suppose you didn't hear anything about *that*, either."

"I haven't heard any news since you hauled me out of the reception earlier to get you your palace landing clearance," Disra gritted. At the time he'd thought it more important to be present and visible at Choard's stupid party than to monitor Caaldra's unexpected arrival. In retrospect it looked like he'd been wrong. "Fill me in."

"First of all, our Imperial agent's somehow managed to get herself unstranded," Caaldra said. "She's here in Makrin City."

An icy shiver ran up Disra's back. "You said you'd gimmicked the last functional ship left on Gepparin."

"Apparently not well enough," Caaldra said. "Ten minutes after I landed at Greencliff she put down not three slots over."

"You mean she *followed* you here?"

Caaldra cocked his head. "If we're lucky."

Disra snorted. "You have a strange definition of luck."

"No, I just have a few new facts," Caaldra said. "On the trip from Gepparin I was finally able to get through to one of the crewers I know aboard the *Reprisal*. It now seems likely that Ozzel's attack on the BloodScars' base had nothing to do with us."

"I thought the Imperials didn't go after pirates these days."

"They do when the attack can serve as a convenient cover for something else," Caaldra said grimly. "A lot of this is still at the unfiltered rumor level, but it appears that our Imperial agent may have seen something in the *Reprisal*'s files that she wasn't supposed to know about, and that Ozzel followed her to Gepparin to shut her up."

"You're joking," Disra said, staring at him. "What did she *see*?"

"Officially, it was something about a secret ISB operation that some of the *Reprisal's* stormtroopers were co-opted for." Caaldra cocked an eyebrow. "Unofficially, rumor has it those stormtroopers aren't on any mission, but that they murdered an ISB officer and deserted."

Disra goggled. "Impossible," he insisted. "Stormtroopers don't desert. Ever."

"They didn't used to," Caaldra agreed. "But who knows? Rot spreads from the top, and Imperial Center these days is about as fetid as you can get." He waved a hand around him. "Hence this whole bid for independence, remember?"

"Yes, thank you, I *do* recall something about that," Disra said acidly, his mind racing. But if the agent wasn't after them . . . "Wait a minute. How many stormtroopers were supposed to have deserted?"

"Very good," Caaldra said, inclining his head. "There were five of them. The same number that the follow-up reports from Ranklinge indicate were on hand when Cav'Saran went down."

Considerably fewer than the three squads the Bargleg swoop gang claimed attacked them on Drunost, Disra recalled. But since when could a bunch of swoopers be trusted for accuracy? "So *they're* the rogue stormtrooper unit running around Shelsha?"

"Our so-called Hand of Judgment," Caaldra agreed. "All rather ironic, really. We've been all worried about an Imperial agent and her private stormtrooper squad, when in fact if she ever actually came across them she'd probably execute all five of them on the spot."

"Comforting to know," Disra growled. "Or it might be, if she wasn't nosing around our doorstep."

Caaldra shook his head. "You're missing the point. It's the *stormtroopers* who've been backtracking the BloodScars, not her. There's no longer any reason to assume she's made any connection at all between us and the BloodScars."

Disra thought about that. It did indeed sound reasonable. "But you said she'd followed you here."

"All she knows is that I was with the Commodore at Gepparin," Caaldra said. "I guess it's just as well that idiot controller on the *Executor* wouldn't let me land here at the palace."

Disra exhaled in relief. So the agent wasn't gunning for them at all. The whole thing had been a gigantic coincidence that he and Caaldra had simply misread. "Then we're off the hook," he said.

"Probably," Caaldra said. "But it's always possible she found something in the Gepparin rubble that points in this direction. We need to be ready, just in case."

Disra shivered. Yes, indeed. Because if the agent made an appearance before Disra was able to get those records to Vader, he would be going down in flames. "Any idea how soon we might expect her?" he asked.

Caaldra shrugged. "I left her a diversion, but there's no way of knowing how long that'll keep her busy." He waved at the computer. "I've raised the security level on your external intruder defenses, but I can't restructure your guard configuration without authority."

"I can do that," Disra said, gesturing for him to move aside. "Will that be enough to stop her?"

"Not if she's on the hunt," Caaldra said, climbing out of the chair and stepping away from the desk. "Which means we need to make our move." He raised his eyebrows. "And we need to make it *now*."

Disra stared at him. "Are you *insane*? Declare independence with Vader and the Five-oh-first right here in the city?"

"If we do it right, they'll have more immediate matters to worry about than you or me," Caaldra said. "I've already ordered the pirate and raider groups into their positions. All you have to do is send out the orders."

And within minutes or hours Shelsha sector would be engulfed in fire and war and death. The pirates would attack and destroy the Imperial garrisons, the raiders would seize and hold critical military equipment plants, and the swoop gangs and carefully placed moles would take major cities and major Imperial officials hostage. The declaration of independence would be made, and Imperial Center would be dared to do something about it.

And there would be no going back. "I can make the calls," Disra said carefully as he activated the comm panel. "But it's going to take time. You'll need to make sure the agent doesn't get in here until I'm done."

"I can do that," Caaldra confirmed grimly. "You just worry about your end." Turning his back, he headed for the secret door.

Disra watched him go, his hand itching to draw the hidden blaster and shoot Caaldra down. But he didn't dare. He still had to collect those records and get them to Vader, and he had no illusions about the palace guards' ability to keep the approaching Imperial agent away that long. Only Caaldra could do that.

Besides, if he shot at the man now, he might miss.

"By the way," he called. "Does anyone know where this Hand of Judgment is now?"

Caaldra shook his head. "Out somewhere being white knights for hope and glory, no doubt," he said. "Don't worry. When Gepparin went, so did their last hope of pinning us to the BloodScars." He opened the door and disappeared into the maze of secret passages beyond.

"Let's hope so," Disra muttered under his breath as he turned back to his desk and switched off his comm panel. No messages were going out to any pirates tonight. Not from *this* palace. Not if he could help it.

Keying the computer, he got back to his records compilation. Ironic, Caaldra had called it. Little did he know. For nearly two years now Disra had been manipulating the man, jumping him through hoops only Disra could see. Now, suddenly, events had effectively pushed Disra to the sidelines, with his life and future resting completely on Caaldra's ability to intercept and destroy an Imperial agent.

Disra could only hope the man was as good as he claimed.

They were still five blocks from the palace grounds when LaRone began to notice the disguised sentries.

"Actually, I think there was one even farther back," Grave said when LaRone commented. "A couple of blocks ago. It was a little hard to tell— he was rigged out to look like a low-class slythmonger."

"Yes, he was a sentry," Jade confirmed from the backseat. "I could see it in his eyes."

"Do Imperial governors typically set this wide a picket screen?" Quiller asked.

"Not usually," Jade said. "Looks like someone in the palace has a guilty conscience."

"So what do we do about them?" Grave asked as they passed another of the quiet sentries.

"Nothing," Jade said. "All they're seeing here is a few more stormtroopers in a city already full of them. I doubt they'll even bother to call it in."

"We'll need more than just familiar armor to get through the front gate, though," Quiller warned.

"Fortunately, we're not going in that way," Jade said. "The governor's built himself quite an estate over the years, with lots of ground and plenty of nooks and crannies. We'll find our own way in."

"Though the perimeter wall's probably rigged six ways from Imperial Center," Grave warned.

"Maybe even seven or eight," Jade agreed. "Don't worry—I've had some experience with these things."

Beside LaRone, Marcross stirred. "There's another way," he said quietly. "We can use the governor's emergency exit."

LaRone looked at him in surprise. "He has an emergency exit?"

"All governors and moffs do," Jade said with a touch of contempt. "How do *you* know about it, Marcross?"

"I grew up in Makrin City," Marcross said. "I used to hang out with Choard's son Crayg when we were teenagers. The exit's in the northeast side of the wall, at the edge of the Farfarn District, one of the city's working-class neighborhoods. There's a door-sized section of the wall that opens up."

"And Choard just let the two of you wander in and out?" Quiller asked.

"I don't think he ever knew we were doing it," Marcross said. "It's pretty far from all the security at the main gate, and it leads into the edge of one of his garden areas. Mostly pools and fountains and trees, with lots of flag-stones so you don't leave any footprints. Crayg used to sneak out at night and hit the clubs and cantinas."

"How did you deflect the security tags?" Jade asked.

"It wasn't tagged," Marcross said. "I think Choard was as worried about his own guards turning on him as he was about trouble from outside. He didn't want anyone inside knowing about the exit. You *do* need a passkey to open it, though."

"Not a problem," Jade assured him. "Let's take a look."

Marcross's chest plate expanded slightly as he took a deep breath. "Turn right at the next corner."

His directions led them off the main road and into a slightly marshy area crisscrossed by meandering creeks. The streets turned narrow and winding as they threaded their way through and between the creeks, and LaRone noticed that most of the houses were built up as much as a meter above ground level. Apparently flooding was a constant concern here.

"There," Marcross said, pointing ahead. "Where the wall bows out a little and almost touches the edge of the street."

LaRone took his foot off the accelerator, letting the speeder truck coast as he peered ahead at the spot framed in his headlights.

"Not very secure," Quiller commented doubtfully. "If your enemies were smart enough to surround the grounds, you'd walk right into their arms."

"There's supposed to be a heavy long-range fighter prepped and hidden in that house over there," Marcross said, pointing to a dilapidated house on the far side of the street from the wall. "There's also supposed to be a force-field tunnel you can activate that'll give you safe passage between the wall and the house. I never saw that work, though."

"What are we going to do about a passkey?" Grave asked.

"We don't need one," Jade said. "We're not going in that way. Keep driving, LaRone—I'll tell you where to stop."

"If we're not going to use it, why did you want me to show it to you?" Marcross demanded as LaRone continued on past the secret door.

"Watch your tone, stormtrooper," Jade warned. "We're not going in that way because it'll be the entrance of choice for the conspirators, and I don't want us bumping into them until we're ready. There—that section between the two trees. Pull over there."

LaRone brought the speeder truck to a halt. "Everyone out," Jade ordered, pushing up her own swing-wing door. "Give me a perimeter."

She strode over to the wall, lightsaber in hand. LaRone had formed the others into a standard, outward-facing guard-box formation by the time Brightwater glided his speeder bike back around and came to a halt beside them. "What are we doing?" he asked.

"I'm not sure," LaRone admitted, watching Jade out of the corner of his eye. She was leaning against the wall, her hands and one ear pressed against the cold stone. Slowly, methodically, she moved herself in a grid search pattern along and down the surface. "We're going in, but I'm not sure exactly how."

"Quietly and without casualties," Jade said, stepping away from the wall. "Ever hear of cryseefa gas?"

"It's an acidic poison," Brightwater said. "Highly corrosive and lethal to most oxygen-breathing species."

"Very good." Jade tapped a section of wall. "There's a canister of compressed cryseefa buried in the wall right here. *And* here—" She indicated another spot. "—and here, and here."

"Ready to kill anyone who tries to punch through the wall," LaRone murmured, a shiver of disgust running through him.

"Along with everyone for fifty meters around him," Jade said. "A simple but very undiscriminating weapon."

"And you can tell where the canisters are?" Grave asked.

"Walls like this collect a lot of sun heat during the day," Jade explained, unlimbering her lightsaber. With a sizzling *snap-hiss*, the brilliant magenta blade burst into existence. "Stone and metal make different contraction sounds as they cool down. You might want to step back for this."

None of the stormtroopers moved. Lifting the lightsaber horizontally, Jade pushed the blade's tip gently into the stone. For a few seconds she continued to force it straight in, then shifted to a sideways motion, carefully carving out a circle. She finished the circle and shut down the lightsaber. "Do you want us to get that out?" LaRone asked.

"No need." Lifting a hand toward it, Jade inhaled slowly.

And with a muffled grinding sound of stone on stone, the cylindrical plug she'd carved worked its way out of the wall. Marcross stepped forward and caught the plug as it came free. Nodding her thanks, Jade reactivated her lightsaber and set to work on the next canister.

Five minutes later there were six stone cylinders lying on the ground beside the wall. "Is that all?" LaRone murmured.

"All we need to worry about," Jade said, turning to face them. "Understand me now. When we step inside this wall, we'll be in enemy territory. If you can get through without killing any of the guards, fine. But if you have to kill, you kill without hesitation."

"Understood," LaRone said for all of them.

A minute later, Jade had carved an opening through the safe parts of the wall big enough for them to get through. On the far side, LaRone could see some of the garden areas Marcross had described earlier. "Commander?" Jade invited as she closed down her lightsaber. "Deploy your troopers."

LaRone nodded acknowledgment. "Brightwater, you'll swing around toward the main gate," he ordered. "I want to know what their security looks like, including how many men they'll have available to draw on when the balloon goes up. Grave, Quiller: you're on flank. Marcross, you're on point. You'll lead Jade to your best choice of entrance and get her inside. I'll take rear guard. We close up as soon as Marcross gets us in and re-form for quiet incursion. Grave, give Brightwater a hand with his speeder bike."

Brightwater waddled his speeder bike to the wall, and together he and Grave maneuvered it through the opening. The scout trooper got on and took off with a subdued whine, heading to the left and the cover of the garden foliage. Grave and Quiller went next, branching to right and left, with Marcross behind them. LaRone took a step forward—

"A moment, Commander," Jade murmured, putting a hand on his arm. "Sensible policy dictates that the second in command knows what the mission is."

"Yes, ma'am," LaRone said, feeling his heartbeat starting to pick up.

"Our target is Governor Choard," she said. "He's committed high treason, both in conspiring with pirates against Imperial shipping, and in sending the *Reprisal* to try to kill me on Gepparin. Those crimes have earned him the death penalty."

"Understood," LaRone said, a strange sense of unreality sifting into him like fine desert sand. It was one thing to sit out in space or at a pirate nest and talk about judgment and duty and principle. It was quite another to stand outside the palace of an Imperial governor and contemplate his execution in cold blood.

"Then let's do it," Jade said. Shifting her lightsaber to her left hand and drawing her blaster with her right, she slipped through the opening.

To defend the Empire and its citizens . . . Making sure the safety on his E-11 was off, LaRone climbed through behind her.

Chapter Twenty-Two

GOVERNOR CHOARD APPARENTLY LIKED HIS GARDENS ROUGH AND primitive. Once they were through the wall and past a narrow brook that ran along the estate's inner edge, they hit a wide patch of trees, closely spaced bushes, and reedy plants growing out of a ground cover composed mainly of flagstones interspersed with flakes of dead bark.

Oddly enough, for the first few minutes it seemed as if the enemy had completely missed their arrival. Mara saw and heard no one as they slipped through the trees, and could sense no suddenly heightened alertness anywhere around them.

The patch of forest ran for about thirty meters, then abruptly gave way to a wide, grassy area, across which they could see a double row of comfortable outdoor chairs set up near the wall of the palace itself.

"That's the game field," Marcross said, pointing to the field. "That door behind the seats leads into a kitchen adjunct where refreshments can be set out for the players and spectators."

"What's past the adjunct?"

"The main kitchen," Marcross said. "From there you can go to the first-floor private dining area, the formal dining room, or the main ballroom."

"Stairs?"

"Closest set is behind the kitchen, off the service corridor," Marcross said. "There's a set of turbolifts there, too."

Mara pursed her lips thoughtfully. It all looked very straightforward, as it was no doubt meant to. But as usual, looks were deceiving. The palace's stylishly crenellated walls had been combined with careful placement of decorative colored lighting to create deeply shadowed indentations at regular intervals along the walls. Most of those nooks probably sheltered sentries—human, animal, or droid—with their eyes and other senses trained on the wide lawn she and the stormtroopers would have to cross.

But Mara still had a few tricks up her sleeve. A couple of minutes to surreptitiously move a small canister into place upwind, and an oddly persistent mist would begin drifting across the critical lines of sight.

LaRone muttered something under his breath and sidled closer to her. "Brightwater's in sight of the main entrance," he reported. "There are nearly fifty civilian landspeeders near there."

Mara frowned. An emergency meeting of Choard's fellow conspirators? "Could they be advisers in for a meeting?"

LaRone relayed the question. "The speeders are all too expensive for even high-ranking civil servants," he said. "More likely Choard's invited the city's upper-class citizens to a dinner or party."

"That could be awkward," Mara said, peering again at the kitchen's lighted windows. If Choard was feeding a roomful of guests, the kitchen might not be a good place to break in after all. "Marcross, what's above the kitchen?"

"Directly above it is a storage area," Marcross said. "Tables and extra chairs. Flanking the storage room are meeting rooms that open into the reception area outside the main ballroom—"

Suddenly, without warning, a huge dark mass of vines rose silently from the garden floor behind them.

There was a single startled curse as the four stormtroopers spun around, their blasters tracking toward the apparition. "No!" Mara barked.

But the warning came too late. Even as she ignited her lightsaber, four blaster bolts lanced out, striking the creature dead center. With a crackling roar, the whole mass burst into flame.

And with that, the stealthy part of their incursion came to an end. "Inside," Mara snapped, closing down her lightsaber and bursting out from the bushes onto the exposed grassland.

"What the hell was *that*?" LaRone demanded as he caught up with her.

"Nouland flare," Mara ground out. Shadowy figures were starting to emerge from the concealed guard nooks, the firelight flickering off their blaster rifles as they moved to cut off the intruders. "They're used some places to smoke out intruders."

LaRone snorted. "Quite literally, I see."

"Exactly," Mara agreed tightly. "Nonsentient, not really dangerous, but big and scary and very flammable. Must have been installed sometime after Marcross stopped coming here."

The closest pair of sentries opened fire, their shots sizzling through the air past Mara's head. LaRone sent a precise pair of shots in return, and one of the sentries flopped to the ground and lay still. Quiller, on LaRone's other side, fired a single shot that took out the other of the pair. "What's the new plan?" he called.

"Same as the old one," Mara told him, slowing her pace enough to let them catch up. "Give me a wedge."

The four stormtroopers moved around in front of her, LaRone and Marcross taking dual point, Quiller and Grave a little behind and outboard from them. Mara set herself in the center of the formation, carefully and systematically targeting the scattered pairs of guards converging on them. The air was filling with blaster bolts now as more of their opponents reached optimum firing range, and Mara heard one of the stormtroopers grunt as a shot found a way through his armor. They were halfway to the kitchen door now, the bolts starting to sizzle ever closer.

And then fifty meters away around a corner of the building two pairs of swoops appeared. Driving hard toward the intruders, apparently with little or no regard for the guards between them and their targets, they opened fire with underslung blaster cannons.

"Keep going!" Mara snapped, jamming her blaster back into its holster and igniting her lightsaber.

"Jade—" LaRone began.

"That's an order," Mara cut him off. Stepping out of the relative protection of their moving screen, she turned to face the incoming swoops.

To her surprise and chagrin, they ignored her completely. Instead they deliberately curved to stay on an intercept course with the stormtroopers.

Swallowing a curse, Mara snatched out her blaster again. Those cannons would make short work of even stormtrooper armor once they got close enough, and Mara had no intention of letting that happen. Thumbing the blaster's setting to full auto to open the valve between the gas chamber and conversion enabler, she hurled it in a high arc toward the approaching swoops. Midway through its flight she stretched out with the Force and caught it in a firm grip, tweaked its trajectory, and guided it to a spot just in front of the lead swoop and directly into the blaster cannon's line of fire.

The resulting explosion, as such things went, was fairly tame. The cannon's next shot shattered the blaster's gas chamber housing, blowing the rest of the weapon apart and igniting a brief fireball as the remnants of the shot then activated the expanding gas.

But if the explosion itself wasn't particularly impressive, its precise placement more than made up the difference. The force of the blast slammed into the swoop's nose, causing the vehicle to rear up and back like a crazed animal.

The rider, the bulk of his attention on the stormtroopers, didn't have a chance. For that first crucial second the swoop thrashed wildly beneath him as he fought to bring it back under control. It slammed sideways against his partner, and now there were two out-of-control swoops flailing across the yard.

The second pair, coming up behind them, swerved hard to get out of the way. They were curving around to bring themselves back on track when Grave and his T-28 nailed them both. Two shots later he had taken out the two flailing ones, as well.

"You coming?" LaRone called back to Mara.

"On my way," Mara said. She paused first to deflect a pair of blaster bolts, then sprinted after the stormtroopers. They had reached the door, and LaRone was blasting away at a surprisingly stubborn door lock, when she caught up with them.

"Get back," she ordered, quickly ending the lock's resistance with a slash of her lightsaber. "You four get inside," she went on as she pulled the door open. Beyond it, she caught a glimpse of kitchen equipment and frantically retreating kitchen staff but—as yet—no blasters. "Anything from Brightwater?"

"He's got the gate personnel pinned down, including most of their vehicles," LaRone told her. "He apologizes for the swoops—no idea where they came from."

"Just tell him to watch himself," Mara said, looking back at the converging guards. "Get inside—I'll take rear guard. Seal the door behind you if you can."

"What? But—"

"You have your orders, Commander," Mara said sharply. "If I don't make it, carry out the mission."

"Yes, ma'am," LaRone said, this time with the proper professional tone. "Good luck." With a final salvo at the approaching guards, he and the other stormtroopers slipped inside and closed the door behind them.

Mara put her back to the door and for a few seconds continued to deflect the incoming blaster bolts. But her opponents were getting closer, the decreasing distance sharpening their aim, and she knew that within seconds even the camouflaging effects of her cloak and combat suit and a Force-driven defense would be unable to handle all of them.

She gave it two more seconds anyway, stretching her margin to the limit to give the stormtroopers more time to seal the door. Then, pushing off the wall for extra momentum, she sprinted outward toward the forest strip and the perimeter wall beyond.

She got two steps before the guards reacted to the move, and managed three more before the blaster bolts were once again tracking toward her. She took two more steps and then jammed her feet into the ground, spinning around as she brought herself to an abrupt halt. Bending her knees, lightsaber at the ready, she stretched to the Force for strength and jumped.

For a second she soared above the fury of the blasterfire as the guards once again tried to react to her unexpected tactic. She was above second-floor height now, nearly to third, the wall rushing up toward her as she hit the top of her arc and started back down again. As she reached the wall she slashed her lightsaber in a wide ring in front of her, cutting a circle through the stone. Tucking her knees to her chest, she slammed feetfirst into the center of the circle.

With a thunderous crash of breaking stone, the section of wall collapsed inward. The impact robbed Mara of her forward momentum, and for a heart-stopping second she teetered on the edge of the hole, fighting for balance. Then her free hand found a grip on the edge, and as the blaster bolts belatedly began to stab at her again she pulled herself inside to safety.

She had ended up in the storage room Marcross had mentioned, empty except for two carts loaded with round fold-leg tables and three dollies stacked halfway to the low ceiling with ornate, high-backed chairs. A single door was visible at the far end. Closing down her lightsaber, she headed toward it.

She was halfway there when the hint of an odd smell twitched at her nose. Still moving, she started into her sensory enhancement techniques.

There was a sudden, loud splash at her feet. She looked down, rapidly cutting back on the enhancement to find that her last step had landed her in a pool of liquid. So far the pool was only a few millimeters deep, but as the edge flowed past her feet she could see it was getting deeper.

And that single enhanced sniff had left no doubt as to what the liquid was.

One of the two table carts was a couple of meters to her left. Instantly she leapt sideways up onto it, nearly braining herself against the ceiling as she did so. The tables rattled together as she hit them, and she had to grab a pair of the edges to keep from sliding off.

"Imperial agent? Celina, or whatever your real name is?"

Mara looked up, her eyes probing the darkened room. The voice had been muffled, which meant he was outside the door. Considering the liquid rapidly filling the room, she reflected grimly, outside was a very smart place for him to be. "I'm here, Caaldra," she called back. The edge of the pool had made it nearly to the back wall now, leaving her stranded in the middle of the room. "Better give maintenance a call—you've got a serious leak in here."

"And just in time, too," Caaldra said. "I was expecting you to come through a window into one of the meeting rooms, not right through the wall like you did. Looks like I've ruined a couple of carpets over there for nothing."

"You're going to ruin a lot more than that if this stuff goes up," Mara warned. "What is it about you and fire, anyway? Were you burned as a kid or something?"

"Not at all," he assured her. "I've just learned over the years that fire and water are the two things even professionals usually aren't prepared for."

"I'll have to remember that," Mara promised.

"I'm sure you will," Caaldra said. "And if you were thinking about jumping me when I came in with my handy igniter, don't bother. The edge of the pool's already seeped out into the reception area, which means I can touch off your private lake of fire without even opening the door."

Mara grimaced. That *had* been the direction she'd been thinking, actually. Scratch that now. "Of course, you could have done that anywhere along the line, without nearly so much talk," she pointed out. "From that I gather you want something."

"Very perceptive," Caaldra said approvingly. "I want to make a deal."

Mara cocked an eyebrow. "I'm listening. Obviously."

"Basically, I just want out," Caaldra said. "*Completely* out. I leave Shelkonwa, you don't file charges, no one comes after me."

"And in return I get to leave here uncrisped?"

"That, plus I give you all the records you need to nail Chief Administrator Disra to the wall."

"So Disra is in this, too?" Mara asked, looking around the room. No windows, no other doors, and the pool of flammable liquid was nearly ankle-deep now.

But there was the hole she'd cut in the outer wall. And there were those three stacks of chairs.

"He's in it up to his neck," Caaldra said contemptuously. "Actually, I think he's been the head mover and shaker on this thing right from square one."

"Really," Mara said, stretching out with the Force to the topmost chair on the nearest stack. For a moment it stuck to the one beneath it, but then it came free. She floated it across the room and eased it to the floor about three meters from the end of her table cart in the direction of the hole. "I'm surprised someone like Governor Choard would let anyone else run his show for him."

"*Choard's* show?" Caaldra snorted. "You must be kidding. That big stupid idiot doesn't know a thing about any of this."

Mara smiled tightly. "Nice try, Caaldra, but I know better. It takes a moff or full governor to order Imperial forces around. Not even a chief administrator can do that."

"Who said he could?" Caaldra countered. "We weren't going to order either of Shelsha's garrisons around—we were going for straight-out destruction."

"Don't be dense," Mara admonished as she moved a second chair into position, three meters past the first one. "I'm talking about the *Reprisal's* attack on Gepparin."

"The *Reprisal*?" Caaldra echoed. "You *are* on the wrong file heading, aren't you? That didn't have anything to do with us—it was Captain Ozzel trying to cover his own sorry tail. Trying to make sure you never lived to tell anyone about his deserters."

Mara frowned. "His *what*?"

"His deserters." Caaldra barked a laugh. "Oh, this *is* rare. Someone sets you up to get killed, and you don't even know why?"

"Skip the gloating and enlighten me," Mara growled.

"To put it in a clig shell, five of the *Reprisal's* stormtroopers apparently killed an ISB major, stole one of their special ships, and made a run for it."

Mara felt her breath freeze in her lungs. *Five* stormtroopers? "You know anything else about them?" she asked carefully.

"Only that ever since they took off they've been wandering around Shelsha sector poking their fingers into our plans," Caaldra said with a snort. "First they spoiled a hijacking of some heavy blaster rifles we had our eyes on; then they knocked off a patroller chief we were positioning to lead the attack on an attack starfighter plant."

And with that, the strange comment Brock had made in the Blood-Scars' command room suddenly, horribly, made sense. *Did you already know about the deserters? Or is that what you were looking for in the* Reprisal's *computer?*

Deserters. Stormtroopers. Five of them.

The Hand of Judgment.

"It makes for an interesting story, anyway," she said, trying to keep her voice casual. "Where are these renegades now?"

"Probably off somewhere doing more good deeds," Caaldra said. "The point is that Ozzel hadn't reported their disappearance and figured his neck was for it after you interrogated his other stormtroopers or whatever it was you did while you were on his ship."

"Actually, I tapped into his computer," Mara murmured, a horrible thought digging into her like a knife blade. It was the *Reprisal*'s attack on Gepparin, and *only* that attack, that had laid the burden of guilt squarely on Governor Choard's shoulders. But if Caaldra was telling the truth, then Choard could very well be a completely innocent man.

An innocent man whom she'd just sent five stormtrooper deserters to kill.

She clenched her teeth. She had to get out of here, and she had to get out now. Lifting another chair from the stack, she added it to the line. One more, and she should have enough. "So what exactly is it you want?" she called, stalling for time.

"I already told you," Caaldra said, a whisper of suspicion starting to creep into his voice. "I want a free pass out of this. What are you doing in there?"

"Waiting for you to spell out the details," Mara countered, silently cursing herself. Preoccupied with her escape plan and even more so with the miscarriage of justice she'd set into motion, she'd completely forgotten that Caaldra had already presented his request. "I know people like you," she improvised. "You'll want everything done to your exact specifications."

"Absolutely," Caaldra said, the suspicion in his voice deepening. "I'll be taking the *Happer's Way*—we'll need a quick repair job on the cargo bay first—and then you'll provide me safe passage off Shelkonwa with enough fuel—"

"Wait a second," Mara cut in as she set the final chair in line. Now all she had to do was figure out what she was going to do once she got outside. "You don't really expect me to let you fly off with a ship full of military property, do you?"

"Consider it my reward for helping you break up a potentially disastrous political crisis," Caaldra countered. "Disra was all set to issue a declaration of independence and take Shelsha sector out of the Empire."

"You must be joking," Mara scoffed, moving another chair to the wall. Unlike the others, she didn't set this one upright but laid it flat with its back sticking out through the opening. "Or else *Disra* must be joking. He'd have half the Fleet in orbit over his head inside of a week."

"You really think Palpatine would take overt military action?" Caaldra asked. "You don't think he'd cut a deal instead to keep it quiet?"

"Emperor Palpatine doesn't make deals like that," Mara said, lifting two more chairs from their stack and moving them to the hole. Setting one of them down temporarily out of the way, she maneuvered the other onto the lying chair's legs, trying to hook them together so that the new chair would brace the one leaning outside.

"Not even if one of his own very special agents recommended it?"

Mara nodded grimly to herself as the reason for this conversation finally became clear. Caaldra wasn't interested in any deals. All he wanted was to sound her out, to try to gauge Imperial Center's reaction to their insane neo-Separatist scheme. "Not even then," she told him as she locked the last chair into position with the other two. "But it's a moot point, because I'd never make such a recommendation in the first place. You're talking treason, and treason carries an automatic death penalty."

Faintly through the door, she heard his sigh. "Too bad," he said. "In that case you're not worth anything at all to me. Good-bye, agent." There was the crack of a blaster shot—

And suddenly a waist-high wall of flame erupted by the door and raced across the room toward her.

Mara reacted instantly, throwing herself off her unsteady perch atop the tables and leaping for the first of her line of chairs. She hit it and bounded off toward the second.

She was in midair on her way to the third chair when the wave front swept past, engulfing her legs in flame. Stretching out with the Force to suppress the pain, she kept going. Ahead, dimly visible through the roiling smoke and heat shimmer, she could see the hole. Landing on the final chair in line, she ducked her head and leapt through the opening onto the chair back sticking out over the yard.

The chair creaked ominously as her weight came down on it, but with the other two chairs providing a counterweight it held. The cool night air rushed over her, and she paused long enough to inhale a couple of breaths into her scorched lungs.

But her position here wasn't significantly safer than the one she'd just left. The guards she'd escaped from a few minutes earlier were still wandering around the grounds, looking for fresh targets. Even as she turned her face back toward the flames, a shout of discovery came from somewhere and the blaster bolts again began flying past. Pulling out her lightsaber, Mara ignited it and shoved off the chair back, aiming for one of the third-floor windows.

The transparisteel proved much easier to cut through on the fly than the stone wall she'd tackled the first time around. The newly cut hole led into a wide reception area, and even as she hit the floor she was racing silently on the thick carpet toward where she estimated the end of the burning storeroom below her would be.

She reached that point, went five steps farther, and stopped. "Here's something you won't expect," she murmured, and slashed a circle around her through the floor.

With a crackle of shattered wood and stone, the circle collapsed. Mara rode it down, bending her knees to absorb the impact as it smashed itself onto the floor below.

There were four of them grouped around the storeroom door: Caaldra and three armed men in civilian clothing. All four heads were turned in Mara's direction as she stepped off the broken section of flooring, their expressions ranging from stunned to dumbfounded. The man at the far left recovered faster than the others, whipping his blaster up for a quick shot. His reward was to be the first to die as Mara's lightsaber threw the shot straight back at him.

The second and third men, despite their civilian garb, were clearly as military as Caaldra himself. Without a word or even a hand signal passing between them, they dived simultaneously in opposite directions, both opening fire while still in midair. Mara deflected one of the bolts, leaping toward that shooter as the other man's bolt sizzled through the air behind her. The first man's eyes widened as she took another quick step toward him; he got off two more useless shots before the magenta blade slashed through his torso. Twisting back around, Mara raised her weapon just in time to send the other man's final shot back at him.

And Caaldra was alone.

"I saved you for last," Mara said conversationally, holding her light-saber in casual guard position against the blaster pointed at her. "Any last words?"

"You're throwing away a big score," Caaldra warned. His voice was tight, but Mara could sense his mind running coldly and dispassionately through his options. "It's still not too late to make a deal."

"The deals ended when you tried to cook me," Mara said, taking a step toward him.

"At least give me a fighting chance," Caaldra said, a note of feigned pleading in his voice. Lowering his blaster, he tossed it away. "You're a fighter; I'm a fighter. Let's settle this hand-to-hand, warrior-to-warrior, no weapons."

Mara raised her eyebrows. "You trying to appeal to my professional pride?" she asked.

"I'm appealing to your sense of fair play," Caaldra corrected. "Or are you like Vader, and don't have one?"

Mara felt her face harden. "You're on." Not even bothering to close down her lightsaber, she tossed it to the side.

As she did so, Caaldra lifted his left hand to reveal a concealed hold-out blaster. "Fool," he bit out, and fired.

Directly into the lightsaber blade, as Mara calmly recalled the weapon to her hand.

Caaldra jerked as the deflected shot burned through the center of his chest. For a moment he stayed standing, staring at Mara in disbelief. Then his knees buckled, and he collapsed to the floor.

Mara stepped over to him, nudging the hold-out blaster out of his limp hand with her foot. "I always play fair," she said softly. "Exactly as fair as my opponents."

The unseeing eyes had no answer. Closing down her lightsaber, Mara looked around. She was in another expansive reception area like the one whose floor she'd just come through. Across the way she could see a pair of carved doors marking an entrance to the ballroom balcony. If Bright-water had been right about the governor having guests, the ballroom might be a good place to start looking for him.

She only hoped she could get to him before LaRone did.

*   *   *

With its lock no longer connected to the main part of the door, the kitchen entrance wasn't really sealable anymore. Grave did his best, blasting a section of plumbing free and wedging it between the handle and the wall. Then, with LaRone taking point, they headed in.

Most of the kitchen staff had made their frantic escape by the time the stormtroopers wove their way through the various work areas and equipment islands and toward a door at the far diagonal end. "Where to?" La-Rone asked.

"Ballroom," Marcross said tersely.

LaRone nodded, remembering Brightwater's speculation that Governor Choard was entertaining. "Okay," he said. "Watch for trouble."

The trouble was waiting in the corridor as they burst through the kitchen doorway: a half dozen guards standing in a semicircle with drawn blasters.

Fortunately for those guards, the Hand of Judgment didn't kill unnecessarily. Even more fortunately, they'd set up their defensive line well within an E-11's stun range. "Set for stun," LaRone ordered, flipping his selector and squeezing the trigger. The blue rings spread outward and the nearest guard twitched and fell over, his blaster sending a final spasmodic shot into the ceiling. One of the others managed to get two shots off, one of which caught LaRone in his upper chest plate, before they were all down.

"You all right?" Grave asked, leaning over for a look at the blackened spot on LaRone's armor.

"No problem," LaRone assured him, wincing as he moved his shoulder. There was definitely a burn there, but the armor had blocked most of the energy, and the injury wasn't bad enough to slow him down. Marcross was already on the move, he saw, heading down the corridor toward an archway enveloped by a gently undulating light curtain. "Marcross, slow it down."

But the other either didn't hear the order or else ignored it. He kept going, lowering his E-11 into hip-firing position as he reached the curtain. There was a ripple of multicolored light from his armor as he passed through it, and then he was gone.

Swearing under his breath, LaRone set off at a quick jog, Grave and Quiller right behind him. They reached the curtain, and LaRone ducked through.

The ballroom was comfortably full of elegantly dressed men and women, clearly the top level of Shelkonwan society. But at the moment they looked more like elegantly dressed statues than living beings. They stood silent and stunned, some with drinks frozen halfway to their lips, staring at Marcross as he strode toward the center of the room.

There, looking as surprised as his guests, was Governor Choard, his huge bulk squeezed into a set of formalwear, his bushy beard glistening in the fancy lighting.

"Close it up," LaRone murmured to the others and set off after Marcross, trying to catch up while still keeping his pace to something professional and dignified. The edge of the crowd melted away at their approach, and they reached Marcross as he came to a halt a couple of meters in front of Choard.

Predictably, LaRone thought, the governor got in the first word. "What's the meaning of this?" he demanded.

LaRone took a deep breath. "Governor Barshnis Choard, you've been found guilty of treason and condemned to death," he announced. "We have been authorized to carry out that sentence."

"What?" Choard said, his jaw dropping in amazement. "That's absurd."

Grave and Quiller, LaRone noted peripherally, already had their E-11s leveled. And Jade had been quite clear about their orders.

But even as LaRone opened his mouth, he found the command sticking in his throat. He couldn't order the others to fire on an unresisting civilian. Not like this. Not after Teardrop. "Will you come with us quietly?" he asked instead.

"Go with Imperial stormtroopers?" Choard snorted. "Certainly not." He jabbed a finger at a tall man wearing a fur-edged drape tunic. "Siner— go get my guards. Tell them the intruders they're looking for are here."

"Everyone stay right where you are," LaRone ordered, trying desperately to figure out what to do. Did Choard's defiance provide enough justification to carry out Jade's orders? Did he really want it to?

And then, to his astonishment, Marcross turned, swinging his blaster rifle around to point at LaRone's chest. "Lower your weapons," he said, his voice low but determined. "All of you."

"What?" LaRone demanded.

"You heard me," Marcross said tightly. "All three of you. Now."

For a long moment LaRone stared at that blank white faceplate, trying to read something—anything—in the other's stance. But there was nothing there. "I mean it, Commander," Marcross said into the brittle silence. "Put them down."

Commander . . . and suddenly, in LaRone's mind's eye, they were back aboard the Suwantek after that skirmish with the swoop gang, their first battle as a team. *That's part of leadership*, Marcross had said as the two of them stood alone in the cargo bay. *Knowing and understanding the men of your command.* And *trusting them.*

Trusting . . .

"Drop your weapons," LaRone confirmed quietly, lowering the barrel of his E-11 and bending over to set it onto the floor in front of him. From beside him came two soft clattering sounds, unnaturally loud in the silence, as Quiller and Grave did the same.

"I don't understand this at all," Choard said, his voice still angry but starting to fill with confusion. "What in the worlds is going on?"

"What's going on," Marcross said, turning his E-11 around and handing it to the governor, "is that I've just saved your life." Taking a step back, he removed his helmet.

Choard's eyes widened. *"Saberan?"*

"Hello, Uncle Barshnis," Marcross said, nodding to him. "It's been a long time."

Chapter Twenty-Three

THE BALLROOM WAS AS QUIET AS A CRYPT AS MARA SLIPPED THROUGH the door onto the balcony. The railing was a solid wall of carved marble, blocking her view of whatever activity—or lack of it—was going on down there. Moving to the edge of the balcony, she eased an eye above the wall.

LaRone and his three stormtroopers were there, facing Choard with perhaps a hundred other people standing dead-still around them. Marcross had taken off his helmet.

Choard was holding Marcross's blaster rifle on LaRone, Grave, and Quiller.

Mara's first reaction was to breathe a silent sigh of relief. Not only had she made it to Choard in time, but Marcross had apparently come forward and stopped LaRone from carrying out Mara's flawed execution order. Now all she had to do was get down there, confirm that the governor was in the clear, and get them searching for Disra and any of his allies who might still be at large.

"Your *uncle*?" LaRone said, his stunned voice carrying clearly up to the balcony.

"I told you I hung out with his son when I was a teen," Marcross reminded him. "You think a sector governor would let just any riffraff do that?"

"I still don't know what's going on, Saberan, but I'm immensely glad to see you," Choard said. "What are you doing here? Are you and these others from Lord Vader's group?"

"No, we're a separate unit," Marcross said. "This is all of us there are, plus a colleague who's keeping most of your outside guards pinned down."

"I presume that's why no one's come to help," Choard rumbled. "Now, tell me about this insane treason charge."

Mara looked around the edge of the balcony. To her annoyance, there appeared to be no stairways leading down to the main floor. She would have to either jump, which wouldn't do her burned feet and legs any good, or else go back out into the reception area and find a way down from there.

"They think you're involved in a plot to use pirate gangs to harass shipping and steal Imperial property," Marcross said. "In fact, there's an Imperial agent in Makrin City right now who was sent here to kill you."

"I see," Choard said, his tone suddenly thoughtful.

"It seems to me the best plan would be to call Lord Vader and have him put you under the protection of the Five-oh-first while we get it all straightened out," Marcross continued. "Let me borrow your comlink—mine won't connect with any of their frequencies." He took a step toward Choard—

"I think not," the governor said quietly, swiveling the blaster rifle to point squarely at Marcross's stomach. "The last thing we want in here is more Imperials."

Mara stiffened, her relief transforming instantly into icy rage. So she'd been right the first time. Only instead of listening to her instincts, she'd let Caaldra and his smooth talk convince her otherwise. And now Marcross and the others were about to pay the price for her failure.

She stretched out to the Force, trying to pull the blaster rifle from Choard's hands. But the distance, the emotional turbulence generated by a roomful of stunned partygoers, and the simmering distraction of Mara's own burns combined to defeat her efforts.

Which left her only one option, only one chance to help LaRone and the others. Digging into one of her belt pouches, she pulled out the mist canister she'd been planning to use earlier to cover their approach across the palace grounds. The device wasn't really intended for indoor use, but with her blaster gone and her useless grenades back at the *Happer's Way* it was all she had.

Thumbing off the canister's safety catch, she stretched out to the Force for strength and prepared for action.

Marcross stopped short, staring at the governor. "Uncle?" he said, sounding stunned. "Uncle, what are you doing?"

"I'm getting out of here," Choard answered, gesturing with the E-11 for Marcross to join the others. "It would have been nice to make the announcement of Shelsha's independence from the palace, but it's hardly necessary."

"What are you talking about?" Marcross demanded as he stepped back to LaRone's side. "Are you saying—you can't be *serious.*"

"You never *did* understand how the galaxy really operates, did you, Saberan?" Choard said contemptuously. "It's all about power, my idealistic little nephew: actual power, potential power, or perceived power. Fortunately, with the forces I now have at my command, I have all three."

"Tarkin had power, too," Grave reminded him coolly. "You saw where it got him."

Choard snorted. "Tarkin was a fool. I won't make his mistakes."

"Then you'll make others," LaRone said. "People like you always do."

The E-11 swiveled to point at LaRone's chest. "No, it's people like *you* who make the mistakes," Choard said. "Now, very quietly—"

"No, Uncle, he's right," Marcross said, his voice suddenly very tired. "The mistakes were all yours. Your first was to give the BloodScars your private unregistered HoloNet contact, the one Crayg always called when he and I were offplanet and he needed extra money. It was the last call the pirates made—I saw it on their comm setup record."

LaRone looked at the other in surprise. So that was what had caused Marcross's reaction back on Gepparin, and why he'd been so quiet and tense ever since. The knowledge that his own uncle was committing treason . . .

"But I wasn't absolutely sure no one else had access to that number," Marcross went on. "So I had to give you this chance to prove it, one way or the other. That was your second mistake: you talk too much. You always did." He waved an arm at the crowd around them. "And this time in front of witnesses."

"They can babble all they want," Choard bit out. His face had gone the color of a thundercloud, and his blaster rifle was now pointed at Marcross. "In an hour Shelsha's message of defiance will be all across the HoloNet."

Marcross shook his head. "No, Uncle. Because you made one final mistake." He pointed at the weapon in the governor's grip. "You think that blaster is loaded."

And without warning, a small object arced over the crowd onto the floor directly in front of Choard and exploded into a cloud of white mist.

Choard jerked back in reaction, the blaster bolt lighting up the mist as he fired. But the sudden move had thrown off his aim, and the shot intended for the center of Marcross's chest shattered instead into his right upper arm. Marcross grunted, staggering a little with the impact.

"Troopers!" LaRone barked, ducking down and scooping up his E-11. But there was no need for orders. Grave and Quiller had already retrieved their weapons and were charging in opposite directions around the expanding mist, moving to flank their enemy. Gripping his E-11 firmly, LaRone charged straight into the cloud.

Only to be bounced straight back again as Choard's huge bulk slammed into him, knocking him out of the mist and throwing him flat on his back on the floor. Spitting a curse, Choard swung his stolen E-11 around to point at LaRone's face, his eyes crazed above the barrel as he squeezed the trigger.

Only this time, nothing happened.

He tried again, and again, the wildness in his eyes turning to sudden horror as he worked the useless weapon. Peripherally, LaRone saw Grave and Quiller charge back out of the mist, their E-11s tracking—

"No!" LaRone barked. "No."

The two stormtroopers came to a slightly confused halt. "Commander?" Grave asked uncertainly, his blaster still pointed at Choard.

"He *is* a traitor, sir," Quiller reminded him darkly.

LaRone looked into Choard's eyes, at the impotent rage and thwarted ambition still simmering there. It was tempting, he had to admit. It was awfully tempting. All the chaos and destruction the man had caused, all the innocent lives his twisted ambition had cut short . . .

Innocent lives. Like those of the people on Teardrop.

And with that, LaRone suddenly realized how very tired he was of killing. "Yes, he's a traitor," he told Quiller as he climbed back to his feet. "But he'll stand trial for it. Let him find his fate there."

Deliberately, he turned his back on the man. "Marcross?" he asked, stepping over to his friend.

Marcross was clutching at his arm, an instinctive if fairly useless exercise with the armored sleeve still in place. "I'm all right," he said. "I guess it still had one shot left."

"I guess it did, you crazy idiot," LaRone said. He looked back at the dissipating mist that had probably saved his friend's life, then turned to the balcony.

She was there, of course, gazing down at them like an avenging angel. "Governor Choard," she called in a clear, cold voice, "you're under arrest for treason."

From the hallway beyond the light curtain came a clatter of running footsteps, and a moment later a liveried servant charged into the ballroom. "Your Excellency—" He broke off, coming to a sudden halt as he caught sight of the stormtroopers.

"What is it?" LaRone asked.

With an effort, the servant dragged his gaze back to his governor. "There's word from the gate, Your Excellency," he managed, the words coming out as if squeezed from a putty tube. "Lord Vader has entered the grounds with—" His eyes flicked surreptitiously back to LaRone. "With a group of Imperial stormtroopers. Chief Administrator Disra is reported to be with them."

"Excellent," Jade called down from the balcony. Startled, the servant twisted his head to look up at her. "Meet Lord Vader at the nearest door and escort him here."

Her eyes shifted to LaRone . . . and in her face LaRone saw that she knew. That she knew everything—who he was, who the others were, how they'd all gotten here. It was over, and they were as good as dead.

But then he looked back at Choard, a man whose path was littered with the corpses of hundreds of innocent people and who would have killed millions more if he hadn't been stopped. LaRone, Grave, Quiller, Brightwater, and especially Marcross, had helped prevent that.

Yes, it was over. But it had been worth it.

*　　*　　*

Grave had Marcross's sleeve armor off and was working on his injury when Jade joined them. "How is he?" she asked.

"Bad burn, but the armor caught most of it," Grave reported. "He'll be all right."

"Good," Jade said, shifting her cool gaze to Choard. "I trust you realize you should have died right then," she told him. "If I'd been here instead of these men you *would* have died."

"I'm sure that matters to someone," Choard bit out. Even at the end, LaRone thought, the man still had defiance to burn.

What a waste.

A nervous ripple ran through the crowd of elite citizens now lined up against the walls. Bracing himself, LaRone turned around.

Darth Vader stood just inside the light curtain, his fists on his hips as he surveyed the situation, his black mask and armor a stark contrast with the gleaming white of the stormtroopers filing quickly and efficiently into the ballroom behind him.

"Lord Vader," Jade said, nodding to him.

"Emperor's Hand," Vader replied, dipping his helmet briefly. He strode forward, his cloak billowing behind him. "I see you've been busy."

"As have you," Jade said. "I understand you have Chief Administrator Disra in custody?"

"Protective custody," Vader corrected. "Two hours ago he came to me with a full accounting of Governor Choard's treason."

"Did he, now," Jade said drily. "Interesting how fast the rock mites leave the ore carrier on the way to the crash. I had one try the same thing on me."

"The administrator's case is different," Vader said, his voice cooling warningly.

"I'm sure it is," Jade said, inclining her head again. "And I'm sure his evidence will prove useful at Choard's trial. My congratulations. Would you be able to arrange prisoner transport back to Imperial Center? My ship isn't particularly spaceworthy at the moment."

"So I've heard," the Dark Lord said. LaRone tried to imagine him smiling behind that faceplate, but it was a futile effort. "What about these?" Vader added, nodding toward LaRone.

"What about them?" Jade asked.

"I'm told they refused to identify their unit earlier this evening," Vader said, his voice darkening. "I also have word now from the *Reprisal* that they have five stormtroopers missing."

LaRone felt his throat tighten. So they wouldn't be going to Storm-trooper Command, or even be turned over to the ISB. Vader himself would be dealing with them.

At least it would be quick. Probably.

But to his amazement, Jade shrugged. "Interesting, but irrelevant," she said. "These stormtrooper are mine."

"*Yours?*"

"You have the entire Five-oh-first," Jade reminded him. "You certainly won't begrudge me my Hand of Judgment."

For a long moment Vader stared down at her. Jade stared back, her face impassive but firm.

Then, to LaRone's relief, the Dark Lord stirred. "As you wish," he said, lifting a hand slightly. "Commander?"

A stormtrooper group commander stepped forward. "Yes, Lord Vader?"

"Take Governor Choard to the *Executor*," Vader ordered. "Then have your men search this palace." He gestured toward the Makrin City citizens lined up against the walls. "Beginning with them."

"Yes, sir." The commander gestured, and two of his men came forward, stepping to Choard's sides and nudging him into sullen movement toward the exit. Another dozen fell into step around them, while the rest fanned out toward the Makrin City elite lined up against the walls.

Vader turned back, and for a long moment the blank black faceplate stared down at LaRone. Then, half turning, he inclined his head to Jade. "Emperor's Hand," he said. With a swirl of his cloak, he turned and strode away.

LaRone looked at Jade, to find her looking back at him. "Orders, ma'am?" he said, keeping his voice professional.

"We're done here," she said in the same tone. "We'll pick up Bright-water on the way out and head back to Greencliff and your ship." Her eyes hardened. "And on the way, you're going to tell me a story. A *real* one this time."

Chapter Twenty-Four

LEIA'S FACE WAS SHEENED WITH SWEAT BY THE TIME HAN LET HER OUT of the cabin's secret armory. "It's okay," he said, offering her a hand. "They've finished and gone."

"They were certainly thorough enough," she commented, ignoring his hand and stepping out of the cramped space on her own. "I could hear them walking around in here at least three times."

"They weren't very happy about the speeder bikes in the cargo bay," Han said as Leia sat down on the bed. She didn't look very much like a Princess right now, he thought, with stray hairs plastered to her neck and her tapcafe server's covergown still wrapped around her. But underneath it he could still see all that royal dignity stuff. It made for a nice combination, actually. "But I did a little song and sync about military surplus and they seemed to buy it," he added.

"They've probably gone off to run the serial numbers," Leia warned.

"Let 'em," Han said with a shrug. "We'll be long gone before they can track any of that down. Brightwater just called—they're on their way back."

"Brightwater being one of these stormtrooper deserters you told me about?"

"Don't worry, we can trust them," Han assured her. "Though we probably don't need to tell them exactly who you are. Anyway, I've got Chewie prepping the engines—a couple of hours out to where we stashed the *Falcon*, and we'll be done with them." He cocked an eyebrow. "Unless you want to stick around and see if you can talk LaRone into joining the Rebellion."

"Former stormtroopers?" Leia countered with a wry smile. "I don't think so." She hesitated. "Especially since I can't even talk *you* into joining up."

Han grimaced. So she *had* noticed. That was a little awkward. Still, it was kind of flattering that she'd taken the time to figure it out. "It's a pretty big step," he reminded her.

"I know," Leia said. "Especially for someone who's used to taking orders only from himself. But it was a step we all had to take." Her eyes drifted to the hidden closet and the suits of stormtrooper armor. "And after Alderaan, I don't think it's possible to be neutral anymore," she added quietly. "Either you support the Empire's oppression, or you fight it."

"I suppose I *could* stick around a little longer," Han hedged. "But I'm not ready to pledge undying loyalty to Mon Mothma and Rieekan and the others."

"Then don't start with them," Leia said, looking earnestly back at him. "Start with loyalty to just one person."

Han looked at her, a funny feeling in his stomach. Was she actually saying . . . ?

"Chewbacca wants to join us," Leia went on. "Do it for him, and for what his people have suffered under the Empire."

The funny feeling vanished. "Oh," he said.

"Oh what?"

"Just *oh*," Han said, back on balance again. "Anyway, I'd better go let Luke out of his closet."

Leia's eyes widened. "You mean you haven't *done* that yet? You've been standing here talking to me and he's still stuck in there?"

"He's got a lightsaber," Han said blandly. "He can always cut his way out if he gets bored."

"Han—"

"See you later, Princess."

But she had a point, Han had to admit as he headed back out into the corridor. Maybe he could start with allegiance to just one person. Someone like Chewie.

Or maybe even someone else.

Jade listened in silence to LaRone's story as Quiller drove the speeder truck through Makrin City's quiet streets. "You should have gone to your unit commander," she said when he'd finished. "There are procedures for dealing with incidents where there's a strong probability of self-defense."

"Procedures that wouldn't have involved us being turned over to ISB?" Grave asked.

"Point," Jade conceded. "But you still should have turned yourselves in. Now it's too late."

"Probably," LaRone said, trying to read her face. All of it wasted effort—he had no idea what was going on behind those bright green eyes. "But to be honest, at this point we don't really want to go back. After Teardrop . . ." He stopped, a lump rising into his throat.

"Yes, and be assured that I'm going to look into that," Jade promised ominously. "Ordering the slaughter of civilians is against everything the Empire stands for. If it's true, I promise you someone's going to suffer for it."

LaRone looked sideways at Marcross. The other grimaced in silent agreement. For all her strength and competence, this Emperor's Hand had an awfully naïve view of what the Empire actually stood for.

But she would learn.

"What are you going to do with us?" Quiller asked.

For a long moment Jade was silent. "You're deserters," she said at last. "You swore an oath of allegiance to the Empire, and you broke it. That's technically as treasonous as Choard's own conspiracy."

"We understand," LaRone said. "But with all due respect, our oath was actually to defend the Empire *and* its citizens."

"And you think that's what you're doing?" Jade retorted. "Flying around the galaxy like loose laser cannons?"

"We're certainly doing a better job protecting the citizens now than we did on Teardrop," Grave said.

LaRone winced. But Jade didn't respond.

They were in sight of the Greencliff Spaceport before she spoke again. "What name is your ship running under at the moment?"

"The *Melnor Spear*," LaRone told her.

"I'll call the *Executor* and give you clearance," she said. "Get off Shelkonwa and don't come back."

LaRone glanced at Marcross, then back to Jade. "Thank you," he said. "May I ask why?"

The young woman gazed out the windscreen as they passed through the spaceport gate. "You helped me identify a traitor and take him into custody." She hesitated. "Besides, a few days ago I was ready to offer a complete pardon to a man who'd done more against the Empire and its citizens than any of you could ever possibly do. He'll never get to use it. You might as well have it instead."

"Yes, ma'am," LaRone said, wishing he knew what she was talking about. "Thank you again."

Quiller drove the speeder truck beneath the Suwantek and came to a stop. "Just stay out of sight and out of trouble," Jade said, pushing up the door and climbing out. "The next Imperials you run into probably won't be so generous."

She looked at Marcross, and it seemed to LaRone that her head inclined ever so slightly to him. She started to turn away, then turned back. "Oh, and one more thing. That *Hand of Judgment* name of yours?"

"Yes?" LaRone said, frowning.

"Lose it," she ordered. "There's only one Hand in the Empire, and I'm it." Turning again, she strode away into the night.

Brightwater had pulled his mangled speeder bike to the controls and had the Suwantek's cargo lift on its way down. "What was *that* all about?" he asked as LaRone climbed stiffly out of the speeder truck.

"Sort of a political conflict, I guess you'd call it," LaRone said. "Fortunately, it's one I don't mind conceding. Let's make sure Solo and the others are aboard and get out of here."

"Sounds good to me," Brightwater said as the lift platform settled onto the permacrete. "So are we actually going to stay out of sight and trouble this time like she said?"

LaRone watched as Quiller drove the truck onto the platform. "I don't see how we can," he admitted at last. "We swore an oath to defend the people of the Empire. There are a lot of other dangers out there they need defending against."

"Actually, I was kind of hoping you'd say that," Brightwater said, resting his hand briefly on LaRone's shoulder. "For all the bumps and bruises, this hero stuff definitely helps you sleep better at night."

"Agreed," LaRone said. "Let's get our passengers back to the *Falcon* and get on with our lives." He looked back in the direction of the palace. "And our duty."

The Emperor leaned back in his throne, his yellow eyes glittering beneath his hood as he coolly regarded the two figures standing before him. "So it would seem Organa has slipped through your fingers," he said, his gravelly voice unreadable.

"So it would seem, my Master," Vader admitted, lowering his head toward his Emperor in contrition. "The search found no one." His helmet turned slightly toward Mara. "But one vehicle *was* permitted to leave before that search was completed."

"My child?" the Emperor invited.

"The freighter was carrying the stormtrooper unit I'd commandeered," Mara said. "There's absolutely no chance Organa could have stowed away without them finding her. Besides, the *Executor*'s scanners detected only five life-forms aboard." She looked at Vader. "Actually, I'm not convinced Organa was ever on Shelkonwa in the first place," she added. "I strongly suspect this was a story Chief Administrator Disra cooked up to make sure Lord Vader would come personally to Makrin City."

"To what end?"

"According to Disra, he'd been collecting evidence of Choard's conspiracy for quite some time," Mara said. "The problem with turning on your superior that way is how to make sure you give the evidence to someone who isn't one of his friends or fellow conspirators." She gestured to Vader. "Who would be safer than Lord Vader?"

"And who better placed to help Disra in his own ambitions?" the Emperor suggested.

"The man does indeed wish to be become governor in Choard's place," Vader confirmed.

"I'm certain he does," the Emperor said, and Mara could sense his earlier annoyance fading. "Not now. Perhaps later." He gestured. "At any rate, the war continues. Return to your duties, Lord Vader." He smiled at Mara. "As for you, my child, your next assignment awaits you in your quarters."

They had left the throne room and were walking down the long corridor before Vader finally spoke. "What is your assessment of Disra?"

"He's a con artist and conniver," Mara said flatly. "I wouldn't trust him any farther than I could see him."

"Agreed," Vader said. "I don't intend to."

"Good." Mara hesitated. "I have a favor to ask, Lord Vader."

There was a short pause. "Continue."

"It's about Captain Ozzel," Mara said. "He claims his attack on the Gepparin pirate base had nothing to do with me, but was based on intelligence supplied by Colonel Somoril."

"And Somoril supports him in this?" Vader asked contemptuously.

"Of course he does," Mara said in the same tone. For all their differences, she reflected, she and Vader at least had the same opinion of the ISB. "And with their stories welded shut that way, there's no grounds for any kind of real interrogation."

"What would you like me to do?"

"I'm not really sure," Mara confessed. "Keep an eye on Ozzel, I suppose. I don't know if the man's disloyal, easily manipulated, or just plain stupid. But I think he bears watching."

Vader was silent another few steps. "Leave him to me," he said at last. "I believe I can arrange something."

"Countess?" a voice called from the cross corridor they were passing. "Countess *Claria*?"

Mara looked in that direction and saw a familiar person hurrying toward them. "Why, hello, General Deerian," she called back, stopping to wait for him. Vader didn't even break stride, but continued down the hallway. "What are you doing here?" she asked as Deerian came up to her.

"I have a new position," Deerian said with a touch of pride. "I've been assigned to the team in charge of upgrading Imperial Center's planetary defenses."

"Congratulations," Mara said. "I imagine you're sorry to leave the glitter of Moff Glovstoak's palace."

"Hardly," Deerian said, his expression going grim. "I don't know if you heard, but just after I was transferred, Glovstoak was hauled up on charges of embezzlement and treason."

"No, I hadn't heard that," Mara said honestly.

"It was a shock to us all," Deerian said, shaking his head. "Imagine a man like that abusing his position and authority."

"Imagine," Mara agreed.

"Well, I'm on my way to a meeting," Deerian said, the gloom fading from his face. "But I saw you and wanted to say hello."

"I'm glad you did," Mara said. "Good luck to you, General."

"And to you, Countess." Bowing to her, Deerian headed off again down the corridor.

Mara watched him go, a warm glow spreading through her. LaRone could talk all he wanted about these scattered abuses of power, and certainly those abuses needed to be dealt with. But as long as the Empire could still produce men like General Deerian, it would be worth defending. Worth her energy, and her life.

And her allegiance.

Turning again toward Vader's cloak billowing in the distance, she headed for her quarters, where her next assignment was waiting.

About the Author

Timothy Zahn's *Star Wars* novels have more than four million copies in print. Since 1978 he has written nearly seventy short stories and novelettes, twenty novels, and three short fiction collections, and won the 1984 Hugo Award for best novella. He is best known for his seven *Star Wars* books: *Heir to the Empire, Dark Force Rising, The Last Command, Specter of the Past, Vision of the Future, Survivor's Quest,* and *Outbound Flight.* He lives with his family on the Oregon coast.

ABOUT THE TYPE

This book was set in Electra, a typeface designed for Linotype by W.A. Dwiggins, the renowned type designer (1880–1956). Electra is a fluid typeface, avoiding the contrast of thick and thin strokes that are prevalent in most modern typefaces.